MADNESS OF THE ELDER VAMPIRE

THE ELDER MADNESS SERIES
BOOK ONE

DARBY VERNON

Published by Star Strix LLC

ISBN 979-8-9932058-0-9

www.darbyvernon.com

www.starstrix.com

 Formatted with Vellum

I

TWENTY YEARS AGO

No magic prevented Adrian from entering the home of Linh Thi Nguyen uninvited, only a simple deadbolt, several security cameras, polite manners, and severe consequences. Locks could be picked, a skill Adrian had learned out of boredom but put to use more often than once. The security cameras were laughable, something meant to deter mortals instead of vampires. Politeness was something Adrian didn't afford often. He could always knock and ask to be let in, but he doubted Linh's guards would open the door for him. And finally, the severe consequences. Those didn't concern Adrian in the slightest.

"What's taking so long?" one of the men behind Adrian growled.

"Think you can do better?" Adrian hissed, keeping his voice low. Partly, it was to prevent alerting the house's occupants of their intrusion, but it was also in restraint from snapping at the other man. Joseph was the Elder Regent, boss of their Coven. Whether Adrian wanted to admit it or not, Joseph owned him. And Adrian hated it. Had it not been for Garrick in the middle, Adrian would likely be dead already for mouthing off to the top-ranked vampire.

The lock gave way, and the door opened into an unlit entryway. Adrian stepped into the foyer, glancing around for any sign of where Linh might be. He turned to wave the gathering of vampires through, but Joseph shoved his way past without invitation. Adrian swallowed his complaints.

There was something uncanny about the inside of Linh's mansion. The exterior appeared Victorian—old, with massive wooden towers holding up pointed roof spires. Inside, the foundation resembled more of a cabin, with large wooden beams spanning the ceiling. The interior was dark, but that wasn't terribly unusual; vampires didn't require light to see. Heavy curtains blocked out any light from the windows.

As the rest of Joseph's crew entered the mansion, a blur of motion caught Adrian's attention. He darted to the left wall just as a long, curved sword cut the air where he'd stood and clanged onto the stone floor. A guard had been stationed beside the door, likely waiting for them to enter before attacking. In his periphery, Adrian saw multiple guards lunging for other members of his Coven, but he kept his attention on his most immediate threat.

The attacking guard raised his sword once more and charged at Adrian. The problem with swords was that they were long, sharp weapons, perfect for stabbing hearts and lopping off heads: the two parts of Adrian's body still necessary to live. But based on the guard's stiff arms and poor balance, it was unlikely the young man had ever held a Vietnamese-style sword prior to working for Linh. Then again, Adrian had little experience fighting against swords either. But he knew how much punishment his body could take.

Adrian dashed toward his attacker. The blade of the sword sliced against the left side of his torso as he closed the distance, and buried his knife into the guard's gut. A devastating blow to mortals, but a minor inconvenience to vampires. Still, the guard froze after the attack. This was likely the first time he had ever been stabbed. Before the guard had time to realize how little it mattered, Adrian took hold of the young man's arm, twisted it onto his shoulder, and then snapped it at the elbow. The guard collapsed to the floor, crying out in pain and clutching his broken arm.

With his immediate threat down, Adrian glanced around to see who needed help. Half a dozen men and women, dressed in dull gray uniforms, either lay crumpled on the ground or in the fangs of Adrian's crew.

Joseph, however, did not finish off his attacker quickly. The man was just as tall as Adrian, but far more muscular. Physical strength meant little to their magically enhanced bodies, but the sight of Joseph holding a guard by the throat, her face bloodied by repeated strikes from his fist, made the back of Adrian's neck bristle. The brutal display was enough to make another guard, short in stature and still unharmed after their failed ambush, turn tail and run. Like a wild tiger, Joseph's attention snapped to the cowardly guard, and he dropped the woman to pounce on his new prey.

Adrian scanned the foyer to make sure they were safe, but deep down, he knew he just needed to look away. The screams and cries of Joseph's new victim echoed through the otherwise silent mansion. Adrian was long past feeling shocked by Joseph's outbursts of violence, but that didn't make it easier to stand nearby while it happened. A whimper from the guard by Adrian's feet, the one with the broken arm, caught his attention. These weren't trained fighters, just kids who had been swept up by the wrong Elder Regent.

When the cries stopped, Adrian looked up to see Joseph's fangs buried deep in the guard's neck. Joseph gnashed his teeth as he fed, splattering fresh blood across his face. Several grueling seconds later, he dropped the cowardly guard at his feet and grinned at Adrian, his teeth stained red with blood.

"What'cha lookin' at me like that for?" he sneered. "Get a drink in while it's free!"

"I'm full," Adrian said.

Joseph grunted, then laughed and kicked the unconscious guard. Twice. A third time.

"Are you done yet?" Adrian snapped. "We're here for a reason."

Like a wild animal, Joseph growled and slowly sauntered up to Adrian. In the darkness of Linh's mansion, his eyes glowed a menacing red, punctuating the blood smeared across his face. All Elder vampires suffered from the Madness, but Joseph could have been its poster boy.

All Elders, save one.

"Let's go," Joseph said in a mockingly jovial tone.

A fearful weight lifted off Adrian's chest as the Elder turned his attention away from him and directed it toward the crew of equally uncomfortable vampires standing nearby.

"You four, go with him. That way." He pointed deeper into the mansion to the right. "You three, with me."

Joseph bounded off to the left, three of his vassals following close behind. Adrian sighed in relief that he wasn't in the group going with Joseph. The Elder may have been his boss, but he wasn't the vampire who had turned him. That honor belonged to Garrick.

"Man, what the hell," one of the vampires in Adrian's group, a woman named Jan, muttered. "Can't believe Garrick made us come along."

"I think we did too good of a job chasing Juliette out of

central LA," another, Quinn, said. "Now Joseph thinks we can do the same with Linh."

"This seems like a really hasty plan, though."

"Let's just get this over with," Adrian grunted. "Garrick won't let us get hurt."

An awkward silence followed before one of the vampires, Everett, finally agreed. "Yeah. He wouldn't send all of us if it was that dangerous."

The four vampires in Adrian's group were all vassals of Garrick. Elder vampires rarely worked together in the same Coven, but Garrick was an exception. Technically, that made Garrick one of Joseph's vassals, but the traditional hierarchy broke down when two Elders were involved. Elders needed the blood of other vampires, not mortals, to sustain themselves. Normally, the vassal supplied blood to the Elder Regent, but with two Elders, the structure had to subdivide further. Adrian and his group of four comprised Garrick's crew. Garrick answered to the Elder Regent, Joseph, who had a dozen other young vassals answering directly to him.

Other vampires might have considered this arrangement a family structure, but Adrian avoided that classification. He didn't think of Everett and the others as siblings, nor did he think of Garrick as a father. They were his crew. And Garrick was...

Garrick had promised to keep Adrian safe.

Adrian's inner magic surged, and he twisted the shadows around him into a cloak of darkness that shielded him from sight and sound—a trick Garrick taught him a few years ago, once his body had aged enough to use such magical powers. The other four did the same, and together they silently crept deeper into the house. Twice, a guard ran by, unaware of the crew's presence in the shadows.

When their incursion led them to the dining room, Adrian spotted a woman seated at a long, ornate table, sipping a bright red broth. The room was warmly lit by a variety of colorful lamps, and the ceiling stretched two and a half stories high. It was an elaborate sight for a room Linh had no necessity for.

As the group entered, Linh flicked her wrist, and the shadows hiding them dissipated. Two more guards rushed in from a door on the opposite end of the room, but Linh held up a finger, signaling them to wait.

"You do know what entering a home uninvited means, right?" Linh asked. She blotted a white cloth against her mouth, and Adrian couldn't tell whether the red residue left behind was from her soup or her lipstick.

Adrian shrugged. He knew. Traditionally, Linh could do whatever she wanted. But Joseph wasn't one for tradition.

"I would have thought Joseph knew better than to storm my home. He can kill a few guards, but that mad dog is nothing compared to an Elder over a century his senior."

"Elder" was a status gained after two hundred years of age. Joseph hadn't been Elder long, only about fifty years, making him two hundred fifty years turned. Linh was at least three hundred fifty. Garrick was six hundred.

Adrian was twenty.

"Which one of you idiots let them in?" Linh hissed at the nearest guard. "Did Joseph plant a spy in my ranks?" She stood and approached the guard. Linh was short and slender, hardly an intimidating woman, but she carried herself like a queen, and her scowl could menace even the strongest steel-hearted man. The guard froze.

"I will make you my next soup unless you tell me!"

"N-no Mistress Linh, please! We thought an ambush..."

Everett caught Adrian's attention with a sideways glance and an uneasy fidget. Their orders weren't specifically to assassinate Linh, but she had to leave Los Angeles. It was unlikely that she'd do so without significant violence.

The nearest guard was only a few yards away. Adrian grabbed his knife again and closed the distance as fast as he could. The guard had just enough time to react and raise his sword defensively, but it didn't do much to stop the attack. Adrian aimed for the gut, like before, but the angle left the slice shallow. The guard's sword caught between them, its sharp edge pointing skyward and nearly brushing Adrian's face. Another stab below the ribcage landed, and the guard loosened his grip. Just what Adrian was waiting for. He tore the sword from the guard's hands, took a moment to adjust the angle, then swung it like a baseball bat at neck height. The cut sliced most of the way through. Enough to kill.

The fighting resumed. The noise attracted more guards from the rest of the house—or rather, servants, based on their lack of weaponry. Adrian spun around to see Linh furious. She ripped the sword out of the hands of the guard she had been intimidating and held it by her side. Unlike these untrained guards, Linh stood with a sword master's grace.

Adrian angled his shoulder forward, protecting his two most vulnerable points: first, his head and neck; second, his heart, beating slowly, but still pumping the blood vital to his existence. A strike anywhere else would just be a waste of time, unless one simply wanted to inflict pain. Of course, that meant Linh was equally difficult to kill.

Linh stopped abruptly. She tilted her head toward the ceiling, then glanced at Adrian with a questioning look.

"Where's Joseph? I heard that dog barking when you first broke in."

Adrian didn't drop his guard at the question, but she was correct. Where was Joseph? Surely he'd want to face Linh himself.

"Oh, I see. You're not one of Joseph's vassals. You're Garrick's, aren't you?"

Adrian didn't answer her, but he imagined his look of quiet panic was answer enough. She was right, but what did it matter? What dots had Linh connected that he was missing?

Linh dropped the sword at her side and sighed heavily. She returned to her soup, still seated at the edge of the table.

"I'm afraid we've both been played, boy."

She tilted the bowl back and drank the rest of the blood greedily. Just as she finished, another servant burst into the room.

"Fire!" the servant shouted. "Fire, spreading quickly!"

Adrian's panic intensified. Was that what had caught Linh's attention moments ago?

"A waste of good food, if you ask me," Linh said. "I'll give your regards to Joseph and Garrick next time I see them."

With that, Linh's form began to shift. Her head morphed into a monster's, and coarse hair sprouted across her body. Skin stretched from her arms to her sides, forming a membrane that joined with her lower half. Less than a breath later, a giant bat stood in her place. With its expansive wings, the bat took flight toward the upper levels of the dining room. It clung to the ceiling and, with a massive claw, shattered a singular skylight window, sending glass shards raining down. Adrian ducked under the table to defend himself, and once the hailstorm of glass subsided, he looked back up just in time to see the bat crawl out through the hole in the roof.

By now, the area had dissolved into disorganized chaos. As smoke began to pour into the dining room, those who had tried to kill one another moments before ran together toward the nearest exit. Adrian was about to follow, but a shout from the foyer stopped him cold.

"It's barred! The doors are barred!"

This is what Linh meant. It was rare for Elders to work together, and Adrian's crew had gained a reputation for disposing of Joseph's rivals. Joseph feared Garrick's crew, and that should have frightened Adrian.

Adrian looked up. He was at least a century too young for the kind of shapeshifting magic that had saved Linh. He scanned the room for a window instead. The dining room had one long window, shrouded by heavy drapes. He pulled them back—only to find a brick wall framed with wood where the glass had once been.

What?

Adrian grabbed a chair. Drywall was easily breakable. He slammed the chair against the wall, only for it to splinter and bounce away. Thinking he got unlucky and hit a stud, Adrian grabbed another and hit the wall a hand's width away from the first strike. The chair splintered again, leaving little more than a scuff against the paint. Disbelieving, Adrian walked over to inspect the graze. Chipping away at the broken drywall, Adrian found brick.

In her paranoia, Linh had built an impenetrable fortress. And a tomb.

Now the panic truly gripped Adrian. He couldn't escape through the doors. He couldn't escape through the windows. He couldn't escape through the walls. The skylight was unreachable. At this point, his only option was to hope Linh, for some crazed, Madness-fueled reason, built hidden tunnels. Or to find some way to survive a burning building until the flames smoldered out.

"Adrian!" Everett called. He and the rest of his crew ran to him. "What do we do?"

He didn't know.

"Get somewhere safe!"

Adrian dropped to the floor. Smoke wouldn't kill him, as his body no longer needed to breathe, but it still stung his eyes and the room was filling up fast. What could he do to survive? A bathtub, perhaps? He crawled on the floor out of the dining room, but the next room over had flames dancing up the interior walls. Those were not reinforced by brick. Adrian had to find some kind of cover, but he was crawling blind through an unfamiliar house. He had no idea where a master bathroom would be located. Or hell, even if this house had a bathtub he could flip over on himself.

He heard the screams of the servants and a loud crash. The house's foundations were starting to crumble and collapse. Adrian didn't have time for doubt. He either got lucky and found something fireproof to hide in, or he died.

Adrian continued to crouch low and moved across the burning room. He didn't have many options for direction. One end was fully ablaze, the other slightly less so. He made his way into what looked like a bedroom. No bathroom attached to it, however. He tried another room, this one appearing to be some kind of office featuring a very burnable wooden desk.

Adrian looked behind him to see Everett run out of a room in frustration. His other two crew members stayed nearby, hoping Adrian had found safety. They flinched and glanced nervously at the ceiling when he shook his head.

He made his way back toward the shouts of the servants, hoping they'd found something. But as he got closer and could hear more clearly, he realized the cries were just as despairing as he felt. He couldn't give up. Giving up was death.

Another loud crack reverberated through the house, and before Adrian could see where it came from, a large, charred wooden beam slammed into his head. When he woke— seconds later, he hoped—Adrian realized his entire body was pinned beneath rubble. He tried to brace his hands beneath him and push free, but his pounding head had sapped him of all strength. He could barely lift his chest before collapsing back to the floor.

He looked around. Jan and Quinn had also been caught in the collapsed ceiling. Jan was still awake, though her leg splayed at an impossible angle. Broken, painfully. Quinn lay completely motionless.

Everett had been the only one spared. He looked down at Adrian in surprise, then tried to free him from the heavy beam. Another loud crack from above caused him to flinch back. Everett took one last look at Adrian, and then turned and ran. Adrian sneered and once again tried to lift the rubble from his back, but even anger-driven strength had its limits.

So this was it? He'd been played, a pawn in Elder vampire grudges, burning not in the sun but in a trap of fire. Alone.

He nearly gave up. He lay on his stomach, waiting for the flames to reach him, listening to the screams of the others.

"Garrick!" The voice sounded like Everett's. Suddenly, Adrian was filled with hope once again. A chorus from Linh's guards and servants echoed Everett's call.

"Garrick! Garrick!"

He was here, and Adrian admonished the brief moments when he'd thought he'd been abandoned.

"Gar..." Adrian tried to call out as well, but he realized just how weak he'd become. The beam pinning him to the floor allowed barely any air into his lungs, making it difficult to shout.

Then the calling changed. Adrian listened as the cries for Garrick took on a fearful pitch. And then despair. Anger. Now they cursed him.

Adrian craned his head toward the doorway, and he saw a man walk in calmly, as if the world around him wasn't burning to the ground. He didn't crawl along the floor like Adrian, but stood tall despite the smoke. Two hellish red eyes pierced through the black haze and landed directly on him. Adrian froze. What betrayal had the others faced?

Garrick walked beside Adrian's body and, with a loud grunt, he lifted the wooden beam off him. He scooped Adrian up and held him to his chest, then turned and walked back the way he came. Adrian gripped the man's shirt tightly and closed his eyes to block out the sting of the smoke. He heard the other voices, louder now, as they called Garrick's name in desperation. It had no effect on the man. He continued walking as if he were deaf to them.

Then, without warning, they were flying. A cold breeze

whipped over Adrian's body, replacing the broiling heat of the burning house. The shock must have knocked him out cold, as the last thing he remembered was a pair of great demon wings pulling him out of Hell.

When he came to, they were on the ground again in a lonely grass field, far away from the city proper. He was still in Garrick's arms, his back resting against a raised knee, his head cradled to Garrick's chest. With his ear pressed close, he could hear Garrick's slow, soft heartbeat, and the vestigial spasms of a man weeping.

And that was when Adrian knew he truly loved him.

2

NIGHT I - ADRIAN

Present Day

I f there was one thing Adrian did not care for, it was parties. Even as a teenager, he avoided invitations to house parties. Not that he got many. This one wasn't even particularly interesting. No music, no excitement, just idle chatter.

Adrian walked up to a massive window that stretched the length of the wall and gazed out over the San Francisco cityscape. From the top of the hill where the mansion stood, the lights of the city below drowned out the stars above. He had to admit, the view was stunning—at least for the small peninsula that was San Francisco.

Of course, for vampires, glass walls were also a death trap. He figured Owen, the owner of the mansion, must have taken a different design approach in his bedroom. If there was a window, blackout curtains were likely bolted to the wall.

Adrian jumped when he felt a hand rest on his shoulder. Garrick stepped up beside him.

"Mingle, would you?" It was a good-natured plea rather than a command.

"You know I don't do that." Adrian lifted his glass of "wine" to his lips. It tasted like some type of animal's blood. He had long since lost the ability to be nourished by animals, but nothing prevented him from drinking it out of politeness. After taking a sip, he twirled the glass by the stem between his fingers.

"I need you to make friends," Garrick said. "For me."

Adrian shot a sarcastic side-eye at the other man. Friends weren't made in a single night. But before he could respond, Garrick turned his attention to something behind him. Adrian turned to see a shorter, broad man in a beige suit and shaved head sauntering toward them.

"Owen," Garrick called, holding out a polite arm to gesture between them. "This is Adrian. He's been my right hand for just over forty years now. Adrian, this is Owen. He's been kind enough to host us in this city."

Adrian tightened his jaw into a stiff smile and extended his hand. Owen shook it with equal lack of enthusiasm.

"Forty years," Owen repeated. "That's quite a long time to have one vassal around, isn't it?"

Adrian pulled his hand away and slowly slid it into his front pocket. No, it wasn't. Most vassals who remained loyal to the Elder Regent lived to be two hundred. Adrian risked a cursory glance at Garrick's face, and to his credit, he did a good job of hiding his exasperation. If Adrian hadn't spent forty years testing his patience, he might have missed the subtle eyebrow protrusion Garrick made when something bothered him but wasn't worth complaining about.

"Adrian's done well. I prefer having fewer vassals. We're not seeking fame or power."

"Well, you've made it this far. You must be doing something right."

Owen slid his eyes from Garrick to Adrian and held them there, as if reading something written on Adrian's face. Adrian stared back, uncowed by the Elder's gaze, until he felt Garrick's hand brush the small of his back. He broke eye contact and brought the glass of blood-wine to his lips, downing the rest as if it held some property that might make the conversation more tolerable.

The unspoken tension went unnoticed by Owen. He turned his head and pointed his nose toward a woman with short, dark hair in a nightshade-colored dress, standing among a group of four but not participating in the conversation.

"See her?" Owen asked. "That's my right hand. Gorgeous, isn't she? Smarter than she looks, too. Incredibly loyal. Only five years turned, but she quickly became my favorite."

Adrian clenched his teeth and stared a hole into the side of Garrick's head, desperately trying to catch his eye. But Garrick didn't take the bait.

"You're a lucky man," Garrick said, his tone pointedly flat.

"You should trust your girl a little more," Owen said, either ignoring or not noticing the other man's sarcasm. "They're not like the women we knew. Smarter these days. Give them some accounting work; keeps their mind busy and their body resting so they'll be ready for you at the end of the night."

Garrick nodded slowly, and Owen slapped him on the arm.

"I have to take care of a few things, but come find me in thirty minutes so we can talk in private."

He turned and left without so much as a glance toward Adrian. Garrick, still facing away, let out a long, heavy sigh. Despite his lungs going mostly unused for the better part of six hundred years, Garrick still knew how to use them to make a point. Then, he finally turned to face him. Good, Adrian's exaggeratedly arched eyebrows and pursed lips were becoming difficult to hold.

"I know," Garrick said.

"Really? This is who we're working for now?"

"*I know.*" Garrick placed his hand lightly on Adrian's arm, just above the elbow. "We're not in a position to be picky. Owen is a new Elder, and he still has some growing to do."

"Of course. Spry young age of two hundred; I'm sure learning and growing is something he's very interested in pursuing."

The touch on Adrian's arm tightened into a firm grip.

"Let's not make any more enemies this week," Garrick whispered, his face falling. "I know this isn't ideal, but we're safe here. Let's lie low and give it some time. We can reassess whether we want to stay once things have cooled off. Okay?"

Adrian dropped his shoulders and stared at his feet. But he nodded. Garrick was right, as he always was, and Adrian knew there was nothing he could do except make things worse. And he hated it.

Garrick's grip loosened. "Mingle," he said again. "There must be someone at this party you can get along with. At the very least, I need you to gather intelligence for me. Everyone's too scared to talk to me, so I need you to pick up the gossip. Understand?"

Adrian rolled his eyes, but the corner of his mouth lifted. Garrick didn't really mean it, but he knew how to reframe the situation into something tolerable for Adrian. Give him a heightened purpose beyond making small talk and friends.

"Fine," Adrian said. Garrick smiled and let him go. Adrian watched him walk over to Val and chat for a minute, then disappear deeper into the mansion.

It didn't take long for Adrian's willpower to engage in conversation to deplete. He scanned the room, looking for someone to make dull small talk with, but it seemed everyone was already in the middle of a conversation—or loitering off to the side, just as disinterested as he was. Adrian turned and set his empty wineglass on a table, then walked to the far wall, which separated the large sitting room at the front of the mansion from a kitchen that had likely gone unused for decades.

A minute later, Val walked up to him.

"Life of the party, I see," she teased.

Adrian shot her a good-natured, sideways glance. He was relieved that Val had come up to talk, but he knew that wasn't what Garrick meant by "mingle." It didn't count if they'd known each other for ten years.

"Did Garrick warn you about Owen?" Adrian asked.

"No, he asked me to make sure you didn't just stand around on the side of the room."

Thanks, Garrick.

"But what's this about Owen?"

Adrian looked around the room at the three dozen or so vampires talking, laughing, and sipping their blood-wine. At least two of those dozen were women, most of whom were young and skinny with plush lips and wearing dresses that accentuated their breasts, their asses, or both.

"He enjoys certain kinds of company," Adrian stated.

Val let out an annoyed grunt. "Yeah, I noticed." She fit right in with the crowd. About a head shorter than Adrian and as thin as a stick, the only thing that made her stand out was her choice of fashion, wearing a casual blouse and skinny jeans. Adrian wasn't exactly dressed to impress either, keeping his thick travel coat on over a faded T-shirt. But it was less of an issue for him, as the men in the room didn't appear to be held to the same standards as the women. The best-dressed among them wore a deep red button-up shirt with the sleeves rolled up above his elbows.

Val grabbed Adrian's arm and tugged him into the center of the room. "Come on," she said. Adrian let out a groan in protest, but allowed himself to be dragged over to a group of five: two men and three women. He felt eyes settle on him and Val as they approached the circle. No one spoke until one of the women—wearing a sundress despite the winter season, with short blonde hair—finished her story. She turned to the two newcomers and smiled.

"You're the two new vassals who just moved here, right?" she asked.

"That's right," Val answered. "I'm Val, and this is Adrian."

Adrian smiled awkwardly and raised his hand no higher than his abdomen in a hesitant wave. One by one, the members of the group introduced themselves, and by the time the last one said his name, Adrian had already forgotten the first.

"So, where are you from, then?" one of the two men asked. His name started with an M—Mark?

Adrian glanced to his side to see if Val was going to answer, only to find that she had slipped away during the introductions. Thanks, Val.

"Oh, um… LA."

"Damn. I heard they're pretty vicious down in LA. Always getting into fights between the Regents down there."

"Oh, yeah, I guess." "Vicious" was certainly a fitting way to describe Joseph.

The other man leaned forward. Buzz cut, tight T-shirt. John? Now he was just taking wild guesses.

"The third guy's an Elder, though," Buzz Cut John said, keeping his voice low. "He's not gonna try to take over, right?"

"Garrick isn't here to cause trouble," Adrian said quickly. "He doesn't like leading Covens. We worked under a different Regent in LA, and we're going to do the same here."

"Then what brought you to San Francisco?" one of the women, Juniper, asked. He remembered her because her name was so unusual.

Adrian hesitated. "We... ran into some trouble."

Sundress girl chuckled. Buzz Cut John didn't seem to find it nearly as humorous.

"It's not funny," he said. "Elders are psychopaths. It's like when a lion takes over a pride, he'll kill all the cubs so the lionesses will be loyal to him."

"Wait, lions do that?" the third woman, blue sweater and skirt, asked.

"That's what Owen did."

"We're really not going to do anything like that," Adrian insisted.

"What kind of trouble did you get into?" Juniper asked. If she was looking for reasons not to trust him, she was good at hiding it. She sounded genuinely curious.

"I... well, I picked a fight with the Regent." Adrian shifted his gaze. This wasn't helping his case. "But he deserved it."

"I don't know, Tyler, I think I like this lion better," Juniper said. "If the new guy tells you to stop grabbing Mia's ass, then I'm siding with him."

Buzz Cut Tyler—that wasn't even close to John—flinched defensively. If his heart still pumped blood at its former rate, Adrian was sure his face would have flushed red. Adrian just rolled his eyes. Apparently, Owen's proclivities had rubbed off on the men working under him.

"You picked a fight and lived?" Maybe-Mark asked. "How old are you?"

"Forty."

"Damn. Everyone here is younger than fifteen. Still, forty's pretty young to be getting into fights with Elders."

Adrian shrugged, but couldn't help taking some pride in the implied praise. Even if the fight in question had been entirely one-sided.

"Hey, we're celebrating Mia's birthday next week," Juniper said. "You should come."

It took Adrian a moment to fully grasp the invitation. "Oh, sure," he answered automatically. She was inviting him to hang out? But he was... It was only after he pulled out his phone to exchange numbers that Adrian realized how strange his thoughts were. As a vassal to Garrick, he was always an outsider among Joseph's lackeys. There were a few vampires he was friendly with, but no one would risk becoming real friends with him. Here, though, that clearly wasn't the case.

"Come on," Juniper pulled him by the arm and dragged him over to another cluster, this time of three women. Adrian found himself standing across from a short woman with blonde hair as Juniper grabbed her arm as well.

"Mia! Have you met Adrian? He's one of the new guys from LA. They're pretty tough down there, but he's made it to forty years. I bet you know some neat magic, don't you?"

Um, well, yes. Unsure how else to respond, Adrian flicked his wrist, sending a ribbon of shadows weaving in and out of his fingers. It was just a little trick, but he realized it had caught the attention of the two other girls. Was this all it took to make friends? Party tricks? But just as he had the group's attention, Juniper drew the two girls on Mia's left back to her.

"Sorry about her," Mia sighed. "She's been trying to set me up for over a year."

Oh, so that's what this was. Adrian fidgeted with his hands after his little shadow trick, wiping them on the sides of his coat before slipping them back into his pockets. Mia chuckled.

"Don't worry, it's nothing you did. My name's Mia."

Adrian introduced himself again. Well, she did have a cute

smile. Not that it was something he needed to concern himself with.

Something on Adrian's periphery caught his eye. He glanced over, then quickly looked back at Mia after uncomfortably locking eyes with Tyler. In that brief moment, he noticed that Tyler now had the attention of another man— young, with a stream of black hair. Or perhaps it was the other way around, and Tyler was his audience. It was hard to tell, as Tyler seemed far more interested in Adrian, his gaze already fixed on him before Adrian had even turned his head.

Right, Mia. The pieces clicked into place. Juniper was trying to set them up because Adrian was now the third-strongest vampire in the city, and the strongest among the non-Elders.

"Don't mind him," Mia grumbled. "He's just an Owen suck-up."

"I know the type," Adrian replied.

They talked a while longer, and Adrian actually made some progress on his promise to Garrick. No one had anything specific to say about them, but Adrian sensed a worry brewing just beneath the surface. Mia seemed to think the party was a poor attempt at placating potentially troubling news. Small quips between her friends were brushed off as jokes if Adrian took a second too long to laugh. Doubt stirred in his gut. Had he been recruited as a fake friend, a means of gathering information?

Well, a fake friend was still a friend. In a way. Better than open hostility.

As members of the group peeled off to talk to others at the party, Adrian sighed and looked down at the new number in his phone's contact list, which was practically barren save for Garrick and Val. Of course, making friends wasn't that easy, but it was a start. He just needed time to prove he could be counted on.

Adrian looked up to see Tyler approaching. His piercing

gaze hadn't lost its edge the entire time Adrian had been talking.

"Hey," Tyler said, keeping his voice low. But he leaned in a bit too close, and his tone came off a little too confrontational.

"Stay away from Mia, all right? She's a liar, loves to chew guys up and spit them out."

"...I thought you liked her?"

"Yeah, so you stay away."

The look of confusion on Adrian's face did not help.

"Something you don't get?"

Yes, this entire conversation.

Tyler leaned in closer, but Adrian refused to take a step back. He hadn't done anything, and he wasn't about to be intimidated by some young lackey with a bone to pick. He had promised Garrick there'd be no trouble. But with every second that Tyler invaded his space, the walls seemed to close in and choke him.

Like a surge of smoke rising from his feet, Adrian forced a ribbon of shadows between them. He was older, with more powerful magic. Tyler didn't want this fight.

But Tyler simply smiled and thrust a cloud of shadows into Adrian's face.

Adrian stumbled back in surprise, crashing into the table of wine glasses and sending it toppling over. A dozen glasses hit the floor and shattered. The room fell abruptly silent as everyone turned their attention toward Adrian, awkwardly sitting in a puddle of pig's blood and broken glass, with Tyler standing triumphantly before him.

For a moment, Adrian considered doing nothing and just accepting his loss. This was petty, and entirely Tyler's fault. Continuing to fight would only make things worse for him.

But he could also make things worse for Tyler.

Adrian picked up the broken stem of a wine glass and hurled it in Tyler's direction. The glass struck Tyler's raised arm, leaving a shallow cut. Adrian seized the distraction to spring to his feet and leap straight into the air. His hand brushed the concrete ceiling, just enough to latch onto the surface and twist his body into an upside-down kneeling position.

There. Tyler was too young for this power. He couldn't continue their fight if he couldn't reach Adrian on the ceiling.

Or so Adrian thought. But Tyler jumped too, executing the same maneuver Adrian had performed just a moment earlier. The two stared at each other, upside down, Tyler still grinning confidently.

So, Adrian punched him in the nose.

The sickening crunch beneath Adrian's fist was louder than he expected. The shock of it made Tyler fall, but he grabbed Adrian's leg on the way down and dragged him to the floor. They crashed hard. Adrian's senses returned just as Tyler snaked an arm around his neck, trying to lock him in a headlock. In response, Adrian bit his arm. Tyler yelped in pain and struggled to push Adrian off, but with one arm pinned, his ability to fight back was limited.

Someone yanked hard on the back of Adrian's head and around his throat, prying him off like a dog. A man built like a military veteran dragged Adrian away and stood between him and Tyler, who now sported a terrified expression, blood streaming from his nose and forearm. Adrian stood and sneered triumphantly.

And then he was slammed against the window, the glass threatening to buckle and shatter beneath the high-speed force that was Owen—his arm pressed against Adrian's throat, fangs threatening to sink into his neck.

"Owen!" The shout came from Garrick. Adrian braced himself for a strike from the Regent, but it never came. Garrick had somehow wedged himself between them, standing protectively over Adrian as he slid to the floor.

"...Come into MY house!"

"I know, it's been a long day."

Adrian wiped the blood from his mouth with his sleeve and stood up. He didn't want to hear this. Despite knowing the danger he had willingly put himself in, Adrian found he didn't care that he had just blown whatever chance he had at a quiet, happy life in San Francisco. He hadn't wanted it in the first place.

As Owen argued with Garrick, Adrian got up and walked toward the front door. He passed behind Garrick and glanced over at the other girls—Mia, Juniper, and everyone else he had met that night. Whatever his status had been with them at the beginning of the night, they wouldn't risk being friends with him now, fake or otherwise. Fine.

"Adrian!" Garrick called just as he moved out of reach. Adrian sucked in a breath and turned to see what his Elder wanted.

Owen was still reeling but didn't try to push past Garrick to continue his attack. Garrick didn't acknowledge him. He simply pulled a white plastic room key from his pocket.

"Wait for me."

Adrian wordlessly took the key and turned around. No one spoke until he was out the door.

The hotel wasn't far, just five blocks south of the hill where Owen's mansion stood. Adrian walked halfway before sitting down on a street curb, his feet suddenly feeling the weight of his self-imposed exile. He twirled the hotel room key between his fingers.

I shouldn't be mad, he thought. He hated pretending to enjoy cheap animal blood and making small talk, so he should have been glad for an excuse to leave. Listening to the cars drive by was far better company than a room full of strangers. If only the cars could make him feel less alone.

But something else tugged at his mind. Adrian licked his thumb and wiped the corner of his mouth, then licked it again. He hadn't imagined it, the blood was different. Sweet.

3
Night 1 - Val

O h no, Adrian got into another fight. Val sighed, bracing herself for yet another week of drama.

Silence, speckled with hushed whispers, fell over the party hall as Adrian stormed out. Garrick reached out as if to follow, but stopped and turned his attention back to Owen, who had begun protesting again. Stepping into Owen's line of sight to the front door, Garrick tried to calm him. Val wished she could hear what he was saying. Garrick was well-practiced in the art of soothing flared tempers, but Owen was a wildcard. Val ground her teeth. If Owen decided to kick them out of the city, then what? Another six hours of driving tomorrow night, most likely.

Val glanced back at the two women she had been talking

to. They whispered to each other, trying to piece together what had occurred between Adrian and the other man.

Doing her best not to arouse suspicion, Val sneaked closer to Garrick and Owen, hoping to eavesdrop on their tense conversation.

"What have you done to that boy?" she finally heard Owen say.

Garrick's voice dropped to a whisper, and Val couldn't hear his reply. But whatever he said seemed to placate the Regent. Owen twisted his face in disgust but ceased complaining. With a curt nod, he turned and marched out of the room, arms crossed. Garrick combed his fingers through his coarse, gray-blonde hair and slumped his shoulders in relief.

"He bit Tyler?" Val heard one of the women behind her say. "How much you want to bet he was hitting on Mia again?"

"Good for the new guy," another said. "Too bad Owen's going to kill him."

Garrick would never let it happen. He cared too much for Adrian.

Something stirred at the back of Val's throat. For a fleeting instant, she imagined Adrian's head cracked open like an eggshell, shattered under the force of a simple toolbox hammer. What would Garrick do then?

The stirring quickly morphed into revulsion—not just at the mental image Val had been burying for the past week, but also at the thought of losing her last two friends.

Garrick glanced around the room and stopped when he saw her. Exhaustion painted his features, and Val mirrored the expression. As he approached, the two women standing behind Val took a few uneasy steps back.

"So…"

"We'll be fine," Garrick sighed. "Owen puts on a big show, but he's far less temperamental than Joseph. We just need to make sure something like this doesn't happen again."

Val wanted to make a snide comment about the likelihood of that, but she stopped herself to stay kind in front of Garrick.

"We're just tired and moody after a long night of travel," Val said.

Garrick nodded in agreement. "I need to go talk to him. Are you going to stay longer?"

Val shook her head and accompanied Garrick out of the mansion. He threw on an old travel coat—something Val had always found odd, given that Garrick, of all people, should be most accustomed to cold temperatures. Adrian wore his as a fashion statement, as far as Val could tell. She didn't bother with one herself. It might have looked strange for a skinny girl like her to be out in the early morning chill wearing nothing but a short-sleeved blouse, but she couldn't care less what the late-night drunkards thought of her.

"Thank you for coming along," Garrick said after a few minutes of walking in silence. "It's nice to have more than just Adrian here, considering it's been..." Garrick looked up at the sky in thought. "One hundred years? Since I've had to move cities."

"You're welcome." Wow, one hundred years living in Los Angeles. Val would have gone insane. "There was no way I was going to stick around with Joseph."

Val's stomach turned. She focused on each footstep, one after the other, to keep her mind from wandering.

"How are you doing?" Garrick asked.

"Fine."

"Are you sure?" Garrick didn't believe her, because she wasn't fine, and she did a poor job of hiding it. But she didn't want to discuss it. What would that accomplish? Sure, she could cry on Garrick's shoulder and feel a little better. And then what? She didn't need to feel better. She needed Joseph to feel worse.

"I'm sure."

Garrick nodded, and then mercifully changed the subject. "Adrian's not giving you trouble, is he?"

"Adrian and I have been fine for years. I think he might actually like me."

Val pulled her lips into a self-satisfied smirk, prompting Garrick to respond with bemusement. It wasn't much of a mystery why they finally got along. Val wasn't the only vampire in Los Angeles who hated Joseph as much as Adrian did. She was, however, the only one who saw Adrian's outbursts against him as something to be celebrated. She was always careful to keep her satisfaction hidden until they were alone, but it didn't take long for Adrian to win her over, despite their rocky start.

"Who would've thought..." Garrick shook his head. "I'm glad he finally found a friend other than me."

Perhaps, if there was one shoulder she would allow herself to cry on, it was Adrian's. She wasn't sure they were that close yet, but this was one area Adrian understood better than Garrick. But, given everything that had happened with Joseph over the past week, Adrian wasn't in a good place to console her.

"Val," Garrick said, catching her spiraling thoughts. His voice was low, serious, as if he could sense what she was thinking. "Do me one favor. Don't go looking for revenge."

Bile gathered at the back of Val's throat. Of all people to tell her not to seek revenge, it had to be Garrick.

"I won't," she lied.

Garrick stared at her for a few intense seconds, then nodded. Whether he believed her or was simply satisfied with the lie, she didn't know. Regardless, she didn't need his approval. Val did not suffer for the sake of others.

4

NIGHT 1 - ADRIAN

The hotel had to be the oldest in all of San Francisco. The room was more spacious than Adrian had anticipated, with a king-sized bed against the east wall and enough space on the west side for a desk and two loungers. Above the chairs, clashing with the aged décor, was a modern television bolted to the wall. When Adrian first entered, he flipped through the channels but ultimately decided he was too tired and closed his eyes for some rest. The walls were steeped in the smell of old cigarette smoke, a stench Adrian was beginning to find unpleasant, even though it had never bothered him before. Forty years without needing a smoke was finally changing him. At least breathing was optional now.

Adrian only got up when he heard a knock at the door. He opened it and stepped aside to let Garrick in. The old vampire shed his gray travel coat and hung it neatly on the coat rack beside a lounge chair, over which Adrian had carelessly tossed his own jacket.

"Cozy. Unfortunate about the smell," Garrick said. He inspected the desk in the corner of the room. Adrian sat at the foot of the bed, arms folded, silently awaiting whatever Garrick wanted to say. The man wasn't in much of a hurry. He examined the windows, curtains, television, even the lock on the door. When the sun was your enemy, carelessness was killer. Garrick returned to the desk and sat on its edge, facing Adrian.

"How are you feeling?"

Adrian didn't meet his eyes, but he lifted his shoulders in a slight shrug.

"So what happened?"

Adrian turned his head in shame. He had one goal: not to make things worse. That lasted all of one evening. And for what? Just so he wouldn't feel pushed around by Tyler?

How did Garrick do it? Always sweet-talking his way out of every confrontation? How could he stand it?

After a moment of silence, Garrick joined him at the foot of the bed. He didn't try to put a comforting arm around him or rest a hand on his knee. He just sat.

"I'm not mad at you," he said softly. "You know that, right?"

He didn't, actually. Garrick had every right to be mad at him. He should have been furious. Instead, Adrian felt Garrick gently take his hand and thread their fingers together. He couldn't bear to look.

"Why didn't it work?" Adrian asked.

He waited for an answer, thinking that maybe Garrick

didn't know what he was referring to. But after a long, anguished pause, Garrick finally responded.

"Elders are tough," he stated. "We're difficult to kill."

That would have been nice to know before he tried to kill one. But he didn't dare say that out loud.

"Don't worry about Owen." Garrick directed the conversation back to the more pressing matter. "We'll go over tomorrow and apologize. I've promised him a few favors to ease his temper. In the meantime, you can learn where the best hunting spots are and stay out of his... Well, not his hair. His scalp."

Garrick chuckled at his own joke, but it didn't last more than a single huffed breath when Adrian didn't return the laugh.

"I'm sure you're tired. I'll let you—"

"Yeah." Adrian stood and crossed the room to a dresser by the door. He reached into his pocket for his room key and haphazardly tossed it on top of the dresser, then picked up a nearly identical key that had been carefully placed on its corner. He grabbed his travel bag and long coat. His hand was on the doorknob when Garrick called to him. Hesitating slightly, Adrian looked over his shoulder to see what else Garrick wanted.

"...I'm going to be busy all night tomorrow. We'll have time after that."

Adrian waited a beat longer to see if anything else was on Garrick's mind. "Yeah," he repeated, then walked out the door.

5

NIGHT 2 - ADRIAN

Returning to Owen's mansion didn't fill Adrian with confidence. The last time he had seen the Regent, Owen had his arm at Adrian's throat, pinning him against a large glass pane overlooking a twenty-foot drop, his fangs bared like a snarling animal. Garrick always had a way of smoothing over slights. Adrian couldn't fathom how he had the appetite for it.

The front door opened to reveal Owen, who immediately fixed his eyes on Adrian, narrowing them in something close to a scowl. Garrick placed a hand on Adrian's shoulder. Whether to protect or calm him, Adrian couldn't tell. Val stood silently behind them. She was always more tactful with her anger.

"Owen," Garrick said, trying to grab his attention. "I wanted to follow up on what happened last night. Can we come in?"

Owen grunted and jerked his head back in a gesture Adrian interpreted as a welcome. He, Garrick, and Val entered the mansion, now devoid of partiers. The house had been thoroughly cleaned and tidied. Even the bloodstain from where he had crushed Tyler's nose and bitten his arm had been removed from the hardwood floor.

"We wanted to offer an apology," Garrick said in his soothing tone, reserved for whenever Adrian dragged him into yet another skiff. He imagined it worked on anyone who hadn't heard it a million times. To him, it just grated on his nerves.

He felt Garrick squeeze his shoulder.

"My apologies," Adrian said, forcing himself to meet Owen's eyes. He did his best to make his rehearsed words sound natural. "It's been a tense week, but that's no excuse for the way I acted. Please let me know if there's any way I can make it up to you."

Please just drop it, Adrian thought. Owen stared at him for an uncomfortably long moment, and Adrian knew he didn't believe the apology. But mercifully, Owen nodded.

"I can think of something that will help," Owen said. "We have a bit of an incident with a rogue vassal. You LA vampires are tough. Shouldn't be too hard to track her down."

Adrian bit his tongue. Great, this rogue vassal probably had a good reason to run, and now he had to play the designated bad guy and enforce Owen's policies. Still, he put on a pleasant smile and nodded.

Behind him, Adrian heard Garrick whisper to Val to go with him. His initial reaction was offense at the notion that he needed supervision. However, he paused and took a slow, deliberate breath. Getting riled up again wouldn't help anything. And he'd rather have Val than go alone.

"Melissa will go with you. Help you navigate San Francisco," Owen continued. "She's out back. In the meantime, Garrick..."

The Elder nodded and gave Adrian's shoulder a small pat before leaving with Owen. Adrian watched them walk away, surprised by the sense of longing that followed.

"That went pretty well," Val said. Adrian turned to see if she was joking, then realized she was completely serious. Well, she was right. Owen could have demanded much worse from him. Hopefully, he'd just have to retrieve this runaway vassal and could start with a clean slate.

The two made their way to the back of the mansion and stepped into a small, fenced-in area with a stone patio and a modest pool. Standing by a small table and chairs were the woman from the previous night—the one Owen had pointed out as his right-hand woman—and Tyler.

Adrian's stomach sank.

The woman's attention shifted to Adrian and Val. "Can I help you?" she asked.

"Owen assigned us to help you track down a vassal," Val said, quickly responding before Adrian could speak.

"Well, I guess you've proven yourself in a fight." The woman weaved around Tyler and approached Val with her hand out. "I'm Melissa," she said, first shaking Val's hand and then Adrian's. Adrian introduced himself politely, keeping his attention firmly on Melissa to avoid meeting Tyler's eyes.

Now that he had met her up close, Adrian noticed just how skinny Melissa was. Unlike Val and the other women he had met the previous night, Melissa was nearly skeletal. She had barely any fat or muscle on her frame, giving her a sickly appearance. Still, she held her head high with confidence.

"Hey," Tyler finally spoke up after his introduction with

Melissa was over. "No hard feelings, just a big misunderstanding. Let's start over?"

Tyler held out his hand. Slowly, Adrian shook it. "Yeah," he said. "My bad."

"Good! You throw a pretty hard punch. I'd hate for us to be enemies."

Adrian forced one of Garrick's good-natured smiles, and Tyler returned it. Then Tyler turned his attention to Val and introduced himself.

Actually, now that Tyler mentioned it, his nose looked pristine. Owen must have healed it.

"Hope I didn't rough up your boyfriend too much."

"Oh! Adrian's not my—" Val paused and bit her tongue. Did she regret admitting she was single around Tyler? Adrian stifled a teasing laugh.

Tyler continued chatting with Val, so Adrian turned his attention to Melissa. She took her phone out of her pocket and angled the screen toward him. On it was a photo of a woman standing with a neutral expression.

"This is our rogue vassal. Her name is Summer Davis. We last heard from her about two weeks ago. She's cut off all contact with us, including failing to show up to give blood. We need to recover her alive."

The woman didn't resemble Owen's typical vassal. She was tall and muscular, with short hair trimmed like a man's and several facial piercings. A rose tattoo stretched from her clavicle up the side of her neck.

"If she's been gone for two weeks, then she's already dead."

"We intercept her text messages. She's alive."

Adrian threw a suspicious glance Melissa's way.

"Owen pays for the basics. That means new phones."

Adrian made a mental note to never let Owen buy him any electronics. Garrick supplied the money for Adrian's phone, but the man was far too old to understand how to set it up. Adrian had to teach him basic texting, even though he was new to the technology himself.

"We know she's meeting with someone tonight to purchase a new car," Melissa continued. "We'll meet her there and capture her."

"If she wants to leave, why not just let her?"

"No one leaves unless Owen allows it." She met Adrian's bewildered look with indifference. "Is that a problem?"

Adrian pushed down his complaints. Just one job. After it was done, he could worry about his long-term plans.

"Hey, we have some time," Tyler called out to them. "Want a tour of the city?"

"Actually, I do need some blood," Adrian said.

The group began walking toward the heart of the city. The sun had set, but the nightlife was still vibrant. The extended nighttime of the winter months was a blessing to vampires, and the warm California weather rarely interrupted prime hunting hours with snowfall.

"So, where are we headed?" Adrian asked.

"Tenderloin District," Melissa said.

"Because the people there taste like tenderloin?"

Melissa glanced at him, humorless. At least Val laughed.

"San Francisco has plenty of homeless, so you don't have to go far. And this neighborhood is particularly infamous for violent crime. So if you get lucky, someone will pull a gun and make themselves your next meal. You can even do it in front of other people and it'll only be the second weirdest thing they've seen that night."

Val would appreciate that. Adrian had long ago stopped being choosy about the people he fed on, but Val still tried to hold on to some shred of morality when it came to picking victims. Criminals, drug dealers, old men cheating on their wives... It was difficult to constantly find someone who deserved it. Adrian was fine with anyone, except for...

Melissa passed a man huddled on the sidewalk, pressed

against the wall of a pawnshop whose doors and windows were barred for the night. He was bundled in several layers of clothing and covered by a quilted blanket. It was hard to tell whether he was asleep or simply ignoring them, but he didn't move when Melissa knelt down. The only indication Adrian had that the man was alive was the way he startled when she bit into his neck, but that reaction quickly ceased. Adrian waited in uncomfortable disgust for several long seconds until she finally finished.

"I don't drink from homeless," Adrian stated as Melissa stood back up.

"Well, aren't we bougie?"

"I was homeless."

An uncomfortable silence stretched between the group, but Adrian refused to feel awkward about it. Still, he could feel the judgmental stares, especially from Tyler. Tyler had likely been searching for his own homeless person to feed on when Adrian spoke.

"...I'll just find someone else," Adrian muttered. He turned and left, doing his best to ignore the next helpless man or woman destined to be haunted by Tyler's fangs. It didn't matter—plenty of Joseph's vassals fed on the homeless. They were easy prey. Adrian realized his hand had risen to his neck, and he forced it back down.

Val ran up beside him, and Adrian felt a little lighter.

"Thanks," he muttered. "You don't have to come with me. I'm not going to wait around for a drunk cheater looking to solicit a blowjob."

"It's fine," Val said. "Though it would be nice. I can wait until tomorrow if we don't find anyone."

The two wandered closer to the main road, which was filled with people leaving work or heading to dinner. A road like this was too crowded to jump someone, but a block or two over would be just empty enough for the minute it would take to grab someone and get his fill.

Adrian found an alley behind a restaurant. He looked around, decided it was safe, and waited by the dumpster. The hardest part of finding someone to feed on was the waiting. He needed someone who wasn't alert and didn't avoid dark alleys. They had to be alone. Sometimes it took hours. Other times, he got lucky and found someone within minutes.

Tonight was one of those lucky nights. About five minutes after entering the alley, a lone man turned the corner. Adrian waited to make sure no one had followed him before making his move.

The man didn't notice Adrian sneaking up behind him until one hand clamped onto his shoulder and the other gripped his hip. With supernatural strength, Adrian whirled him around and slammed him against the wall. Before the man could scream, Adrian sank his teeth into his neck. Mere seconds later, the man relaxed under Adrian's grip, offering no resistance. Adrian drank from the wound, occasionally scraping his fangs along the man's neck to force the blood to flow again. As he fed, the man went from tense, to relaxed, to completely limp. Adrian adjusted his hold and leaned further into him, pinning the now-unconscious body against the wall, even as the man's knees buckled.

"Hey," Val said, tugging at Adrian's coat. "We're not here to kill him. Grab another if you're still hungry."

Adrian took a step back, allowing the man to collapse at his feet. He drew a few instinctive breaths, invigorated by the feeding.

"That's all right. I'm done." He licked his thumb and knelt down to wipe away the blood dripping from the puncture wounds in the man's neck, which were already starting to heal. "He's a big man. He'll be fine."

"Right." Val didn't sound too convinced. She helped Adrian sit the man up against a crook in the wall so he appeared to be merely sleeping. "Do you always go this rough when feeding?"

"Sorry. Just hungry." Adrian rifled through the man's pockets until he found a wallet. He took the cash but left the credit cards, then slipped the wallet back into the man's winter coat. A mugging, just in case the man remembered being attacked. No need to spark rumors about mysterious assaults leaving only puncture wounds in the neck.

They exited the alley and hurried several blocks away to put distance between themselves and Adrian's victim.

"Where did Melissa and Tyler wander off to?" Val mumbled. Adrian looked around. They had strayed from the nearest major street and now stood along a dark, quiet road. The only other people nearby were huddled inside tents for the night, except for a lone woman checking her phone on the other side of the street.

The woman had short hair, piercings, a rose tattoo... It was the woman from Melissa's phone—the rogue vampire they were hunting. She looked up and noticed Adrian staring. Though it was awkward, he didn't look away. He had to be sure and couldn't risk her slipping away. She glanced over her shoulder before locking eyes with him again.

Then she morphed into a bat.

"Wait!" Adrian shouted. He sprinted across the road in desperate pursuit of the bat, trying to keep up as it flew over the roof of a nearby stone building. He jumped, lifted his legs, then continued his sprint up the side of the building. As he reached the rooftop, he spotted the bat perched on the far corner. It took flight again but floundered in the air. The woman must not have been very experienced with flying yet.

At full sprint, Adrian hurled himself off the edge of the building, feet slamming onto the roof across the gap. The bat darted ahead, wings beating frantically, before veering wide to cross the street. Adrian didn't hesitate. He launched from the rooftop and swiped at the air with an outstretched hand. His palm struck the creature with a snap, and it tumbled to the pavement in a twitching heap. The force of his leap carried him too far, and he braced with hands and bent legs before colliding hard with the opposite wall. He clung to the vertical face a moment, then dropped lightly to the ground below.

No longer able to hold her animal form, the woman, Summer, lay on her shoulder. Adrian quickly ran over, turned her onto her back, and straddled her chest.

Then he took his knife from his pocket and thrust it toward her heart. Before the blade could pierce her chest, she caught his arm and held it in place. The knife quivered just above her breast, locked between their equal strength.

"Wait," she grunted. "I'm not an Elder!"

"Shapeshifting is Elder magic." Adrian pushed harder. If he let up, she might transform again and slip away.

"Please!" Summer begged. "I'm only fifteen years turned. I'm not mad yet!"

Sometimes new Elders lied about their age. Crossing that threshold was often a death sentence. The greatest threat to a mad Elder was another mad Elder, and the last thing vassals wanted was a second mad Elder to serve. Killing a new Elder wasn't something to punish. It was celebrated.

"Please!"

But didn't the man at the party say all of Owen's vassals were young? Summer didn't look like a woman from the nineteenth century. It was possible, but strange.

"I'm not mad!"

All Elders went mad. All, except one—and Adrian desperately wanted to find another.

Slowly, he eased the pressure on his arm. "Don't run," he warned, then withdrew the knife. Summer sighed in relief, her arm trembling. She seemed so genuine.

"Thank you," she breathed. "I won't."

Adrian stepped off her. She sat up with a wince and cradled her shoulder. He helped her to her feet.

"How can you shapeshift?" he asked.

"Owen. He rewards his most faithful with increased power."

Summer shook her head when she saw Adrian's look of confusion.

"I don't know how. He knocked me out for it. But once he finds out that I need vampire blood…"

"So, you are an Elder." Adrian's grip on his knife tightened again.

"No! I'm only fifteen! I'm not mad yet, I'm not!"

Summer shook. This wasn't the rehearsed lie of someone with a cover story. It was genuine shock. She'd been caught off guard.

"Okay," Adrian said. "I believe you." Partially. But it was worth hearing Summer out.

She nodded, then limped between the buildings. Adrian followed. It was a good idea to talk somewhere private, in case Melissa or Tyler had seen the chase. Val would listen to Adrian if he insisted on sparing Summer, but the other two…

"Thank you again," Summer sighed. "I don't know how to prove I'm not mad, but…"

"I know someone," Adrian said. "My Elder. He's like you. Not mad."

Summer's eyes lit up, even beneath her furrowed brow.

"Your Elder? You're not with Owen?"

"No, I just moved—"

Summer's attention darted over Adrian's shoulder, and her eyes widened. Before he could question it, she grabbed his arm and whirled him around toward the wall. Two gunshots shattered the silence of the quiet backroad. Summer hissed through clenched teeth.

"It's silver!" she spat.

Just as the weight of the situation registered in Adrian's mind, Summer grabbed his arm and dashed farther into the alley. Several more gunshots rang out, and thankfully, none of them hit Adrian. Summer, however, stumbled.

Adrian yanked Summer to the left, steering them down a dark, narrow road. He cloaked them in shadows and pressed her against the side of a building. A few seconds later, two men burst out of the alley, frantically scanning their surroundings. Adrian had never seen them before.

Silver bullets. Hunters.

The two ran in the opposite direction of him and Summer. Adrian held his shadows in place, just in case they returned.

Summer whimpered beside him.

"Can you heal?" Adrian asked.

Summer shook her head.

"Really? You're an Elder."

"Yeah, and the first thing I did was learn this." Summer flexed her hand, transforming it into a beastly claw. "Way cooler."

Adrian rolled his eyes. Well, she was fifteen years turned. One didn't have to be an Elder to heal wounds, but they did have to be older than fifteen. Yeah, when presented with a plethora of new powers all at once, shapeshifting was pretty cool.

"You should have let me take that bullet," Adrian said. "I'm only forty. Silver doesn't hurt that bad yet."

"Getting shot hurts pretty bad, regardless."

Adrian glanced up to see her crack a teasing, if highly strained, smile.

"Besides, I'm the Elder. I'm tough. It's my job to protect you."

Adrian felt his heart skip a beat. "Thanks, but you really don't have to," he muttered. Now wasn't the time for conflicted feelings. He dropped the shadows, figuring they were clear of the hunters, and walked beside Summer in silence. Until she started whimpering again.

"We need to get those silver bullets out of your back," Adrian said. But how would they accomplish that? He supposed he could take Summer to Garrick, but would

Garrick spare her? Keep her safe from Owen? Adrian could attempt the surgery himself. It wasn't terribly dangerous—their bodies healed quickly on their own once the silver was removed.

Summer hesitated, then nodded. The two found another alley between buildings to stay off the road. Finally, Adrian got a good look at Summer's back. Three bullet wounds wept blood through her tight-fitting shirt. Slowly, she peeled the fabric up her midsection, then turned her head slightly.

"Could you turn around?" she asked over her shoulder.

"Oh! Sorry." Adrian turned his back.

And saw the two hunters at the entrance of the alley.

Adrian pressed his back against the wall and raised his arm to shield his head, just in time for another round of bullets. Nothing hit him, and after a brief pause in the barrage, he decided to sprint toward the hunters.

The hunters must have known how to track them, or they had gotten extremely lucky. Either way, Adrian was tired of running. To avoid the gun's line of sight, he jumped onto the side of the building next to him and launched himself toward the head of the nearest hunter.

But instead of landing on him, he slammed into a barbed wire net, silver-laced strands searing his face like a lattice of burning coals. Barbs tore into every patch of exposed skin. A third hunter planted a boot on the net, pinning him in place. Adrian thrashed, but the silver bit deeper, leeching the strength from his limbs until his body betrayed him.

Adrian opened his eyes when he heard a roar. Standing in the alley was a large bat, hunched over like a wolf. It charged toward the hunters fearlessly, snarling with monstrous fangs. The beastly Summer leapt at the nearest hunter.

And then she collapsed beneath another volley of bullets. Her form shifted back to that of a human, and she curled slightly into herself—the only sign she was still alive. Adrian struggled again against the barbed wire netting, but a hunter stomped on his head to stop him. His cheek burned like fire.

The third hunter kicked Summer onto her back, then thrust a long wooden stake into her chest.

"No!" Adrian cried. His head was kicked again.

Summer rolled her head toward him. "Sorry," she said, just before the life faded from her eyes.

6

NIGHT 2 - VAL

V al watched in shock as Adrian dashed across the road and up the side of a building. There had been a woman... Was he chasing her? And if so, was she a vampire too? The most likely scenario was that she was the rogue vampire, and Val was wasting precious seconds standing around in awe.

Unfortunately, Val couldn't run up walls like Adrian. At only ten years turned, she barely had more than enhanced strength. Still, that strength helped her sprint down the street. She searched for an alley between buildings, but none appeared until she reached a major intersection. There, she managed to round the line of buildings and dash into a narrow parking lot. She jogged a few yards in before realizing Adrian was nowhere to be seen.

"Shit," she muttered to herself. Val looked up, just in case Adrian was hopping across roofs, but she didn't see any movement. Where had she gotten lost in this labyrinth of buildings? She considered calling out to him, but drawing attention to a group of vampires bending the laws of physics didn't seem like a good idea. Val ran to the end of the parking lot to make sure no one was around, then turned back toward the street.

She retraced her steps. Perhaps Adrian would return, or she'd find another path. But as she approached the spot where Adrian had run off, she saw Melissa and Tyler on the other side of the road. Val ran to them.

"Where's Adrian?" Melissa asked. Val was about to answer and describe what she had seen during his hasty departure, but a series of gunshots interrupted her. She flinched, then turned her head toward the sound. It came from the same direction Adrian had dashed off.

"He didn't bring a gun, did he?" Melissa asked, this time with an accusatory undertone. Val shook her head.

"We'll split up—cover more ground that way." Melissa turned and hurried down the street in one direction, leaving Val to cover the other. Val began jogging but realized that Tyler was following close behind.

"I thought we were splitting up?"

"I don't want to leave you alone. What if it's dangerous?"

"I'm fine," Val grumbled. She passed another alley and cast a brief glance down it. Empty.

"Don't want you to get lost. You don't even have my phone number in case you need to call."

The corner of Val's lip twitched in disgust. Apparently, Tyler had never learned the meaning of "no."

Another alley, this one with a person curled up by a

dumpster. Val paused just long enough to confirm it wasn't Adrian.

"Hey, I've got an idea." Tyler hopped onto the side of the building and climbed up half a story before turning toward the ground, arms held out at his sides for approval. "Easier to spot him from the roof!"

At first, Val wanted to snap at him for using magic in an area where anyone turning onto the street could easily see. But then she paused.

"How are you doing that?" she asked. "I thought you were only fifteen."

"I must be special." Then he winked. Tyler turned and lightly jogged up the rest of the building wall—roughly three stories high—before disappearing over the edge of the roof. Val waited, looking up for some sign. She could run away now that Tyler's back was turned, but he was more likely to find Adrian this way. She could tolerate his flippant comments a little longer.

But more importantly, how did he run up that wall so young? Adrian only just learned to do so last year.

Val waited several long minutes and wondered if Tyler had abandoned her. For all his chivalrous talk about not leaving her behind, he seemed to have no problem doing so now. How much longer was she supposed to wait?

Another round of gunshots echoed through the streets. It was hard to pinpoint their exact origin, but Val took a guess and ran in that direction.

A minute later, she heard Tyler call to her from above. "Hey!" he shouted, waving. "Fourteenth and Anton Street. Two blocks ahead, one block right!"

Well, for as annoying as he could be, Tyler was at least helpful in a pinch. She sprinted in the direction he had given her and rounded the corner at the intersection. Despite his suggestion that Adrian was a full block away, she encountered a gathering just a few yards after making the turn. Three men looked up at her, none of whom she recognized. Adrian lay face down on the concrete, pinned beneath a netting of barbed wire and the boot of one of the men. And finally, the woman he had been chasing lay face up, a wooden stake piercing her chest.

Val snapped her mouth shut to hide her fangs. Only vampire hunters used such barbaric methods.

The three hunters glanced at one another.

"Hey, miss," said the hunter closest to Val. He was the oldest, with gray hair and a wrinkled face. He raised his arms slightly, and Val noticed the gun in his right hand. "I think maybe you should just turn around and forget what you saw."

"Dude, she's gonna call the cops," hissed the pale, lanky hunter beside Adrian.

"We're not killing a civvie," the third hunter with a long beard hissed back.

Adrian shifted beneath the net to look up at her. Thankfully, he had enough sense not to call out or struggle further. Val slowly raised her hands and backed away. One step, two steps...

Finally, a dark fog blanketed the area, muffling any sound from the hunters. Val imagined they must have been confused by the surge of magic. She rushed forward, hoping to catch the old hunter with a tackle. Just as she entered the fog, she slammed into him, knocking him to the ground. The two flailed, and the gun in the hunter's hand fired harmlessly into the air. Val felt for the man's head and pushed it to the side to bite into his neck. When the old hunter finally stopped struggling, she stood—though the dense cloud of darkness made it impossible to tell what her next move should be.

Less than a moment later, the pitch-black fog lifted, revealing the second hunter on the ground and the third caught in Tyler's fangs. Val felt a flicker of jealousy that Tyler had incapacitated two hunters in the time it took her to defeat one, but she pushed the feeling aside to focus on Adrian beneath the silver netting. Without the pale hunter forcing the barbs into his hands and face, he was able to slowly push himself up onto his hands and knees. Val peeled the net away and helped Adrian to his feet.

"You all right?" she asked.

Adrian nodded, but his distant gaze suggested otherwise. He glanced back at Summer, lying dead at the entrance to the alley. Something saddened him. What had happened between the two of them between their chase and now?

Before Val could formulate a question, she saw Melissa sprinting toward them. Well, someone finally showed up a minute too late.

Melissa's first response to the scene was to address Tyler. "Drop him," she commanded. "Injuries are gang work. Murder is an investigation."

Tyler did drop the hunter, but he threw a scowl at the woman. "What evidence are we going to leave?"

"Plenty of eyewitnesses, judging by all the noise. No one's going to help you when the police track you to your apartment in the middle of the day."

Melissa shifted her attention to Adrian and Val, nodding quickly to confirm they were unharmed. Then she looked down at Summer, with the wooden stake lodged in her heart.

"Damn," she muttered under her breath. "I'll take care of the body. You three are dismissed."

Val scanned Summer's motionless body. She couldn't bring herself to feel grief—not after exhausting it all over the past week. But Adrian grieved silently, for reasons she couldn't quite grasp, and for that, she could sympathize. Worse still, hunters were killing in the dead of night, armed with silver weapons. Val felt a little less safe than she had just a moment ago.

Tyler shrugged. "I'm heading to the arcade. Val, want to come?"

Val ignored him, offering only a dismissive wave over her shoulder. She focused her attention on Adrian.

"Are you sure you're okay?" she asked again.

"Yeah, just a little rattled. I just want to be alone for a while."

Val wasn't convinced it was a good idea, especially with the hunters due to wake soon. But Adrian was a grown man, and she wasn't his mother.

"Text me if you need anything," she said, then turned and ran up to Tyler, much to his surprise.

"Oh, changed your mind?" he asked.

"Yeah," Val said, injecting a bit of enthusiasm into her reply. "The arcade sounds fun. And while we walk there, maybe you could teach me a few of those magic tricks of yours?"

7
NIGHT 2 - VAL

Tyler and Val entered a large building with a bright neon sign out front, though it paled in comparison to the flashing lights inside. Val suddenly felt fifteen years younger just walking through the front doors of the arcade. They wove through row after row of old machines, blinking and buzzing with electronic jingles, each one trying to entice Val to stop and play.

"Do you come to arcades often?" Val asked.

"Yeah, it's always fun to try and win some prizes. I know where all the best machines are."

They stopped at one of the shooting games, the kind with

plastic guns and tracking mechanisms that never quite worked. After Tyler inserted several quarters, a small pixelated horde of zombies shuffled in from the edge of the screen. One by one, Val shot at the zombies, leaving behind chunky explosions of pixelated gore. Tyler was clearly practiced, as he seemed to know where each zombie would appear even before it entered the screen.

"You're good at a lot of things," Val said as the screen advanced through a haunted warehouse, then paused to allow more zombies to stumble in. Tyler beamed with pride.

"I get a lot more free time than most. Being close to Owen has its perks. It means more time to have fun."

"Is that how you got so good at magic?" Val asked. Tyler had shrugged off her question before, but she wouldn't let him brush her off now.

"Nah. Well, actually… yeah. I helped Owen take over as Regent fifteen years ago, and in return, he gave me power."

"Gave you power?" Was that even possible? "How?"

"Well, to tell you that, I'll have to take my shirt off."

Val stopped shooting at the zombies. For a moment, she genuinely considered accepting Tyler's proposal. The idea that an Elder could somehow transfer power to her burned at her core. There was a time when Val wouldn't have thought twice about prostituting herself for one night if it meant getting a taste of sweet revenge. But she wasn't that girl anymore, and certainly not a mere week after Raymond's murder.

"Guess we'll never know, then," she said. She took a few aimless shots at the screen, suddenly feeling like sabotaging their game. Without her help, they failed the level quickly. Tyler sighed.

"You sure?" he asked. "You seem awfully curious. It'll only take a minute…"

"Tyler." A woman with dark skin, wearing a professional black blazer, suddenly spoke up from behind. Tyler looked over his shoulder, just as surprised as Val. "Seth wants to talk to you."

Tyler paused, then gave a strained smile. He nodded at Val and walked away, heading to the back of the arcade.

"Girl, you're going on a date with Tyler?"

Val recognized the woman who had interrupted them from the night before. They had talked at the party, just before Adrian's fight.

"It's not a date!" Val insisted. "We were on a mission together, and I just wanted to ask some questions."

"Well, this is Tyler's favorite date spot. He has a deal with the guy who runs the prize counter. He slips him free tickets when you're not looking."

Val scoffed and rolled her eyes. As if those little tricks could have won her heart anyway.

"Well, thank you. Our 'date' was going sideways anyway."

The woman smiled and pulled Val through the arcade, away from the machine. She reintroduced herself as Nora and led her toward a second woman, who was wearing a modest blue blouse and playing an old retro fighting game. Val had spoken to this woman the night before, too.

"Sophia," Nora said. "We're saving Val from Tyler."

Sophia tore her eyes away from the machine. "Really? After last night?"

"Hey, don't be so hard on her. I'm sure she had a good reason." Standing next to Sophia was a much larger man with broad shoulders. Val flinched when she saw his face. It was the same man who had torn Adrian's fangs out of Tyler's arm during their fight. Thankfully, he appeared relaxed when he turned to address her. If he held any ill will from the previous night, he didn't show it.

"Actually, I'd really appreciate that," Val said with a sigh of relief. Having these three by her side meant Tyler would finally stop the flirtations.

53

"We got you." Sophia reached out and patted Val on the arm, then nodded her head to the side. "Come on, do you like fighting games?"

Val was terrible at fighting games, but she didn't turn down the invitation. Sophia won easily, then the man, Devin, stepped in and beat her. Val joined again, and although she didn't come close to defeating Devin, she appreciated how naturally the group of friends welcomed her. On Val's third attempt, Sophia blocked Devin's side of the screen with her hand, giving Val a chance to land a winning punch. Nora, stoic the entire time, sided with the girls when Devin protested.

A few minutes later, a young man with black hair approached them. He looked barely older than a high school kid, but age could be deceiving when it came to vampires. "Tyler's taken care of," he said. "Well, as much as I can wrangle him, anyway."

Val turned to make proper introductions. As she had assumed from Nora's earlier comment, the young man was Seth. Somehow, he seemed to have some influence over Tyler, but Val wanted to drop the subject. She was enjoying herself too much to ruin the moment by dwelling on her failed date.

"You're one of the new vampires from LA, right?" Seth asked.

"Yeah, sorry about what happened with Adrian last night."

Seth waved the comment off. "Whatever. I'm sure Tyler was the one who started it."

"Tyler doesn't seem very well-liked. How did he become Owen's favorite?"

"Sucked up to him. What did you expect?" Seth said as he took over from Devin at the fighting game cabinet to face off against Val. "Same with Melissa. You don't have to be liked—just liked by Owen."

"Not like we can say anything bad about them," Sophia

added. "If Tyler complains about someone to Owen, then Owen is more than happy to make their life a lot harder—not to mention how awkward things get at Blood Ritual."

"Blood Ritual?"

"How Owen takes blood from us," Sophia clarified. "It's not as bad as it sounds. How does your Elder get his blood?"

"Directly from the neck," Val said. "You know, like a vampire."

"Ugh, with just the two of you? How often does he have to do that?"

Val bit her tongue. Actually, Garrick only drank from Adrian, and it was an arrangement that kept everyone happy. But Val wasn't in the mood to get into the politics behind that decision.

"About once a week," she lied.

"Once a week... split between the two of you, right? So, like, he feeds on Adrian, waits three days, and then feeds on you?"

Val nodded and hoped it sounded plausible. Feeding once every three days was uncomfortable but manageable. Garrick rarely had to exert himself, anyway. The lie would hold.

As their game ended, Val glanced back at Seth, and for a moment, she thought he was looking at her with suspicion. That somehow, he could sense the lie. But he quickly shifted to a friendly expression and told her, "Good game." Val returned the gesture.

As Sophia and Nora took their turn at the game cabinet, Val looked around to see what Tyler was up to. Whatever Seth had said to him seemed to have worked, as she spotted him chatting with two women who were playing a single-player game, having completely moved on from her. While it was difficult to tell from behind, the women didn't appear particularly interested in what Tyler had to say.

The girl at the game cabinet snapped at Tyler, causing him to raise his hands defensively. But he still didn't leave. Val could only imagine what Tyler was saying in response. "Whoa! Sorry, I didn't mean anything bad!" She rolled her eyes.

Someone had to do something about him, someone with subtler tactics. Thankfully, Val was well-practiced in such things.

8

NIGHT 2 - THEA

"**I** am really fucking hungry."

Thea grumbled as she searched for a pub open at eleven in the evening. She still hadn't grown accustomed to the reversed sleep schedule. Without a normal frame of reference for time, Thea generally ate whenever she felt hungry. She hoped the other hunters would have a proper schedule when she finally met them.

Thea parked her motorcycle in front of a small bar just off the main road. She lifted her helmet from her head and ran her fingers through her long red hair, then tightened her ponytail to smooth the tousled strands the helmet had left behind.

Thea walked into the pub, helmet tucked under one arm. All pubs had the same grungy look, one she wasn't particularly fond of. The furniture was always wooden, hastily nailed together, and slightly broken. The floors had been mopped, but years of spilled beer had left a permanent layer of stickiness, just enough to keep them from ever feeling truly clean. Still, Thea wasn't in a position to be picky, and pubs always had the best burgers.

She sat at a table and ordered a meal. Behind the bar, two television sets silently played different college football games. She scanned the pub, watching people chat with friends and yell at the screens. Thea didn't mind sitting alone, but tonight she was acutely aware of just how alone she felt. Given the choice, Thea would be eating a burger with friends or family. But her family was gone, and her friends were... Well, maybe they'd be fun in person.

At the far end of the pub stood a single pool table. Thea hadn't played in years, but she still knew the basics. A lone man was shooting, his hair frizzed as if he'd just taken off his own helmet and hadn't bothered to fix it. He intensely focused on the table, running what looked like drills, lining up the balls in a peculiar pattern and pocketing them one by one. He looked slightly intimidating, but Thea pushed aside her gut reaction. She still had two hours to kill, and most people preferred to have someone to play against.

After finishing her burger and fries, Thea got up and walked over to the pool table.

"Mind if I play?" she asked.

The man glared up at her, and for a moment, Thea thought she had stumbled into something dangerous. But he simply shook his head and gestured toward the table. Perhaps she had imagined it. He dropped a few quarters into the coin slot and began racking the balls as Thea grabbed her own cue.

"Ball-in-hand, or do you prefer kitchen rules?"

Thea froze. Maybe she didn't know how to play pool as well as she'd thought.

The man, reading her expression, cracked a small smile amid his otherwise dreary demeanor.

"The correct answer is ball-in-hand, by the way. If you foul or scratch, the opponent gets to place the ball anywhere on the table, no restrictions unless it's on the break. Then it has to be behind the kitchen—those two markings on that side of the table—and the ball must hit something on the other side of those markings. If the cue ball doesn't hit your color first, it's a foul. If an object ball or cue ball doesn't hit an edge or pocket, it's a foul. If the cue ball hits your cue at any point after the initial hit, it's called a double tap and it's a foul. Don't try to hit an object ball less than half an inch away from the cue ball; you will double tap and I will know. Call your shots if it's not obvious what you're aiming for."

Thea wilted. Turns out, pool had a lot more rules than she thought.

"Sorry if you knew all that," the man continued. "Everyone's got their own house rules, and it's better to make sure we're both on the same page before hitting balls around. Not interested in getting kicked out because of a bar fight over scratch rules. Again." The man placed the cue ball on the table and gestured toward it. "Break?" he asked.

Thea nodded. The man turned his hand toward her.

"Adrian," he introduced.

"Thea."

Thea lined up her shot and struck the cue ball as hard as she could. The balls scattered across the table, but none fell into a pocket. Adrian went next. His first shot pocketed a solid, but his second missed. They took turns shooting back and forth.

Thea made a good shot that pocketed one of her stripes, but every attempt after that missed. Meanwhile, Adrian had a consistent pattern: pocketing his first shot, then missing the next. Thea quickly realized he was going easy on her and missing on purpose to avoid ending the game too quickly. At first, she felt annoyed, but then decided it was better to be given a chance than to lose in a single round. However, by the time Adrian was down to his last ball, Thea noticed his demeanor had changed. He started to take his shots more seriously, considering each one longer, and scowling slightly each time he missed. She observed that with so many of her balls still on the table, Adrian struggled to line up a clean shot. This made him foul more often, allowing Thea to score a few easy shots.

Eventually, however, enough balls were cleared that Adrian was able to sink the final solid ball, followed quickly by the eight ball.

"Again?" he asked. Thea nodded, despite the clear difference in skill.

"You come here a lot?" Thea asked as Adrian racked the balls again.

"I just moved here a few days ago," Adrian replied. "But I do play a lot of pool, if that's what you were asking."

"Oh really? I'm new here too. Meeting up with some online friends."

"Oh, nice. How did you meet?"

Thea didn't really believe Adrian when he said "Nice." The subtle drop in his voice and flat tone betrayed how little he actually cared. But conversation was conversation, and he was polite enough to keep it going.

"True crime," she said.

Adrian furrowed his brow and darted his eyes to the ceiling. "As opposed to fake crime?"

Thea chuckled. Adrian didn't seem that old, late twenties maybe. Only slightly older than her. "It's a community," she said. "We get together and discuss cold cases and mysteries that fell through the cracks of law enforcement."

"And this is popular?"

"It's huge! There are entire internet forums, podcasts, and conventions…"

Something Thea said seemed to spark an interest in Adrian's mind. His eyes darted around in thought, but what he was thinking, Thea could only guess. Eventually, Adrian leaned over to break, seemingly finished entertaining whatever idea had captured his attention.

Once again, Adrian went easy on her, but Thea was improving. Not improving enough to win, however. Adrian always seemed to play at a level slightly above hers, much to her annoyance.

After their initial small talk, Adrian fell silent. Not one for conversation, apparently. Thea tried to discern whether his drooping frown and heavy eyelids signaled a bad day or if he simply had a resting-tired face.

When their game came to a close, he offered to play a third time. But Thea shook her head, saying she needed to meet up with her friends. Adrian wished her well, and she returned the favor.

Thea exited the pub at twelve-thirty. She still technically had some time before she needed to find the others. Walking back to her motorcycle, she pulled out a key, different from the one used for the ignition. The small key opened a box fitted to the side of the bike, and Thea pulled out a black handgun. She slipped it into an inner pocket of her jacket, then turned and headed for a dark alley. Maybe she'd get lucky.

As she aimlessly wandered down dark streets, Thea realized it was far more likely she'd run into a petty criminal trying to rob her than encounter her real target. She tried to gauge which of the two was more dangerous. Criminals had guns but generally weren't interested in murder if you cooperated. Vampires, on the other hand, had no need for guns because they were deadly enough without them.

She thought she saw movement in the shadows and jumped, dropping her helmet to the ground. She stood perfectly still, her eyes darting around. Her hand slipped inside her jacket, ready to draw her gun if necessary.

Maybe she imagined it. But just as she was about to lean over to pick up her helmet, she heard it. Footsteps. A rustling of clothing. Thea whipped around and pulled her gun on the pursuer. The woman stood paralyzed, just a few feet away, her hands raised.

A woman, that was promising. Women were rarely muggers. But Thea had to be sure.

"Smile," Thea commanded. "Show me your teeth."

The woman pushed her lips up in what was almost a snarl, but kept them closed.

"It's silver," Thea warned. "Though I'm not sure that matters if it goes through your head. Don't think I can't get away with a self-defense charge."

The woman pulled back her upper lip, though it was more in disgust than a smile. Sure enough, two pointed fangs hid beneath.

"Do you know Melissa Fowler?" Thea asked. "About five foot seven, too skinny for her own good?"

"Melissa?" the woman vampire asked, her expression shifting from aggressive to surprised. "What do you want with her?"

"So, you do know her?"

"What's it to you?"

Thea wobbled her gun, drawing attention to it.

"Yes!" the woman shouted in panic. "She works directly with Owen, but that's all I know. We're not close or anything!"

So, she was right. Melissa was here. After years of searching, Thea finally found her.

"Thank you," she said. "Now back away. Next time I see you, I won't bother asking questions first."

The woman slowly walked away until she rounded a corner. Thea kept her gun raised, just in case the woman was waiting for her to follow, but the alley remained silent. She lowered her weapon slightly and peeked around the corner to confirm the woman had gone. Then she ran back to her parked motorcycle.

9
NIGHT 2 - VAL

Val closed the door to her hotel room quietly. She wasn't sure whether Adrian or Garrick had returned yet, but she didn't want to alert them to the fact that she'd been out in the early morning hours.

She rummaged through her bag, finding the items she had shoved between clothes before their flight from the city: candles, an amethyst geode, salt. Would she need anything more specific? It was a bit late for a store run, so this would have to do.

How did she want to hurt Tyler? Killing was too extreme

—and likely not something she could pull off with mere witchcraft, despite her growing connection to magic. If she could have, she would've used it on Joseph long ago, karma be damned.

What she wanted was to make sure he hurt for a long time, and that every time he thought of women as nothing more than objects of desire, the memory of that pain would flare again. It was difficult to achieve when the consequences of his actions were hidden behind closed doors, miles away. Still, she could give it a try. A splitting headache every time he looked at a pair of breasts would certainly get the point across.

Using magic with the intent to harm was a fraught subject among witches. Some strictly banned the practice, while others followed the Rule of Threefold Return: the belief that any energy one put into the world would come back three times over to the caster. Val wasn't sure she believed in the rule. Based on the number of times she had cast spells wishing love, harmony, and good fortune for her friends, she herself should be in the arms of the love of her life, living in her million-dollar mansion.

Still, it never hurt to spin it in a positive light. She wasn't wishing Tyler harm, she was just hoping a police officer with a vampire-hunting hobby had good aim.

That sounded a little ridiculous and difficult to set up. Headache it was. If the universe had a problem with it, she could endure a little pain.

Paper. Scissors. Val felt a little silly using such simple materials for specific people, but she worked with what she had. Paper was malleable and could serve multiple purposes. A pin through the head, and… moonstone. She placed the paper Tyler in the center of the five-candle circle, two amethysts at the head, and the moonstone on the heart.

Val stood and took a deep breath. That was the most annoying part of her vampire transition: having to remember to reconnect herself with air. Vampire magic was more forceful, masculine, like taking a fistful of the fabric of the world and bending it to her needs. Witchcraft required a more delicate hand.

"Feminine spirit," Val began, waving her hand over her circle of candles. Each one lit, one after the other. "Gentle, sweet, beautiful, kind... Let each of these traits take root in Tyler, Vampire of San Francisco, growing like the roots of a tree in his mind, until he learns to accept these qualities within himself and others. Let his lust water the thorns, let his ego provide the sun. And let this great tree stand as a warning to all who may see. Let it be."

Another wave of her arm, and the candles blew out in an unfelt wind.

Val looked down at the spell circle. It always felt a little weird to clean up the ritual space before the spell really took hold, but leaving stones and candles in the middle of the floor usually drew unwanted attention. Usually. But this was her room, and Owen had made sure room service wouldn't bother them. No harm in leaving it. She cast one last smirk at the little pin in the paper doll's head.

Now, to wait. That was always the hardest part. There was no guarantee how quickly the universe would cash the check she'd written, and until then, she just had to go about her day, twiddling her thumbs.

10

FORTY YEARS AGO

Adrian learned quickly that having nothing did not save him from those who wanted to take. He now slept in a crevice between two buildings in a dark alley. Hiding was his only option at night. It didn't matter if he was on a major, well-lit road—no one was awake to protect him at three in the morning. He hid from the other homeless people who tried to steal his clothes, his bag, or any food he was saving for morning. But he also hid from the rich, the drunk, the party-goers, the walk-of-shamers. He'd been mugged and beaten before, always by someone he didn't expect, always for reasons that left him confused. Whenever he was about to fall asleep, he'd startle awake at the slightest sound of a footstep. Paranoia had become normal.

The nightmares started not long after he began sleeping on the streets. They were always the same, and they always felt so real. He would "wake" to see a man walk up to him, kneel down, and bite him on the neck. Then he'd wake for real, curled up and shivering. For a while, he tried running in his dreams, but the man—always the same man—caught him every time.

The only reprieve from his night terrors was his daytime routine. If necessary, he'd panhandle until he made just enough to get started. First, he'd buy a pack of cigarettes and do his best to make them last as long as possible. Then he'd find a nearby pub, order the cheapest item on the menu, and exchange whatever he had left for quarters. Finally, he'd play pool.

It started entirely as a way to distract himself from the melancholy of homelessness. But he improved quickly, learning from a variety of strangers who passed through. Eventually, he got good enough to start betting. The amounts were small, to avoid angering the pub owners, but to Adrian, a twenty-dollar bill felt like winning the lottery.

The best trick to winning money from people was, as Adrian had observed one night, to be a woman. For several weeks, a young woman named Claire visited the pub every other night and took bets from men. By then, Adrian had been learning how to gracefully sandbag his opponents to boost his winnings. But Claire didn't need to sandbag. In fact, the opposite was true. The more she won by, the more the men insisted on playing again, sometimes even increasing the size of the bet. They always went home broke and angry.

Adrian couldn't be a woman, but he found other ways to appear more feminine. He made sure to shave as often as possible, usually in public or fast-food bathrooms. Instead of skulking off to the side while his opponent took shots, he began leaning on one hip and picking at his nails. He saved up for a new shirt that exposed his neckline, and he even started pitching his voice up, just a little. Adrian wasn't sure how much it all helped, but he thought he noticed his opponents playing more aggressively. At the very least, it helped speed up his games.

One night, a group of young men visited a pub with multiple pool tables. They were odd in number, so Adrian offered to fill in as the extra player. During his first match, he carefully gauged each man's skill level. Most weren't very good, except for one. He was the best target. Those who knew they were bad wouldn't bet money.

He played his first game against one of the weaker players, and kept it close. He waited until both he and his opponent were shooting on the eight ball so as not to alert his real target. After a friendly "good game," he offered to play again and casually suggested putting money on the table. The man he had just played seemed interested in a rematch but shied away from betting. The other, the one with some skill, took him up on it.

Adrian won with his opponent still having one ball left on the table. Sometimes, he could string along a single player for multiple bets if they thought they had a chance of winning. It was a difficult line to walk: win by too much, and they'd realize they'd been hustled; keep it too close, and their ego wouldn't take a hit. Adrian smiled coyly and held out his hand for his winnings.

What he didn't account for was the group dynamic. These were the types of friends who ribbed and taunted one another for fun. His opponent's ego was damaged regardless. The man snarled and angrily fished a five-dollar bill from his wallet.

"We can go again, if you want," Adrian offered.

"How about I give you twenty dollars to suck my dick?"

"Okay, never mind..." Adrian mumbled, pocketing his

new money. He was about to turn away, thinking the man was done playing, when the man called after him.

"I'm serious."

The man held up a twenty-dollar bill. Adrian was stunned.

"N-No... that's..."

The man pulled out another twenty. "Forty, then?"

Adrian froze. Forty dollars was more than he made on most days, but he also knew it was a cheap price for what the man was asking. Not that he wanted to make the exchange. Still, his hesitation betrayed him. Behind the man, his friends began jeering, whispering just loudly enough for Adrian to hear.

"He's actually considering it!"

"Wait, can I get in on this?"

"Can I borrow some cash?"

Adrian gripped his pool cue nervously. Suddenly, bruised egos turned against him. He wanted to lash out at the group, to tell the man exactly where he could shove his forty dollars. But forty dollars could buy food and new clothes. Panhandling was also uncomfortable, demeaning, dehumanizing—and it lasted longer.

Without looking up, Adrian nodded toward the back door. He did what he had to survive.

Adrian never visited that pub again. By virtue of trying to trick his opponents out of their money, he never stayed at one pub for too long anyway. The regulars didn't want him around either. Some found his sharking entertaining, but most were too honest for that. When they started warning Adrian's potential targets, it was time to cool off one pub and find another.

One regular seemed to like him, though. His name was Garrick. He had wiry hair in a color somewhere between gray, blonde, and brown—the shade hair turns when it starts to age. Adrian guessed the man was in his forties, or maybe a healthy early fifties.

The first time he offered to play, Adrian successfully got him to bet money. He wasn't bad, he knew more strategy than the average player, but he still lacked the control needed to position the cue ball for his next shot. Adrian didn't have to hold back as much as he normally did with his targets, which was a welcome change. After taking his ten dollars, he offered another game.

"I'll give you twenty if you don't hold back this time," Garrick offered.

Adrian paused, then accepted the deal. If Garrick realized he'd been sharked, there was no point in continuing to sandbag. This would be the last money he'd get from Garrick anyway.

Adrian broke and sank two balls. After a moment analyzing the table, he determined that stripes offered the better position and pocketed three more before missing. Garrick sank two, and Adrian missed only once more before clearing all of his balls and winning the game. Garrick was smiling as he went to collect his twenty-dollar bill, and Adrian initially interpreted the expression as barely hidden spite, given the way he kept his lips firmly pressed together. But Garrick freely gave the money without complaint.

"You're quite impressive," he said. "Do you play in a league?"

No. Leagues cost money, and his time was better spent trying to earn it.

Adrian shook his head without explanation.

"So, you just enjoy cheating old men out of their cash?"

He hesitated to answer. Adrian preferred to keep his homeless status private. Eventually, he just shrugged and punctuated his reply with a simple, "Yeah, sure."

Despite his callous answer, Garrick returned to the bar at regular intervals and offered to play on slow nights. Not for money, but simply to keep his practice up, which Adrian accepted.

They talked over their games. Garrick worked "a boring business position" at "a boring big company." When Adrian pushed for more details, he realized Garrick was right. The job did sound quite boring, and he understood little of it. Eventually, Adrian admitted he was homeless. He hadn't wanted to, but Garrick recognized his evasive answers for what they were.

When he finally told Garrick, the man pulled out his wallet and immediately fished out a crisp fifty-dollar bill.

"What? No..."

"It's a gift. Take it."

Adrian hesitated. Nothing was ever free. But Garrick wasn't trying to bargain for anything. He slowly took the money and looked down at it. Fifty dollars. He could eat for a week on this.

"If there's anything I can do to repay you..."

Garrick hung his head and shook it gently.

"You don't understand the meaning of a gift, do you?"

When Adrian didn't respond, he changed tangents.

"Stop overthinking it," Garrick commanded. "Let's say you got hit by a car tomorrow. Would you have deserved that?"

"No."

"And you don't deserve fifty dollars either, but sometimes it's not about who deserves what. Sometimes you just get lucky and make friends with an old man with money who wants to play some pool. So take the good luck, it'll offset the bad luck later."

Adrian gently slipped the small piece of paper into his pocket. If only it could offset the bad luck that had defined his life up to this point. Still, he felt slightly more secure. Slightly more in control. For a week.

"Thank you," he muttered.

After Garrick left, Adrian had his first full meal in months —a burger, fries, and a beer—and he still had more money than he usually did at the end of the day. Adrian's mind flitted to schemes of how he could use his newfound friendship with Garrick as a source of income. He admonished the thought. That would be an excellent way to ruin it. Friendship was a rarity these days.

Adrian didn't act on his ideas and continued to enjoy games with Garrick, asking nothing in return. One night, as he surveyed the table, a figure entering the pub caught his eye. Tall, lanky, and wearing clothes that hung off his shoulders like drapes. Adrian's head snapped up in recognition.

Garrick looked over his shoulder to see what had caught Adrian's attention.

"Do you know him?"

"I…" Adrian fumbled for an explanation that didn't sound completely deranged. "Sorry, he just looks familiar."

Too familiar. The coincidence was uncanny. But how was he supposed to explain that the man who haunted his dreams every few weeks had just walked into the pub?

His opponent just nodded calmly, not taking his eyes off the new stranger. He hummed, deep in thought, and then asked no more. It was a coincidence, surely. Garrick left soon after, and at close, Adrian left as well.

Like a premonition, Adrian had the same dream again. He snapped his eyes open at the sound of gravel crunching underfoot and saw the man approaching once more. Adrian lay still, paralyzed with fear. He had long ago stopped trying to run or fight. He tried to force himself awake, but his dreams always felt so real.

In a blur, another man snuck up behind the first. Adrian barely saw him approach. The newcomer clasped one hand over the first man's mouth, then sank his teeth into his neck. The tall, lanky man tried to scream, but his cries were muffled. His flailing arms quickly went limp and dropped to his sides. A few seconds later, he collapsed to the ground, slipping from the second man's grip. He clutched at his neck, but his movements were sluggish. He couldn't quite manage to scramble back to his feet.

"Have a little class and feed off someone else for a change," the second man growled. Adrian instantly recognized the voice. The first man shuffled away on his knees, panicked by the sudden assault.

Garrick finally acknowledged Adrian. He looked down at him forlornly, and a chill ran through Adrian's core. This was not the man he had played pool with night after night. Garrick regarded him without the warmth of a friend or the kindness he showed with his charity. Adrian shrank back into himself, realizing he was still not free of monsters in the night.

But then, without any fanfare, Garrick turned and left. Adrian hesitated, every instinct telling him he had narrowly avoided the jaws of a beast, and any movement might remind the creature of its prey. But pushing through that fear, Adrian jumped to his feet and followed. He wasn't dreaming. The whole time he knew, but admitting that vampires were real was too much for his waking mind to accept.

"Wait!"

Garrick stopped and turned to face him. Adrian couldn't see his expression clearly in the dark, but he still seemed unhappy.

"Go lie back down," Garrick commanded. "And forget everything you saw."

Adrian stopped. "But..."

"No one will listen to a homeless man rambling about vampires. Still, I don't need you making things difficult for me. So, thank you for the entertainment. I sincerely hope things start looking up soon."

"You're leaving?"

"Safer for me, in case you do start talking. Which I

wouldn't recommend. No one will question a homeless man beaten to death on the side of the road, either."

Adrian froze in fear. The smart thing would be to turn around, go back to sleep, and do as Garrick said. He could return to his life of panhandling and pool sharking, every day, hoping that one day he'd catch his big break and escape that life. He could continue his routine until he froze, or starved, or was stabbed, or overdosed.

"Please wait," he pleaded. "You can turn people, right? Into vampires?"

Adrian's heart sank into his stomach when Garrick turned to address him once again. He had warned Adrian, and the blank look on his face made it clear he wasn't bluffing. It showed not anger that was ready to kill in a fit of passion— only a chilling indifference toward the life of a mere mortal. Adrian thought he'd pushed too far, and that he'd sealed his fate, dying on the side of the road.

Then Garrick sighed and rubbed his temples. "If I turned everyone who wanted to become a vampire, there wouldn't be many mortals left."

Hope punched Adrian through the gut. He was shaking, but he was alive. "Well, why'd you get to be one? Are there requirements? I'll do anything."

"My wife turned me."

"Oh." Adrian paused, eyeing Garrick up and down. "So, not into men then?"

Garrick didn't answer. He just rubbed his temples even harder.

"Do you need an assistant? Apprentice? Accountant?" Adrian's mind flitted back to the forty dollars in the bar. He swallowed the lump rising in his throat. "…Companion?" he added hesitantly.

"No," Garrick said. "I don't need any of that."

Adrian withered. Not that he spent much time thinking about vampires specifically, but he had always imagined them as evil beings out to corrupt anyone who crossed their path. To think he'd have to beg, and still be rejected. Of course, why would a vampire trust him when no one else did? Even vampires had standards. He leaned against the side of the building, dejected.

"Whatever," he mumbled. "Just go. Save your fifty bucks next time, too."

Adrian dropped to the ground and looked up at the starless sky. He fumbled in his coat pocket for a box of cigarettes, doing his best not to acknowledge Garrick, even though the man lingered nearby.

"It's not an easy life, you know," Garrick said. "You'd never see the sun again. You'd spend several hours a night waiting for someone to walk by alone. You'd have to dodge cops, lest they recognize your description from an assault charge."

Disgusted, Adrian gestured toward his street-side hovel.

"Point taken. Come on, let's get going, then."

Garrick extended his hand to help Adrian to his feet, but Adrian didn't take it. He leaned away, eyes darting between the offered hand and Garrick's face, trying to read his intentions.

"What?"

"Come on, we don't have all night." Garrick rolled his eyes in exasperation. "Look, you're pathetic, pitiable, and making me feel bad. So let's put a pair of fangs on you and see if you can fix that."

Adrian still didn't move. "What's the catch?" he asked.

"Smart man. Now, do you want this or not?"

He didn't take Garrick's hand, but Adrian cautiously pushed himself up off the ground. He still didn't fully believe Garrick's complete one-eighty.

"Why?"

"I told you, you're tugging on my dead heartstrings. And…" He shrugged. "It would be foolish of me to turn everyone who asks into a vampire. But we're friends." Garrick paused ever so slightly at the word. A small smile broke through the hard lines of his face. Amusement, probably. "Maybe this is what you need to turn your life around. So, I'll make an exception."

Adrian nodded slowly. He still wasn't convinced, but what did he have to lose?

"Okay," he said. "Thank you."

II

NIGHT 3 - ADRIAN

Adrian fell asleep immediately upon returning to his hotel room, even before the sun rose and banished him to slumber. He awoke the next night facedown on his pillow, still dressed in the clothes from the night before. It was the mundanity that made him forget, at times, that he was a vampire. He was feared, even if his prey no longer believed in his existence. He was immortal. He was strong, fast, capable of wielding dark magic. And he had to do the laundry.

But first, a shower. Adrian turned the water to cold. There was a time when hot showers had been a small pleasure in life, but those days were behind him. Running water was one of the few things that could hurt vampires. He had never heard of that before turning, but he couldn't argue with it now. Something about it being a "purifying agent." Same as silver and garlic.

Purifying agents worked better as the vampire aged and, apparently, became less pure. Less pure of what, Adrian didn't know. Garrick never bothered to give a satisfying answer. Purity from disease, Garrick had originally believed, hundreds of years ago, before anyone understood how disease worked. Spiritual purity, he supposed now. Adrian didn't believe in the soul or in God, but he was a vampire who used magic. So maybe now was a good time to start believing.

Adrian felt the water and flinched. It wouldn't kill him, but it stung. Soon, he'd have to take baths like Garrick. Adrian hated baths. Took forever to fill, made it harder to wash his hair, all so he could sit still in a basin of tepid water while flecks of dirt and grime floated by.

After a quick and painful shower, Adrian rummaged through his travel bag and slipped on his last set of clean clothes. Then he opened his hotel door and stepped into the hall. A small sigh of relief escaped his lips when he saw that it was empty.

Which was strange, because he had nothing to hide.

Adrian knocked on Garrick's door. A moment later, Garrick let him in. Adrian walked to the foot of the bed and paused, waiting for the sound of the door closing behind him.

"You were out late last night," Garrick said. "I was surprised I wasn't the last one back. Owen kept me until early morning. Mostly just rambling. Unfortunately, he has no idea how to run a Regency. I know fifteen years isn't that long for us…"

Adrian was only half-listening. He slipped off his shoes, then his socks. Reaching over his shoulders, he pulled his shirt over his head. He hesitated for a moment, then finally worked his pants off. Garrick walked around to the opposite side of the bed, halfway through unbuttoning his own shirt. Adrian climbed onto the bed and rested his back against the headboard. He waited patiently for Garrick to finish undressing, twisting the bedsheet between his fingers.

Garrick climbed on next and sat on Adrian's thighs. His body had long decomposed its unneeded stores of fat, leaving his skin stretched taut over a skeletal frame interwoven with muscle—just enough to keep him from looking sickly. Lean was a better term, or perhaps statuesque. A few scattered scars hinted at centuries of battles lost to history, but the most striking was a long, vertical mark running from the center of his breastbone to his navel.

Garrick leaned forward to kiss him, and Adrian obliged, rolling his head to the side. He felt Garrick snake a hand around his shoulders and pull him close. Then Garrick broke from Adrian's lips and bit his neck.

Adrian winced at the initial sting, then closed his eyes and tried to relax. Though their venom caused mortals to slip into unconsciousness, other vampires were immune. It still had a euphoric effect, however. He felt his body lighten, almost as if he could float, and a tingling spread through his extremities. His eyes opened, staring at the back wall, unfocused on any one point, as he patiently waited for Garrick to finish.

A minute later, Garrick lifted his fangs. He softly kissed Adrian's neck where he'd previously bitten him, then ran his lips up behind Adrian's ear and nuzzled the crook beneath his jaw. Adrian slid his arms around Garrick's shoulders in a loose hug and waited for him to finish with whatever tasted so good behind his ear.

He held there a moment, then broke away. Garrick brought his face around in front of his, then leaned back, sitting up straight.

"You're not interested," he accused.

Adrian snapped back to reality, away from the fog where

his mind had drifted. "What?" he said. "No, I..." He stared into Garrick's eyes, and it became clear that whatever excuse he was about to offer would be easily seen through.

Adrian lowered his gaze. "I'm sorry. I'm just not feeling it today. Not with everything else going on."

Garrick nodded, crestfallen, then swung his legs over the edge of the bed. He picked his shirt up from the floor and threaded his arms through the sleeves. Adrian leaned his head back against the headboard. He felt like apologizing again, but his stomach twisted at the thought of drawing attention back to himself. But the silence that followed was unbearable.

"I'm..."

"It's fine," Garrick interrupted, pulling on his pants. "It's been a difficult week." He stood and adjusted the collar of his shirt. A subtle jolt betrayed his intention to head for the door, but instead, he gently sat back down on the foot of the bed. Looking down at his hands, fidgeting and flexing each finger in turn, he spoke in a low whisper that barely reached Adrian's ears—words Adrian wasn't sure were even meant for him.

"What am I doing wrong?"

Adrian wanted to answer, just to talk and clear his head of every turbulent thought that had plagued him and his actions over the past week. But what did he have other than baseless accusations? What would Garrick say in response? He'd explain his side, it would sound reasonable, and Adrian would be happy. That's what he wanted, right?

A single word occupied Adrian's mind. A beautiful little lie.

"Nothing," he said. "Just tired."

A shadow blanketed Garrick's features, the hard lines of his face creasing as his eyes narrowed to shoot a damaged, hurt glance in Adrian's direction. It lasted only an instant—

Garrick never revealed his anger for long—before his expression softened into something listless.

"Remember, we have a meeting with Owen in an hour. I'll meet you there."

Garrick exited the room without looking back, leaving Adrian alone to stare up at the ceiling. He found it difficult to hold on to any coherent thoughts, just emotions. He felt dirty, dejected, and, most of all, hungry once again.

It had been some time since Adrian had visited the beach. He had never been overly interested in the ocean before he was turned, but with so much time on his hands, he found himself drawn to the sand and waves. Adrian slipped off his shoes and stepped into the wet sand, feeling his feet sink as the waves washed over them. Stung again, just like his shower. Guess the ocean counted as running water.

The best part about the beach were the people. On a cold day like today, Adrian wasn't sure if anyone would also be taking a nightly stroll along the waves. But he was thankful that someone had the idea. Saved him time later, prowling the streets.

A light appeared in the distance—small and bright, seemingly from a handheld phone. It didn't illuminate much, making its owner the perfect unsuspecting prey. Adrian casually sauntered toward the light, shielding his eyes with a hand to preserve his night vision. He could see better in the dark than the mortal could with the tiny phone light—well enough to notice he wasn't alone. There were two people behind the light, one boy and one girl, both looking like they were still in high school. He didn't need two, but that was an easy enough problem to fix.

With a flick of his wrist, the phone light shut off. He heard the boy stop and swear, and now, with his night vision unobscured, Adrian could see the man turning the now-dead phone over in his hand. The girl started reaching into her pocket for her own phone, but Adrian was quicker. He hastened his pace, and within a second, he was standing right by her ear.

"You should run," he whispered. The girl screamed and scrambled back toward the city. The boy, startled, called out for his date. But when he reached out a hand, he found Adrian instead. Before he could voice his confusion, Adrian pounced on his neck and bit down. The boy went limp in his arms almost immediately, so Adrian threw him to the ground and knelt on top of him, holding his neck up to avoid getting hit in the face with saltwater as the waves lapped in and out.

Minutes stretched by. When he was done, when he was finally full, Adrian raised his head and took several invigorating breaths. Much better tonight, without Val worrying over his shoulder. It was the first time since Los Angeles that he had felt content, if only for a fleeting moment.

Adrian picked the boy up by the arms and began to drag him above the tide line when something about him made Adrian pause. He wasn't breathing. Adrian placed two fingers beneath the boy's chin to check for a pulse, but found none.

His mind was silent. Slowly, he let the boy's body slip from his grasp, then sat beside the boy's head. This happened sometimes. Adrian hadn't accidentally killed anyone in over thirty-five years. He was too experienced for rookie mistakes like that.

He looked at the boy's face. If not for the absence of a rise and fall of his chest, there was nothing to suggest he wasn't simply asleep. Adrian held his head in his hands and tried to restart his brain.

Sorry, kid. It was just an accident. A careless, tragic accident. Technically, he could still do one thing. A dead body fed vampire blood before the next sunrise would rise as a new vampire the following night.

Would that be all right? He wouldn't be able to see his family, his friends, or his girlfriend anymore. His entire life would be different—stuck as a seventeen-year-old for two centuries, which Adrian would have hated.

With a single, sorrowful sigh, Adrian got up. The signature puncture wounds had already healed, despite the body being dead. He took out his knife and made a cut along the boy's neck, close to where he had bitten him. Just a mugging gone wrong. Then he dragged the body to the ocean and, with a heave, hurled it several yards into the deep. Depending on the tide, maybe no one would ever find it.

Adrian waited several minutes, watching the ocean to see if the body would reappear above the waves. A cry of frustration remained trapped in his lungs, unable to escape. No, he wouldn't let it escape. He was Adrian Rowe, big bad vampire, and sometimes that meant accidentally killing a man or two. Because he wouldn't go back to his old life.

He *couldn't* go back to his old life.

12

NIGHT 3 - ADRIAN

A drian wished he had asked why the entire city had gathered at Owen's mansion before stepping through its threshold. He assumed it was yet another meeting between Garrick and the Regent that he was required to attend, despite never being asked for input. They had held many such meetings with Joseph.

Unlike their first night, there was no pretense of a party. Various groups split off into their own circles to chat, as was typical of large gatherings, but there was little indication of why anyone was there, except for a large bowl sitting suspiciously empty on a desk by the back wall. Had it been a normal party, Adrian would have assumed the bowl was for punch. But that would have seemed oddly festive for a group of vampires.

Adrian scanned the crowd for Garrick and spotted him chatting with a sickly-looking woman in a flowing dress—Melissa. The first thing he noticed about her was the low neckline exposing her breasts, and a scar that reached up to her clavicle. Kind of like Garrick's, curiously enough. Adrian couldn't hear what they were discussing, but it must have been funny, given how they both laughed.

"Oh, there you are," Garrick said as Adrian approached. "I was worried you might be late."

"Can we talk?" Adrian asked, glancing over at Melissa, who was still lingering. "Alone?"

Garrick gave a polite nod and walked toward the back wall with Adrian in tow. Then he gave him his full attention.

"There was an attack," Adrian whispered. "Last night. Hunters."

Garrick's eyes widened. "What? Adrian, why didn't you tell me sooner?"

"Sorry, I didn't want to worry you."

Garrick shook his head. He cupped Adrian's face, and for a moment, Adrian truly believed he loved him.

"I've done nothing but worry all week. Are you all right?"

Adrian nodded. "I'm fine, but… there was a woman, the rogue vassal we were chasing? She was an Elder, despite being only fifteen years turned. And she didn't have Madness. Like you."

Adrian had hoped the revelation would ignite some kind of hope in Garrick, as it had within him. Instead, Garrick's brow furrowed in confusion, and Adrian's heart sank.

"Adrian… you couldn't have known that, not from just a brief meeting."

"But she protected me," Adrian insisted. "She sacrificed herself for me. I know it!"

Garrick didn't look convinced.

"And she was only fifteen! How is that possible? She said Owen did something to her…"

Garrick's reaction remained frustratingly muted. Why wasn't this as shocking to him as it was to Adrian?

"I… You're right. I'm sorry," he finally replied. "I trust your judgment. It's a shame this woman perished before I could meet her. I'm still suspicious that she wasn't just lying about her age. It's very common for vampires nearing Elder age to lie out of fear for their lives. But I'll ask Owen what he knows."

Adrian nodded. It was a reasonable position, given how strange it all sounded. Perhaps, in time, more evidence would surface. Or better yet, maybe Owen would be forthcoming with a fellow Elder and confirm everything.

"I'm sorry," Adrian whispered. "I'm not trying to pull away. Things have just been stressful lately."

Garrick gave him a soft smile and clasped Adrian's hand tightly. Garrick was never one for public displays of affection, especially with another man, but he still felt the warmth in the gesture.

"I understand."

"Let's spend some time together tonight. Just the two of us?"

"Of course."

They returned to the center of the room and stood next to Val, who was talking with another woman in a blue blouse. The two seemed to be getting along well. Adrian even overheard the woman invite Val to a concert after the meeting, and he felt a pang of jealousy at Val's ability to make friends so easily. Well, he had just made plans with Garrick, anyway.

A few minutes later, Owen finally made his way to the back of the room and stood by the table with the large bowl. He placed a roll of cloth bandages on the table but kept a sheet of paper in one hand and a knife in the other.

"All right, everyone, let's get this started so you can all be on your way," he announced. "Alice Nunes."

A woman with a sleeve tattoo approached Owen. She took the knife from him and stepped twice to the right. Without flinching, she slid the blade across her wrist and held the bleeding wound over the bowl. Blood trickled steadily as she waited, bored, for it to pool at the bottom of the container. Finally, Owen waved her off. She handed the blade back to him, then grabbed a bandage from the table and quickly wrapped her wrist.

"Basir Rahman."

The chatter in the house continued as its inhabitants remained disinterested in the roll call. One by one, names were called, and someone from the crowd would approach the table to spill blood. Slowly, the bowl filled.

Adrian looked to Garrick, confused. He didn't have to ask anything specific—Garrick understood his meaning. The other man leaned in close and whispered.

"It's not as uncommon as you think. Just another method for Regents to obtain blood from their vassals. It's more prevalent in the South and Midwest. Some of the more conservative vampires prefer it, as it allows them to avoid the... intimacy of biting their fellows."

A small smirk tugged at Adrian's lips, and a quick glance at Garrick showed he found it just as amusing.

"Of course, some also appreciate the obvious parallels to Communion. They find spiritual meaning in giving blood back to the chalice and into the mouth of their Regent. Others consider it blasphemous. Owen is keeping things quick and professional. I've seen this become highly ritualized before."

Based on the alphabetical order of the names being called, Adrian realized his had been skipped. He let out a sigh of relief.

The crowd thinned. Once each vampire had given blood, they were free to go. Most did, while others waited to leave with friends. By the time Owen reached Zach Wallach, he was the last one remaining, and the bowl was nearly full of blood.

"Adrian Rowe."

Adrian frowned and looked at Garrick. The man pressed his lips into a thin line but made no move to object.

"Yes, you too," Owen chided. "You are a part of us now."

Garrick glanced at Adrian and gave a slight nod toward the bowl. Adrian scowled but obediently stepped up to Owen. Like everyone before him, he took the knife and made a deep cut across his wrist. Disdainfully, he watched the blood run out. He was already hunting enough for two, and now he had to add Owen to that burden. Adrian wasn't counting the seconds, but it felt like he'd held his wrist over the bowl long enough. Perhaps Owen was punishing him by making him give more than the others. He glared at the Regent, watching for any sign of glee at his submission.

Owen had a blank expression, just as bored as everyone who had come before him. Maybe Adrian was overreacting. A few seconds after receiving his deathly stare, Owen waved him off. Adrian didn't bother with the bandages and simply walked back to Garrick, his wrist still bleeding.

"Valeria Santoro."

If Val was annoyed at having to partake in the ritual, she hid her displeasure better than Adrian did. He turned to Garrick and held out his wrist. Garrick placed two fingers on the bleeding cut and slowly rubbed the wound closed. A few minutes later, Val returned, opting instead to wrap her wrist in a bandage.

"Garrick Leach."

Garrick snapped his head toward Owen, a frown creasing his features. "Owen," Garrick rebuked, "really?"

"No exceptions, Garrick." Owen held firm and humorless.

Garrick's face fell with disdain. He huffed, then walked over to Owen. "You've got to be kidding me," he muttered under his breath. Still, he cut his wrist over the bowl like everyone else.

Adrian's first reaction was smug satisfaction, watching Garrick endure the same indignities he had been forced to accept. But then disappointment crept in. A part of him had wanted Garrick to refuse, even if it meant being treated differently. As far as Adrian could tell, there wasn't much Owen could do to enforce his rules against another Elder. Kick them out of the city? Adrian could use a fresh start anyway.

After contributing his own blood, Garrick marched back to Adrian and Val, forgoing the bandages. He gave a small nod—though hardly a polite one—to Owen as he rejoined them.

"Before you leave," Owen addressed Adrian, surprising him, "I have another task for you today. Melissa has to make her daily rounds, and I want you to go with her as extra security."

"Security?"

"Because of the hunter's attack last night."

Adrian hesitated. He had hoped to return to the hotel and immediately begin repairing his relationship, but a glance at Garrick confirmed that arguing against Owen's orders was out of the question.

"Fine," he said, trying to hide his disappointment. Well, this would give Garrick an opportunity to question Owen alone and, hopefully, uncover some information about Summer's condition.

Satisfied, Owen whispered something into Garrick's ear, then disappeared deeper into the mansion. Garrick cast one last remorseful look Adrian's way, then dutifully followed the Regent.

When they were alone, Val finally spoke up. "Cool. I guess I really am just chopped liver, then."

"Lucky," he muttered.

"You'll be okay? Please call me if someone points another gun at your head."

Adrian gritted his teeth. "Thanks. You'll be the first to know," he said.

With a friendly wave, Val stepped out the front door, leaving Adrian standing alone in the middle of the large room. Alone—except for Melissa, off to the side, a smoldering cigarette between her fingers. Adrian approached, stopping just a step too close for comfort.

"Don't flirt with him," he threatened.

Melissa didn't flinch. She exhaled, blowing a stream of smoke into his face. A warning for getting too close.

"Can't steal what doesn't want to be stolen," she replied.

13
NIGHT 3 - THEA

There were seven vampire hunters who decided to join up in San Francisco. That was a large number, from what Thea understood. While she had traveled to cities before to hunt vampires, those had all been solo expeditions. Sharing a house with six other people didn't sound like fun, but she agreed when it was suggested in their group chat, nonetheless. It would only be a week, she told herself, and this way, she'd have a better chance of making friends.

What disappointed Thea when she arrived at the house was that she was the only girl. She didn't mind making male friends, but it was one more thing they didn't have in common. Vampire hunters were a special breed of crazy. When one believed in one conspiracy, several others weren't far behind. If vampires existed, what else was the government hiding? As it turned out: a flat Earth, lizard shapeshifters, mind-controlling radio waves, Satanic blood rituals to keep elite politicians young, and a whole host of other things. Thea did her best to hold her tongue whenever someone in the group launched into a crazed rant about this or that hidden organization making the world a terrible place.

Although, she was willing to believe in the Satanic rituals. Because the vampires were likely doing them.

Thea knew most of the hunters by their online names, and that persisted even in person. However, there was an odd shift in seeing their faces for the first time. She was used to talking to someone whose only image was a picture of a wolf, so it felt strange to see them now as a person, even if talking to a giant wolf would have been stranger, logically.

Geo (username: Geodian) was unexpectedly tall. Like his online persona, he was generally quiet unless spoken to directly, but he had a cutting sense of humor that appeared out of nowhere. Thea liked Geo but found him difficult to connect with, and meeting him in person wasn't helping.

Wyatt (username: Wyatt) was the oldest, which Thea knew beforehand. He frequently mentioned his age—fifty-nine, soon to be sixty—during online discussions. Somehow, he always had a story about meeting a vampire, though his evidence was questionable. Along with Geo, he helped bankroll their trip to San Francisco, covering extra expenses like taxi fare. He wasn't objectionable, but Thea had little patience for his old-man stories.

For some reason, everyone thought Salem (username: SalemHunter) was a girl—everyone except Thea, the one actual girl in the group. Salem never listed his gender in his bio, but he posted in pink text and used an anime girl as his icon. Thea had never met a girl online who projected that hard, except maybe trans women who hadn't yet come out or realized their identity. If Salem was questioning his gender, he wasn't making much effort to present himself in a feminine manner, as he proudly sported a thick red beard and wore ragged beige shorts, despite it being November.

Noc (username: Nocturnebird) was the biggest surprise. Thea liked him and had been the most excited to meet him, but she quickly found something unnerving about his real-life persona. He never shared his real name, and his pleasant yet blank affect felt plastic and fake. His grim sense of humor, while amusing online, quickly wore out its welcome once the safety of distance was gone.

Carter (username: ForkLiftCertified) appeared oddly normal—late thirties, secure job, fresh haircut, wife, kid. Thea wondered if his wife also believed in vampires, or if she thought he was away on a week-long business trip.

Finally, there was Striga. He was the only one missing from the house when Thea arrived. As a relatively new addition to the forum, she hadn't gotten to know him well— very few of the hunters had. Still, he had provided solid evidence of vampire activity in the area, which had sparked their trip.

The group waited two hours past their agreed-upon meet-up time before Striga finally called Geo's phone.

"What the hell, dude? Why are you so late?" Noc said over the speakerphone.

"Sorry. Work called me in." Striga's voice sounded slightly distorted, more than the usual artificial tonality of speaking over the phone.

"We've literally had this planned for weeks. You couldn't get any vacation days?"

"Couldn't get my shift covered. You know how it is."

Thea glanced around the group to see how many "knew how it is." Salem frowned but nodded along. Carter rolled his eyes. Wyatt didn't react. Thea thought it was bullshit that Striga couldn't get out of work too, but she wasn't going to make a big deal out of it.

"I heard several of you went out yesterday and tracked down a vampire," Striga continued.

"Yeah! We—"

"You were supposed to capture them *alive*." The vitriol in Striga's voice caught Thea by surprise, as did the news that the group had killed a vampire. Thea stopped herself from blurting out a question, though she ached for more information. The chance that they had killed the vampire she was after was slim, but she wondered.

"We did capture one alive," Carter said, rubbing a bruise on the side of his face. "But he got away. And I'm not even sure the girl was a vampire. I think she was a werewolf."

"Vampires can turn into wolves too," Salem said. "Any creature that's a predator of the night."

"Come on, they can't just take—"

"Back to the problem at hand?" Striga interrupted. "No more staking. When you shoot, aim for the gut. A dead vampire disintegrates within hours. They're no good to us."

"Says you," Wyatt grumbled. "What are you doing this for, if not to remove monsters from the streets?"

"Proof," Striga said, "and I'm not interested in continuing this partnership if you can't stick to the plan."

"Hey, hey, it's fine, guys," Noc said. "I'll just bring out the big guns next time!"

The room fell silent. "Big guns?" Striga asked.

Excitedly, Noc got up and retreated to his bedroom. He soon reemerged, carrying a large metal device with a chain slung over his shoulder. He whipped it onto the couch, causing Thea to flinch. The heavy contraption featured a jaw of savage, silver-lined teeth beside a pair of large springs.

"What was that sound?" Striga asked.

"A... bear trap." Thea's skin crawled at the sight of it. She leaned forward cautiously, tracing a finger around its closed jaws. "Aren't these things illegal?"

"Only to use, not to own."

"I think you're genuinely insane," Wyatt muttered under his breath.

Thea wasn't new to odd weaponry, especially since picking up her new vampire-hunting hobby, but the bear trap sent a special kind of chill down her spine. Her toes wiggled with built-up stress, anticipating the disaster that would inevitably occur when Noc set up the trap in the house and snapped someone's leg clean off. She would have to watch her step carefully from now on.

"By the way," Striga said, "does anyone have a spare gun with silver?"

"Really?" Salem scoffed.

"Yes, really—I pay San Francisco rent. I don't have the money to spend on silver bullets."

"They're not that expensive. I know a guy who makes them for fifteen dollars a round."

"Then those aren't real silver," Geo said. "They're probably just silver-coated."

"Works just as well."

"Don't worry, I got you." Noc got up again and ran out. The room fell silent at the pep he displayed upon announcing that, yes, he had brought a bear trap and two guns. Thea didn't need anyone to say it out loud, she knew they were all thinking the same thing. How many weapons did he bring in total?

"Someone keep an eye on him at all times," Wyatt said before Noc returned.

"Good. I'll let you know when I'm off work and can meet up. As for our next target, you're lucky. I already have a tracker on him."

"Already?" Geo asked. Thea agreed, that was fast. She was willing to believe that Striga had a connection to the first vampire, the one he had used to entice them all into joining him in San Francisco, but to replace her so quickly?

"Yes, so don't fuck it up this time." Striga hung up the phone before anyone could argue.

A silence stretched between the group until Geo spoke up. "We can all agree that Striga's a little suspicious, right?"

"Guy just happens to know every vampire in the city, I guess," Carter muttered.

"Think he's trustworthy?"

"If Striga wanted to hurt us, we wouldn't be alive right now," Wyatt said to Noc and Salem. "I find it more suspicious that those vampires left us unharmed."

"There's still something weird about this..."

The room fell quiet once again until Carter groaned and rubbed his eyes. "We're heading out again, right? Let's be a little more careful this time."

The room murmured in agreement. They each split off to gather their weapons: guns, stakes, silver barbed wire. Thea retreated to her room to prepare. She traveled light, arming herself with a single handgun loaded with a few silver bullets. Her phone buzzed as she was strapping on her helmet. She pulled it from her pocket to find a message from Striga, addressed to the entire group. The attached photo was poorly cropped and digitally brightened to offset the bad lighting, but the figure in it was clear enough to make her stomach drop.

It was the man from the pub.

14

FORTY YEARS AGO

Between the many nights he spent at the pub, wasting hours playing pool, and the ring he wore on his right hand, Garrick didn't seem like a man particularly close to others. So it was a surprise when Adrian entered his home and saw two people sitting around a small table in the middle of the living room, playing cards. They both looked up when Adrian entered and stared at him.

"Everett, Jan, this is Adrian. He'll be joining us from now on."

The two were quiet but kept their eyes on him. Suddenly, he felt like a zoo animal, his every move and fidget scrutinized for information. If Garrick noticed the tension, he didn't bother to address it.

"Give me a minute to get set up. Once you become a vampire, your body will stop aging and growing. So, if you'd like to grow out any facial hair, we can wait a few days."

Adrian shook his head. With his pointed chin and soft jawline, beards never actually made him look older or more mature. Certainly not tougher, especially with the way his stubble accentuated his cheeks. Never having to deal with it again would be a blessing.

Once Garrick left the living room, Adrian found himself lost, awkwardly standing by the door, unsure how to properly make himself at home. The stares from Garrick's two housemates did nothing to put him at ease.

"So," the man—Everett, apparently—finally spoke first. "What's he want with you?"

That question told Adrian everything he needed to know about Garrick's relationship with the two, and that doing favors wasn't something Garrick was well known for.

"Um, what does he want with you?" Adrian asked in return. The dodge was obvious, and though he was clearly agitated, Everett at least answered honestly.

"Finances. The government gets suspicious when the same name is linked to a bank account for centuries."

"And I'm the government," Jan added. "Gave him a new driver's license, and I got immortality. Pretty good trade, I'd say."

Ah, so Garrick did need things, just not anything Adrian could provide.

"So," Everett repeated, "what are you here for?"

Adrian didn't answer. Nothing, he was here for nothing. That was even worse than if Garrick had taken him up on his awkward prostitution proposal. At least then he'd be providing some kind of service.

"Oh, lay off the questioning," Jan chided, coming to Adrian's rescue. "I've been begging Garrick for months to take someone new in, just so we can have an extra buffer in the feeding schedule. Personally, I hope he brings in four more."

"Feeding schedule?" Adrian asked.

"Garrick's an Elder vampire," Everett explained, taking the deck of cards and shuffling it to start a new game. "It means he has to drink the blood of other vampires, not regular humans."

Adrian froze, his hands halfway through twisting the strap of his bag. His greatest fear from living on the streets had returned—this time, his savior was the perpetrator. Though he didn't dare turn around and reveal his fear to the others, he could have sworn he felt the ghost of the vampire who had fed on him countless times creeping up behind his neck, hovering once more for another bite.

He nearly jumped when Garrick returned, calling for Adrian to join him. He followed into what must have been the master bedroom. A heavy bed dominated one wall, its carved posts glinting faintly in the light from the streetlamps outside, while an adjoining bathroom yawned open like an afterthought. But what caught Adrian's eye was the single bar stool planted in the middle of the floor, its low back stark and exposed. Garrick gestured for him to sit on the stool.

"So," he began, "this process sounds more uncomfortable than it actually is. From your point of view, it'll feel just like falling asleep."

Adrian set his bag down by the door but didn't take the chair. "And from your point of view?"

"Well, you'll die. That's how it works. I drain all your mortal blood and replace it with my own. You'll wake up at the next sunset a vampire. And hungry."

"Oh. Well, that is a bit unnerving." He half-heartedly smiled, forcing himself to play off the sudden mortal panic with humor. A pit in his gut told him to run for the exit as fast as he could. But his legs wouldn't move. Even if he genuinely believed he was making a mistake, what could he do now? He was in the heart of the lion's den. He wasn't leaving this room alive, it was what happened after that mattered.

"Let me know if there's anything I can do to make you more comfortable. The venom usually puts you to sleep before your body reacts."

Venom. Sleep. That was why, every time the last vampire preyed on Adrian, it had felt like a dream. A clever way to stay hidden from mortals.

Adrian slowly settled into the chair. Garrick walked around behind him, and Adrian felt him brush his overgrown hair away from his neck. His shoulders tensed in anticipation of the bite, until he realized what he was doing and forced them down. Memories of running away, only to be grabbed and bitten, came flooding back. He snapped his eyes shut and waited, wondering what was taking so long. Then he felt the telltale sharp sting of vampire fangs. Adrian lifted his arms reflexively to push him away, stopping just short of hitting Garrick in the face.

Then the venom kicked in, and, despite his best efforts, Adrian was pulled into slumber.

If it hadn't been for the fact that he was now a predator of the night, Adrian would have been concerned about following Garrick into a dark stretch of uninhabited plains with no light or weapons. Even though he could now see clearly in the dark—the short trees and scattered shrubs appearing gray, as if viewed through a night filter—the plains were so empty that it still felt like something was lingering just out of sight.

Following a dirt road, they finally approached a lone workshop, with a small, barn-like cabin about half an acre away. Garrick knocked on the workshop's door, barely more than a rough metal sheet that rattled on its hinges with each strike, before letting himself in.

The centerpiece of the workshop was a flat, roofless car, riding low on its wheels with its hood open to reveal the machinery inside. A toolbox sat on the ground next to it, several tools spilled out or lazily tossed aside. The car's red paint glimmered around the image of a flaming skull painted on the driver's side door. Along the sides of the workshop were several workbenches, each cluttered with tools and parts whose purposes Adrian couldn't identify.

Two men stood at the far side of the garage, leaning against one of the workbenches. They both looked up as Garrick entered. The man on the left was well-muscled, wearing a tight-fitting, faded shirt and sporting a beard of dirty-blonde stubble—more late evening than a five o'clock shadow. But it was the man on the right who made Adrian's blood run cold. Taller, leaner, with dark hair—it was the vampire who had fed on him night after night. The vampire seemed to recognize Adrian as well, as their eyes locked in mutual surprise. Adrian's first reaction was fear, ingrained from years of being the man's prey. But the vampire's eyes flicked nervously between him and Garrick, and he slowly edged behind the shorter, muscular man. The vampire's cowardice unlocked something in Adrian, and his fear began to bleed into anger.

Garrick placed a hand on Adrian's shoulder. It tempered his fire, but he continued to stare down the other man, feeding off his trepidation.

The muscled man, apparently the only one in the room who didn't grasp the connection, gave a slight sneer and jutted his chin at Adrian.

"Who the fuck is this guy?" he asked.

"Joseph, meet Adrian," Garrick said in a tone much lighter than the tension in the room. "I've met him a few times over the past few months and thought he'd be a good addition.

Clean break, no family or close friends who might get suspicious."

Joseph raised his hands to stop Garrick.

"So, in addition to biting one of my guys, you're telling me you made a new vamp without my authorization?"

"Well, I just assumed..."

"Assumed?" Joseph leaned forward and tilted his head, as if this were the most ridiculous thing he'd heard all week. "What part of 'no new vassals without my explicit permission' did you not understand?"

"Wh... Joseph..." Garrick held his hands out to his sides. "Chelsea died less than a year ago. I would have thought it obvious that I could replace her. I'm sorry if that wasn't clear. My mistake."

Despite Adrian's impatience to confront the person who had terrorized him, now standing across the room, he couldn't help but shoot Garrick a confused side-eye. His uncharacteristically friendly tone felt forced, and Adrian found it hard to believe he meant half the words coming out of his mouth. Joseph, it seemed, didn't believe it either.

"Oh, that's it? You're just going to apologize, and this whole thing is going to get swept under the rug?"

"Of course not," Garrick said in his falsely soothing voice. "Let me make it up to you. Do you need anything picked up from Vegas?"

"You can't keep using Vegas as a get-out-of-jail-free card! I should be telling you to start making it up by separating this guy's head from his shoulders!"

Adrian flinched and glanced over at Garrick, relieved to see that his unflappable attitude remained intact.

"Please, there's no reason to punish him for my mistake. Besides, I see potential in him. He's quite the sharpshooter."

Adrian lifted an eyebrow. Was Garrick actually bragging about his pool skills, or was it a clever play on words, not technically false?

Unfortunately, the lanky man snickered in response, but fell silent when the room's eyes turned to him.

"You're not serious, right?" he asked. "This man is homeless. He's worthless."

Adrian shrank into himself. He had thought becoming a vampire would improve his lot in life, but it felt meaningless when the people he consorted with were also vampires. They managed to be vampires and still contribute something meaningful.

"Ed," Garrick said, "you're one hundred seventy years old. Why are you hunting homeless men? Have some self-respect."

The lanky man jerked as if he'd been slapped when Garrick said his name. Ed. Adrian's shame slowly morphed back into anger. An utterly mundane name for a pathetic, small man.

"Like I said," Garrick continued, "I've known Adrian for a while. He's got more balls than some in present company."

Garrick's praise made Adrian's stomach flip. It was completely undeserved, but he did his best to hide it. He stood with back stiff and hoped the worried look on his face didn't betray his true feelings. Joseph, however, paid him no mind and glanced over at Ed instead, one eyebrow raised and a disgusted sneer on his lips.

"You one-seventy?" he asked.

For some reason, Ed didn't answer right away. He rapidly shifted his attention between Joseph and Garrick, his eyes widening in horror.

"W-well, yes, but... come on, Joseph, I'm not... I still have thirty years."

Joseph glanced back at Garrick, and the two shared a moment of unspoken agreement. Then he rolled his eyes and walked to the far end of the workbench. Adrian didn't see what tool he grabbed, not until Joseph raised a handgun and shot Ed twice, once in each knee. The lanky vampire cried out in pain and collapsed to the ground, whimpering. Adrian froze in terror.

Then Joseph pointed at him and curled a finger. "You. C'mere."

Adrian didn't move, and Garrick placed a protective arm in front of him.

"I ain't gonna hurt him," Joseph reassured. Something in his voice convinced Garrick of his sincerity, and he placed a steadying hand on Adrian's back, gently urging him forward. Adrian took a hesitant step, then pushed down his nerves once more. Putting on a far more confident facade than he truly felt, Adrian walked forward, locking eyes with Joseph in silent hope that the vampire would respect feigned bravery over honest fear. When he stood an arm's length from the muscular vampire, Joseph thrust the gun's grip into his chest.

"Shoot him," Joseph instructed. "In the head."

Automatically, Adrian took the gun in hand, but his mind went blank with horror. If he refused or hesitated too long, would Joseph shoot him instead? That seemed likely. Adrian turned the gun toward Ed's head, but his trembling hand betrayed his true emotions.

"It's fine," Joseph reassured. "He's mad. You're doing him a kindness."

Adrian glanced back at the other vampire, his face clearly painted with confusion. Joseph clarified.

"You haven't told him yet, Garrick? We go mad after two hundred years—give or take a bit. Minds break, turn into nothing but monsters. 'Cept Ed here. He just lost his balls."

Adrian furrowed his brow and did his best to think through the implications, even though his thoughts were clouded by fear. He glanced back at Garrick, who hung his head. Joseph was telling the truth. A wave of nausea hit Adrian's gut. Even though death was something he lived with every day, being reminded of its presence somehow felt worse now.

"Get a good look, kid. 'Cause one day, I'm gonna do that to you." Joseph nodded toward the crumpled Ed, too paralyzed by fear to crawl, beg, or even flail. "But maybe, if I like ya, I'll keep it nice and peaceful, like puttin' down your favorite dog."

That did little to relieve Adrian's nerves. But with a forceful slap on the back, he realized he wouldn't be getting any more reassurance. He turned back to Ed. What had this man done to deserve his mercy? He had haunted Adrian's dreams for years. This was just revenge. He was a vampire now, and if there was one thing Ed had taught him, it was that vampires weren't kind.

Adrian had never fired a gun before and was surprised by how easy it was. Not the actual mechanism of firing, but the result. One moment, Ed was alive; the next, he lay on his side, hands twitching, a pool of blood slowly spreading beneath his head.

"Not bad. You ever killed someone before?" Joseph took the gun from Adrian's hand. "You can keep him."

With another slap on the back, Adrian returned to Garrick, slowly and in a daze. With a polite nod, Garrick silently ushered him out of the workshop.

Finally, out in the darkness of the moonless night, all the repressed horror Adrian had pushed away clawed through his defenses. He choked back his feelings to prevent the flood of terror from overwhelming his senses, but his body wouldn't cooperate. His chest convulsed in strange spasms, as if it couldn't decide whether it needed to breathe or not. The strength in his legs waned, and he had to focus on the blurring ground beneath him to maintain his balance.

"Hey."

Garrick stepped in front of him and swept Adrian into a hug. At first, he flinched at the unexpected gesture, but then, realizing he was safe, he let the built-up torrent of fear pour out.

"I'm sorry," Garrick whispered in his ear. "That was... not a normal initiation."

Despite the initial overwhelm, it didn't take Adrian long to calm down again. The pressure of Garrick's arms against his back sheltered him against the cruel, outside world, and his firm voice reassured him like an oath.

"I wish I could promise nothing like that will happen again, but vampires can be a violent bunch. If it's any consolation, though, you handled yourself well back there."

It was, just a little, even if the thought of going through something equally harrowing made him ill.

"Was he telling the truth?" Adrian asked, the words catching in his dry throat.

"About Madness?" Garrick paused, and Adrian felt his chest rise and fall in a sigh, pressed against his. "Yes, unfortunately. But I won't let Joseph harm you. It's not his place to make that call for vassals under my care."

"But," Adrian trembled at the thought of bringing up the point, "aren't you...?"

"Older than two hundred? Yes. Would you believe me if I said I'm the exception to that rule?"

Exception? Was that possible? But nothing about Garrick felt mad. He could be a bit frightening at times, like the night he revealed himself to be a vampire, but the way he held him now? Adrian felt only kindness.

Adrian nodded, then slowly pushed himself away, feeling better. He wasn't calm, his heart still fluttered, but not from fear. He couldn't look Garrick in the eye without the embarrassment of accidentally revealing the emotions he now felt.

"And Joseph?" he asked.

"Joseph... No, he's quite mad. You saw his penchant for violence yourself."

Before Adrian could ask the obvious follow-up question, Garrick continued. "Sometimes Elder vampires fall through the cracks and become powerful enough that no one wants to enforce the rules on them. We don't have any kind of vampire council overseeing that. Even if we did, I'm sure you can imagine how corrupt and mad they'd be. No one wants to voluntarily end their life just because the rules say so."

"How..." Adrian paused. The implications of his next question were fairly obvious. It wasn't something he should have felt ashamed about—anyone would ask the same—but the idea of trying to make himself seem special, when there was nothing particularly special about him, made him feel foolish.

He continued when he noticed Garrick's attention, patiently waiting for him to finish his thought. "How often are there exceptions?"

Garrick hummed. "Not often," he said, his voice apologetic. "Not impossible, but quite rare."

That was better than the one-hundred-percent chance of death he faced as a mortal, and he'd be able to live twice as long regardless. Still a far better deal than before.

They slowly began walking again, side by side. Though his emotions had calmed, his mind remained barbed; letting it wander inevitably touched on some painful thought he didn't want to confront. From the execution to Madness, from the glee of revenge against his abuser to the sickening dread of taking a life. Finally, his mind settled on a subject he could interrogate further.

"Why did you turn me?" Adrian asked, breaking the silence. Garrick glanced over, a subtle hint of surprise on his face.

"Still don't believe me about last night?"

"You tried to lie to Joseph," Adrian said. "Everett and Jan both provided you with important services. So what do you want with me?"

"You saw Joseph. Unfortunately, he's the most influential vampire in northern Los Angeles. Our Regent. If you want to live here, you report to him. But he can be a little... unpredictable. It's possible that one day Joseph will decide he's done with me, and I'll be out on my own. That's why I need friends. Everett and Jan provide me with blood to feed on and file my paperwork when needed, but they wouldn't risk their lives for me. There's nothing wrong with that, as long as everyone understands what the relationship is. But I need someone who'd rather raise Hell than willingly work under Joseph."

Adrian smirked. Yeah, that sounded like him all right.

"Also, I do like you. That's usually the only requirement for being friends."

"Your only friend is a homeless man?" Adrian asked.

"Give yourself some credit. A homeless man who beat me at pool." Garrick smiled playfully, and for a brief moment, the world wasn't so cruel. "Which, by the way, maybe you can help me with. It's pretty embarrassing to be old enough to remember when it was invented and still lose."

15
NIGHT 3 - VAL

Val pocketed her phone as she stood idly at the end of the long driveway outside Owen's mansion. She bit her thumbnail while she waited—probably worrying over nothing. Still, Val realized she was being a poor friend by letting Adrian go off on his own once again. But if her concerns were valid, then learning how Tyler had gained his enhanced powers would help not just her, but Adrian as well.

Would Adrian approve of Val's plan to get revenge on Joseph? He had already attempted it and failed. Now, they were in San Francisco, hundreds of miles from home, with Adrian and Garrick sleeping in separate rooms. She wouldn't have blamed him if he wanted to lie low and lick his wounds. Val had no interest in that. It merely meant she had to figure out how to become more powerful than Adrian—powerful enough to kill an Elder. And Tyler, unfortunately, was her best lead.

Sophia finally left the mansion and joined Val outside.

"Where are we going?" Val asked.

"Neat venue, other side of the city," Sophia said. "Live band, seemed fun." Then she lowered her voice. "Are you sure about inviting Tyler along? I thought you were trying to get away from him?"

"I know, I just..." How much should Val say? Did Sophia know about the enhanced powers? "I need something from him."

Sophia gave an exaggerated shrug and raised her eyebrows just enough to let Val know she didn't approve of her weak excuse.

A silver sedan pulled up to the curb next to the mansion. The driver rolled down the front window, and to Val's annoyance, it was Tyler behind the wheel. He grinned and waved, his face showing no sign of a headache. Val and Sophia climbed into the back seat.

"All right!" Tyler said, far more cheerful than Val felt. He drummed his hands against the leather-lined steering wheel. "Classic rock cover band! Good choice."

Val tried to catch Tyler's expression in the mirror, hoping to spot an inordinate amount of glee at being alone with two girls for the entire ride. The car pulled out onto the road and, shortly after, merged onto the highway. Sophia made little effort to engage in conversation, leaving Val in the awkward position of having to answer Tyler's overly friendly questions. How are you liking San Francisco? Must be hard moving to a whole new city. Did you leave a boyfriend behind?

Val sighed and watched the street lamps pass by in

rhythmic succession. "I'm not looking right now," she said, anticipating Tyler's next question.

"No? Whole new town, new people. Someone might catch your attention."

"Mmhm." San Francisco wasn't that big of a city, from one end to the other. Hopefully, their destination would be close. Val eyed Tyler in the mirror again. That was the problem with witchcraft. She could ask the universe to deliver justice, but timing was unpredictable. Sometimes it happened right away; other times, it took painfully long. As Val gained more experience, her spells seemed to work faster. But Tyler didn't look pained.

"How long have you been in San Francisco?" Val asked, figuring it would be easier to get Tyler to talk about himself than to constantly dodge his flirtatious advances.

"Moved here after college. Hard to believe it's been a little more than twenty years now. That was right before the dot-com bubble burst, and I lost my job. Then Owen found me and said he had an opportunity. A startup, if you will. I didn't think it would involve vampires, but hey, it turned out to be way more exciting than building websites. I even helped Owen take over as Regent."

"And that's how you became loyal to Owen?"

"Hm? Don't think I can't see what you're getting at." Tyler threw a smirk over his shoulder, and Val immediately shut her mouth. "I told you, if you want to know how to get enhanced magical powers," he added a mocking flourish to the last few words, "then I need to take my shirt off."

"Tyler," Sophia interjected, "shut up."

Tyler scowled, but it did succeed in redirecting his attention back to the road without further comment.

"You know," Val said after a moment of silence, "I had a boyfriend. His name was Raymond. He died a week ago. Murdered."

Neither Sophia nor Tyler commented, though Val could

feel their attention shift to her, waiting for more information. She didn't have much else to say, but it felt good to finally tell someone other than Adrian and Garrick. All the emotions she had bottled up for an entire week threatened to spill out at once, so she turned her head to look out the window and blinked back the tears welling in her eyes.

"And I'm going to kill the man who did it," she continued. "That's why I want your enhanced magical powers."

Tyler glanced over his shoulder to meet Val's eyes. "Well," he said, "it doesn't sound like you want it enough."

Anger flashed hot in Val as time seemed to stop between them. He eyed her like a hawk, his overly friendly mask slipping for one brief moment.

"I'm Owen's best man. One word from me, and you'll have all the power you want. I just need you to—"

Then she saw the headlights.

Val knew, for a single frozen moment, what was about to come. She had time for only one thought, a brace for impact, before the car slammed to a halt. The sound of metal crunching and scraping exploded around her, and her body lurched violently against the seatbelt. She shut her eyes and lifted her arms to protect her head. Then, as suddenly as it began, it stopped.

Val opened her eyes, her arms trembling beside her face. Well, she was alive—that was a good start. She didn't feel any immediate pain and glanced over her body to confirm she had no major injuries. A dull throbbing in her head suggested she'd hit it against the seat in front of her during the crash. Sophia, slowly lifting her head from the protective barrier of crossed arms and drawn-up knees, seemed to be going through the same thought process.

And then there was Tyler, slumped over the steering wheel, the deflated airbag beneath his chest. Val couldn't immediately tell what his injuries were, but he remained motionless.

Sophia reached for the car door, but the warped frame kept it from budging. Val's door opened without issue, and on shaking legs, the two women climbed out.

Val didn't realize the extent of the damage until she saw the car from the outside. The entire front end had crumpled and warped beneath the hood of a larger SUV. The driver of the oncoming vehicle appeared to have survived, judging by his movements, but he seemed disoriented.

Traffic stopped. Most drivers slowly maneuvered around the wreckage, but a few pulled over to comfort her and Sophia. Val noticed one woman on her phone. Then, police and paramedics arrived on the scene with surprising speed.

One paramedic led Val to the back of an ambulance to check her vitals. The shock of the crash left her too dazed to react quickly. Val didn't have vitals. Or rather, her vitals should have been fatally low. The paramedic clearly thought the same.

"This can't be right," she muttered, unclasping a small device from Val's finger. She picked up an arm cuff from the floor of the ambulance and began wrapping it around Val's arm.

"Um, it's all right," Val said. She couldn't go to the hospital. What was she supposed to say? Yeah, I have low blood pressure. Really low blood pressure. Don't worry about it.

"I just want to check you for internal—"

"No." Val jerked her arm back forcefully. "I'm refusing help."

The paramedic furrowed her brow, a hint of confusion in her expression. "Are you sure?" she asked, matching Val's intensity. "I'm not sending you to the hospital. I just want to make sure you're not in danger."

"Yes." It was easy to be a jerk when her life was on the line. The paramedic looked over at Sophia, who simply said, "Same." She sighed, frustrated.

"Fine," she said. "Let me get the paperwork that shows you're refusing assistance."

Once the paramedic was out of view, Val flashed a strained grimace at Sophia, then looked back toward the cars. The driver of the oncoming vehicle had been rescued and was undergoing an evaluation himself. Just how bad his injuries were, Val didn't know, but they couldn't be worse than Tyler's.

Tyler was still unconscious. It had taken several tense minutes to pull him from the wreckage, and now he lay on the pavement, face up and motionless. Val noticed a long gash along his temple. For a mortal, such a wound would have required immediate attention. For a vampire, it was hard to say. Several paramedics shouted to one another, and one leaned over him, compressing Tyler's chest. Val winced. She had never witnessed CPR before and hadn't realized how hard one had to push. Even if Tyler suddenly sat up and refused help, he'd still have quite the recovery ahead of him.

But Tyler still didn't wake up.

"Is he... dead?" Sophia whispered.

Honestly, Val had no idea.

Another paramedic brought over a briefcase-like device. In one swift motion, he cut Tyler's shirt open across the front and began attaching wires.

Despite the distance between them, Val noticed a curious scar across Tyler's chest, running from the top of his sternum to just below his breast. How often was he getting into car accidents?

Though now that she thought about it, it reminded her of...

The paramedics watched the device eagerly, then, with a disappointing lack of fanfare, ripped the wires off him.

It was possible Tyler's heart still beat so faintly that the paramedic couldn't detect it with a simple finger beneath his chin. Vampires didn't need a lot of blood pulsing through their systems at all times. Hell, their systems were, by all detectable means, dead during the daylight hours. That didn't mean Tyler, given enough time for the swelling in his brain to subside, was truly dead himself.

And yet, Val found herself grinning as she watched his body being loaded into the back of the ambulance.

A splitting headache indeed.

16

NIGHT 3 - ADRIAN

The cold winter air rarely bothered Adrian anymore. Back when he was homeless, winter nights had been his greatest enemy. They could mean an entire night of shivering, desperately trying and failing to fall asleep. When he became a vampire and his body no longer cared about the outside temperature, he had laughed in glee at the thought of never feeling that desperate, smothering chill again.

Adrian could never have anticipated the icy tension between him and Melissa now.

About ten minutes into their walk, after turning down an empty residential road, Melissa pulled out a second cigarette.

She lit it and blew the smoke off to the side. Adrian no longer needed to breathe, but he scrunched his nose in disgust as he walked through her smoke several paces behind.

"You're judging me," Melissa said. She hadn't turned to see his face, so he must have been that obvious. "I only started after becoming a vampire. It's not like I'm using my lungs for anything."

No, but talking required moving air through the vocal cords. Better to keep them free of a layer of tar. Or so Garrick had told him forty years ago, as he snatched a cigarette from Adrian's mouth.

"I was the perfect girl before. Didn't smoke, didn't drink, no drugs. Always wore sunscreen. Guess what? I got leukemia."

Ah, that explained Melissa's figure, with skinny arms and bony neck, devoid of any muscle or fat. He didn't respond, though. He was angry and had no interest in letting her manipulations slide just because she had a sob story.

After another minute of silence between them, Melissa turned on her heel to face him.

"Look," she said. "I'm not trying to cut you out of the picture here. I'm just trying to secure my place in the hierarchy. When Garrick takes over as Regent, I don't want to go down with Owen's ship. It's just a little harmless flirting to get him to like me, nothing more. Men always treat women who flirt with them more nicely."

He didn't! Adrian gritted his teeth and held himself back so as not to snap at her. He forced himself to take a calming breath and played her words back in his head.

"You think Garrick is going to betray Owen?" he asked, steering the conversation away from her generalization.

"Seems obvious. Since when have two Elders ever worked together?"

"That's what we did with Joseph."

"And how did that work out?"

Well, that was Adrian's fault, not Garrick's. But he wasn't interested in giving Melissa a play-by-play of the circumstances that had brought them to San Francisco.

"You don't seem particularly loyal to Owen," Adrian said.

"We met the same man, right? I didn't exactly interview different Regents before becoming his vassal. If I had a choice, I would've picked someone a little more handsome. It would make servicing him a bit more pleasurable for me. Honestly, I hope your Elder does rip Owen's head off. He seems nice."

"Services?" Adrian knew what she meant. He just wanted to be a jerk about it.

Melissa stared him in the eyes for a moment, and Adrian recognized the calculations going on in her head. Garrick was a master at deciding exactly how to answer Adrian's uncomfortable questions. Perhaps he and Melissa had more in common than he'd realized.

"If you want to get ahead with Owen, it helps to have loose legs," she finally said. "Shocking, I know. But there are far worse things than sharing a bed with him. I get to live in his mansion instead of a dingy apartment and do real work. Many of the other girls are prostitutes anyway."

"What kind of work?"

"Managing technology, for the most part." Melissa shrugged. "He was completely lost with modern banking five years ago. I handle his accounts, file the necessary paperwork, help him communicate with the other vassals. Not the most glamorous life, but probably better than most of the jobs available to us."

"You have to keep a job?"

"Owen's got money, but not that much. Not enough to spend on apartments for three dozen vampires. If you want to work for him, you need to find a way to pay."

Joseph had a slightly different system. If you had enough money to pay for an apartment or house, you were free to continue living there. But he also maintained an underground bunker for anyone who couldn't afford it. Joseph wanted his vassals ready for territory wars, not tied up with jobs.

Adrian was always grateful that he had ended up with Garrick. He'd had enough of that kind of life in homeless shelters.

"How do most people pay?"

"Everyone has their thing—prostitution, driving, bartending. Owen has opportunities to help if you're struggling to find work."

"Like what?"

Melissa ignored him and turned up a driveway. The house had a deep blue door and garage, but the upper half of the walls was a beige-white. Adrian knew people couldn't be picky about where they lived, but who chose those colors?

Just as Melissa was about to ring the doorbell, the garage to her right opened. A tall woman in a stylish denim jacket stepped out. She looked up, surprised to see the two of them at her door, then frowned with disgust.

"Ugh, I already told Owen I'd pay next week," the woman said with a scoff.

"Leaving an email and not responding to the reply isn't 'telling,' Nora," Melissa responded flatly. She held out her hand and curled her fingers, motioning for cash.

"Don't have it, slow month. I'll pay next week, with interest."

"You know the rules. Either you pay rent on your own, or you make runs for Owen."

"Seriously? This is my first late month!"

Another man exited the garage, and Adrian flinched when he saw him. Broad shoulders, square face—it was the man who had pried Adrian off Tyler after their fight. They briefly locked eyes before Adrian looked away, nervously tapping the tip of his shoe against the pavement. If he had to be the bad guy, he could at least try to show just how uncomfortable he was with it.

"Here." Devin tossed a package wrapped in brown paper toward Melissa, who had to lunge forward to catch it. "There's double in there for Nora."

Melissa opened the package to check its contents, while Adrian curiously looked over her shoulder. He had a hunch about what was inside, and the several baggies of white powder confirmed his suspicions.

"How long have you been...?" Nora asked her housemate.

"Just a one-time thing," Devin muttered, barely loud enough for Adrian to hear. "Just until Seth gets his act together."

"Thank you," Melissa said, just as enthusiastically as with her initial greeting. "Don't make me hunt you down next month."

They left, and only after a few steps away from the house, Melissa handed Adrian the package of drugs.

"Here," she said. "Sell these for me. Owen expects the cash in a week."

"What?" Adrian shoved her hand away. "No! Why are you even selling drugs? Are you trying to rub elbows with mortal gangs?"

"It's fine." She shoved the package back into his chest. "You're not afraid of a few mere mortals, are you?"

"When they can walk around in the sun, break into my house, and shoot me in the head while I'm in a forced sleep? Yeah! We already had enough problems with rival vampire gangs, we didn't need to piss off the mortal ones too."

Melissa stared at him, her hand still holding the drugs against his chest, waiting impatiently for his objections to stop.

"Take the damn drugs, Adrian," she replied.

Glowering, Adrian stared her down. He would not. Between the two of them, Melissa was far less likely to be shaken down by the police. This was her stupid Regent's idea, so she could bear all the risk and responsibility. The least she could have done was ask if it was something he wanted to do, instead of thrusting it upon him. If Owen had an issue with him disobeying orders, he could tell him personally.

Melissa met his gaze, unwavering. Swearing under his breath, Adrian took the drugs and shoved them into his pocket. Damn it!

"I don't know how to sell drugs," Adrian grumbled.

"Really? Didn't you used to live on the streets?"

"Broke! I was broke!" he snapped. Sure, he had tried a few, but only because they were given to him secondhand. Thankfully, he never found out where the other homeless people had bought them, and after a few rough withdrawals from quitting cold turkey, he didn't go looking. "What do you do? Stand on a street corner and ask, 'Hey, wanna buy some drugs?'"

Melissa rolled her eyes. "Come with me."

They soon found their way to a moderately busy street, even at seven in the evening on a cold day. Melissa slipped into a narrow alley behind a row of buildings and finally positioned herself next to the back door of one. She pulled out her phone and began typing.

"I'll add you to this chatroom," she said. "There's still some risk doing it this way. I once had a Fed get in. When that happens, just wipe the whole chatroom and start over from scratch. I have a few regulars I know are solid, so I'll text them to get it going again."

Adrian shook his head as he listened. Who would have thought that, between the two of them, it was the skinny woman in a velvet dress and perfect hair teaching him, the homeless man in a ratty old coat, how to deal drugs?

"And the Fed?"

"Just bite him in the neck and stitch up the bullet hole."

They waited around, like Adrian would if he were on a hunt. He supposed this was one way to find people to sneak up on and bite, if necessary. What were they going to do, go to the police because their illegal drug deal went south?

Finally, two men wandered into the alley and nervously approached the pair. They must have been new, as they addressed Adrian instead of Melissa.

"Hey," the younger of the two men asked, "you Sparkles?"

Confused, Adrian shot a glance at Melissa, who gave a small nod. Sparkles? That was her dealer name? Wait— because of that one vampire novel? His confused expression shifted into one of judgment. Melissa just shrugged.

Adrian pulled one of the baggies from his pocket and held it up so the men could clearly see what they were buying. "Money?" he asked. Even though he had no idea what he was doing, acting tough and irritable came naturally to him.

The older of the two men pulled out a wad of cash, folded in half, and began counting the bills to prove the amount was correct. Adrian realized he had forgotten to ask what they were actually selling the drugs for, but figured Melissa would step in if he was being shortchanged. When the man finished counting, Adrian held out his hand to take the money, only to be met with the barrel of a gun from the other man.

Adrian instantly responded. He yanked the man forward by the arm, sinking his teeth into his neck. The gun fired into Adrian's side, but the shot caused only a sharp sting. Melissa ducked behind a dumpster, dodging the second man who had also drawn a gun. Adrian released the first man and slammed his fist into the second man's face, sending him stumbling backward, away from the attack.

"Noc!" the man screamed. "Noc, get in—" His shout faltered as Adrian bit into his neck. After holding on just long enough for the venom to take effect, Adrian looked up to see a third man appear at the end of the alley, gun drawn and held high. He fired, and thankfully missed.

Adrian reflexively pressed his back against the alley wall

and raised his arm to shield his head. The third man—dark-haired, with piercings—fired again, this time grazing Adrian's arm. Adrian charged at him, hoping the sudden advance would startle his attacker enough to throw him off. The pierced man managed to get off another shot, hitting Adrian in the right shoulder. Adrian tackled him to the ground and slammed his head against the pavement—not hard enough to cause serious blunt force trauma, but enough to stun him. In that moment, Adrian sank his teeth into the man's neck, intending to render him unconscious without killing.

But before he could wait long enough to be sure the venom had taken full effect, a fourth person stepped in front of him, this one wearing a leather jacket and sporting tied-back red hair.

Bar girl?

"Thea!"

Upon hearing her name, Thea looked up and immediately dropped her gun arm to her side. She ran past Adrian, heading straight for Melissa. Adrian jumped to his feet to follow, but before he could reach her, Thea embraced Melissa in a hug. A look of surprise spread across Melissa's face as she slowly raised her hands to gently pat Thea's back.

"Hey, whatever this is," Adrian called to the two, "we need to get out of here." The gunshots had already sent nearby pedestrians scattering. No doubt the police would be on their way, though how long it would take, Adrian couldn't say. Regardless, it was best that the two—or three—of them were long gone by the time they arrived.

17
NIGHT 3 - VAL

Only scattered shrapnel remained from their accident by the time Val and Sophia pulled themselves away from the bustle of emergency workers, who were working quickly to clear the road for traffic. The two women walked for two blocks before calling the others, neither wanting to dwell on the crash. They sat on the curb in front of a café, closed for the night. The ambulance had left soon after loading Tyler's body. Dead or undead, Val couldn't be sure.

Seth's car pulled up to the curb in front of them, and Nora jumped out of the passenger-side door before it had fully stopped. Devin had the good sense to wait two seconds longer before opening his door.

"Oh my god, are you hurt?" Nora ran up to Sophia and gave her a hug. Val watched them for a moment in silence. She couldn't help but feel a little jealous. It made sense, though, as she was the new friend. Then she felt Devin's hand on her arm. She gave him a reassuring smile and nod.

Val chastised herself for not making up her mind. Did she want comfort, or not?

She longed for Raymond's comfort.

Well, Raymond wasn't here, and Devin wasn't a half-bad second choice. But the moment had passed, and reaching over for a hug would be awkward now. Next time she was in a dangerous situation, she'd hug the first person who offered. Hopefully not anytime soon.

"Shit," Seth swore as he rounded the car's hood. "What the hell happened?"

"Freak accident," Val said. "I think the other guy was drunk."

"Where's Tyler?" Seth asked, his concern evident.

Val and Sophia glanced at each other. Who would break the news?

"On his way to the hospital," Val said, "or the morgue."

"Shit…" Seth scratched the back of his head, twirling a lock of black hair through his fingers as he fidgeted.

"I'll call Melissa," Nora offered. "She can pass it along to Owen."

Seth nodded, groaned, then turned and waved. "I need a fucking drink."

Val glanced over at Sophia, who remained expressionless. Val didn't think Tyler deserved any concern, and from what she could tell, neither did Sophia. Maybe Seth and Tyler were better friends than she had originally thought, though their conversation the previous night suggested otherwise. Val followed Seth into a small bar a block away, along with Sophia and Devin, and took a seat at a raised bar table. Seth immediately made his way to the bartender to order.

Val watched, amused, as the bartender took five... six... seven seconds staring at Seth's driver's license. Seth was fifteen years turned but didn't look a day over twenty. That put him at around thirty-five years old in total. Pretty soon, he'd need a fake ID with a more recent birthdate if he wanted his license to be believed.

Val had the opposite problem. She appeared old for the age she'd turned—or, well, "mature" for her age. She could probably keep her license another thirty years.

"Really?" Val asked as Seth sat back down, beer in hand. "You're trying to rescue Tyler by getting into another accident?"

"I'm just sipping," Seth grumbled.

Vampires could drink just about anything if they were careful. Blood was half water, after all. The catch was, without kidneys, nothing flushed out. Val learned that the hard way after a single night of drinking. She remained buzzed for a week. Fun at first, annoying as hell after.

"Is there a reason to be concerned about Tyler?" Val asked. "I didn't think we liked him."

"Well, we don't," Devin said. He shrugged and glanced over at Seth to see if he would elaborate.

"The coroner's going to be really surprised when he finds out he has a vampire on his hands," Seth added from behind his beer.

Unlikely, Val thought. Either Tyler was really dead, his body already in the process of disintegrating into dust as they spoke, or he was fine and about to give a few paramedics the scare of their lives. Either way, Val was aware of strange stories about people who appeared to be dead and then were fine hours later. Just another medical mystery to be shared online and assumed to be fake.

How hard had Tyler hit his head against the steering wheel? A large gash had split his temple. Was that enough to kill him? It was enough to kill Raymond, but Raymond hadn't suffered a single blow. Unless the car that hit them had backed up and collided again and again, Tyler's head injury had to be far less fatal.

A lump caught in the back of Val's throat. Raymond's death had a way of worming its way into her thoughts, no matter where she was. Had she been thinking of it when she cast her spell? Was that why it turned out so much more violent than she intended? She had smiled when she saw Tyler's head split open on the pavement. He didn't know Raymond. He hadn't smashed his head with a hammer. He didn't deserve her smiling at his pain like that.

And yet, the thought of someone else suffering like Raymond, suffering like she had, made the rage and despair easier to swallow. And Tyler was a good victim.

"You okay?"

Devin snapped Val out of her thoughts. She nodded, realizing she had shed a tear while thinking about Raymond. Dammit.

Devin reached over to put a hand on hers. "Hey, it's fine," he said. "Sounds like it was a really scary wreck."

"It's not that," Val said. "I... I lost my boyfriend last week."

"Shit, just one week ago?" Devin asked. Nora had returned and was whispering in Seth's ear, but he still took a moment to glance at Val.

Devin continued. "Damn, I'm so sorry. What happened, if you don't mind me asking?"

A small smile twitched onto Val's face. She realized this was the first time she told the story. Adrian had been there, and Garrick got the quick, delirious version right after it happened. After that, it was just a blur of moving between inns and motels, everyone too tense to talk about the event further. A full week passed before someone finally offered comfort without any extra baggage. It was like a cool breeze, and it threatened to make her tear up once again.

"He... He was murdered," Val began, "by our last Regent. He just walked up, unprovoked, and killed him right in front of me." Val opened her mouth to say how Joseph had struck multiple times to make sure Raymond was dead, but found those words particularly difficult to voice. It wasn't necessary to the story anyway.

"Just... walked up and bang?" Devin asked. "No argument or anything?"

Well, smash—but yes. "That's his Madness," Val said. "Violence. He was never that bad, though."

"Madness?"

"Yeah." Val looked around the table and realized everyone was staring at her like she'd said something strange. "Elder Madness?"

The three younger vampires looked at Seth, who simply shrugged.

"Really? Owen never told you?"

"Tell us what?"

"Vampires go mad when they become Elders," Val explained. "They start losing their minds. Joseph became violent, but Adrian said he met others who grew paranoid."

"Well, yeah, I could have told you that," Seth scoffed. "It's nothing special, though. All Elders are assholes."

"But this is like... they just can't help themselves."

Seth squinted at Val and brought the beer to his lips for a long sip. "Who told you this?"

"Garrick..." Wasn't this common knowledge? All the vampires in Los Angeles knew about it. Then again, no one here besides her had ever met an Elder other than Owen. Was he keeping this a secret from them?

"So, what's Garrick's Madness?" Seth pressed.

Well...

"Garrick doesn't have one."

Seth's eyebrow arched so high it looked ready to break through the roof of his forehead.

"I know that sounds awfully convenient," Val explained, "but I've known him for ten years. He's... well, normal."

Garrick had his faults, sure, but compared to Joseph? Garrick was a saint.

"Owen is normal," Seth countered.

"Owen is a misogynistic pig."

"So's Tyler," Seth shrugged. "And most of the men who work for him. And some of the women, to be honest."

"Yeah, but..." Sure, Owen wasn't special in that regard, but he fit the pattern just like all the others. "Look, if you knew the other Elders, you'd understand."

"You mean the garden-variety violent criminal, the guy who conveniently is the exception to your own rule, and...?"

Val couldn't answer. She had heard stories but never personally met another Elder besides Joseph and Garrick. There were others in Los Angeles—it was a large city, after all—but ten years before Val turned, Joseph had successfully expanded his territory to the northern quarter, nearly one hundred square miles. There was little reason to meet anyone else, and many reasons not to.

"A lot happens once you become an Elder," Val retorted, though she didn't feel terribly confident in her argument. She was only ten years turned, arguing with someone fifteen years turned, about what happens to vampires two hundred years turned. Neither of them were in a good position to know anything. "Why wouldn't your mind break?"

"Why would it?" Something about Seth's tone suggested genuine agitation. "I bet if you took a step back, you'd see that your Elder isn't such a great guy either. He'd probably seem insane if you weren't so close to him."

Val's mouth went dry. Garrick might have been a saint compared to Joseph, but he was far from one himself. He was human, with all the foibles that entailed. The times he lied, the sly smile when Val caught those lies, knowing the pieces would still fall exactly as he needed them to, avoiding any real repercussions. The way he encouraged her worst behavior.

And yet, Val wouldn't go so far as to say he was bad. Even if he was, Val was no better, and she was tired of being good.

"How's he get his blood?" Seth followed up. Sophia had asked the same question, and Val had dodged the details.

"From... Adrian," she said, assuming the question was aimed at the who rather than the how.

"Just him? Not you?"

"I don't want Garrick near my neck," Val answered quickly. "Adrian... he's fine with it."

Seth let the reply linger, simply holding Val's gaze in response, a knowing smile indicating he could read between the lines. Devin and Sophia shifted uncomfortably at the heightened tension, but it was clear they shared Seth's opinion, given how they continually looked to him for direction. Nora sat furthest from Val and didn't bother to engage, other than offering a few bored glances.

If there was any doubt that Seth was the leader, it was now obvious.

"Your Elder certainly has a lot of conveniences," Seth teased. "The only one who isn't mad. A dutiful lover who doesn't mind having his own hard-earned blood drained night after night. If poor Adrian weren't around, then what? Oh, good thing you're close. He doesn't need anyone else, though—just his ill-tempered juice box and the spare, who also conveniently lost her boyfriend, freeing her to follow her Elder across the state and call it a kindness."

A flash of anger flared in Val at the mention of Raymond's death, and at using it to attack her friend. She wanted to think of a retort quickly, but she needed a moment to process Seth's implications. Unfortunately, he noticed her hesitation.

"Sounds to me like he's got you two wrapped around his little finger. Or am I wrong?"

He was, partially. But some of his assumptions were

correct. And the more Val thought about it, the more she came to the uncomfortable conclusion Seth was leading her toward.

Did Madness really exist? Suddenly, it didn't seem to matter. Whether its origin was supernatural or not, her trust in Garrick felt a little less certain than it had moments ago.

And if he were mad, just how deep did it run?

"Of course, feel free to find evidence to prove me wrong," Seth said with a shrug, returning to his beer. The conversation then shifted to whether the group had caught the latest television episode, and from there, the tension lifted as the friends laughed and joked as if Val's sanity wasn't crashing down around her. Discreetly, Val pulled out her phone and texted the one person she still trusted, even if he might not have any answers.

> Can we talk when you get back? I've had quite the night.

18
NIGHT 3 - ADRIAN

The two vampires, plus mortal, agreed to meet in a motel room—somewhere neutral and away from prying eyes. Thea arrived last, carrying a first aid kit. One of the many advantages of being a vampire was that Adrian's heart pumped blood much slower than it had when he was alive, which meant he hadn't completely bled out on the way to the motel. Still, he made sure not to lean back in his chair, avoiding a large blood smear as his wound slowly oozed into the fabric of his shirt.

Being a vampire also meant that pain didn't register as intensely as it once had. The bullet wound in his side was merely a minor annoyance, no worse than a cramp. His shoulder, however, burned like a small hellfire. It was the difference between lead and silver.

When he took off his shirt for the two women to dress his wound, he realized the bullet hole in his side was worse than he'd expected. That would explain the slight dizziness and the gnawing pain aching through his body.

"Looks like you don't have an exit wound on your shoulder," Thea said, helping to wrap it in bandages from behind. "Guess silver doesn't actually work against vampires. But just so you know…"

"Actually," Adrian said with a smirk, "it's a kind of, sort of situation with silver."

"Really?" Thea perked up, clearly intrigued by the finer details of vampire biology. She leaned into his line of sight, eager to hear more.

"What? You want me to reveal all our secrets to a mortal?"

"Come on, I'm cool," Thea said. "I'm just doing this vampire-hunting crap to find Melissa."

"Yeah? How do you two know each other?"

Melissa rubbed her shoulder now that Adrian's wounds had been tended to. A smattering of dried blood clung to her skin, and the motion caused a bullet graze to start bleeding again. Melissa didn't mind. She placed her palm over the wound and held it there, then removed it half a minute later. It was gone, save for a fresh smudge of blood. So, she could heal too.

"We're sisters," Thea answered. "Melissa disappeared five years ago and didn't tell anyone where she was going."

There was a hint of disdain when Thea said it. Adrian glanced between the two of them. Even now, knowing they were related, he didn't see the resemblance. Melissa was taller, had a more pointed face, and darker hair. He supposed the two women shared a similar way of speaking and carrying themselves—a similar inflection on certain words—

but if lined up side by side, he wouldn't have assumed they were sisters.

"I'm sorry," Melissa whispered. "I couldn't... Vampires can't mingle with humans, not even family."

"Yeah, I guess..." Thea didn't seem placated by that excuse, but she didn't press the issue. Unfortunately, Melissa was right. Maintaining ties to the mortal world rarely ended well. If you weren't aligned with a Regent who enforced strict rules on mortal contact, the facade could only last so long. It was nearly impossible to stay in touch without questions piling up. The inability to visit friends and family during the day, the lack of aging...

Adrian had lucked out. His family stopped contacting him years before he ever met Garrick. Sometimes, he wondered if they ever thought about what happened to him. He'd been homeless before the age of cell phones and the internet, so if they ever started caring again, there'd have been no way to find him.

"So, how did you find Melissa, then?" Adrian asked. "Your sister disappears under mysterious circumstances, and you think, 'Ah, definitely vampires'?"

Thea, finished with her first aid and sat across from the two of them on a small sofa. "Because we saw one once," she said simply. "We were out in the city and saw one creep up on this other person, and—chomp!—right into her neck. Mom thought they were just kissing when we told her, but we knew better! So I figured, if I were dying of cancer in my mid-twenties, what would I do? I'd totally go find a vampire. So when I wanted to track down Melissa, I went searching for vampires. And I was right!"

Melissa shook her head and buried her face in her hands. "I see my suicide note wasn't believed at all."

"No one bought that!" Thea griped. "Well, except for, like, most of the news and the internet. But Mom and Dad and I didn't! Especially since you were last seen getting on a plane and never left a body. God, could you have been more suspicious? What did you expect us to think? That you wanted to go to the beach by yourself one last time?"

"Fine, fine!" Melissa snapped. "I'm glad you didn't believe me, actually." Her face lightened, and she smiled. She got up, walked over to the couch where Thea sat, and hugged her. A real, genuine hug this time. Melissa turned her face away from where Adrian sat, but he could see tears welling up in Thea's eyes.

"But you can't tell Mom and Dad, okay? I'm serious. We're really not supposed to have connections with mortals. If the others find out..."

Thea broke their hug and looked at Melissa with despair. "You never heard," she whispered. "They're dead."

Melissa's face contorted like she had been punched in the gut. Her eyes became unfocused, as though she were searching for the right words somewhere in the far-off distance.

"I'm sorry." Thea placed a hand on her sister's knee. "It was three and a half years ago. They were driving home one night, and a car just..."

Adrian didn't interrupt what was obviously an emotional moment between the two sisters. But some things started clicking into place. "True crime," Thea had called it. Her sister left behind a suicide note and disappeared. Her family, refusing to believe that their daughter had really killed herself, began investigating every clue they could find. Then, a year later, they were killed in a car wreck. Even without the vampire angle, it was an odd set of coincidences. Thea, the lone survivor of her family, dedicated her life to finding answers, finally bringing her here to reunite.

Adrian waited in silence while the two women finished connecting and reminiscing about old times.

"So, now what?" Thea asked at last.

"Now what?"

"Yeah, I finally found you! So, like—"

"You leave," Melissa cut her off, "knowing that I'm safe and doing well, and then we don't see each other again."

"What? Come on! Being a vampire isn't a full-time job! I'm cool with having a vampire sister!"

"Weren't you paying attention?"

"First things first," Adrian finally interjected into their conversation, "we need your hunter friends out of the city."

"Yes!" Thea snapped her fingers. She seemed oddly excited about the task, but Adrian figured she was clinging to any angle that might keep her in Melissa's life a little longer.

"Fine," Melissa grumbled. "But once they're gone, you go too. Understand?"

"Yeah, sure," Thea said. Adrian wasn't sure he believed her, and it was obvious that Melissa didn't either.

"What? Promise! In the meantime, is there anything you need? Come on, having a mortal around who can do things during the day has to be useful."

Melissa shook her head again, but Adrian accepted the offer. "Actually," he said, "I'm pretty hungry."

"No!" Melissa sat up straight, glaring daggers at him.

"What? I lost a lot of blood. You don't want a literal, bloodthirsty vampire sitting right next to your sister, do you? It's taking everything I have to hold back…"

In the theatrical way he said it, Adrian hoped Thea knew it wasn't a real threat. But he was hungry, that much was true, and vampires were known for making poor decisions when hungry.

"No," Melissa said again. "There's still time. Find someone else."

"But I'm weak…" Adrian's eyes drifted over to Thea, pointedly ignoring Melissa. She sat with her arms crossed, a look of bemusement on her face. "Come on," he goaded. "You've heard the stories. You must be curious what it's like. Don't tell me you never…" He threw his head back and dramatically draped an arm over his forehead. "Oh, handsome vampire, take me away from this dull, boring life."

"Ugh, fine!" Melissa stood up and walked over to Adrian, thrusting her wrist toward his face. "Just be quick about it."

Adrian smirked and gave Thea a small wink. The gesture was met with a chuckle. He pulled Melissa's wrist closer, then nearly flinched when the blood touched his tongue. Sweet, like Tyler's. Thick like syrup and sweet as cherries—Adrian's hunger seemed to grow as he drank. Though he couldn't see her glare, he knew Melissa was watching him like a hawk for any sign of over-eagerness. He drank slowly, savoring the taste and calculating how much more he could get away with. When he felt her muscles tense beneath his hands, Adrian withdrew his fangs from her arm. He did his best not to lick his lips immediately afterward, resisting the urge to chase any spilled sweetness.

"Thanks," he said, trying to act natural. "Appreciate it."

Adrian thought back. Both of the men from the previous two nights had tasted normal. Was it vampire blood? He'd tasted that before. There wasn't much of a difference between vampire and mortal blood. Could it be something specific to Owen's vampires?

"Now that we have that out of the way," Melissa growled, "perhaps it's time for you to leave. I'm sure you want to get those bullet holes patched up. Thea and I have five years of catching up to do."

"Wait!" Thea jumped out of her seat and fumbled through her pockets, checking her jeans first, then her jacket, until she pulled out a small phone. "There's something you two should know." She turned the screen toward Adrian and Melissa, revealing an internet chatroom. In the middle was an image.

A picture of him and Garrick, taken at Owen's Blood Ritual meeting just hours earlier. A chill pricked at Adrian's neck. How did Thea get that? Based on some of the replies surrounding the photo, he could tell the chatroom belonged to the hunters.

"What?" was all Adrian could manage to say.

"Yeah, I know," Thea said.

If the picture had been taken at Owen's mansion, that meant Thea was in contact with a vampire. He tried to recall who had been standing nearby while he and Garrick were talking, but his mind had been on more important matters at the time. The only person he knew for sure was there was Melissa.

Adrian couldn't help but hazard a glance her way and found Melissa staring back at him, her expression blank. He returned his attention to the phone screen, realizing he had likely given away his scathing suspicions about her.

He didn't have proof. Plenty of other vassals could have taken the picture. He just knew Melissa had an interest in removing him.

"Who took this?" Adrian asked, pretending he didn't already have someone in mind.

"His name's Striga, but that's just his username. I'm guessing he doesn't use it in real life."

"He?"

Adrian mentally kicked himself for sounding so disappointed. He was trying not to let Melissa know he suspected her. She'd know now.

Thea shrugged. "I mean, I've never met him. Could be a girl. We talked on the phone, but he might have been using a voice modulator."

So, it was still possible.

"That's concerning," Melissa muttered. She finally looked away from Adrian, allowing his disgust at her feigned ignorance to surface. No, he was being hasty. It was still possible someone else was behind this. Perhaps Owen himself, still angry over Adrian's transgressions on the first night. Or maybe a third party. The picture also included Garrick, so

Adrian might not even have been the intended target. Based on Melissa's earlier comments, it was possible that any number of vassals feared the emergence of a new Elder and wanted him gone.

"I'll tell Owen about this when I get back. In the meantime…" Melissa gave him a curt nod. Adrian did his best to appear unfazed by being dismissed without further questions, but he needed time to collect his thoughts anyway.

Upon leaving the hotel, Adrian immediately cloaked himself in magical shadows, no longer feeling safe anywhere near Melissa. He didn't drop the shadows until he had spent twenty minutes walking through dark, empty side streets. This "Striga" and their hunters shouldn't be able to track him out this far.

As soon as his shadow fell to the ground and faded like smoke, his phone buzzed in his pocket. Adrian checked it and saw a text from Val. Adrian laughed.

Can we talk when you get back? I've had quite the night.

You and me both.

19
NIGHT 3 - ADRIAN

Adrian spotted Val a block before he reached the gaudy red brick facade of Owen's old hotel. The time was well into the early morning, just a few short hours before sunrise, so even the major streets were completely barren. It made it easy to speak frankly, though Val still glanced over her shoulder, as if someone had followed her.

Adrian was about to greet Val when she stopped short and stared at him. Or, more accurately, at the bloodstains on his shirt.

"What happened to you?" she asked.

"Hunters."

"What? Again?"

Adrian wanted to laugh. Yes, again, and she should see the other guy. Adrian was a little roughed up but still in a far better state than being caught beneath a silver net. Still, it was nice that Val understood the severity of encountering the hunters twice in two days.

"They're tracking me." Adrian wished he had insisted on getting the photo from Thea, but with Melissa watching them, he hadn't wanted to push his luck by voicing his suspicions. So instead, he described what he saw. The photo was from Blood Ritual with Owen, a place where only vampires were in attendance.

"Shit. Adrian, this is really bad. Someone wants to kill you! Do you know why?"

He had been wondering that his entire walk back. He simply shrugged in response.

"Ugh, can you please take this seriously?"

"I am," Adrian snapped. He hadn't meant to come off so terse, but Val voicing her fears only compounded his own. Melissa was his best guess, though he admitted that was mostly because they'd clashed that day. It was possible someone Adrian had never met was simply afraid of the three new vampires entering their city, starting rumors of a violent turnover.

"Have you heard anything? Do you know anyone who isn't a fan of Garrick or me?"

"I could ask my new friends," Val offered. "They seem to be in the know. Actually, that's what I wanted to talk to you about. You know how Tyler has more power than he should, right?"

He noticed, especially during their fight that first night. Despite being only fifteen years turned, Tyler's power matched Adrian's. Or, as much as Adrian didn't want to admit it, possibly surpassed it. It aligned with what Summer had said, she was only fifteen as well. There was something

Owen could do to accelerate their age. What that was, however, Adrian didn't know.

"Well, I was trying to figure out why that was, and, well, we were in a car accident."

A car accident? Adrian scanned Val for any sign of injury, but she appeared unharmed.

"…And Tyler might be dead."

"Might be?"

"I'm not sure. He had a deep gash across his head and was completely knocked out, even when the paramedics took him away. Do you think that could be enough to kill him?"

It was hard to say, given how little they knew about Tyler's power. A vampire turned for only fifteen years probably wouldn't survive a fatal head wound like that, but older vampires could shrug off incredibly debilitating injuries. Even so, that wasn't the most dangerous part of Val's story.

"Even if he survived the crash, I don't think he's going to make it out," Adrian said. "He's not breathing, and his heartbeat might be so slow it's undetectable. They probably moved him to the morgue. Unless someone happens to be working late, they won't hear him wake up. He'll spend the next few nights trapped in a metal coffin—until he either starves, gets cut open during the day, or is cremated."

Horror gripped Val, causing her to tense. Yeah, it wasn't a fate Adrian wished on people lightly. Tyler, despite his annoyances, probably didn't deserve it. But rescuing him wasn't worth the effort or the danger.

"There was something interesting, though," Val said. Her voice cracked slightly after the harrowing description. "Tyler had a scar on his chest. He kept saying something like, 'I'll need to take my shirt off,' which I thought was just him coming on to me. And maybe it was. But maybe Owen put something inside him?"

"Wait. What did this scar look like?"

"Like…" Val hesitated. "Like Garrick's."

Tyler too? This was getting too odd to be a coincidence. Between him and Melissa...

"They also had sweet blood," Adrian mumbled. Noticing Val's look of confusion, he elaborated, "Their blood tasted sweet when I bit them." Val's judgmental stare only intensified, and Adrian shrugged sheepishly. "I bit Melissa *consensually*, okay? I was hungry after the hunter attack."

"Okay." Val continued her accusatory glare, which Adrian chose to ignore for the sake of his sanity. "Have you ever bitten Garrick before?"

"Yes, many years ago." It was unusual for vampires to bite each other. Adrian hadn't been in a fight that required him to use his fangs in at least five years, until his fight with Tyler. "It wasn't sweet, if that's what you're asking."

"It's still a weird coincidence, though."

It was. Adrian would admit that. Tyler and Melissa—both scarred, both sweet, both with enhanced powers. He hadn't gotten a look at Summer, so he couldn't say if she was an exception. Meanwhile, Garrick had the same scar but not the sweet blood. What did it mean?

"I'll have to ask him about it," Adrian conceded. "Maybe he knows something."

"Sure, but..."

Adrian waited, but Val bit her tongue. Did she not want to finish her thought? Yes, he should ask Garrick, but...

Finally, Val asked her question. "Are you and Garrick... okay?"

Just the question itself caused a small panic in Adrian. Yes. Yes, of course they were. Sure, Adrian had insisted on sleeping in a separate room for the past week, but... he was on his way right now to fix that. Because he loved Garrick.

"Of course," he said, then bit his lower lip to hide the sneer.

It seemed unlikely that Val believed him, but she just nodded and let the interrogation rest.

"It's just an odd coincidence, is all I'm saying." Val opened the hotel door and went inside. Adrian lingered outside for a moment before following her. It was an honest question. A strange curiosity. Of course Val would be suspicious. So why did he grab the door handle with white, tense knuckles?

Once inside, Adrian knocked on Garrick's door and braced himself for the inevitable interrogation about his bloody, sorry state. As expected, Garrick opened the door and flinched.

"What—?"

Adrian pushed past and threw his coat to the floor. "Silver," he stated. The bullets weren't bothersome enough to keep him from functioning, but the longer they remained in his body, the more they would drain his strength—until one night, he might fail to rise with the setting sun. Thankfully, Garrick was well-practiced with a scalpel.

Without pressuring him for more information, Garrick walked over to the desk against the far wall and cleared it of a lamp and an old landline phone, then pulled it into the center of the room. He retreated into the bathroom to fetch a few towels, grumbling under his breath about them being white and easily stained.

"I met the hunters again today," Adrian said, finally letting Garrick in on the details. "They're tracking me." He pulled off his shirt and winced as Garrick helped him with the bandages. Dried blood peeled away from his skin along with the cotton fabric.

"Tracking you?"

"I talked to one of the hunters."

Garrick paused to show his disapproval. Adrian had expected that reaction. Garrick was careful, often to the point of distrust.

"She's Melissa's sister. She became a hunter after Melissa went missing, but I don't get the sense that she's truly interested in killing vampires."

A low grumble told Adrian that Garrick didn't agree with his assessment. "She's not interested in killing vampires *today*, but as long as she knows about us, she's a threat."

After spreading a towel over the desk, Adrian lay down on his back. "People aren't interested in killing vampires on sight anymore, old man. They think we're sexy. Mortals want to become vampires now."

He heard Garrick rummaging through his bag for medical supplies—a scalpel, rubbing alcohol, more bandages. Ever the prepared doctor. Adrian wasn't sure if Garrick carried the items out of habit, forged by centuries of needing first aid equipment, or if he just knew Adrian would find trouble again.

"If we're so beloved, then why are these hunters trying to kill us?"

"Well, *most* people are fine with vampires."

"For now, until they find a reason to hate you. Then they'll conveniently remember that you're an inhuman monster. Left side."

Adrian turned onto his side and crossed his arms over his chest. He couldn't blame Garrick for his distrust. For most of his life, Garrick had lived in a world steeped in superstition, where even minor mysteries were blamed on evil, demonic forces. Adrian didn't press the issue any further.

Garrick stood behind him and brushed his fingers lightly across Adrian's chest, back, and hip. They were warm. The warm touch of another vampire was a rare luxury.

"This isn't what I had in mind when you said you wanted more intimate time with me," Garrick said.

Adrian's chest lurched with a laugh. "Sorry."

Garrick didn't share in his humor, making Adrian wonder if he had laughed too readily. He clamped his mouth shut and simply lay in the quiet of the room as Garrick's careful touch glided over his skin. Occasionally, Garrick pressed firmly near his bullet wound, sending a jolt of pain arcing up his shoulder. But despite that, Adrian's muscles slowly released their tension.

"I'm sorry, by the way, for acting so stern with you." Garrick's voice was quiet, each word spoken slowly, imbued with thought to ensure they were the right ones. "This past week has been difficult for me too. Perhaps more difficult than I'd like to admit. And I don't want that to cause a schism between us."

His fingers paused, settling on Adrian's side. Garrick fell silent, and Adrian wondered whether the man had gotten lost in his own thoughts.

Then he continued, "I know we sometimes disagree on the best way to approach things, but I still care about you and your opinions, and I don't want you to think otherwise."

Adrian crossed his arms tighter over his chest. He had grown skilled at ignoring the fights with Garrick, especially lately. He was glad he was facing away, so the man couldn't see the tears welling in his eyes, though he could always blame them on the bullet.

Garrick commanded Adrian to roll onto his back. He picked up the bottle of rubbing alcohol once more and wiped down a spot near Adrian's shoulder, just to the right. "Please let me know if there's anything I can do for you. We can't go around sowing chaos in Owen's ranks. I've lived long enough to see the problems that causes, but I still love you. Okay?" Garrick sighed. "And please don't read too much into earlier. I'm not here to demand anything from you. We don't have to be intimate until you're ready."

That. Adrian closed his eyes and felt a wave of relief wash over him. No matter how much he pretended otherwise, he had steeled himself for the intimacy he'd promised Garrick, determined to provide everything he wanted. He couldn't lose him. A pit of worry still lingered—a small fear that Garrick was just trying to placate him, and that his offering had its limits—but at least, for now, Adrian was free from any uncomfortable obligation.

"Thank you," he said.

"Now, unfortunately, I'm going to have to hurt you."

Adrian's head snapped up. Garrick held a scalpel in one hand, hovering it over Adrian's body, and a pencil in the other. Adrian simply rolled his eyes and opened his mouth to accept the pencil bit.

"Punishment for getting shot?" he asked, his words slurring around the wooden obstruction.

"Maybe a little."

Pain dulled for vampires, but lying down with nothing to do except think about the sharp knife cutting into his chest? That hurt a lot. Though it lasted only a few seconds, the feeling of the scalpel slowly slicing through skin and muscle was agonizing. The pencil in Adrian's mouth cracked under the pressure of his clenched jaw.

"Just a little longer," Garrick mumbled. Adrian felt various instruments poking and prodding around the newly created hole in his chest. He tried to occupy his mind to ignore the pain. Finally, he felt the surgeon's tools withdraw from his body, along with a small lump. The burning sensation finally subsided.

Adrian opened his eyes to see Garrick holding a small metal scrap up to the light. He rotated the bullet between his fingers, then let it rest in his palm.

"Real silver, not the fake stuff. These hunters aren't cheap."

Garrick washed his wound with plain water and returned his healing touch to the bullet hole. Adrian spat out the snapped pencil from his mouth, shards of wood and graphite leaving behind a dry, gritty taste. Next time, Adrian would do without.

When the wound finally closed, Garrick helped Adrian sit

up on the desk and placed a palm over his left breast to check his vitals. How he managed to assess them, he wasn't entirely sure, given the slow, dull beat of Adrian's heart even at the best of times.

"When are you going to teach me healing?" Adrian asked. "It seems like an important thing to learn."

Garrick hummed as he lifted his hand. "I suppose you're about that age." He pulled Adrian's hands close and clasped them between his own. The heat intensified.

"Focus on the energy within you and try to ignite it, like a flame drawing fuel from your blood. Then, extend it to the area you're trying to heal." He let go of Adrian's hands and reached for the scalpel once more. He made a small cut on his fingertip. Blood pooled in the newly formed crevice until Garrick placed another finger over the wound. A few seconds later, he removed his hand, revealing that the cut had fully closed, leaving behind only a small scar.

"Please make sure to practice on small cuts for now. Don't let me catch you out in the sun because you thought you could heal a major, gaping wound instead of calling for help."

"I will." Adrian pinched his index finger and thumb together, trying to see if he could warm them using Garrick's small fire metaphor. Maybe he could, or maybe his mind was just playing tricks on him.

"Does the scar ever go away?"

"If you're concerned about the appearance, you can continue the healing process until the scar fades. However, it can take a long time, especially for larger scars. Most don't bother with the trouble."

"Like the one on your chest?"

Garrick grunted. "I gave up on that one long ago." He took the scalpel and towels in hand, moved to the bathroom, and began filling the sink with water. Once the basin was full, he scrubbed his tools to wash away the blood.

"How did you get that scar?"

"A fight with another Elder."

Adrian hesitated. It would be far easier to simply accept Garrick's words and believe it was all a coincidence. But he needed to know.

"Melissa has a scar just like that."

"I noticed, but to be honest, I was keeping my eyes above her breasts."

"Val said that Tyler had the same scar, too."

Adrian watched Garrick intently. Garrick picked up a bar of soap, rubbed it across his palms, then placed it back onto the small dish by the sink. His back was turned and his reflection gone, so Adrian couldn't see if his thoughts leaked onto his facial expressions. And yet, Adrian knew that inside Garrick's head, he was flipping through every possible response, making careful note of what information was safe to share, and crafting a reply designed to yield the best possible outcome. Adrian had seen that process many times before.

"Interesting coincidence," was his final response.

Adrian's fingernails dug painfully into the wooden desk as his shoulders seized, his muscles straining as if to hold back an explosion from deep within. What a coincidence, indeed.

"Val said Tyler promised her increased power from Owen," he continued. "Summer said the same. Melissa could heal minor wounds, and I know she's not lying about her age. Strange that they all had the same scar as you."

Still, Garrick didn't turn to face him. Adrian waited, silently daring him to offer another lie or comforting reassurance. Garrick left the towels to soak in the sink and gripped the edges of the granite countertop, his head slightly bowed.

"It's just a coincidence," he said. "There's no grand conspiracy."

Adrian pushed himself away from the desk and stormed out of the room. He had to leave, or he'd provoke Garrick further. And if that happened, he wouldn't be able to lie to himself any longer.

20

Night 3 - Val

Val retreated into her room. She still wanted to interrogate Garrick but knew Adrian had the same idea. With sunrise only two hours away, Val decided that conversation could wait until tomorrow night. Instead, she spent the time picking up her spell circle. She thanked the spirits, returned the crystals to her bag, and burned the paper.

Her spell had gone well. Too well. Val found herself torn between unease at having caused Tyler immense harm and glee at finally delivering punishment he'd managed to evade for so long.

Glee? He might have died. Did that make Val a murderer? No, she only meant to give him a headache.

Anything beyond that was just his own karma catching up with him.

The sound of a door slamming announced the end of Adrian and Garrick's conversation. Val cracked open her door and peeked out just in time to see Adrian march past. He stopped at his door, swiped his key card, and slammed the door behind him again.

So, their talk went poorly.

Shortly thereafter, Garrick opened his door. He stood in the middle of the hall, paralyzed, until he let out a despairing sigh and ran his fingers through his hair. Val had initially decided she was done for the night, but if her goal was to get information from Garrick, it was best to strike while the iron was hot.

Val ran to her bag, pulled out a deck of cards, and met Garrick in the hallway.

"Everything all right?" she asked.

"Fine," he said quickly, dismissing the concern. "Just stress from everything."

Val could easily tell it was a lie, but she chose not to press the issue.

"I have some time to kill," she said, changing the subject. "Want to play cards?"

Garrick regarded her with suspicion but relented quickly. "Fine," he sighed. "Of course you brought cards."

The two found a small lobby area near the hotel's front entrance, empty and dark in the early morning hours. Val shuffled the deck a few times before handing the cards to Garrick, letting him choose their game. He always knew interesting, antiquated ones. Val wasn't very good at anything he taught her, but she found the history fascinating.

"Piquet?" he offered. Val nodded, and Garrick began to split the deck.

"There's something I've been wanting to ask you since this morning," Val said. She noticed Garrick tense up, but he didn't try to stop her. "Your last name is Leach? That's a little on the nose for a vampire, isn't it?"

Garrick stopped his shuffling and let out a hearty laugh. "Legally, my last name changes every half-century or so, just so the government doesn't get suspicious. But yes, my real surname is Leach." He dealt the cards. "You have to realize that when I was born, surnames weren't passed down the way they are now. Or rather, that was something reserved for royalty. We common folk just had descriptors. But had I known my ultimate fate, I might have insisted on going by Garrick Medic or Garrick Doctor. Alas, it was the leeches that left the biggest impression."

"So, wait, you were a leech doctor?"

"Physician. Bloodletter. Surgeon. Barber, if needed. It was all the same thing for much of my life."

"Have you ever drunk blood from a leech?"

Garrick scowled in disgust. "Yes, unfortunately, though it was rare that I needed to. My profession provided a good cover during the early years of my vampire life. I worked night shifts, and people would knock on my door asking to be bled for all kinds of maladies."

They began their game. Val vaguely remembered how to play and let Garrick guide her through the first few hands until the strategy came back to her. The best part of playing Piquet was teasing Garrick about its French origin, something that had mattered much more hundreds of years ago. Garrick took the ribbing in stride, even played along, daring her to report him to the king.

Piquet was a trick game in which players earned points based on the strength of their hands, as well as their ability to guess the strength of their opponent's. Val wondered if Garrick liked the game purely because of a quirk in its vocabulary, where the dealer was called the "Elder."

"No, this game was taught to me by a friend," Garrick

answered when Val asked him the question. "I suppose it is a funny coincidence, though."

"You're full of coincidences today, Garrick Leach."

The pleasant smile disappeared from Garrick's face, replaced by a grave stare devoid of warmth. "I see you and Adrian talked before you found me," he said flatly. "Is that why you were so eager to play cards?"

Val shrugged. She could play coy, too.

"Ask whatever you like, but don't expect a different answer just because you're not Adrian."

"Prove to me that Madness is real."

Though the coldness remained, Garrick slowly raised an eyebrow in response. "Was Joseph not proof enough?"

"He's just one Elder," Val challenged. "I only know of two."

"Lucky." Garrick flipped his cards onto the table and clasped his hands together. "I've met many. Adrian told you about Linh, correct? How she nearly trapped and killed him inside her own home? She was always paranoid, saw enemies everywhere. Her own vassals were always one scheme away from stabbing her in the back—when, in reality, she was the only threat in the room. Then there was Juliette before her. She raised her vassals like cattle. Slaves, really. They weren't allowed outside her ranch and fed on her cows until they aged out of being satiated by animal blood. Then they were drained and discarded. And if you ever want to flee California, stay away from Houston. Otto, the Regent there, is a fan of experimentation. So, is that enough examples for you, or do you need more?"

With a dry mouth, Val nodded. She shrank in on herself for even asking the question. Technically, more examples didn't necessarily prove that something supernatural broke the brains of Elders, but assuming Garrick hadn't made up his story, the pattern was obvious. Garrick had effortlessly named more evil Elder vampires than she could name living evil mortals, despite the much smaller sample size.

But that did not bode well for her next question.

"Have you ever met another exception like yourself?"

"It's rare," Garrick responded quickly. "But I've met a few. No one currently alive though."

"That's convenient. Especially considering that, from the outside, you look just as mad as everyone else."

Garrick waited a moment before replying. Though nothing about him changed physically, Val knew that inside, a fire had ignited beneath his cold exterior. "And what Madness would that be?" he asked slowly, carefully.

Val paused to sort the cards in her hand, arranging the suits together from high to low. Finally, she placed the Ace of Clubs onto the table.

"I want you to know that I'm not saying this to provoke you. I've known this about you since the night you turned me, and every day since, I've chosen to be your friend regardless. I was willing to believe you when you said this wasn't part of some supernatural Elder curse or whatever, even though I'm not sure I believe that myself. But here's the thing. You have always been a complete and unrepentant liar."

21

TEN YEARS AGO

Val's chest tightened when Garrick entered the bar. Her mind reflexively tried to calm her nerves, telling herself he could just be here for a drink. But Garrick was never just here for a drink. Though it was difficult to see in the dim lighting, he briefly locked eyes with her, then casually walked over, without so much as a smile, a frown, or a moment's hesitation to suggest he understood the weight of their meeting.

Val didn't move from her table, which was decorated with amethyst and blue agate stones, a bowl of cut wild jasmine, and a stack of tarot cards, each the length from the base of her palm to the tip of her fingers. In the far corner sat a glass tip jar, pre-loaded with five one-dollar bills. Normally, she draped the wooden table in maroon velvet, but tonight she had forgone it in favor of two tall, thin candles to avoid creating a fire hazard. Garrick sat across from her, elbows resting on the table. He met her eyes again and smiled, lips taut, the candle flames dancing in his eyes.

"Why are you here?" Val asked, arms folded. She kept her voice steady. She wasn't mad. Or at least, she didn't want to appear that way.

"I thought we should talk."

"Should we?"

Garrick paused, his eyes darting to the table. "How about a reading, then?"

"You had one two nights ago."

"So?"

Garrick reached into his pocket and pulled out a wallet. After thumbing through it for a moment, he took out a crisp bill and dropped it into the tip jar. A twenty, based on Andrew Jackson staring back at her. Val rolled her eyes but made no move to stop Garrick from picking up the tarot deck and shuffling it. The readings worked better when the person receiving them did the shuffling, but most people didn't know how to do it properly, and she didn't want to risk her cards getting bent.

That wasn't a concern with Garrick, though. Despite his feigned ignorance of tarot, he expertly shuffled the oversized cards, dropping them hand over hand until both halves of the deck rested in his right hand, then repeated the process. Val knew Garrick was gentle with those hands, for all the wrong reasons.

"What do you want to talk about?" Val finally asked, giving in.

"I should apologize."

"You should."

Garrick glanced back up at her, unamused, though his

shuffling continued uninterrupted. "I'm sorry I didn't inform you of my relationship status two nights ago."

"Are you sorry that you cheated, or just sorry that you got caught?"

"Adrian can worry about that distinction," Garrick said. "As for you, I'm sorry that I made you an accomplice to my cheating."

"And yet, here you are once again. I don't get the sense that you're sorry at all."

"I just want to talk, something I can't do if my lips are otherwise occupied."

Val felt her cheeks flush, and she bit down on the tip of her tongue to keep herself from showing any more embarrassing reactions. She had never imagined herself as the type of girl who would go for older men. Garrick had to be at least twenty years her senior, and yet here she was, crushing on him like a teenager again. His easy smile, sharp features, and continual interest in her life didn't help matters.

"So… you want to talk about more than just two nights ago?"

Garrick shrugged, then nodded toward the two candles. "Those are new," he said. "Do they mean something?"

The candle closest to Val was made of red wax; the other, of green. Both were originally the same size and had been lit at the same time, but the green candle burned ever so slightly faster.

Val hesitated to answer. Was he dodging the very conversation he had sought her out for?

"It's…" she began, trying to think of the best way to put it. "It's an experiment. I'm racing them. There's a spell at the bottom that will release once the candle fully melts. I couldn't decide which one I wanted to use."

Garrick kept his gaze fixed on her eyes, waiting for further explanation. His hands continued to shuffle.

"The green candle is a karma spell. It just asks Karma to

mete out justice a little more promptly than usual. The red candle..." Val paused. "The red candle contains my suggestion for what appropriate karma looks like."

"And that is...?"

Using magic to cause harm was a fraught subject. And yet, plenty still cast whatever spells they pleased, and Val wasn't sure if they ever faced any consequences.

"It's nothing bad. Just, like, a bee sting. Or stepping on a shard of glass and spending an hour digging it out of your foot."

Garrick continued to stare at her in silence. He pointedly raised an eyebrow.

"Just a little cosmic slap on the wrist. To, you know..." Val sighed and shrugged. "It's nothing bad," she repeated.

"It's not directed at me or Adrian, is it?"

"No."

Garrick set the deck of cards on the table. "Well, if you want to know what I suggest..." He reached over and took the red candle—Val's karma—and, before Val could protest, snapped it in half. He placed the top half back onto the candlestick. Val could have sworn the flame had blown out in the motion, but when Garrick removed his hand, it was still alight on the wick.

"There. I think that's a bit more fair."

Val sighed. Well, her experiment was ruined now. The goal was to let the universe decide, to maybe put some distance between herself and whatever consequences transpired. It wasn't up to her, or to Garrick, for that matter. She blew out the two candles.

Instead of picking up the deck of cards, Garrick cut it and drew three cards from the top. He placed them in a line in front of him: the Page of Wands, the Devil, the Ten of Swords. Garrick frowned.

"Perhaps you ought to translate for me," he said. "These cards don't look promising."

160

Val tried to keep herself from smirking. At least the universe had a good sense of humor.

"The Page of Wands," she began. "Wands represent fire, energy, creativity, and spiritual potential. The Page grounds this energy, but he's young. What will he do with such potential? In your past, you may have seen the world as full of opportunity, and yourself as having the energy to forge ahead. Think not just of what inspired you, but how you acted on it.

"The Devil. Think not in terms of good and evil, but rather how the Devil operates. He offers quick rewards in exchange for long-term pain. A perversion of The Lovers, he sits between a man and a woman, binding them not by love, but by chains. This card represents your present. Think about what binds you, even if you don't want to admit it. The Devil often appears when one is struggling with addiction, negative thoughts and behaviors, or—quite commonly—sex."

Ever so subtly, Garrick wilted. He kept his eyes on the card rather than looking up at her.

"The Ten of Swords," Val continued, "is in your future. The man lies on the ground, ten swords stuck in his back. It is a card of betrayal and endings, but without the rebirth that Death brings. No glorious phoenix rising from the ashes to create something better. The man must simply accept his pain and move on."

Garrick tapped his index finger against the table, his gaze fixed not on the cards, but through them.

"So that means…"

"It means you cheated on your boyfriend, and he's about to break up with you."

"Hm," he grunted. "I don't think the cards approve of me today. Although..." His eyes lifted, finally meeting hers again. "You got one thing wrong. This isn't a Past, Present, Future spread."

Val furrowed her brow and glanced back down at the cards again.

"This is you," Garrick said, pointing to the leftmost card—the Page of Wands. "This is me." He moved his hand over to The Devil. "And this is Adrian." The Ten of Swords. He picked up the card. "Though, now that I think about it, that didn't change much, did it?"

"Well, it changed from him betraying you to you betraying him. Which, actually, makes a lot more sense."

Val picked the cards back up, took the Ten of Swords from Garrick, and placed them back on the deck. She lingered on the Page of Wands. Not a bad card to assign to her, she thought.

Garrick rubbed his eyes with his thumb and middle finger. He suddenly seemed so tired, shedding the vitality that made him appealing despite his apparent age. She didn't want to pity him. Whatever inner turmoil Garrick was going through now was a product of his own making, and one he should have known better.

Still...

"You know, the thing about The Devil card is that the chains binding the man and woman are deliberately drawn to be loose. The Devil's hold over them is imaginary. The only thing keeping them there is their belief in their own hopelessness."

Garrick snorted, keeping his eyes closed while pulling his mouth into a condescending, incredulous smile. He leaned back in his chair, his left elbow firmly planted on the armrest as he moved his fingers to stroke his temple instead.

"Thank you for the attempt," he said, just honest enough that Val didn't take offense. His eyes slowly slid open, still unfocused. Deep in thought. Val waited in silence, wondering if he wanted to get something off his chest.

Ah, that's why he had sought her out tonight. Her shoulders tensed. He had no one else to talk to.

"Well, don't expect any sympathy from me," Val mumbled. She cleared the table of the rest of her baubles just in time for a salad to arrive. She ate in silence, waiting to see if Garrick would try to vent any other worries that were on his mind. Blissfully, he kept to himself. But annoyingly, he still lingered at Val's table. If he was going to take up potential customer space, the least he could do was leave another tip.

"Why'd you do it?" Val finally asked. She didn't care, and he probably wouldn't provide anything insightful. From what Val could tell, having never cheated herself, was that people didn't exactly think about the repercussions. They were driven entirely by libido, apparently. But Garrick had a unique way of always sounding so well-spoken. Whatever lie he'd told himself to feel better might at least be interesting.

Garrick kept his eyes closed. "I'm worried about him," he said.

"Odd way to show you care."

"I'm losing him." There was genuine pain in Garrick's voice. He let the statement linger just long enough for Val to wonder what he meant. Had this Adrian found someone closer to his own age? Or worse, was he sick?

"He's growing up so fast. He so badly wants to run straight into danger and resents me for stopping him. I just needed someone else for a little while."

Oh, no, just normal relationship problems. Ugh, was that it? Why couldn't men form close friendships the way women did? "That's what happens when you date someone half your age," Val said through a mouthful of lettuce and beets.

Garrick opened his eyes and frowned. "He's older than he looks. Young face. And there's no one else my age."

"Use online dating next time, old man. Now, is there anything else, or did you just want to use me for support again?"

Garrick took a moment to express his displeasure at Val's sharp comments, then reached into his pocket and pulled out a small bottle filled with various organic materials. Val's heart sank when she saw it, and she resisted the urge to check her own bag to see if the identical bottle she had made two nights ago was still inside. She didn't leave it at Garrick's house, right?

"I'm a little rusty on my witchcraft, but if I'm not mistaken…" Garrick held the bottle up in front of his face, pinching it between two fingers so the dim bar lights shone through. "Crushed rhodonite mixed with salt, forming a layer over wilted rose petals. Above that, fresh rose thorns, topped with a layer of soil. This is purely a guess, but I'm going to say it's soil from the foundation of my own house, based on your rather insignificant fascination with a small flower growing nearby when I took you there."

Val's entire body went cold. Garrick had not only found her spell jar but also knew exactly what was inside it. How long had he been lying to her? What did he want from her? Damn it, she had slept with him—and the whole time, he'd been feigning ignorance in order to…? If Garrick wanted something from her, the perfect time to blackmail her was two nights ago.

"Not exactly a love spell, is it? My first thought was that it was a break-up spell, but you're missing a component used to represent binding. Rookie mistake for someone as experienced as you. A heartbreak spell, then. Seemed to work well enough. Although, you didn't use it on me, did you? I'm too… experienced for witchcraft like that to harm me. Adrian, though…"

Garrick's face went cold as he stared into her eyes, his fist clenched around the small bottle. His gaze pierced her like an icy spear through the heart.

"Although I suppose you wouldn't have known that. I'm just a normal old man, unversed in the ways of magic. I'm sure Adrian happened to come home early that night purely by coincidence."

Val stared, eyes unfocused, unable to face Garrick's accusation. She felt more exposed in front of him now than she had without her clothes.

Garrick set the jar on the table and leaned forward onto his elbows. His expression softened once more, though Val knew which emotion was false.

"For the record, I'm impressed. Twice over," he said, a polite smile returning to his face. "First, for the unexpected deviousness. You got me, and that doesn't happen very often. Second, for the fact that your magical talents seem legitimate. I've met a lot of charlatan psychics. I was starting to think nobody had real power anymore."

Val didn't respond. The compliment felt anything but genuine. She waited to see what Garrick was really here for. Pressuring her into another night?

A server came by before Garrick could say more. Last call for drinks. Val nodded, said she was done, and asked for the check. Garrick didn't make a move to pay for her, thank God.

"Walk you to your car?" he offered instead. Val wanted to say no, but the quarter-mile walk to the lone spot along the street always made her uneasy.

"Sure," she said. She knew it was a bad idea. Garrick was undeniably angry. But even if she refused, she wouldn't be able to stop him.

They walked in silence through the dim streets, illuminated only by the occasional street lamp, Val waiting for the catch. Probably a suggestion that she come back to his place for another go. Damn it, how had she gotten into this situation? Was it too late to turn around and ask the bar owner to walk her instead?

"So," there it was, "why'd you do it?"

"Do what?" Val knew what he meant, but the question was unexpected, and her mouth moved before her brain caught up.

"You knew Adrian and I were a couple before we slept

together, and yet you still went through with it. Why? I wasn't coercing you. Or at least, I don't believe I was."

"I…" Val struggled to come up with a spin that wouldn't make her sound like a terrible person.

"You just spent the past thirty minutes berating me for my mistakes. Do me the honor of being honest."

Shoulders hunched as if to hide her shame, Val steeled herself in anticipation of revealing her own faults, bare and raw.

"I didn't always know. The bartender noticed how we were getting friendly and told me he'd seen you and your boyfriend together a few times. Then you walked in a few hours later and offered to take me to your place." She had declined but said she'd meet up the next night to give herself time to prepare her spell. "I started that day fantasizing about what it would be like to get into your pants, and then was crushed to find out it was all a lie. But why not? I'm not your moral compass."

Her words took on a note of spite. To Garrick's credit, he didn't flinch. He looked Val straight in the eyes as she spoke.

"Whether we actually slept together doesn't change the fact that you cheated just by asking. So let me have my fun. How it affects your relationship is none of my concern."

"Most people would say that, despite everything, what you did was still morally wrong."

"You're right. I should have just gone home and cried into a bucket of ice cream. 'Poor Val, nursing her sweet, broken heart. I'm so sorry. You did the right thing.' Or," Val stopped, hands on hips, "I could have gotten my fucking rocks off with a little revenge on the side."

Garrick watched her display with a smirk. Hell, he approved—judging by how the edges of his lips curled into a full grin, his two canines oddly elongated into sharp points. Kind of like a…

He couldn't really be a vampire.

"Give me those candles," he said, holding out his hand.

Despite her better judgment, Val slung her bag off her shoulder and rummaged through it to find the two candles. She didn't approve of him further derailing her plans, but his demand had been oddly forceful, and she was curious. She handed him the green candle and both halves of the red one.

"What spell was in this?" Garrick asked. "And be honest this time."

"It's a little vague," Val muttered. "But it was something along the lines of his car ending up at the bottom of a lake. I didn't specify whether he'd be in it, but…"

Val held her breath, waiting to see if Garrick would ask who 'he' was. It wasn't him or Adrian, she had been honest about that.

"Sounds like a bad guy doing something to deserve a new submarine. Funny how the universe loves to take its sweet time with these things, giving guys like that plenty of second chances they love to ignore. That's why Hell exists, right? Because justice likes to sleep on the living—unless we step in."

Garrick threw the green candle callously over his shoulder and took the top of the red, broken one between two fingers. He pinched the wick, and a flame flickered to life as he pulled away. But how…?

"I promise you this, Val: I will never mislead you, pressure you, or coerce you into anything physical ever again. I don't currently have any spell-crafting materials, so you'll have to take my word for it. At least until we can do this more formally, if you'd like. But I can't rely on Adrian forever. One day, someone will have to take over his responsibilities, and you would make an excellent candidate. If you say no, I'll disappear, and our paths will never cross again. But I think there's something we can agree on."

The flame doubled in size, turning an eerie, intense blue. Candle wax flowed down the sides and over Garrick's motionless fingertips like an open wound. Within seconds, the candle had melted completely, leaving behind only streaks and a puddle of hot wax.

"Don't suffer for the world's sake; it won't suffer in return."

22

NIGHT 4 - ADRIAN

Adrian had no intention of sitting around while a group of hunters searched for him. If Owen or one of his vassals wanted him dead, he wasn't about to stay in one place, waiting for the hunters to discover where he slept. Nor could he ignore his need to feed. He didn't know where the hunters were staying, but he figured he could do his best to draw them out and get some fresh blood in the process.

The nightclub was smaller than Adrian had expected, but it was plenty busy. It was surprisingly well-lit, with several stage lights that danced over the crowd in shades of pink, blue, and green. A sleek black granite bar stretched from one end of the room to the other, its shelves lined with an impressive array of liquors. Adrian pushed his way across the dance floor to claim an unoccupied barstool and ordered something small and fruity. The staff were always kinder when he spent money, even though he'd always find someone to take it later. He scanned the room, mentally noting the people who stood out. Most of the men were shirtless, many wearing little more than underwear. A few drag queens livened up the dance floor with their vibrant presence. Adrian had never fed from a drag queen before. In addition to being far more noticeable if they disappeared for ten minutes, he found them too nice. Also, heavy makeup tasted bad.

Adrian's phone vibrated, and he saw a text from Melissa. Melissa? Of course she found a way to get his number.

Owen wants to talk to you.

Adrian slipped his phone back into his pocket without replying. He wasn't interested in talking to Owen right now.

Despite the venue, there were a few girls scattered throughout, one of whom walked up right next to Adrian at the bar. She placed her elbows on the counter and flagged down the bartender without looking at him. In the dim light, it took a moment for Adrian to realize it was Thea.

"What are you doing here?" Thea asked through clenched teeth, her lips pulled into a forced smile. She still didn't look at him, but it was obvious whom the question was directed toward.

"Getting a drink," Adrian replied casually. "I should be the one asking you that question. I don't think this is your kind of crowd."

"I'm hunting vampires, which is why you shouldn't be here."

"Oh, really? What a coincidence."

"Coincidence?" Thea's shoulders seized up as her teeth

clenched. "Everyone knows vampires flock to gay nightclubs, yet here you are, fully aware there are hunters who recognize your face."

"And that's why I'm here. I'm doing reconnaissance."

The bartender returned with a bright red drink in a martini glass, with two cherries skewered on a toothpick. Adrian took a small sip. It was sweeter than he preferred.

"You ordered the Vamptini?" Thea hissed past her clenched jaw, still trying to hold her fake smile. "Are you trying to get yourself killed?"

"Have you found anything about Striga yet?"

"It hasn't even been twenty-four hours! I just spent all my time gaslighting everyone into thinking I wasn't actually nearby when you attacked everyone. You nearly sent Noc to the hospital."

"Are any of them here with you?" Adrian asked.

"Just Geo for now. He's pretty reserved, so I don't think he'll do anything rash, but…"

"Cool. Distract him for me. I'm hungry."

Adrian slid his drink and jacket over to Thea. Despite her hushed protests, he hopped off the barstool and made his way into the crowd on the dance floor. One man stood out. He had been talking with several others at the bar, likely a regular. Adrian did his best to appear relaxed and sidled up next to the man, shoulder to shoulder.

"Hey!" he said, raising his voice over the music. "Do you come here often? I just moved here last week."

The man, wearing only a pair of navy blue boxers above his ankles, gave Adrian a friendly smile.

"I do! Name's Jake!"

"Adrian! Nice to meet you. I'm a vampire."

"Rock on!"

Kink communities made hunting so much easier.

"I was wondering if you happened to know someone I might, you know, pair up well with."

"Sure, man! Let me go find him for you!"

The man slapped Adrian on the ass before disappearing into the crowd. Adrian looked back at Thea and gave a thumbs-up. She looked ready to burst, her eyes bulging as she held in a scream.

Adrian spent the next minute awkwardly dancing with another man until Jake returned, dragging along a young man with dark hair and a plain black shirt. Before Jake could properly introduce them, he ran off, seemingly caught by someone else.

"And there he goes," the man mumbled. "Jake said we have... similar interests?"

"Hope so! It's kind of loud in here. Mind if we find somewhere quieter to talk?"

The man grabbed Adrian's hand and nodded toward a back corner. It was a convenient spot, away from the lights and crowd.

"So? What do—?"

As soon as the man turned around, Adrian sank his teeth into his neck. But as the blood touched his tongue, he froze. Sweet—again. This man also had sweet blood. In fact, it tasted even sweeter, somehow. Adrian stood, trapped between the implication and the desire to drink more—to finally get his fill of the irresistible blood.

Then the young man's hand grabbed hold of his throat.

"Well, this is really awkward," he whispered into Adrian's ear. "But you're supposed to ask permission first."

The man shoved Adrian off him with one arm, and Adrian stumbled back, nearly colliding with another dancer. The man rubbed the side of his neck with his palm, and the bleeding stopped quickly.

"You're..."

The man grinned and pulled back his lip, revealing two long fangs.

"And they're just as real as yours."

"I'm so sorry, I thought—"

"You thought I was a mortal and would forget this conversation ever happened. I get it." The vampire scowled. "But we still don't do that here. You must be Adrian. Sorry we haven't had the chance to properly meet yet. Val's had a lot to say about you."

Adrian froze in embarrassment. He'd been to two gatherings at Owen's and still didn't recognize him. In fact, he probably wouldn't recognize most of the vampires in the city.

"Seth, nice to finally meet you. I'm sure Val's filled you in on me."

When Adrian didn't respond, Seth clapped him on the back.

"Come on, I'm a forgiving guy. Let me help you find someone to get a drink from the proper way."

Adrian's mind felt numb. The social embarrassment was absolutely paralyzing, but something about Seth's reaction gave him pause as well. Seth played the part of the carefree, forgiving man, but his arm wrapped around Adrian's back like a coiling snake, preventing him from slipping away.

"Your blood…" Adrian said, trying to push aside his feelings. "It's sweet."

"Is it now?" Seth searched Adrian's face. His friendly facade slipped as he stared into Adrian's eyes with uncharacteristic intensity. Perhaps he had revealed too much. Did Owen's vassals know what their own blood tasted like?

Then Seth's friendly demeanor returned. "Well, can't say I've ever tried it myself. But you're not getting any more, if that's where the next question is going. I worked hard for my blood, and I'd like to keep it."

It was more jovial, but Adrian recognized the fake pleasantries from decades of experience with Garrick. This time, however, instead of mild annoyance, Adrian felt a flicker of fear at the insincerity.

Seth beckoned over a shockingly tall, muscular man with

a full beard, built like a football linebacker. "Julio! You up for helping a newbie out?"

He whispered back into Adrian's ear. "Julio's usually up for anything. He's never questioned me when I get up in his neck. Just have to give him what he wants first."

Seth's hand gripped his shoulder tighter, renewing that constricting feeling from before.

"Um, I'd rather…"

Julio held out a hand in introduction. By all accounts, he seemed like a nice guy—polite, warm smile, beard well-mani-cured. It wasn't anything Adrian hadn't grinned and beared before, and he was large enough to get a nice, filling drink that would last him until his wounds healed. Being a vampire wasn't a glamorous life. Sometimes it meant getting a little uncomfortable.

Suddenly, Thea grabbed his elbow, holding her phone to her ear.

"Adrian! It's Melissa, it's an emergency. We gotta go!"

Melissa? What kind of emergency could she possibly have gotten herself into, and why did it involve him? But before he could ask any of those questions, Thea pulled him out the front door of the bar and shoved his jacket into his arms.

"Phew. Maybe it's a good thing I was here after all."

"What? What's wrong with Melissa?"

"Oh my god," Thea said, dramatically rolling her head in exasperation. "That's literally the oldest bar safety trick in the book. I'm pretty sure you were the only one there who actu-ally thought there was an emergency."

"What?" There was no emergency? Then what the hell was that all about?

Thea shrugged and shifted her weight back and forth. Her mouth parted as if she wanted to say something, but she hesi-tated. Adrian had the feeling she was waiting for him to put the pieces together himself, that there was something obvious he was missing that didn't need to be said. But with every second of silence, it became clearer that the implication was lost on him.

"You know," Thea said, gesturing vaguely up and down Adrian's height. "Look, sorry, maybe I misread you. But you had that look, like you're in a bar with some guys, debating doing something you know you don't want to do but don't know how to say no to. I've seen that look before."

Adrian shrank into himself. He slowly put his jacket back on, suddenly feeling cold. He fidgeted with the collar and buttons, trying to avoid meeting Thea's gaze a little longer. Somehow, it wasn't just the feeling of being used or trapped —it was also knowing that Thea had accurately pinpointed exactly what he was feeling. Even his emotions weren't private.

"You shouldn't have done that," Adrian snapped. "I mean, I appreciate the concern, but sometimes being a vampire means putting yourself in situations that are a little uncomfortable. I don't have the luxury of going to the supermarket for my dinner."

Not to mention, he wanted to stalk the hunters for more information, but Thea didn't need to know that. She may have been Melissa's sister, but if she started to suspect that Adrian meant her friends harm, there was no guarantee she'd continue to protect him.

Thea flinched at his statement. "Wow, okay. Never mind, just waltz right back into the club, then. Say hi to my hunter friends while you're at it, too."

Adrian flipped up the hood of his jacket in an effort to signal he was done talking about it. But she was still right— he didn't want to go back inside. He marched off, the hunger for blood making him feel restless. Behind him, he heard Thea jog to catch up.

"Hey, I have an idea if you still need to eat," Thea said. "I just need you to promise you won't hurt anyone."

Adrian looked over at the girl. He could pounce on her. It

would be easy, with her guard down. According to her, she'd never been bitten by a vampire before, meaning she likely wouldn't even know what happened when she finally woke up. That would take care of his hunger right here and now.

"What about you? Won't your hunter friend find it suspicious that you disappeared?"

"I made up a story about how my period came early, and Geo ran to the drugstore. I'll just tell him someone slipped me a tampon and I went home."

"Devious," Adrian muttered. His instinct was to rebuff Thea and wallow in his melancholy alone, but he reminded himself of his goal. Thea was his best lead in discovering who was trying to capture him, if not outright kill him. He noticed a subtle shift in Thea's posture as the silence dragged on—a small, listless shrug of her shoulders. Disappointment?

"I'm still a little hungry, I guess," Adrian admitted. "What's your idea?"

That instantly perked her back up. Her smile returned, and her brows lifted in excitement.

"Come on!" Thea grabbed his arm and tugged him toward a nearby parking lot. They approached a large black motorcycle, hastily parked along the side of the lot, not quite in a proper space.

"Sorry, normally I'd offer you my helmet to be courteous, but I think if we get into a wreck, you're more likely to walk away fine than I am."

She slipped the helmet onto her head before throwing a leg over the seat and patting the space behind her, inviting him to hop on.

Despite being tougher than when he was alive and needing far fewer functioning organs to survive, Adrian hesitated at the idea of getting on a vehicle with no barrier between him and the asphalt. But of all the emotions to show a hunter, fear would be the worst. He climbed onto the back of the motorcycle and sat at the very edge of the seat, though he had the sense that the bike wasn't meant for two riders.

Thea turned to face him and slapped her hips. "Hold on tight, yeah?" she said, her words muffled by the helmet.

Adrian wanted to be respectful, but he realized he didn't have much of a choice in the matter. He placed both hands on Thea's waist. She revved the engine, and the motorcycle suddenly lurched forward. Whatever courtesy Adrian had begun with instantly vanished as he grabbed Thea tightly and leaned into her back.

A few minutes into the ride, Adrian finally found himself relaxing, becoming enthralled by the rush of wind beating past his face. At first, Thea weaved through traffic at a slow pace, but once she hit the open road, she sped up, causing Adrian to cling a little tighter.

All too soon, they turned into another parking lot. Thea stopped the bike and turned her head expectantly. Adrian realized he had to get off first, and he wobbled onto his unsteady feet as soon as they touched the pavement. Thea laughed.

"How was the ride?" she asked, taking off her helmet.

"Fun... I think." When his balance returned, Adrian looked around. "Where are we?"

Thea pointed to a neon sign that read "Karaoke."

"There! I saw it yesterday but didn't have anyone to go with. Melissa was all, 'I have too much important vampire business to attend to,' and the other hunters are... well, not my type of crowd. But this will be perfect! I'll make a distraction, and you chomp-chomp some blood when no one's looking."

"Chomp chomp?" It was pretty brilliant, now that he thought about it. Adrian had never wanted to sing in front of a crowd, so the idea had never crossed his mind before. The two entered the bar and found a spot to sit in the back. The interior had a much dingier feel than the gay bar, with dim lighting and wooden tables, but Adrian almost preferred it. A pool table would feel right at home here, if they cleared out some seating to make space.

"I'm going to stand in line to request a song," Thea said. "Don't worry, the trick to singing karaoke is to pick a song everyone sings along to. That way, they're having too much fun to notice how bad you are. How much time do you need?"

Was that the trick to karaoke? Adrian's instinct was to pick a soft, easy song so no one could tell if he was off-key.

"Thirty seconds," he answered, "once I've found my target."

"You've got three minutes." Thea gave him a thumbs-up and made her way to the stage at the far end of the room. Adrian looked around. He needed to find someone in the back, preferably alone with a glass of something alcoholic.

After the current singer finished her song—a popular tune overplayed on the radio—Thea bounced up on stage, slightly elevated above the wooden floor and surrounded by a stack of speakers. The lights dimmed, except for a few focused stage lights. She took the microphone and pointed at the crowd.

"Come on, everyone! You know the lyrics!"

Adrian's ears perked up when he heard the opening line. A classic rock song he hadn't heard in decades. It was on the first album he ever bought with his own money. Well, Garrick's money, gifted to him. He'd tried to get Garrick to listen, but it was clear the older man's taste hadn't quite caught up to the electric age.

And Thea was right. It took only a few words of the opening line for the entire bar to start singing along. As the music swelled, so did the crowd, rising to their feet, clapping and cheering.

Adrian snapped himself out of his reminiscing and scanned the room for his mark. A middle-aged man sitting alone against the back wall, nodding his head and tapping his feet, seemed like a good target. Adrian did his best to nonchalantly wander over next to him. The man didn't notice, too absorbed in Thea's spirited rocker impression on the stage. Once Adrian was close enough, he clamped a hand over the man's mouth and sank his fangs into his neck. He quickly checked to make sure no one was watching as he drank, working fast. But everyone remained too captivated by Thea's performance to notice anything happening in the dark corner of the room. Once he'd had his fill, he let the man slump limply in his chair and slipped back to his original seat. A clean mission, no witnesses.

His deed was done before Thea reached the bridge. Sitting at an empty table with his chin resting in his palm, he watched as Thea jumped, pointed, and even air-guitared on stage. At some point before starting the song, she had unbound her hair, letting the strawberry-red strands whip and twirl with her movements. Sure, her stated goal was to be as much of a distraction as possible, but it was a rare day that Adrian met someone with so little concern for others' opinions and the energy to back it up. She looked like she was having genuine fun, and her singing wasn't even that bad.

Adrian caught himself smiling. Oh no.

Thea finished her song and returned to the table, skipping slightly as she walked, still energized from the performance. She gave him a thumbs-up.

"Did you get it? I couldn't see you from the stage, the lights were too bright. I can go again if you need me to."

"I'm all good, thanks."

They talked over drinks. Adrian wasn't one for making small talk in a bar unless it led to feeding off someone's neck, but he'd come to the unfortunate conclusion that he liked Thea. It wasn't a feeling he was used to, being genuinely interested in another person. But when Thea talked, Adrian listened. Her history, her unusual opinions, her basic opinions

—for some reason, Adrian actually cared and wanted to hear it all.

"I'm regretting getting shot. Just a little," Adrian said as the conversation shifted back to the hunters. "Can't believe you actually got ahold of real silver bullets."

"Yeah! What *is* the deal with it?" Thea shouted, with little concern for who might be listening. "How does it work? This has been a huge debate in vampire-hunting communities."

"Wait, you want me to tell you, a hunter, all my secrets?"

"Oh, come on. I'm on your side now!" Thea smiled, trying to convince him. "If I don't know what's a real threat, how am I supposed to protect Melissa and you?"

"And me? So, you've warmed up to me."

"Oh, don't let it go straight to your head. Maybe I just feel a little bad that I almost killed you."

"You wouldn't have killed me."

"Ooh, I'm the big bad vampire. I'm so dangerous," Thea teased. "You don't know how many of your kind I've staked. Maybe I'm more dangerous than you are."

Adrian lifted an eyebrow. Shit, he even found enjoyment in her offensive ribbing. Still, it made his situation easier. Garrick worried about earning her ire, but Thea seemed difficult to scorn.

"Fine," he said. "But this stays between us. No telling your hunter friends or spreading it online."

"I'm pretty sure that even if I did spread it online, everyone would still insist that everything I said was false. But I promise."

"Silver," Adrian stated, "does affect vampires, but how much depends on age. It's merely an annoyance for younger vampires, but it burns to the touch for older ones. It can also drain the magic from our blood, so removing silver bullets is important."

Thea clasped her hands together and smiled. "Knew it. Not the age thing, but I knew silver was important. How does that work, vampire blood and magic? How much do you need?"

"Only a pint every few days," Adrian shrugged, "but more if we use a lot of magic. Same as a normal metabolism. You need to eat more if you run a lot."

"I mean, that makes sense, but, like, do vampires cry blood?"

"Only if we're crying really hard. Otherwise, our eyes would be dry all the time. Or bloody all the time. Can you imagine how annoying that would be?"

"Are there werewolves? Are you enemies?"

"There are werewolves, but that's mostly an old grudge. I met a werewolf from Vancouver once. Nice girl."

"Is it possible to have half-vampire babies?"

"No," Adrian snorted. "Unless you're asking whether we can *try* making some."

For a brief second, Adrian thought Thea was going to press further. Instead, she gave a playful smirk and then moved on.

"What about crosses? That's an even more fraught subject than silver."

"That depends on whether the vampire was baptized before turning. The ritual leaves some sort of... spiritual branding, I think. It works for other religions too, along with their holy symbols. So it's effective if you're in the Bible Belt, but I wouldn't count on it stopping a vampire in the Bay Area."

"Oh, weird. Hold on, I need to write this down..."

Thea paused her barrage of questions to pull out her phone. She began typing, presumably to record what he'd told her so far. A part of Adrian worried about giving away information so freely. Garrick was always so careful, insisting that keeping their existence a secret was paramount. Adrian wasn't so sure. As Thea had said, anything posted on the internet would instantly be disregarded as fake.

"Hey," he said, "sorry if this is a bit forward, but would you mind if we exchanged numbers? It's just difficult to make friends these days."

Thea's eyes brightened, and the corners of her mouth pulled into a grin that folded her cheeks. It was an absolutely infectious smile that Adrian couldn't help but return. He'd never asked for someone's phone number before, but with her, it felt completely natural. Seeing her joy, knowing that Thea craved the same connection he did, gave Adrian an energetic rush that made him forget, just for a moment, that his body was supposed to be dead. He felt his heart with every beat, his lungs expanding for air long past needed, his stomach aching, empty.

"Yeah!" Thea responded energetically. "You're a cool guy. I promise to send you funny vampire memes." She fumbled with the touchscreen on her phone before finally handing it to Adrian. "Um, I'm going to stand in line for another song. Don't go snooping through my pictures, okay?"

She winked at him before standing, accidentally bumping the table and stumbling over her first few steps. It was hard not to laugh—not at her clumsiness, but at the shared, awkward energy between them. He took her phone and found her number, then had a thought. Not to look at her pictures, though he wondered if Thea almost wanted him to, given her gesture. But no, there was something far more valuable on her phone.

23
NIGHT 4 - ADRIAN

I t was late, and closing time at the karaoke bar was approaching. Several used napkins and an empty glass of beer littered the table where Adrian and Thea sat. Thea held a club sandwich in one hand and used the other to scroll through her phone resting on the table. The lull in conversation gave Adrian a moment to remember an important text he needed to send to Val.

> Hey. Met your friend Seth. He has sweet blood.

What?

> Wait, why did you bite him?

> Got a little frisky at the gay bar. Don't worry about it.

> Does he have enhanced powers too?

> Not that I know of.

> I'll investigate.

Adrian put his phone down and looked up. Back to the matter of Thea.

"Hey, now that we're officially friends, there's something I want to tell you."

Thea looked up from her phone, intrigued by what Adrian had to say.

"You said your parents died in a car accident. Did they ever find the person who hit them?"

Thea shook her head. "Hit and run. Everyone was surprised the other guy was in good enough shape to run."

"And this accident, did it happen within a few hours of here?"

Thea raised a suspicious eyebrow at Adrian's digging. "Sacramento," she answered. "We lived in Fort Worth, but the last thing Melissa did was get on a plane to Los Angeles. So, they came out to the West Coast to look for her. Why?"

"I don't have any proof, but Owen probably ordered a hit on your parents."

Thea's face hardened. "Who's Owen?" she asked gravely. Adrian found himself impressed by how she handled the news. Perhaps her status as a vampire hunter wasn't as much of a facade as he had initially believed.

"He's the vampire Melissa works for, the Regent. We organize ourselves like gangs, and he's the leader. It's likely he knew your parents were getting too curious and made sure they were taken care of."

"But do you think Melissa knows?"

Adrian shook his head. "She didn't even know your parents were dead. He probably kept it from her."

"Shit." Thea leaned her head on her hand and stared through him. "Do you think we should tell her?"

Adrian shrugged. It wasn't uncommon for ties to the mortal world to be forcibly severed if a vampire or their family couldn't fully break contact. Joseph enforced this with fear—find a way to silence your family, or he'd do it for you. If they lived too far away for him to arrange something, the easiest solution was to silence the vassal, permanently. Owen's organization was new, so it was possible his methods were still a secret.

Thea's phone rang. She picked it up and held it to her ear.

"Hey, Geo… Nah, I bounced. Sorry, the gay bar wasn't my thing. Found a new spot to stake out… Stop worrying about me. If I see one, I won't engage. I'll be back at the house before sunrise."

Thea hung up without a polite goodbye. "Hunters," she stated.

"Have you found a way to get them off Melissa's tail? And mine?"

"No," Thea sighed. "They're pretty bold. We were going to cap our search at a week, but now they're talking about staying for two, maybe three. At least it gives me more time to spend with Melissa, except she doesn't want to see me. Well, I guess for good reasons.

"Am I in danger?" Thea asked suddenly.

That was a question that deserved a serious, truthful response. "If another vampire sees you and Melissa together for more than just a casual conversation, then probably."

"What about you? You don't seem to have a problem being seen with me."

"I don't work for Owen," Adrian answered. "So I have more freedom with this kind of thing."

Adrian tried to keep his words steady, hiding the half-truth within them. Owen didn't have quite as much oversight over Adrian as he did over Melissa, but he still wouldn't approve. Worse, neither would Garrick. But Adrian desperately needed a new friend, and now that he had finally found one, he wasn't about to give that up just because some old vampires with outdated rules demanded it.

"Good." Thea sank deeper into the hand she was leaning on. Despite his reassurance, her despondency only seemed to grow.

The bar manager walked over to inform the two that the bar was closing, and they left. It was two in the morning, typically the time when Adrian went home to watch television, read a book, or browse the internet until going to bed at sunrise. By then, the nightlife usually dwindled enough to make hunting no longer worthwhile. Still, Thea lingered in the parking lot, hesitant to say goodbye.

"I want to tell Melissa," she declared suddenly. "She deserves to know. Can you come with me?"

Adrian shuddered. The last thing he needed was to give Melissa even more reason to want him dead. Trying to drive a wedge between her and her boss seemed like a bad idea at the moment. Still, he didn't want to leave Thea to deliver the news alone, especially when he was the one who had shared the theory with her in the first place.

"Sure," he relented. Thea called her sister and asked if they could meet. Considering how much Melissa usually tried to avoid Thea, he was surprised that she didn't resist, at least from what he could gather from Thea's side of the conversation.

They met on a quiet street corner. As Melissa approached, her face immediately twisted with dismay, her eyes accusatory. Adrian tried to muster a pleasant smile without appearing smug. He was under strict orders not to flirt with Thea. He'd done the exact opposite. Technically, it hadn't been his idea. And even if it had, he didn't feel obligated to bow to Melissa's demands.

"Oh, so this is what you were doing instead of answering my text. I see you two have become fast friends," she said, sarcasm dripping from every word. "What is this? Some kind of intervention?"

"Well," Thea stood up straight, trying to appear confident, but Adrian noticed her hand shaking slightly at her side. "Do you think Owen might have killed Mom and Dad?"

The question completely blindsided Melissa. Her mouth hung open, a single sound caught in her throat, as if Thea had spoken in an entirely different language and she didn't know how to respond. "What?" finally escaped.

"Adrian was telling me—"

Adrian clenched his teeth. Somehow, this was going to end up being his fault.

"—that sometimes vampire gang leaders like Owen will kill people who learn too much. And Mom and Dad were looking for you…"

"Yes, and that's why I can't be seen near…" Melissa took a calming breath and paused to collect her thoughts.

"Maybe he did," Melissa said. "It's certainly possible. Is that all?"

Thea recoiled, her shaking hands tightening into fists. "Well… that's bad! If he killed them…"

"Yes, it's bad. But I'm a vampire now. I can't be bothered with my old mortal life."

When Thea began to protest, Melissa interrupted her.

"I'm not going to kiss Owen's ass forever. There are plenty of reasons to hate him beyond this one. Just give me some time, and he'll get what's coming to him."

So, Adrian's hunch was right. It wasn't enough for Melissa to get revenge, she had to come out on top, in a more powerful position than before. Of course, she was Owen's favorite, and she had made sure of that.

"Come on, then. I'll walk you back to your motorcycle."

"No," Thea spat. "I can walk by myself, thank you."

Adrian just stood by, hands buried in his pockets. Melissa flashed him a vile look, and he met it without flinching. It wasn't hard, he hadn't spoken a word throughout the entire conversation.

Melissa nodded and walked away. Thea waited until she was out of sight before burying her face in her hands and sobbing. Adrian stood uncomfortably, realizing he'd gone nearly his whole life without ever once comforting someone. He hesitated, unsure of the appropriate response, before awkwardly placing a hand on Thea's shoulder.

She looked up at him, eyes red and rimmed with tears. "Can I get a real hug?" she asked wryly.

Adrian opened his arms to her, and she wrapped hers around him, pressing the side of her face against his chest.

24
NIGHT 4 - VAL

V al tapped on her phone with a grumble. So, Seth had enhanced powers too. She shouldn't have been surprised. He was fifteen years turned—same as Tyler, same as Summer. It seemed Owen rewarded his earliest vassals. Seth had implied that he hated Owen, but a lot could change over fifteen years.

The man at Val's feet groaned and sluggishly propped himself up on his hands and knees. Tonight, Val had to settle for a catcaller. Normally, after feeding off someone on the street, she would hastily flee the scene to avoid complications with onlookers. But sometimes, if no one else was around, she'd wait for her victim to wake up. This man was bigger, taller, and far more muscular than she was, yet he was still no match. With his eyes straining to focus, he jerked his head up at Val, who smirked in return. Then he bolted, but not before tripping over a discarded metal beam lying in the middle of the alley.

Satisfied, Val returned to her text messages. Sophia had replied with Seth's phone number, without asking any questions about why Val wanted it. Val then texted Seth, asking to meet up and continue their conversation from the previous night. About five minutes later, Seth responded and sent her an address where they could meet.

Val started to slip the phone back into her pocket when it rang in her palm. Curiously, it was Garrick. She hesitated for a moment, wondering what could be so important that it warranted a phone call instead of a text message.

"Hello?"

"Val," Garrick's voice greeted on the other end. "I, um, wanted to follow up after our conversation last night. I meant to catch you before I left to meet Owen, but…"

"Sorry, I slept in." She hadn't been avoiding Garrick, even if it seemed that way. She was just genuinely tired. "What did you want to talk about?"

"I know I've been… not the most forthcoming with you and Adrian," he said slowly, carefully. "But I don't want you to think I'm a liar. Or mad."

"Well, you could start with a little honesty."

"I'm not sure how I'm supposed to prove a negative to you. Or convince you that an answer is the honest truth if it's not the ground-shattering revelation you want it to be."

Val's reply died before it passed her lips. He had a point. Now that she already thought him a liar, he would need to present irrefutable proof of his claims, proof that might no longer exist.

That was something that worried Val. If Garrick had the same scar as Tyler, did that mean he had lied about his age? He had quirks that convinced Val he was old, but no older than her own grandparents. How would someone even begin to verify that they were six centuries old?

"How about this," Garrick continued. "I'll trade my honesty for yours. Are you seeking revenge for Raymond's death?"

Val bit her lip. She'd promised Garrick she wouldn't. That was an obvious lie.

"Yes," she answered confidently. She didn't need Garrick's permission to seek revenge.

Garrick went silent for a beat, and Val wondered which emotion struck him the hardest. Disappointment? Anger? Fear? He didn't let any of them show when he spoke again.

"Meet me on the rooftop of the hotel three hours from now, and let me plead my case. Don't expect all your questions to be answered, but hopefully, we can at least come to an understanding."

He hung up. Three hours. Plenty of time to meet with Seth first.

The location Seth sent her was at the intersection of two major roads, roughly a twenty-minute walk from the alley. The walk was stiflingly empty and silent, with only the occasional car passing by on her right. Big cities were never truly dark in the early mornings, as street lamps, traffic lights, neon signs, and distant skyscrapers all kept the streets well lit. But somehow, the extra light only highlighted how dead the world felt between midnight and morning, before the sun would rouse mortals once again.

A layer of thick fog heightened the atmosphere, allowing Val to see only half a block ahead. For a moment, she thought she had passed the meeting point. A quick glance at her phone confirmed she was in the right place.

"Over here."

Val jumped at the sudden noise, even though she recognized his voice. Seth stood leaning against the stone wall of a building, hidden in the shadows of another alley. The last two times she had seen him, Seth had worn loose, baggy clothing with little regard for fashion. Now he wore a form-fitting shirt beneath a light jacket and a small silver pentagram necklace. So he did know how to dress, sort of.

"So," he said, "what have you got?"

Val braced herself for the coming conversation. Tyler hadn't been straight with her, nor Garrick, and she didn't want to scare Seth out of giving her information, either. But what other strategy was there besides being direct?

"I know Tyler had powers beyond his age, and I know it's because of that scar on his chest. He had some kind of surgery, didn't he?"

She watched Seth's face for any sign of surprise. Oddly, he gave none.

"Someone's been investigating," he commented, then waited for Val to continue.

"What's the surgery?"

"You think I know just because I'm friends with Tyler?" Seth laughed.

"I know you have a scar, too."

"Oh?" That finally elicited surprise. "And how did you figure that out?"

"Adrian told me. Your blood is sweet." Val hoped she wouldn't have to explain the connection between sweet blood, the scar, and the powers. While there was a clear link, the cause remained unknown. Perhaps Owen had inserted some device or magical artifact into their bodies.

Seth narrowed his eyes, and Val guessed he wasn't aware of the connection. Why would he be, unless he was biting his fellows? Where to begin the explanation? Probably with Adrian's involvement. But wait, why did he bite Melissa again?

Interrupting her thoughts, Seth smirked and shrugged. He tugged down the neckline of his shirt, revealing a scar between his collarbones.

"Correct," he said. "And you're wondering what the surgery is that gives you a boost in age, right?"

Val nodded.

"It's a heart transplant."

He said it so casually that the statement caught Val off guard. A transplant—not a device or magical artifact.

"It's our hearts that turn mundane blood into magic," Seth continued. "Over time, it gets stronger, allowing us to use the excess magic for more than just keeping our bodies alive. But once it grows old enough, it requires more refined fuel to keep functioning. That's why Elders need to drink vampire blood. So, what happens when you take the heart of one vampire and place it in another's body?"

"You… keep the magical strength of the heart?"

Seth grinned and nodded. "Just like upgrading an engine."

So, Tyler was able to use more advanced magic because Owen took the heart of an older vampire and gave it to him. Apparently, he did the same for Seth, Melissa, and Summer. And possibly others.

So, if Val wanted the power to kill an Elder...

Her stomach twisted. She had been so close. A solution right in front of her, only to have it snatched away at the last moment. Of course. There were never easy solutions.

"It takes an Elder to kill an Elder. Bummer." His grin widened, revealing his fangs. He enjoyed watching her dilemma.

"Whose heart is in your chest?"

"Don't know. Some vampire from the early days who worked for the Regent before Owen. That Regent's name was Bartolomé, got his fangs during the conquistador era. I was just a kid, desperate, and Owen made big promises. Really made me believe I was going to do something good against this evil man. Bartolomé saw anyone with dark skin as less than human. Hell, he barely listened to anyone who wasn't

193

Spanish. Owen cut Bartolomé's head off when his back was turned, then ordered the rest of us to slaughter every one of his followers, no matter how much they begged. We told ourselves they deserved it, because how could they not see how evil he was? I've heard people say you LA vamps are the tough ones, but that's because everyone likes to selectively forget the real horrifying stuff that happens."

Seth dropped the cruel smile. Despite his youthful appearance… No, at that time, Seth truly was as young as he looked. Just out of high school and being manipulated into committing mass murder. Even now, he would only be in his mid-thirties, the same age Val was when she turned. Yet the deep creases beneath his eyes betrayed the simmering rage of a man wronged by the world.

"Then Owen was in charge, and what happened next? The same damn shit, just a new target. Though it's not like Bartolomé was all that kind to women either. Kill one evil man, and another springs up in his place. It's almost like the problem isn't with the people. It's the entire system that enables it.

"But enough about me. What's your plan? Say you get a new heart, go back to LA, and kill your old Regent. Then what?"

Val swallowed through a dry throat. The aftermath wasn't important, she just wanted Joseph to suffer, to finally see a little justice done. She didn't really care what came next.

"I'll tell you what happens: someone new takes his place and continues being a violent asshole because that's all they know. Let's say you take Joseph's place as Regent. One of his friends or lovers will come looking for revenge against you."

"Don't give me that 'cycle of violence' bullshit," Val snapped. "If someone has a problem with me taking out Joseph, let them come for revenge. I'll deal with them all the same."

That visibly irked Seth. "Good luck," he growled. "But you still need an Elder heart if you want a chance. How do you plan to get one?"

Val wanted to answer confidently to maintain her position, but she didn't know. It was a glaring hole in her plan. She doubted she would find a willing Elder donor anytime soon.

Seth pounced on her hesitation. "You want power to get revenge on an Elder who did what all Elders do. You're just mad it finally happened to someone you know. If you want revenge, real revenge, then don't stop at Joseph. All Elders are the same. They feed on their vassals until those vassals become a threat, then they discard them and move on to the next. There is no innocent Elder. You need to think bigger."

"What are you suggesting?"

"You have an Elder heart right in front of you, and he wouldn't even see it coming."

The realization hit Val like a wild bull. "No, I'm not killing Garrick."

"Why? He won't think twice about killing you."

"Garrick wouldn't…" She paused. Yes, he would. He'd made it clear that once the Madness hit, it would be a kindness to put her out of her misery. "I'm not killing an innocent person."

"Look around you, how innocent are we, really?" Seth shrugged. "Death is a natural part of life, one we hijacked by surviving at the expense of others. And Elders figured out how to game that system. They've lived for centuries, had more than their fair share of life, and yet they refuse to give us the same chance. We're doing the world a favor by cleaning them out. The biggest threat to an Elder is another Elder. So keep them culled before they reach that stage. Keep them dependent so they give blood freely. That's how Elders operate. We're just cattle to them."

No, not Garrick. Not her friend. He could be a bit of a liar, sure, but about their entire relationship?

Seth waited patiently for a reply, but pushed himself off the wall when she failed to respond. He began walking toward the parking lot at the end of the alley. As he passed Val, he formed his fingers in the shape of a gun and mimicked firing it.

"A bullet through the head doesn't kill them. That's the mistake everyone makes. It knocks them out, though, long enough to cut off the head. Keep a butcher's knife and a cooler full of ice nearby. Bring me Garrick's heart, and I'll stitch it into your chest. Don't go after Owen. He's mine."

Val leaned her back against the alley wall and watched him walk away. Was she really going to kill Garrick for power? Seth's words echoed in her head. *He won't think twice about doing it to you.* He'd lament it, but he would do it. And perhaps that was the worst part. For all the things Garrick may have hidden, the most damning was the one he didn't even need to lie about. Because Seth was right, she was wrapped around his little finger all the same.

Two hours later, Val took the hotel elevator to the top floor and found a separate door leading to the roof. Good thing it was accessible. Trying to catch Garrick's attention to fly her up, or having Adrian carry her vertically up the wall, would have been awkward.

Garrick sat on the edge, legs dangling over the side. He turned his head when Val approached but remained seated. With a small gesture, he invited her to sit next to him. Val sucked in her cheeks. She wasn't afraid of heights, but standing so close to a five-story drop without any safety harness unnerved her all the same. If she fell, Garrick wouldn't let her hit the ground. Probably. Slowly, she sat beside him on the ledge, keeping her legs firmly planted on the solid concrete.

"So," she said, "what do you have?"

Garrick reached into his pocket and pulled out a small coin. He held it out to her. Val took it in her hand and admired the tarnished gold, rubbing her thumb over its face. She couldn't quite make out the figure on its head, except that it was some kind of man.

"What is this?"

"A florin from the Renaissance."

"Are you trying to buy my trust?"

"Can it be bought?" Garrick teased. "No, it's merely a token. I know you like old things, and you witches love a good symbol."

Val peeled her eyes away from the florin and waited for an explanation.

"Five years," he said. "Five years, and I will answer every question you have, no matter how uncomfortable it makes me. The florin is a reminder of that promise."

"Five years? Why the wait?"

"That's a very small amount of time from my point of view, but..." Garrick caught his trailing thought, sighed, and continued. "You think I've never wanted revenge in my six centuries of life? I've witnessed countless injustices, watched loved ones murdered. I know revenge feels good now, but is it really worth it? Is it worth risking the loved ones you still have? If the sting still burns in five years, then I'll help. But until then, give it some time to heal."

Val flipped the florin between her fingers. Flipped it again. Rotated it. Five years. In truth, it was unlikely she'd be able to match Joseph's power by then. She was limited to finding an Elder heart in a place—or from a person—she could easily take it from, ideally someone who deserved it. Meanwhile, if

Garrick actually helped, Val had no doubt he could rend Joseph in half, even though he hadn't done it when Adrian tried to enact justice.

"What was Raymond like?" Garrick asked, interrupting her thoughts. "I never had a long conversation with him. He must have been special to earn your love. I'm well aware that you don't suffer fools."

"Raymond? He..." Was Garrick trying to deflect? Val wondered, a bit too late. "He was kind, but devious. Loved alcohol. Never forgot when it was only served behind closed doors. Knew exactly how much he could drink without staying buzzed the next night, and sometimes he drank more anyway. Once, he mixed it with human blood. I didn't ask where he got a bottle of that. Tasted great, though."

She wiped a tear from her cheek. "He always knew when I was feeling down, often before I did. He gave great hugs. Sometimes, all I wanted was a hug from him. He didn't have to say anything; just being in his arms made everything better."

Another tear. Val rubbed her eye. Garrick sat with his hands politely clasped in his lap, lost in thought, nodding slowly. She almost asked him for a hug. Maybe she would have, a week ago.

Five years. If she waited that long, Garrick would help her kill Joseph. It was hard to believe he'd actually keep his promise. The florin was nothing more than a placation, something to quiet her feelings. And yet, he had kept his first promise to her. In ten years, he had never once suggested, let alone joked, that she return to his bed. Even now, he respectfully kept his distance. Inaction was a bar so low it shouldn't have counted, but Val had to admit that, compared to the man she'd met a decade ago, Garrick had improved.

Val handed the florin back. "Thanks, but I don't need a token to remember your promise," she said. Garrick took it without comment. Suddenly feeling worn, she stood and walked to the rooftop door, ready to retire for the night.

She would not give up revenge. Raymond deserved his justice. But she would not lose herself to it either. Garrick could keep his florin and his heart, because in five years, it would be Joseph's heart beating in her chest.

25

ONE WEEK AGO

"Wait, so you never got your driver's license?"

Adrian rolled his eyes as he listened to the crunch of gravel beneath his feet. Of all the potential Joseph suck-ups Val could have fallen in love with, Raymond wasn't the worst. As long as Adrian didn't take him or his teasing seriously—and according to Val, he never meant it as more than friendly ribbing—then he was pleasant to be around. From what Adrian could tell, Val liked his old-fashioned mannerisms and style, as Raymond always dressed like he had walked straight out of the Prohibition era. Adrian would be a hypocrite to judge her for it, though Garrick at least tried to keep up with modern sensibilities.

But there was an advantage to being in good graces with a few of Joseph's favored. It was not lost on Adrian that whenever Raymond stood a little closer to him, Joseph's scowls and attempts to provoke him lessened.

"No," Adrian sighed. "I never got a license. I couldn't afford a car, and now Garrick does all the driving."

"Oh, don't tease him," Val reprimanded playfully, giving Raymond's arm a light slap. "You never had a license either."

"Because they weren't mandatory yet!" Raymond snickered. "And I've had several licenses, they were just forgeries."

Val's car needed repairs, and despite how much Adrian hated him, working under a two-century-old car repair expert had its perks. Both he and Raymond offered to walk Val home, even though walking alone at night wasn't really a safety concern for them. Adrian didn't trust Joseph, and Raymond just enjoyed spending time with his girlfriend. It was grossly adorable.

Only about three minutes after leaving Joseph's workshop, Adrian heard the Regent behind them, calling for Raymond. He turned to see Joseph's silhouette framed by the workshop's light, jogging to catch up with them. It had to be something important, as Joseph still gripped a hammer in his hand. Adrian looked down at his feet, doing his best not to draw Joseph's attention.

"Yes?" Raymond asked. "Is there something you need?"

Joseph didn't answer with words. It was the sound of a sickening crack that grabbed Adrian's attention, just in time to see Raymond collapse to the ground beneath Joseph's hammer. Then Joseph knelt down and smashed his head twice more. Val screamed, and Adrian nearly lost his balance as he jumped back from the carnage.

Then, as suddenly as it had begun, Joseph stood up and walked back to the workshop.

Adrian couldn't take his eyes off Raymond's head, lying flat on the ground, skull smashed open. Like a melon. A wave of intense nausea hit Adrian's stomach, and he was sure that if it weren't empty, he might have hurled. At some point, Val had fallen to the ground, rapidly switching between screaming and whimpering.

Finally, Adrian's mind began to move beyond the bloody scene before him. His shock had frozen him in the moment, and he suppressed the instinct to confront Joseph now, lest he share Raymond's fate. Val must have had similar thoughts, as she scrambled to her feet and turned toward the workshop, but didn't move any closer.

With hands trembling so badly he could barely press the right buttons, he called Garrick. Less than five minutes later, an owl descended from the sky and transformed into the Elder. He saw the body and raked his fingers through his hair, a look of disgust spreading across his face.

"Are you all right?" Garrick asked.

Adrian nodded slowly before turning back toward Raymond's body. "Well, not him."

Garrick nodded in return and got to work. He made sure the body was far from the dry grass, pulled a matchbox from his pocket, and dropped a lit match onto Raymond's body. Like tinder, it ignited into a large bonfire. Garrick stood nearby to ensure the stray embers didn't grow into something more dangerous.

Thus was their fate. Vampire bodies crumbled to dust upon death. Burial could preserve the skeleton, but most didn't bother to honor their compatriots in such a way.

"What happened?" Garrick asked once the body had smoldered into ash.

Val had sat again during Garrick's cremation, her chin resting on her knees. She stared through the black and gray dust, her eyelids heavy. "Joseph," she repeated. "Just... unprovoked."

Garrick rubbed the back of his neck, deep in thought. "Come on, you can rest at our house tonight," he offered Val.

He extended a hand to help her up, and the three walked back slowly and in silence. Dead, tense silence.

What had happened? Had Raymond said something to Joseph earlier? Did it even matter? They were working for a loaded gun, a live grenade. How long until it was Val's or Adrian's skull that was attacked without warning?

Joseph didn't even have the decency to acknowledge them during his act of manslaughter. No asking them to leave. No pulling Raymond into his garage for privacy. Just walk up. Kill. Leave.

The silence remained unbroken until Val retired to the guest room to rest.

"Talk outside?" Adrian asked curtly.

"Yeah," Garrick said. "That's a good idea."

Quietly, they walked back out the front door and put a few yards of distance between themselves and the house. Only then did Adrian turn to Garrick and seethe.

"What the fuck?" he hissed, keeping his voice low but letting his anger show. "Joseph's out of control!"

Garrick nodded, his eyes darting everywhere—other than into Adrian's.

"I'll talk to him," he said, his voice infuriatingly calm.

"Talk?" Adrian spat. "About what? Remind him that murder is wrong? Ask him to say he's sorry?"

Garrick's eyes finally met Adrian's, held its gaze, and then looked away again.

"Talk about what, Garrick?"

Softly, Garrick shook his head, his eyes still darting from point to point as he tried to find the right thing to say—not to Joseph, but to Adrian.

"This isn't a fucking 'talk-it-over' problem!"

"I'll handle this."

"Handle how?"

Finally, Garrick's eyes snapped to Adrian—along with his

frown. He took a step forward, pushing into Adrian's space, and raised a finger up to Adrian's chest.

"I'll handle it," Garrick stated forcefully. "And you're going to go inside and comfort your friend."

Adrian stumbled back slightly, surprised by Garrick's sudden command. "B—" he began to protest, but Garrick cut him off before he could say a single word.

"You are going to go inside," Garrick repeated, and at last, Adrian felt the fire behind his words. His heart trembled.

"Fine," he said, barely louder than a whisper.

Garrick held his gaze a moment longer, then patted him on the arm before briskly walking down the driveway and onto the sidewalk toward Joseph's workshop.

Adrian stood alone in front of their house, the air suddenly ice-cold against his skin. How long had he waited for Garrick to stand up for himself? How long had he wanted Garrick to get angry, to say no, to acknowledge that he was the biggest threat in the room?

And he finally did. Against Adrian.

He went inside, but he had no intention of staying. He looked around. Garrick didn't carry guns, not since their territory wars with Linh. He said no self-respecting vampire needed one. A knife wouldn't pierce Joseph's skull or reach his heart from behind. A hammer, from Garrick's toolbox— that would do. If it was good enough for Joseph, it was good enough for him.

Once retrieved, Adrian left the house, locked the door, and cloaked himself in the night's darkness. He walked in silence, both from muting his own footsteps and the quiet of his mind. The thought of cold, calculated murder made him feel oddly empty, not the anger he had felt minutes earlier. It almost made him reconsider and turn back. Almost.

The garage door was open, and Garrick stood inside, talking with the other Elder. Adrian cut to the side so the light from the garage didn't illuminate in his direction, then crouched low. The California countryside didn't offer much foliage to use as cover, but he managed to glide between patches of small bushes and paused to make sure he hadn't been spotted. Thankfully, both men seemed focused primarily on their conversation. With his heart pounding in his ears, Adrian slowly crept closer until he could hear them.

"...Got a problem with the way I'm handling my boys?" Adrian heard Joseph first, his voice booming compared to Garrick's silver tongue.

"Just... a bit more..." Adrian couldn't quite catch the last word. Slowly, he moved forward, making sure to stay out of the direct line of sight of both men.

"What's your problem?" Joseph shrugged and leaned forward, pointedly showing his aggression. "Because I don't see what the issue is."

"You killed him right in front of his girlfriend," Garrick growled. "Was that necessary? What do you think is going to happen once she starts talking to the others? You already have a reputation for being a loose cannon, and now everyone's going to think their lives are in danger just by being around you."

Adrian's hand tightened around the hammer. Apparently, Garrick knew exactly what he wanted to say to Joseph. He wanted to chastise him for being sloppy with the murder.

Maybe he was jumping to conclusions. Maybe Garrick knew something Adrian didn't, some secret about Raymond that justified the slaughter. But if Garrick couldn't trust Adrian with that information, then why should Adrian trust that such a justification existed?

"So, what? You saying I should have killed her too?"

Garrick stepped forward, intimidating Joseph just as he had done to Adrian earlier. Adrian watched him intently, hoping that Garrick would do what he himself had come here to do.

"Threaten any of my vassals again," he spat, "and I'll stake your heart to your front door for all to see."

In all the years he'd known him, Garrick had never made a direct threat before. But Joseph wasn't fazed.

"All bark and no bite, Garrick. Did you finally grow a spine?" Joseph taunted. "You work for me. And the people who work for you work for me. I do what I want with the people who work for me. Now, do you have a problem with the way I'm running things?"

The two men stood perfectly still, locked in place, until Garrick finally backed off. He didn't say anything, no confirmation or denial of Joseph's rhetorical question. Instead, he simply turned and left.

Adrian's fingernails dug into his palm as he gripped the hammer handle. He clamped his jaw shut, reminding himself to stay silent, else he feared he might cry out in anger at Garrick's cowardice.

Right before Garrick approached the line where Adrian crouched in hiding, he stopped and brought a hand to his face. He rubbed the corners of his eyes, and despite the darkness, Adrian could see the weariness in them. A six-hundred-year-old man who survived by sucking up from one Regent to the next.

Despite the well of emotions building inside him, Adrian remained silent, determined not to let them spill out and blow his cover. No matter how much it hurt, he couldn't let his heart shatter—not until he was safe, with Joseph dead by his hand.

Garrick finally resumed walking, and Adrian turned his attention back to Joseph. The Regent fumbled through a nearby bucket, searching for some kind of bolt, and then turned his back and walked to his workbench. Now.

Adrian made a brisk walk toward the garage entrance. No sound. No hesitation. Don't stop until Joseph's head was crushed.

Once he was within arm's reach of the man, Adrian raised the hammer above his head and swung it down with all the force he could muster. He didn't know what to expect when the hammer made contact, but the crack it produced, and the way Joseph's head lurched forward, was promising. Adrian lifted the hammer again, but in a sudden whirl, Joseph's arm struck the side of his head, slamming him into the workbench. The sound of a heavy object scraping against the wood made Adrian stumble back several steps.

Joseph gripped a large wrench, his face twisted in fury. One eye stained blood-red. Adrian hesitated for a moment, surprised by how agile Joseph was after receiving what should have been a debilitating blow. Joseph, however, wasted no time rushing forward and swinging the wrench at Adrian's head. Adrian raised his arm to block, doing his best to ignore the searing pain from one blow, then another. He lunged forward with a strike of his own but managed only to hit Joseph's shoulder. Joseph retaliated with a clean blow to Adrian's temple, and Adrian found himself on the ground, the workshop spinning around him.

By the time Adrian regained his wits, he saw Garrick standing over him, gripping Joseph's arm as the two shouted at each other. Joseph shoved Garrick's hand away and hurled the wrench to the ground. He walked a few steps away, then turned and pointed a gun at Garrick.

Garrick raised his hands to his chest. "Joseph," he warned.

Joseph flicked the gun. Step aside.

"Let's calm down, and—"

Joseph fired a bullet into Garrick's chest. All three men froze, as if suspended in time. Adrian stared, wide-eyed, at the back of Garrick's head. A single bullet wasn't enough to kill him, right? Not his Garrick.

Then, the violence began again. Garrick slammed Joseph's head against the workbench, much like the Regent had done to Adrian earlier. This wasn't the time to be useless on the ground. Pushing through his pulsing headache, Adrian scrambled to his feet. He found his hammer on the ground nearby and stood, ready to help. He turned toward Joseph, who was now locked in a hold from behind by Garrick. Garrick's right hand pushed Joseph's head into his shoulder, exposing his neck for Garrick to bury his fangs into. But Joseph didn't struggle. His bloodshot eye locked onto Adrian, and he grinned. His right arm freely raised the gun.

This time, three shots were fired, and time did not stand still. The strength in Adrian's legs left him, and his knees buckled beneath his weight. He found himself on the ground once more, staring up at the harsh fluorescent lights of Joseph's workshop. Seconds later, Garrick knelt over him, eyes wide and mouth agape. As a fourth gunshot rang out overhead, Adrian suddenly felt weightless, the world rushing past him—before, all too soon, snapping back into place.

Now, Adrian stared up at the dark night sky while Garrick held him in one arm and pressed a trembling finger to his lips. Garrick glanced over his shoulder, his face still taut with fear.

"Garrick!" Joseph shouted from... beneath him? "You're fucking dead, you hear me? You and that boy are fucking dead!"

Ah, the roof. Garrick had somehow transported the two of them to the top of Joseph's workshop to hide. Judging by the fading sound of Joseph's screams, it seemed to have worked.

Garrick turned his attention to Adrian's chest, pulling his shirt down to inspect the bullet wounds. Adrian had no idea how bad the damage was. He couldn't feel his heart, but that wasn't unusual. Maybe the bullets had missed it entirely, and he'd just collapsed from the shock. Or perhaps one had nicked a major artery and a few minutes under Garrick's healing touch would fix it before any serious harm was done. Or maybe one of the bullets had been a direct hit, his heart now reduced to mush, and he just had to wait for the blood in his brain to run dry.

Garrick's eyes widened again, a look Adrian could only interpret as despair.

So, mush.

Adrian cracked a grim smile. How familiar. Lying at the edge of death in Garrick's arms once again. How had he felt last time? Relief? Hope? Love? He felt none of that now.

And to think, he never once asked Garrick why he'd been in that burning building in the first place. Never asked why Garrick hadn't been there, until the last second. He could never bear the thought of what the answer might be.

Surely there were worse ways to go than being held by the man who had pretended to love him for the last forty years, but nothing immediately came to mind. Adrian closed his eyes and waited to slowly slip away.

He wasn't sure how long he waited, but it was Garrick's voice that finally roused him.

"We have to go," he whispered.

Adrian opened his eyes. He was going to live. Damn.

26

NIGHT 5 - ADRIAN

An unread text from Thea greeted Adrian when he woke the next night. It was a cartoon of Dracula, identified by his slicked-back black hair and high-collared cape, with the caption, "What's a vampire's favorite holiday? Fang's-giving!" He snorted. It was dumb, but of all the ways to wake up, answering a silly text wasn't a bad start to his night. Adrian got out of bed and carefully pulled his shirt over his head, exposing Garrick's handiwork over the bullet wound. After showering, he pressed two fingers gently against the wound on his side. Energized, fire... Adrian understood the basics of magic, he tapped into it every time he performed his shadow powers, so this couldn't be that different. He held his fingers there, concentrating, until he thought he felt warmth beneath his skin. He lifted his hand. Maybe he was imagining it, but the wound looked a little less red.

A knock on the door signaled to Adrian that Garrick was ready to feed. Steeling himself, he opened it.

Garrick looked him up and down. "Good, you're keeping clean," he said. "I see you've resisted the urge to make things worse."

Adrian rolled his eyes and beckoned him in. He looked around for a chair, but the only one available had an unusually high back and was carved to look like an antique. Adrian sat on the edge of the bed instead, with Garrick joining him at his side. The tension between them made Adrian fidget, bouncing his knee, unsure of the appropriate amount of affection to display. He hadn't felt this way in almost forty years, right before he started to not abhor Garrick's fangs on his neck, but enjoy it—along with the alone time to talk, joke, and laugh.

But this time, when Garrick pulled him closer, Adrian did his best to sit still and resist the urge to pull away.

When Garrick finished, he wiped the corner of his mouth with a small handkerchief and then remained seated in stark silence. Even Adrian felt uncomfortable, despite typically being fine with quiet moments. Perhaps Garrick was waiting for Adrian to show some sign of affection. Some indication that their relationship wasn't in shambles.

Obliging, Adrian leaned into his side and wrapped his arm around Garrick's. With his other hand, he pulled out his phone.

"I've got some information about our hunters," he said.

That seemed to lift Garrick's mood, even if only out of curiosity.

Adrian decided to skip the part where Thea had told him that the hunters wouldn't give up easily. He didn't need

Garrick's opinion about spending time with a mortal, and a hunter at that.

The phone displayed a map, with a small circle blinking in the center. Directly beneath it lay a narrow street situated halfway between two blocks.

"This is where they're located," Adrian said. "I was able to…" If Garrick was okay with lying, then so was he. "I stole one of the hunters' phones when they jumped me and turned on location tracking."

Garrick squinted at the tiny map on his phone, then dragged it around with one finger. He frowned.

"You can do this?" He pulled out his own phone and looked at it. "Are you doing this to my phone too?"

Adrian pulled back his phone defensively. "For emergencies!" he clarified.

Garrick rotated his phone in his hand, eyeing it like an exotic animal. He could use it better than most older men, meaning he could text, make calls, and perform basic internet searches. Anything beyond that remained a mystery to him.

"Mortals are becoming too magical," he muttered before slipping the phone back into his pocket. "Good. We can keep an eye on the hunters and make sure they don't pick up our trail."

Garrick stood up and smoothed the crease in his collar, even though it was already perfectly in place. "I have bad news. Owen wants to talk to you."

The muscles around Adrian's jaw tightened. He wanted to make a lighthearted quip to ease his annoyance, but he wasn't in the mood for joking. He wasn't even sure if Garrick was trying to be funny or if he already knew what the meeting was about and was trying to warn him. Adrian simply stood and silently took his long coat from its place, draped over the antique chair.

After they both exited the hotel room, Garrick spoke in a more lighthearted manner, perhaps concerned by Adrian's lack of humor. "I'm sure it's nothing bad," he said. "I told him how you saved Melissa from the hunters. He seemed genuinely pleased."

Adrian nodded but offered little else. It wasn't exactly a good thing if Owen's goal was to have Adrian captured. Their walk to the mansion was a silent one. Garrick didn't attempt any more comments or try to comfort him. Thank God.

The two were ushered into the sitting room of the mansion and shared a seat on the long leather couch across from Owen's chair. Behind him, Melissa was busy typing away on a small laptop. She briefly glanced up when they arrived but didn't make an effort to welcome them.

"Good," Owen said once they were settled. Adrian stared down at the small coffee table between them. Was this going to be about the hunters? Would Owen brazenly try to put him in a position of danger?

"You specialize in break-ins, correct?"

Adrian looked up in surprise, then glanced over at Garrick, hoping he'd provide an answer in his stead. "I've done a few," he replied when Garrick didn't.

"Good. This is an important assignment, and I want it done right. We called around and believe Tyler was taken to this hospital." He pushed a paper toward them. Printed in black and white ink was a map with a rectangular area circled in red. It read, "San Francisco General Hospital."

"The staff said someone named Tyler Henderson was in their care, but they wouldn't give us any specifics. Some kind of privacy law, unless we could prove we were family. He would have been moved to the morgue by morning. I need you to break in and recover his body, alive or dead."

A morgue? Owen genuinely wanted Adrian to break into the hospital morgue for someone who might not even be alive. He turned back to Garrick to gauge his reaction, but the man remained stone-faced.

"I've done home invasions," Adrian clarified. "I've never

broken into a major facility like that. I don't even know what a morgue looks like."

"This is an important assignment," Owen repeated, punctuating each word with a growl. "You are the oldest and most experienced in this area, aside from us Elders. Tyler is a vital member of the Coven. The risk is well worth it."

"A hospital is staffed around the clock," Adrian snapped. "Where's the morgue located? What kind of locking system do they use? Are there alarms? How am I supposed to walk out with a dead body? Wait, no. Why do you even want it? If he really is dead, he'll be dust by now."

"The disintegration process can be stalled in freezing temperatures." Owen leaned forward, staring Adrian in the eyes from beneath his thick brow. "I am your Regent. So when I say to carry out an important mission, you say, 'Yes sir,' and do it."

Adrian's gaze flicked over Owen's shoulder and briefly met Melissa's before she returned to her typing. A hospital was a public place, but the morgue would likely be tucked away in a windowless back room, maybe even the basement. It wouldn't have many people going in or out. Not a bad place for an ambush. No, that was the paranoia talking. How would a group of mortals gain access to the morgue to ambush him? Unless Melissa or Owen had grown tired of the hunters and decided to take Adrian out themselves. Then they could return to Garrick and claim it was an accident.

"No," Adrian said. "I'm not doing it."

A flash of surprise crossed Owen's face before it sank into a snarl.

"Adrian," Garrick reprimanded.

Adrian stood up before he could protest further. "Handle it yourself, if it's that important."

He turned his back and made for the door, then heard Garrick spin reassuring words for Owen before running up behind him and grasping him on the shoulder. Adrian shrugged him off at first, but allowed himself to be turned to face him.

"What are you doing?" Garrick scolded. "We just made amends with Owen and now you want to undo it?"

"I'm not going." Adrian held firm. "It's too dangerous. Owen wants me dead."

"He doesn't want you dead. I talked to him, he's not the one behind the hunters tracking you."

"Then who is?"

"I don't know. But Owen knows full well that I wouldn't stand for you to get hurt."

"Good." Adrian took a step back toward the door once again. "Then I have nothing to fear while I enjoy a nice, relaxing bath for the rest of the night."

Garrick looked down at Adrian, his eyes slowly narrowing as scorn etched itself across his face. In all the years he'd known him, Adrian had never seen Garrick truly angry, and he worried he was dangerously close to witnessing it for the first time.

Then Garrick turned his head back over to Owen. "It'll be done," he said.

Adrian turned to leave. He didn't need to argue. If Garrick wanted him to go on this mission, he'd have to drag him there himself. Adrian marched halfway down the driveway before Garrick finally caught up.

"What's gotten into you?" Garrick hissed.

"Just a sense of self-preservation." Adrian thumped the wound in his right shoulder. "Thought you'd appreciate that."

"Self-preservation isn't about giving Owen reasons to run you out of town! Or worse, put a silver bullet in your head."

"Why won't you support me?" Adrian tried to make the question accusatory, but the words came out as a plea, surprising even himself. "Why am I always second to everyone else? You're constantly defending the Regent, but you won't tell me the goddamn truth?"

Garrick opened his mouth to reply, then paused and took a calming breath.

"Look, sometimes there are things that have to stay among Elders—"

"Don't give me that!" Adrian seethed. "If you can't tell me what's going on with your scar, or why you didn't care that Raymond died, or—"

"Because you'll do something stupid!" Garrick snapped. "What did lashing out at Joseph accomplish? You would have died if I hadn't been there! And even if you had succeeded, then what? You think his vassals would have just bowed their heads to you? Or that there would be a clean transfer of power? And now you're paranoid about Owen. I don't want you causing unnecessary problems!"

"Then maybe you could step the fuck up!" Adrian shoved forward, chest to chest, refusing to flinch this time. His voice trembled with rage. "If you really love me, then maybe you'd start taking me seriously!"

"Not when you're acting like this!"

It was conditional, and he hadn't said the exact words, but the last thing Adrian needed to hear was "I don't love you." He couldn't lie to himself anymore. Adrian yanked the hood of his coat over his head and turned away before Garrick could see the crack in his expression. He stormed down the street, almost running. He'd let Garrick see his anger, maybe even his disgust, but never his hurt. That, he would save for the dark of night, when no one else was watching.

"Where are you going?"

"Bottom of the ocean," Adrian snapped. "Feel free to join me if it doesn't burn your skin off."

27
NIGHT 5 - ADRIAN

G arrick did not follow Adrian to the ocean. Thank God, as the tide sent a surge of knife-like pinpricks as it lapped at his feet. It wouldn't kill him to sit beneath the pitch-black waves if it meant getting away, but it would be painful.

Not that it mattered, as the light patter of evening rain drummed against the hood of his coat. Rain counted as running water. Adrian had never realized just how often water ran until it started stinging his skin. It was just a drizzle, easy enough to ignore as long as he kept his head bowed. He wished he could at least look up at the stars for something to keep his mind occupied, rather than being alone with his thoughts and the roar of an unfriendly ocean.

The rumble masked the sound of someone approaching from behind, causing Adrian to startle when he realized he wasn't alone. His first thought was that Garrick had returned to continue their argument, but he was relieved to see Val standing next to him instead.

"Hey," she said, her voice so quiet it was nearly lost in the sound of the rain and waves. "I heard what happened."

Adrian didn't respond. He appreciated Val checking in on him, but he wasn't ready to confront his raw, battered emotions just yet.

But Val didn't ask about that. "Want to take a walk?"

After a moment of consideration, Adrian nodded. It was a good idea to give his sore feet a break anyway. He and Val took a position just above the tideline and began walking down the length of the beach. At first, they moved in silence, as was customary between the two whenever one was upset. Val understood the value of simple presence.

A few minutes into their walk, Val broke the silence first. "I wanted to apologize."

Adrian looked up at her from beneath his hood. Apologize? "For what?" he asked.

"Yesterday," Val said, "it's not my place to ask about you and Garrick."

"Oh. No, it's fine." And she was right, in the end. It was hard to admit, but he trusted Val more than he trusted his own lover at the moment.

"Still, I didn't want to cause you any distress."

The silence returned between them, but Adrian felt a little lighter thanks to Val's kindness. How ironic that the person who had first exposed the cracks between him and Garrick was now his closest confidant. Silver linings, he supposed.

"Hey, Adrian?" Val said again. "Thank you for standing up to Joseph."

"Huh?" That was unexpected. "I mean, I'm not sure how good a job I did with that."

"True, but I'm still glad you did it. I think we've both been waiting for someone to step up like that, even if it meant moving here."

Adrian pulled his overcoat a little tighter around himself and looked away, trying to hide the shame he'd buried for over a week. But at the corners of his mouth, a small smile peeked through.

"Thank you," he whispered.

They returned to their silence for a moment longer, until Val suddenly stopped and bent down to pick up a small stone. Then she turned toward the ocean and flung it across her body. The soft plunk of the rock barely registered over the sound of the waves.

"What are you doing?" Adrian chuckled. "Are you trying to skip it? On the ocean?"

"Oh, I'm sorry, are you a rock-skipping expert?" Val smirked and looked down by her feet again. She picked up a chipped shell and repeated the motion with the same result. With a mischievous smile, Adrian scanned the ground and found a much larger rock. He held the oblong shape in one hand, braced it against his forearm, and chucked it like a discus into the ocean. The splash was far louder than Val's small stone and sent a visible spray of water into the air upon impact.

"Darn. Didn't skip."

Val playfully shoved him. "I have some new information for you. Those scars? They're from heart transplants."

A heart transplant? Yes, he supposed that would work, if he remembered Garrick's explanation of their magic correctly. But that meant "increasing" one's power wasn't quite accurate. They stole power.

"Where'd Owen get enough hearts?" Adrian asked.

"The previous Regent. You know how people were saying

Owen slaughtered all the vassals when he took over? He probably took their hearts and put them in his own vassals."

"Damn."

"And..." Val's posture tightened, her shoulders squaring to the ocean with a look of authority, as if the tide roared for her. "I'm going to find a new heart for myself. Thank you for standing up to Joseph, but I'm going to finish the job."

"Val," Adrian cautioned, "I tried that, and it didn't end well. If Garrick hadn't been there, I would have died."

"I know." Val didn't turn to address him, but she paused, hopefully contemplating his warning. Her conclusion remained the same.

"I'm still going to do it," she said firmly. "It's not just about Raymond. I'm sick of people like Joseph doing whatever they want without consequences. He's just an easy target because it's personal."

Adrian relented. Too quickly for his liking, though he'd be lying if he said he disapproved. He didn't want to lose Val to a foolish suicide mission, but the thought of her succeeding where he had failed brought a smile to the darker corners of his mind. Val was an adult. If she wanted his help in her reckless revenge plot, who was he to say no?

"Where are you getting this heart?" he asked.

"I've been thinking about that," she said. "And I think Owen made the choice easy."

She turned her head toward him and smirked, waiting for him to puzzle out the answer. Adrian thought for a moment, then shook his head.

"Why do you think Owen wants Tyler back so badly?"

Then it clicked into place. "The heart," he said. "He wants the heart back."

"We go into the morgue, grab Tyler's dead body, put his heart in me, and give Owen my younger heart instead. No one will be any the wiser."

"If Tyler's dead," Adrian muttered. It was a wild plan, so

crazy that he couldn't help but approve, just to see if she could pull it off. Still, he frowned.

"Sorry, I'm not going," he said. The thought of an underground morgue made his skin crawl as his mind became obsessed with visions of Melissa slamming the only door shut, trapping him until morning. "I'm not going back on my word. Have Garrick go with you, since he's the one who committed to it."

The tension in the air returned, the rumbling of waves once again unfriendly. Val's face darkened, but she nodded regardless. "I get it," she said. "But how do you plan to do that? Garrick is right, Owen won't just let you sit around and brood. You need to at least contribute blood."

Adrian sank into himself. His plan, if it could even be called that, was flimsy at best. All he was really doing was testing Garrick, hoping he'd finally step up and treat him not as an equal, but as someone greater than that. As the most important person in Garrick's life. The moral, good part of Adrian's nature bristled at the selfishness of that desire, but right now, he wasn't even on par with Joseph and Owen. How could he kiss his lover with that kind of acid boiling in his heart?

"I'd support you if you took out Owen."

Surprised, Adrian replayed Val's sudden words to make sure he had heard her correctly. He searched her face for any sign of a joke but found only serious determination.

"I…" Take Owen out? Like he tried to do with Joseph?

"Nobody likes him," Val said. "And you're not as unpopular as you think. Besides, with my support, that should smooth over any concerns. And we're not Elders, so we won't need to take blood from anyone. I think a lot of people would appreciate that."

She had a point. Adrian was also the oldest vampire in the city, aside from Garrick and anyone else who might have received heart transplants. His experience made him a natural choice for guarding against any newly mad Elders seeking territory.

"How are we going to kill Owen?" he asked, seriously considering Val's plan. "I hope you're not going to suggest hitting him in the back of the head with a hammer."

"If only we knew some crazy mortals trying to kill a few vampires."

The hunters. If he or Val could somehow leak the location of Owen's mansion, they could break in during the day and kill Owen while he was completely defenseless. Then, hopefully, their bloodlust would be sated and they'd leave, killing two birds with one stone.

It was a good plan. It just had one problem.

"Thea might ruin things," Adrian stated. "If she knows Melissa lives with Owen, she won't risk it. There'd be no way to tell the hunters to kill Owen and not the vampire sharing his bed. Or she'll tell Melissa, who'll tell Owen, and... who knows what he'd do."

"You're in contact with Thea, right? Is there any way we can get Melissa out of the mansion for a day?"

"Yeah, I'm sure she'd be real interested in coming over for a sleepover," Adrian joked. But the more he thought about it, the more a plan formed in his mind. A devious plan. A cruel, amoral one. But it could work, and Adrian would be free. He was long past the point of being a good man. He needed to be a successful one.

"I could distract Thea," he said, "and keep her from going to the mansion."

"How? They need to go during the day, while you'll be asleep."

"I think she'll be... receptive to a sleepover."

Val's brow furrowed in confusion before she finally read between the lines.

"You sure about that? You'd be..." The sentence trailed

off, as if Val were afraid to speak the implication. "You and Garrick…"

He'd be cheating on Garrick. He should have felt ashamed for even entertaining the idea. And yet, he didn't. That old wound, scabbed over from a decade of apologies and soothing words, ripped open once again. At least his cheating had a purpose. And afterward, how would Garrick respond? Beyond the betrayal, would he scorn Adrian for going behind his back? For betraying an ally?

He was going to lose him regardless.

"It's fine," he said. "I don't love him anymore."

28

NIGHT 5 - VAL

The irony of the situation was not lost on Val. She had put Tyler in the hospital, only to discover he had something she needed. Now, she was getting him out. Or at least parts of him.

Val wasn't sure if having Garrick along was a blessing or a curse. Logically, his Elder magic was a blessing, as it made the potential break-in far safer should Val be caught and arrested. But the dark storm cloud hanging over his head didn't just sour the air around him. Garrick was never angry. Outwardly. But inside? Lightning only announced its presence after it struck.

What was Tyler's fate? Val didn't believe the crash had

killed him, but surviving the hospital and morgue process seemed unlikely. If his skin touched sunlight, it would incinerate. If the morgue performed an autopsy immediately, his blood would be drained. She didn't know if Tyler still had a valid driver's license or a will. What if he had signed up to be an organ donor? What if he wanted to be cremated?

The best-case scenario was that none of that had happened, and his dead body was simply frozen, waiting to be claimed. And the second-best scenario? It was a difficult call between the heart being dead, or Tyler being alive.

The hospital campus, now visible behind towering steel buildings, glowed with curved glass windows and white scaffolding. Val couldn't speak much about architecture, but the building's modern design was impressive. Certainly more pleasing than the endless rows of metal boxes that filled most cities.

"Are you sure you're up for this?" Val hazarded an ask. "We can wait—"

"No," Garrick snipped. "It's fine."

Val wanted to reassure him, but after her talk on the beach with Adrian, any soothing words would likely be a lie.

Adrian, I hope you know what you're doing, she thought.

The inside of the hospital caught Val by surprise. Instead of clinical, boxy white walls and the off-putting stench of sterilizing cleaners, the lobby was large and inviting. High ceilings rose above walls that stretched multiple stories. The floor was painted in a rainbow of cascading colors, the walls adorned with artwork, the banisters painted a playful blue. Val took a moment to take it all in. If she had to be wheeled into this hospital, at least she'd have something pleasant to look at before perishing.

Garrick took a few glances around before making a sharp left turn and proceeding to the front desk, not in the mood to appreciate the finer things in life.

The front desk was empty, except for two women shuffling papers and typing on computers. That was to be expected, given the evening hours. Garrick walked up to get their attention.

"Excuse me," he said in his soothingly pleasant voice, "I was wondering if you have someone by the name of Tyler Henderson in your care. I'm his boss, you see, and he hasn't called in to work for the past few days."

The younger of the two women looked up at him and returned his stiff, obviously fake smile. "I'm sorry, sir, are you listed as an emergency contact?"

Garrick paused. "I don't believe I am."

"Unfortunately, due to HIPAA laws, we are unable to disclose information about patients without their direct consent. Have you tried contacting his family?"

"Hi, I'm sorry," Val said, hurrying up to Garrick. "I'm his girlfriend. I tried calling his parents, but they're stuck on the East Coast. Flight problems. They're worried sick about him. They just want to know if their son is stable. It sounded like a dreadful car wreck."

"I understand, ma'am," the woman said. "But unless you are listed as an emergency contact or are direct family, we are legally unable to provide any information. Have his parents tried calling us directly?"

Well, this wasn't going anywhere. Val tugged on Garrick's sleeve. "Come on, let's try again when Tyler's parents arrive in the morning," she said, though it took a few harsh yanks to peel the tense Garrick away from the front desk.

They walked away and rounded a corner, out of sight of the front desk. Only then did Garrick drop his fake smile.

"Val," he growled. "What is HIPAA?"

Val lurched, stifling a laugh. She knew the girlfriend angle wasn't likely to work, but that didn't mean everyone prioritized the law over the pleas of a worried lover.

"Exactly what she said. Health information is private. It's against the law to give it out to just anyone who asks."

"Since when? What if it's important? What if we have to exile his family for twenty days?"

"I think that's exactly why they don't tell people," Val said with a chuckle. "Come on, looks like we're doing this the hard way."

Making sure to avoid the attention of the two front desk workers, Val and Garrick explored the hospital in search of a directory. It didn't take long to find one, and Val scanned the map for any mention of a morgue. Eventually, she realized it wasn't listed, if it existed at all.

"Does this hospital even have a morgue?" she mumbled.

"People die here. They must put the bodies somewhere."

Owen was certain Tyler was located here. Val didn't trust Owen's judgment, but it was more likely that Melissa had done the actual research. Melissa could be a bitch with a stick up her ass, but she was a competent bitch with a stick up her ass.

"Maybe they just don't list it for guests," Val theorized. "There's no reason for anyone to go there unless they're specifically invited."

"Is this another part of your 'hippie' privacy laws?" Garrick mocked.

"Possibly. People can be peculiar about dead bodies."

"You get over it quickly. My grandfather stacked bodies up to his waist during the Black Death."

Val could only nod in reply. Thanks for the input.

"The morgue is probably in the basement, if this building has one," she said, deflecting from the subject of mass death. "Let's search for a stairwell or elevator."

Thankfully, no one asked any questions as the two of them wandered through the hospital halls. Garrick's commanding presence kept him from ever appearing lost, even when he had to turn on his heels after reaching a dead end or a section of the hospital clearly not leading to the morgue. The first elevator they found had a button for an underground level, but pressing it didn't make the elevator move.

"Is it broken?" Garrick asked.

"It needs a badge," Val said, pointing at the scanner next to the elevator buttons.

Val could feel Garrick's frustration seeping out beside her. Is this what Adrian had to deal with regularly? How did he even teach him to use a smartphone? Had Garrick ever owned a computer?

"We could kill someone," Garrick grumbled, "and then follow them to the morgue that way."

"No!" Val hissed. "No killing innocent people!"

"There are old people here! They've lived long lives!"

"Let's just go steal a badge." Val pushed Garrick out of the elevator and began wandering the halls again. A few minutes later, they passed a woman in scrubs, alone. In one fluid motion, Garrick wrapped an arm around her shoulders and bit her neck. The swiftness of the act gave her no time to cry out, and Garrick gently lowered her to the ground. Val unclipped her badge.

"Come on!" she insisted. They re-entered the elevator and swiped the badge. The reader beeped pleasantly, and Val pressed the button for the basement. The elevator didn't move. Val tried a second time, with the same result.

She did her best to ignore Garrick's judgmental stare.

"I… I guess we need a higher security clearance," she said. Adrian had been right to throw a fit—this was far more complicated than she had initially thought. They'd already assaulted one worker, and they didn't even know if they were heading in the right direction.

"We could kill someone," Garrick repeated, "and then follow them to the morgue that way."

"No! Don't you have some kind of Elder vampire magic that could help?"

"With what?" he asked. "The Ancient Ones never had to develop anti-elevator magic!"

"Can't you call to the flesh of the dead or something?" Val was grasping at straws now. She had no idea what Elder magic was truly capable of.

"Wait." The realization struck Val like a bolt of lightning— or more like a small static shock, jolting her out of the fog that had kept her from seeing the obvious solution. She lightly slapped Garrick's arm. "What the hell are we doing? We're dead."

Garrick made to argue again, but then his eyebrows lifted. "Oh," he relented. "You are correct."

They exited the building and walked around to the emergency entrance. Val played the part of the newly deceased while Garrick ran in, begging for help. He cried fake tears, claiming Val had complained of chest pain before suddenly collapsing. Though her eyes were closed, Val heard multiple nurses rush to her side. They checked her pulse and breathing, both of which were still. Garrick had said he'd help make her heartbeat completely undetectable. How, she wasn't sure, but it seemed to have worked. Her body was lifted onto a gurney, and a veil was placed over her head. Good, she didn't want to blow her cover by smirking at a plan that had finally gone right.

"Don't worry, I'm right here," Garrick whispered in her ear. She didn't dare move to see how, but she thought she felt a small animal brush against her cheek.

After a surprisingly long walk, the veil lifted from Val's body, and the gurney rolled into a freezing cold room. When the sounds around her subsided for more than a minute, she opened her eyes and found herself staring up at the underside of a metal shelf, in what appeared to be a large walk-in freezer.

And Tyler, standing next to her, wide-eyed and famished.

Goddamn it, he was still alive.

Tyler smiled in recognition. "D-Did you come to rescue me?" he asked.

"Yes," Val answered, unable to hide her disappointment. It didn't appear that Tyler caught the emotion, as he giddily jumped with excitement. Or was he trembling from cold and hunger?

Val rolled off the gurney, stood up, and looked around the freezer. Television portrayed morgues as rows of metallic crypts, but this area looked more like it was designed for storing meat than bodies. Before she could panic about the confined space, the wall opened to reveal Garrick with a nurse slumped behind him.

"Oh good, you're alive," he said, eyeing Tyler. "I was starting to prepare our escape with your dead body, but walking out the front door sounds much easier."

Val glared at Tyler's bare chest, showing through the cut shirt. Inside that chest beat a heart of indeterminate age and power, and if she just had a minute alone, no one would ever suspect that Tyler hadn't died on the pavement in a gruesome car crash.

Garrick stared at her with an intensity that made her shudder. She wasn't sure if he knew what she was thinking, but he clearly disapproved. Subtly, but his look was a warning. A warning was different than a threat.

Val fixed her eyes on Tyler's neck. Like a tiger pouncing on unsuspecting prey, she latched onto his throat and tore through his arteries. Despite their difference in size, Tyler could barely put up a fight. His blood was thin, and his veins dried quickly. Val dropped him, limp, to the floor of the freezer. Garrick closed his eyes, frowning deeply.

She ignored him. She walked out of the freezer and into the larger room to search for tools—a saw, a knife, a cooler for live organs, ice, and a bag. She quickly got to work. Val didn't know how to properly open a ribcage to retrieve the organ inside, but she didn't care about preserving the rest of the body. She sliced through skin, muscle, and tendons. She broke ribs. She tore through other organs, atrophied from disuse, to make room. Thankfully, the heart was easy to find, spasming from a lack of blood to pump. She sliced above the aorta to cut it free, then dropped it into the ice-filled bag.

Garrick didn't say a word during the entire procedure. He just stood, watching her with that signature blank, disappointed expression. She didn't care. She washed her hands and arms at a small sink in the corner.

"Don't give me that look," Val grumbled, flicking the water away. "Don't pretend this is a matter of morals."

"I'm just trying to protect you," Garrick said. "Even if you succeed, you'll be making a lot of enemies."

"I never asked for your protection, but your help would be appreciated."

Garrick's initial reply was silence. But when Val reached for the cooler containing the heart, Garrick rolled a metal gurney into the middle of the morgue. She paused, watching him, curious—until she realized what his outstretched hand toward the gurney implied.

"If I can't stop you from chasing revenge, then at least let me make sure you survive your back-alley surgery. I want you to regret fighting an Elder, not your poor choice of doctor."

Val hesitated. The about-face was unexpected. Still, Garrick was the closest thing she had to a surgeon. And she had asked for his help, even if it was meant as a jab.

Unlike the rest of the hospital, the morgue was as cool and clinical as one would expect. The harsh metal gurney made for an unpleasant deathbed. Slowly, Val climbed onto it and tried to rest her head as best she could. Her heart pounded at the reality of what she was about to do. Strange to think it wouldn't be her heart much longer.

Garrick stood over her, knife in hand. "If we do this," he said, his tone neither worried nor encouraging, "everything that follows is yours to bear. Don't curse me when you need my protection and I'm not there."

Determined, Val gave a nod.

"This is going to hurt. A lot."

"Worse than watching your love murdered in front of you, and your friend make excuses for it?"

Garrick paused. "You'll have to tell me."

29
NIGHT 6 - ADRIAN

This time, Adrian sent Thea a good evening text. He lay in bed, phone held above his head, pondering how to start the conversation. She was clearly smitten with him, so even a simple "Hey, want to hang out?" would probably do the trick. But he didn't want to come across as disinterested or unappreciative of her previous message. It had to be a vampire joke. Surprisingly, even after forty years of being one, he couldn't think of a single joke off the top of his head. The internet offered nothing but painfully groan-worthy puns. Come on, he had to send her something actually funny.

He finally texted, "Why don't vampires eat cows?" It was

DARBY VERNON

because large animals were actually very dangerous, they spooked easily, and vampire venom wasn't strong enough to knock them out like it was with humans. Plus, vampires stopped being satiated by animal blood after five to ten years. But none of that was funny.

"Why?" Thea replied to his text.

"Because we don't like stakes."

On second thought, it really was a painfully bad joke. If Thea never wanted to see him again, he would understand.

Thankfully, she sent him a laughing emoji instead.

> Want to hang out today?

Yes! Do you need more help getting blood?

> Yeah, thanks.

> But also want to catch a movie?

> Or something?

That was smooth, right? Sixty-eight years, and Adrian still never learned how to flirt. It had been easy to break the ice when, essentially, his last relationship began because his soon-to-be boyfriend kissed his neck every other night. Before that, he was just an awkward teenager, and then a worthless homeless man.

Mm, nah.

Shit, what? How did he blow it already?

I want to get to know you!

Can't talk during a movie.

Wanna laser tag?

Oh good, she still liked him. And her reasoning made sense.

> Sure. I've never done laser tag though.

Really? Ok now we HAVE to do it!

Adrian found himself smiling. He confirmed their meeting place and time, then dropped his arm and gazed aimlessly at the ceiling. An uncharacteristic radiance flowed through his body, urging him to bask in its warmth, his mind blissfully blank—if only for a moment longer. Just as long as he ignored the ugly darkness lurking behind it.

There was no need to worry about the fallout. It was too difficult to predict what might happen after tonight. Perhaps Thea would never learn of his hand working behind the scenes, and this, too, would become a permanent part of his new life.

The phone vibrated in his palm, and he eagerly lifted it to see what Thea had to say. Garrick's text met him instead.

Can we talk?

Adrian's mood immediately came crashing down. He stared at the single sentence like the corpse of a pest that had crept into his room—something he wanted to ignore, but knew would only rot the longer he did. His thumb hovered over the touchscreen keyboard, unsure how to respond, until he settled on something suitably noncommittal.

> Just woke up. Give me a minute to shower and change.

Groaning, he got up and quickly went through his morning routine: a cold shower, brushing his teeth by the sink, and staring at his phantasmal reflection in the mirror—

the details of the figure before him obscured and translucent, like a human-shaped fog. Young vampires could use magic to turn their reflections off. Older vampires had to use magic to turn theirs back on.

After changing into fresh clothes, he braced himself and exited his room. Garrick waited in the hall, leaning against the wall just outside the doorframe, his attention unfocused as he stared at the phone in his hands. He straightened and stiffly pocketed the phone when he saw Adrian.

"What's up?" Adrian asked, as if they hadn't had a huge fight the last time they saw each other.

"Right, I…" Garrick shifted on his feet, searching his mind for whatever perfect words would placate him. "Adrian, what's wrong? Where is all this coming from?"

His jaw tightened in response. Had he not been clear? Despite hoping otherwise, it was becoming obvious that their conversation was once again hurtling toward another fight.

Adrian spoke, each word emerging in a punctuated hiss as he struggled to keep his voice steady. "I'm not doing anything Owen asks of me. No missions, no blood, no favors."

"We can't do that," Garrick replied in a hushed tone, either to keep Adrian's anger from flaring or to maintain control of his own temper. "If we want to stay in San Francisco, we have to do as we're told."

"Then I don't want to stay in San Francisco."

"Where would we go?" Garrick begged. "Every city is like this. Seattle, San Jose, San Diego, Las Vegas… They're all just as bad as Joseph, many worse."

Adrian bit his tongue to keep himself from snapping. Yes, God forbid them, there was absolutely nothing they could do. If Adrian so much as breathed a word of his plan to kill Owen, would Garrick go so far as to stop him? There was no way he didn't know it was a potential option. He was, quite literally, the only vampire in the city who didn't expect—or didn't want—him to do it.

Adrian pushed past him, finished with the conversation. Garrick's words were worthless to him.

"Wait!" Garrick called after him. "Can we please just talk this through?"

"No!" he snapped. Then, before Garrick could argue, he added, "We'll talk about it tomorrow, okay? I'm just... I'm still too raw about this. Just give me some space today." Please, just one day, and everything would change. Garrick wouldn't be able to soothe him into obeying Owen if the Regent was dead.

"I promise," he continued. "We'll talk about it tomorrow."

Garrick hesitated, then pinched his eyes shut and nodded, resigned. "Tomorrow," he agreed.

"Thank you." With a stiff nod, Adrian strode down the hall and out the doors before Garrick could change his mind. He tried to remain composed, walking at a normal pace, head high, rather than skulking with hunched shoulders and clenched fists. Just one night, and everything would change. He wouldn't let it ruin his plans, or his mood.

Adrian checked his texts from Thea again, telling himself he just wanted to make sure she hadn't changed the meeting place at the last minute. Instead, his eyes drifted up to the emoji, laughing at his stupid joke. So dumb, she couldn't have actually laughed at it, but the thought that she might have let out a small chuckle lifted his spirits, just a little.

He met her sitting on a park bench, a fifteen-minute walk away. Her eyes actually lit up when she saw him approaching. Suddenly, his worries about Garrick melted away. No more of that, he was out to have a good time.

"Hey! How's it going?" she said in greeting.

"Pretty good, you?" It was a lie, but he wasn't about to tempt her with topics he didn't want to discuss.

He joined her on the park bench, catching up on gossip about the hunters and Melissa. Thea didn't have any new information, just confirmation that the hunters were still restless, and her communication with Melissa remained short and curt. It seemed Adrian's insistence on keeping his distance from Melissa and Owen was working, as Striga hadn't given the hunters any new leads on where to ambush him next.

"You know..." Adrian had contemplated bringing up the idea ever since he and Val had their talk on the beach. It wasn't something to suggest over text, and he wasn't sure how Thea would take it. But his plan would be much simpler if she agreed.

"You're a vampire hunter. Have you considered, you know... getting revenge on Owen?"

Thea hesitated before answering. "I'd be lying if I said I didn't consider it," she said. "But... look, I wouldn't lose any sleep if he ended up with a stake through the heart. I'd do it myself if I knew I could get away with it. But I'm not about to risk prison time on attempted murder charges over this. Besides, I hate that Melissa's working with him, but I don't want to accidentally cause her any trouble." She finished her explanation with a quiet "bitch" under her breath.

Then she changed the subject. "So, what are we doing for your meal tonight?"

It was worth a try. This would have been so much easier if Thea just agreed to break into Owen's house alone during the day. Throwing Owen's body into the sun wouldn't leave evidence of a murder, but he couldn't guarantee there'd be no consequences. It was best not to push it.

"Good question," Adrian answered. "Bars and nightclubs are always an option, or we can jump a random stranger on the street."

"Mmm, I guess you can't be picky as a vampire."

Right, Thea might have been cool with him being a vampire, at least in theory. But it was hard to maintain that acceptance once she had to confront the fact that his survival meant physically assaulting someone every other night. Vampires who couldn't come to terms with that moral conundrum didn't last long.

"So, what does a vampire bite feel like?" she asked.

"My offer's still on the table," Adrian teased. It would be an easy way to get his blood for the night, if a bit quick and boring. He needed to burn almost ten hours for their plan to work. "Vampire bites have venom that puts mortals to sleep," he clarified, before Thea could respond to his flirting. "You wake up wondering if it was all just a dream."

"Oh. I guess that's not too bad," she trailed off, looking out over the park before finally saying, "Okay."

"Okay?"

She rolled her head to the side and tapped her neck.

"You sure?"

"It's fine," she complained. "Like you said, it shouldn't hurt. This way, we can get going on, like, fun stuff."

He couldn't argue with that, not if she was offering freely. Adrian took a quick look around to make sure no one was nearby, then leaned in. He tried to embrace her like a lover unconcerned with public displays, but even though it was just pretend, it was still embarrassing. He bit her as neutrally as possible.

"Ow."

Adrian rolled his eyes. Drama queen.

It didn't take long for Thea to go limp in his embrace. After forty years of placing his lips on complete strangers every other night, the act no longer held any intimate meaning. Usually. But this time, he became oddly aware of every movement, every sensation. What did his tongue normally do while feeding?

Finally, he pulled away, mortified, even though no one was around to judge him. He held Thea close, resting her head on his shoulder as if she were merely asleep, trying not to appear stiff or uncomfortable. Minutes of silence stretched by until she finally stirred awake.

"Mmm... Huh? Oh, you're done already?"

Adrian released his arm from around her shoulders, slipping it behind the back of the park bench.

"Damn, I can barely remember a thing," she muttered, sitting upright. "I could've been bitten before and never even known."

An awkward pause was Adrian's only reply. Fear of saying the wrong thing kept him quiet. Thea stretched, rolled her neck, then stood and offered her hand.

"Right, laser tag! Trust me, it's a lot of fun."

"Isn't it for kids?" Adrian teased.

"No! Adults play it too." She pulled him toward her motorcycle, and to Adrian's delight, the ride to the arcade was an exhilarating fifteen minutes.

To Thea's credit, the laser tag line wasn't entirely filled with kids. A group of three college-aged adults stood ahead of them, but the line was still mostly made up of young children. Once they were allowed into the waiting room, an employee made sure to split the teams so that Adrian and Thea were together on the red side, and the three students were on the blue side.

Lining the walls were racks of black, bulky vests with electronic plates attached to the chest, back, and shoulders. Following Thea's direction, Adrian slipped one over his head. A large, rectangular toy gun dangled off the vest by a wire. Adrian looked it over, weighing it in his hand. It was considerably heavier than a typical handgun. Maybe it would be easier to hold the barrel like a rifle. He tested his theory by bringing the laser gun up to his eye. A little short to be comfortable, but it offered more control than using one arm. Then again, the laser gun wouldn't have any recoil.

"How many gunfights have you been in?" Thea leaned in close and whispered.

Suddenly self-conscious about his appearance, Adrian quickly dropped his arm to his side.

"Don't worry about it."

A small television set bolted to the wall explained the rules. Shoot the other team in the sensors on their suits to score points. Get shot three times, and you had to retreat to a "recharge" station on your team's side of the room. Every few minutes, a target would appear somewhere in the arena, and shooting it would earn even more points. No running, climbing, crawling, or anything else fun was allowed.

They were let into the arena, a dark room illuminated by neon and blacklight. Adrian imagined the effect would look more impressive if his vision didn't naturally adjust to the darkness. Instead, he was left with the suffocating atmosphere without the allure of mystery. Numerous maze-like walls partitioned the room, some with holes, others with mirrors tucked into the corners. Heh, cute.

As Adrian followed Thea to the far end of the room, marked with glowing red trim, he spotted a bright Exit sign glowing in the corner. It was on the red side, thankfully—not that it mattered. The room wasn't going to catch fire. Probably.

A buzzer signaled the start of the match, and Adrian held his gun up to the recharge station. An electronic "whoop" sounded as a display lit up on the back of his gun, showing his score and the number of hits he could take.

Thea immediately scurried through the glowing maze walls, and Arian followed.

"Cover my back," she instructed, holding her gun up with two stiff arms like a hero in an action movie. Adrian chuckled and did as he was told. They crept around corners, shooting and ducking for cover when necessary, until a whistle echoed through the arena. A bright yellow target lit up on the other side of the room.

"Let's go," Thea said, moving toward their new goal. But soon after, the plates on her vest flashed.

"Dam—Drat." She stopped herself mid-swear, realizing there were kids nearby. "Gotta recharge."

"Bye," Adrian teased. He still had two hits left before he needed to retreat, but as soon as Thea was out of sight, he felt helplessly alone.

Ridiculous. He peeked around a corner and shot his laser at a kid, probably ten years old, hitting him in the shoulder. The kid jumped and retreated behind a wall, allowing Adrian to sneak by. A second kid hid behind the next wall, and Adrian shot her in the chest. She just stood there, staring down at the vibrating vest. Adrian considered taking a second shot but decided to wait for her to realize what had happened and retreat instead.

Adrian's own shoulder buzzed, and he quickly ducked around the corner for cover, doing his best to resist crouching low in accordance with the "no fun" rule. Peering back, he spotted one of the college students doing the same around a corner about five yards away. Adrian held his gun around the corner as if to aim at the student's head, even though—unlike in a real fight—shooting at the head wouldn't accomplish anything. Still, it caused the student to duck.

Glancing over his other shoulder, Adrian realized he was within shooting distance of the yellow target. He landed a single hit before his chest vibrated and the gun refused to fire again. Confused, he looked around and saw the second college student peeking through one of the small holes in the wall.

Damn, they were good at this.

Adrian followed the Exit sign back to the recharge station, and his gun blinked back to life. Two other small girls stood nearby, whispering to each other, seemingly too timid to stray out of sight of the station.

Thea reappeared at the recharge station as well. "Ugh, those college students are targeting the kids for easy points," she grumbled. "Bullies."

242

Adrian looked up at the large scoreboard hanging high on the side wall. They were significantly behind.

"Take those two to the main checkpoint," he said, pointing to the two small girls. "I'll handle the adults."

Before Thea could ask what his plan was, Adrian wove through the maze walls once again. Then, convinced no one was watching, he cloaked himself in darkness. He could play dirty too.

As nothing but a shadow, Adrian prowled through the arena unseen. Giving himself a new goal helped focus his mind and kept him from constantly checking the Exit sign over his shoulder. He ignored the smaller children and searched for the adults, finding them by the yellow target. He shot one in the shoulder, prompting her to look around for her attacker. Then he shot one of the two men in the back, and the other in the chest. They scattered, and Adrian followed, choosing a new target each time to keep them from figuring out his position. One by one, the students peeled off to recharge, glancing in all directions, still trying to determine where the shots had come from.

But that was only the first part of his plan. Following them halfway back to the Blue Team base, Adrian then dispelled his shadows, except for two small patches on his shoulders, just enough to cover the sensors. He positioned himself in the center of the room, making sure he could be seen.

One of the male students saw him first and tried to fire at him. Adrian ducked halfway behind cover and raised his laser gun to return fire, but he kept his attention on the other hallways. As expected, the female student used the scuffle as a distraction, so he quickly peeled himself off the wall and stalked after her, tagging her in the back. She jumped and ran off, away from the precious yellow target.

Adrian spotted the third student and approached him directly, turning so his shoulder faced him. The student attempted to return fire but found that Adrian was far more successful at landing hits.

Adrian's gambit successfully held off the three adults for several minutes, until they finally managed to tag him in the back enough times. But by then, Thea and the kids had made huge gains based on the updated score. A few minutes later, the obnoxiously loud buzzer went off, signaling the end of the game before the blue team could catch up.

Returning to the waiting room, Adrian overheard the male student he had dueled against complaining, loudly enough that Adrian knew it was directed at him just as much as at his friends.

"He was covering it with something, I'm sure of it!"

Adrian raised his laser gun to his lips and blew away imaginary smoke.

Thea discarded her vest and high-fived the two girls who had been cowering by the recharge station. A beaming smile spread across his face as he watched the three celebrate. After Thea said goodbye and they exited the laser tag area, she leaned over to him and whispered under her breath.

"You cheated, didn't you?"

"No," Adrian insisted. "The rules didn't say anything about using dark magic."

Thea snickered and gave him a good-natured push. "Now what? The night's still young."

"Could find a bar with a pool table, or maybe a concert. Clubbing, perhaps."

"I told you, as long as it's not a gay club."

Adrian scoffed. "Gay clubs are way more fun."

"No, they're not!"

"How many have you been to?"

Thea smirked. "All right, I see. You just don't know how to dance with girls. Well, we'll just have to fix that."

Adrian complained but allowed himself to be led back to

the motorcycle, his destination apparently a nightclub. He climbed onto the back behind Thea and wrapped his arms around her waist. Leaning forward, he spoke near Thea's ear, or where he assumed her ear was beneath the helmet.

"Take the long way around."

Thea gave a thumbs-up and lurched the motorcycle forward. She weaved through traffic on the large, busy road before turning away from the towering skyscrapers at the city's heart. She merged onto a road along the edge of the peninsula, the long plane of dark ocean unfurling to Adrian's right. Wind whipped past his face, salty and cool, as the engine revved and they zipped past a slower car. Adrian held on to her tightly, resting his head against her shoulder, watching the swelling ocean waves roll by.

Finally, they turned back into the city and pulled up to a large, warehouse-like building.

The club was much larger than the previous gay bar. It had a proper stage, a closed-off VIP section in the back, and black-painted walls that drowned everything not hit by spotlights in darkness. Loud, thumping dance music pounded Adrian's ears as Thea pulled him into the heart of the crowd, just beneath the DJ's stage. She took his hands and began swaying to the music, then laughed.

"You're so stiff!" she shouted over the music.

"I am not!"

"Just sway your hips to the beat!"

"That's what I'm doing!"

That's what he thought he was doing.

Thea took hold of his hips to guide him in what was apparently the correct way to dance. Begrudgingly, he placed his hands on her shoulders and mimicked her steps and sways, doing his best to relax and loosen up. It seemed to be working, as Thea finally lifted her eyes from his hips and shoulders to meet his gaze, her lips parted in a smile.

"Well?" she asked after a beat. "Are you going to kiss me, or what?"

Adrian pressed his lips to hers, losing his rhythm until Thea guided his body once more.

30
NIGHT 6 - ADRIAN

Vampire hearts were weak things, kept alive only by magic. But they still remembered a time when they were alive, and they beat with full strength in times of high emotion. Such moments were almost painful for Adrian. It was easy to ignore a beating heart when it was constant. Now, it felt like a bad muscle twitch, constantly distracting him from whatever emotion had triggered the annoying affliction. Fear, or excitement, or anxiety, or something more primal. One of those.

The hotel Thea brought him to was far nicer than any he'd stayed in before. Located in a skyscraper in the busiest sector of the city, it featured sleek, modern decor instead of something decades out of date. Even though it was past two in the morning, a man in a suit gave them a welcoming bow as they entered, making Adrian shift uncomfortably while Thea secured their room.

The room was located on the twelfth floor, with a large glass window for the wall, like the ones in Owen's mansion. Adrian hung a Do Not Disturb sign on the outer door handle and threw the deadbolt, ensuring room service wouldn't walk in on his seemingly dead body during the day. He closed the blackout blinds as Thea flipped various lights on and off, trying to find the right mood.

"That good?" she asked, deciding to keep the lamp in the corner on while turning everything else off.

"I can see in the dark, so it's up to you."

Adrian shed his coat and adjusted the neckline of his shirt, absently standing by the king-sized bed. The phone in his pocket vibrated, and he pulled it out to find a text from Val.

> About to make my move. You good?

>> Unless I fuck it up in the next 10 min yeah I'm good.

> Be safe have fun.

> If you run out of ideas before she's worn out just text me.

> I know it's been a long time since you've been with a girl.

>> I'm turning my phone off now.

Adrian rolled his eyes and powered off his phone.

Thea stood on the other side of the bed, dressed in a metal band T-shirt, her hands stuffed in her pockets. "You good?" she asked.

Adrian snapped his head up, suddenly very self-conscious

about how unsexy he felt. Val's teasing hadn't helped matters, nor had the reminder of why he was here.

"Um, yeah. Sorry," Adrian muttered. "I'm just... not actually that smooth."

Thea chuckled. "Yeah, nothing sexier than standing around at the hotel front desk for ten minutes while they see if they can get a room last minute. Don't worry about it. At least they gave us this." She picked up a bottle of wine from the nightstand and popped the cork. Instead of pouring it into one of the two wine glasses, she took a sip straight from the bottle. Then she climbed onto the bed, atop the neatly pressed sheets, and rested her back against the headboard, patting the spot beside her to invite Adrian to join. He slid in next to her and awkwardly draped his arm over her shoulders.

"What's it like to be a vampire?" Thea asked suddenly.

The question took Adrian by surprise. There was so much to it that he wasn't sure how to respond. Where should he begin?

"It's... well, a lot of staying awake at night and sleeping during the day."

"Yeah, no shit," Thea mumbled. "Do you like it?"

Adrian took another moment to think before he answered. "It's the best thing that ever happened to me. But my bar was pretty low. I was homeless before that."

"Damn, sorry about that."

He shrugged. It was so long ago now. "It's not an easy life. The food situation is... well, it's not like I can just go to the store. And it's not as freeing as you'd expect. Traveling is hard. I have to make sure I always have secure shelter. Need to stay in big cities, where the police will just shrug off casual assault..."

Adrian trailed off. He was really making a case for what a great catch he was.

Thea shifted further into his side embrace. "I've been

wondering whether I should ask you to make me a vampire," she said.

Adrian's brows lifted in surprise, and his chest ached. He wanted that. He wanted her. What he didn't want was to impose his life on her—but he also didn't want her to leave once everything with Owen, Melissa, Garrick, and the hunters was over.

"But..." Thea continued. His ache turned to sharp pain. "...I don't know. After Melissa disappeared and my parents died, I lost a lot of friends. We mostly drifted apart, if I didn't push them away first. They thought I was a crazy conspiracy theorist. I chased rumors of vampires while they went on with their lives. And then I found Melissa, and... she doesn't even want me around. My online friends were disappointing, to say the least. You're the only one I've..."

She leaned over to place the wine bottle back on the night-stand, then slipped her arm around his waist.

"But I don't know, it doesn't sound like a very glamorous life. Certainly not the castles, crypts, and fancy aristocratic parties folk tales make it out to be. I like you, I really do, but maybe I should consider it a success that I found Melissa and confirmed she's okay. And then... move on. Get a job, find new friends..."

Adrian leaned his cheek against her head and held her shoulders a little tighter. No, he wanted her to stay. But looking around at the fancy hotel room, he knew she deserved better than the life he could offer. He couldn't deny that.

"But, I mean, it's not like I have to decide right now." Her unusually somber mood lightened. "Let's be real, I'm totally going to change my tune in twenty years when my back hurts just getting out of bed. Even if it's not right away, I have a new vampire best friend I can call anytime."

He smiled. Yes, at least she had that.

"But if it's all right with you, even just for a short time, just... one night where I'm not alone."

Adrian's heart fluttered painfully. If nothing else, he could give her that. He pulled her in front of him, kissed her lips, felt her breath quicken against his face, and held her close until sunrise.

Night 8 – Adrian

Adrian woke to the soft, comforting sound of Thea shouting his name and slapping his face. In his initial grogginess, he appreciated that she had stayed until the next sundown, until he registered the panic in her voice.

"Adrian, wake up!" she yelled, standing beside the bed fully dressed. She slapped his face again, which finally got his attention.

"Stop hitting me!" he said, raising his arms to shield his face.

"Oh thank God you're finally awake," Thea said. "It's Melissa! Something's happened!"

"Yeah?" Adrian rubbed his eyes. Right, Melissa was dead now. The hunters should have hit Owen's mansion during the day and taken everyone out. Time to play the part of the comforting, gentle shoulder to cry on.

"I don't know what's going on. She left me a voicemail, told me to get away from the hunters, said she was in trouble, and..."

"Wait, what?" Now Adrian was fully awake. How did she send a voicemail? But did it matter? Melissa should be dead. Her messages must have been sent before sunrise, and then the hunters should have struck. As concerning as it was, it shouldn't matter anymore.

Adrian looked over at his cellphone on the nightstand, still powered off from the night before. He hesitated, then turned it on. Please, let there be a confirmation text from Val saying everything went smoothly on her end.

Adrian's stomach dropped as the text appeared.

Help.

No further clarification. He quickly sent Val a text asking for information.

Thea held her phone up to her ear. She was silent for a few seconds, then her face lit up.

"Melissa?" she asked. "Oh, thank God. Is everything all right?"

No, it was impossible. What happened? Adrian sent Val another text, telling her to call as soon as she woke up. He jumped out of bed and quickly pulled his clothes on. Then he called Val in a panic.

"Pick up, pick up," he prayed. Four rings, then the call went to voicemail. He swore and hung up.

"I'm at the hunter house," Thea said. Adrian gave her a glance, trying to overhear as much as he could. Every piece of information he gathered could be vitally important.

"Nothing. I was up late and went to bed at sunrise. What? No. Why do you think I'm with Adrian?" Thea glanced at him and gritted her teeth. Who told her? Val?

"No, I didn't sleep with him last night! Look, does it matter? I'm an adult, I can make my own bad choices."

Adrian folded his arms. Thea regarded him with a finger to her lips, signaling him not to blow this for her. To be fair, at that moment, he was scared of Melissa too.

"Well, I'm not with him right now, so tell me whatever you want." Thea listened intently, her face slowly falling.

She then looked back at Adrian with nothing short of horror.

"Listen," she said, her voice suddenly quiet. "Can I call you back? ...I'm not, but this isn't a conversation suitable for public. Okay, I'll call you back soon."

Thea hung up and immediately rushed to the door. "I'm sorry," she said. "It's an emergency, I really have to go."

"What? What did she say?"

"I'm sorry, I just... I'll tell you later."

Thea ran out the door. Confused and panicked, Adrian followed but stopped cold at the exit. Standing in the hallway just outside was Garrick, arms folded, leaning against the wall. He made no effort to stop Thea as she ran by. Instead, he kept his eyes fixed on Adrian.

Adrian knew he should have kept running. Thea was the more pressing concern than his complicated relationship with Garrick, but the man's cold, indifferent stare held his attention just long enough for Thea to get away. He waited for Garrick to start yelling, to get angry, to make some kind of aggressive move, but Garrick only continued his judgmental stare.

"It's... it's not..." Adrian stammered. He didn't know where to start. Should he apologize? How had Garrick found him? "We had a plan, Val and I. We'd leak the location of Owen's house to the hunters. I'd distract Thea while the others kill Owen in the morning. No more orders, no more looking the other way and making excuses for that asshole."

Garrick's expression remained unchanged. "So this is why you didn't want to talk until today."

Adrian approached Garrick, getting right in his face to avoid yelling for the whole hotel to hear. "Maybe if you actually listened to me, I wouldn't have had to go through all this!"

Slowly, Garrick's eyes narrowed. "Really? That's the angle you want to take?" he growled, each word slow and weighted. "'You made me cheat?' At least I spared you that excuse."

Before Adrian could snap back, Garrick cut in with his usual indifference.

"So, how did your plan turn out?"

Adrian's face fell. His eyes darted toward the elevator. He needed to catch up to Thea.

"That well," Garrick said, accurately interpreting his panic. "Congratulations, you've made an enemy of everyone, and for nothing."

Adrian shirked back as if Garrick had punched him in the gut. His mind raced—too fast, too desperate to gather the million shattered pieces of his plan—to fully comprehend the extent of Garrick's threat. But he knew Garrick was right.

"We had visitors this morning," Garrick continued, and Adrian froze. "They had a lot of silver on them, so maybe it was best that you weren't there after all."

The hunters? But how? What had gone wrong?

"That hunter girl—she doesn't have a reason to hate you, does she?"

Adrian shrank into himself. His hands trembled, his knees threatened to give out, as fear overshadowed every thought.

Garrick reached beneath the hem of his shirt and pulled a gun tucked into his belt. He held the grip out to Adrian.

"Why do you have that?" Adrian whimpered.

"The hunter girl is a problem."

Bewildered, Adrian looked up at Garrick, silently pleading with him, but was met only with his stone-cold expression.

"This is your plan, Adrian. Fix it."

He hesitated, but Thea was only getting farther away. Adrian grabbed the gun and sprinted down the stairwell, out through the hotel exit. As soon as he stepped outside, he cloaked himself in shadows. The illusion worked better once the sun had fully set, rather than during the dark blue twilight that stained the sky just after sunset. He hoped Thea wouldn't notice the shifting darkness nearby. He raced to the back lot where she had parked her motorcycle and spotted her standing nearby. She held her phone to her ear, helmet tucked under one arm, jacket hanging loosely off her shoulders. No doubt she was talking to Melissa again. How much she knew, Adrian could only guess.

He hid behind a car, shadows still obscuring his figure. Was killing her really the only option? No doubt Garrick had other motives for wanting her out of Adrian's life. For Garrick, killing Thea solved two problems at once. He didn't need to toe Garrick's line.

But what was his other option? Letting Thea go? The look on her face... she had to have known about his plan to kill Owen and Melissa. Even if he and Garrick ran, Thea would still be a danger to Val, if she was even alive. She'd always be a danger.

But there was no guarantee that Thea would choose vengeance. She might curse his name but still take the higher road. As long as their paths never crossed, she could move on and forget him. Could, yes, but would she? This was the girl who had spent five years searching for her dead sister. Yet last night, she told him she wasn't interested in revenge against Owen, that she didn't want to cause trouble. But that was before he used her and tried to kill what remained of her family.

Adrian grabbed his phone and tried calling Val once again. Surely, by now, she was awake—especially after such an unexpected night. He needed her to throw him a lifeline. There had to be something that could shed light on his situation, something that would make his choice clear. Four rings, then voicemail.

Thea finished talking on her phone. He could only guess

what Melissa had told her. Probably something along the lines of how the guy she had just confided in was a monster, a traitor. Time was up to choose.

Adrian held up the gun and fixed the problem.

31
NIGHT 7 - ADRIAN

No bullet wounds. Fourteen rounds remaining.

Adrian considered knocking on the front door. He didn't need an invitation, but should he leave evidence of a break-in? He didn't care. He kicked the door off its frame, the wood around the lock splintering as it gave way with ease. He stepped aside from the entrance, still just outside the two-story house. No bullet wounds.

He heard shouting. Someone ran out onto the front porch to see what had happened to their door. Adrian shot him in the arm, and he dropped to the ground. Thirteen rounds remained. An arm shot wouldn't be enough to kill, so he fired again at the man's head. Twelve rounds.

Adrian pulled a cloud of darkness over himself and ran into the house. The lights were on, so he was far from invisible, but a shifting mass of shadows could buy him precious seconds of confusion, seconds the hunters weren't spending to shoot at him.

He slid behind a nearby sofa as he heard a gunshot. Nothing hit him, so he peeked out from the side to assess how many hunters were in the room and where they stood. He counted two, both near a small table in the dining room. One was running toward him while the other stayed back, gun raised. Adrian tested the weight of the sofa. Probably still too heavy to lift, even with vampiric strength, but flipping it was doable. He flipped the sofa over, primarily as a distraction. Then he darted out from the side and fired a shot—eleven—at the hunter who hadn't moved from the dining room table. It missed, but Adrian kept running. The hunter flinched at the sound, perhaps anticipating a bullet, and was left completely unprepared when Adrian slammed into him. He tumbled to the ground, making an easy target for Adrian's next shot. Ten.

He kept moving as another gun fired. Ducking behind the kitchen counter, he waited for the bullets to stop flying. After several seconds of silence, Adrian peeked around the low wall and saw the third hunter behind a corner, doing the same. This one, at least, knew how to handle himself in a gunfight.

Adrian fired another round as cover—nine—and dashed out from behind the counter. He fired two more shots to keep the hunter from peeking out from around the corner—seven —then rounded it himself, catching the hunter by surprise. Six.

The house was quiet, but that didn't mean he was safe yet. Thea hadn't mentioned how many other hunters she was staying with. It was possible they were out of the house. That would be unfortunate, but he couldn't stay here for long.

Adrian slowly crept up the stairs to the second floor, gun

held high in case he needed to shoot. Halfway up the stair-case, he saw a man peek out from behind a door. Adrian jumped and pulled the trigger as the man ducked back behind the door, but the gun didn't fire. Empty. Adrian had assumed the gun had a full clip—it's not like he'd seen Garrick use it. He swore under his breath, discarded the gun, and drew his knife.

Adrian glanced up at the light fixtures at the top of the stairs and, with a slight wave of his hand, they flickered out. He silently crept toward the door, cracked open, that the hunter had darted behind. Inside the still-illuminated room, he heard two men whispering to each other, wondering if the lights going out was just a coincidence. Standing behind the doorframe, Adrian gently pushed the door open. He expected to hear gunshots, but none were fired. The door creaked slowly as he nudged it with little more than his fingertips, until it was open wide enough for him to peek in and spot the ceiling light. Finally, that light went out as well.

Now encased entirely in darkness, Adrian could move freely into the room. He spotted two men—one squatting by the bed, the other pressed against the back wall, clutching a heavy bookend. He dealt with the man by the bed first. The man didn't even notice Adrian approach until a hand clamped over his mouth and a knife slit his throat. The second man clearly heard something happen to his compan-ion, but couldn't shake his paralysis before Adrian drove the knife into his chest.

The lights flickered back on, revealing Adrian's bloody scene. Aside from the last dying gasps of the hunters, the house was uncomfortably silent. Adrian didn't know how many there had been in total, but if anyone was still here, he hoped they'd be smart enough to hide until he left.

Unfeeling, he searched every room. It didn't take long to locate each of the hunters' stashes of vampire-hunting tools. Crosses, stakes, rotting garlic. Adrian finally found what he was looking for in an ornate wooden box: an old six-shooter revolver, with half a dozen silver bullets lying nearby.

Adrian picked up the gun and inspected it. The revolver looked straight out of an old Western movie, except for the scuffs, the chipped wood on the grip, and a dent near the barrel. The cylinder held only one bullet. Uncertain, he rotated it so the bullet was in position and aimed at the hunter's body. Despite its worn appearance, the gun fired without issue.

Content, Adrian reloaded the cylinder to full. As he finished, he heard footsteps climbing the stairs just outside his room. He braced himself against the wall beside the door frame, gun raised. Then he reconsidered and switched to his knife. Silver bullets were precious, and he didn't want to waste them on a mortal hunter.

When the man stepped into the room, Adrian whirled his blade toward his chest, but it was caught before it could pierce the skin. And good thing, too, as Garrick pulled Adrian to his knees in front of him, the knife clattering to the ground. Hell, he'd even aimed for his heart.

"What are you doing?" Garrick shouted. For the first time, he was truly, passionately angry. "What the hell is this?"

Irritated, Adrian returned to his feet. "Fixing the damn problem," he grumbled.

"By committing mass murder?"

Adrian rolled his head, exaggerating the gesture to ensure Garrick understood his annoyance. "Yep. If it was good enough for Thea, then it was good enough for all of them."

Surprisingly, Garrick stepped forward and grabbed Adrian by the collar of his coat, pulling him close so he couldn't escape the full force of his fury.

"Have you learned nothing?" Garrick yelled. "This is exactly what you did in LA! And for what? You almost died! You can't keep lashing out like this! You understand that, right? We're here because of you!"

"No, we're not!" Adrian shouted back. "You could have helped me! You could have stood up to Joseph, but you were too much of a coward! What's the point of being six hundred years old if you don't act like it?"

Garrick's grip loosened, and Adrian took the opportunity to push himself away. His eyes narrowed in confusion—or was it disgust?

"Coward?" Garrick spat, clearly not expecting the insult.

Adrian slowly backed toward a window at the far end of the room. "Yeah," he said. "What did Joseph call you? All bark, no bite, Garrick. Unless it's with me, of course. You can push me around all you want, because what else am I supposed to do? Go work for Joseph? Buy my own apartment? I can't even go back to the streets anymore."

He opened the window and heard sirens in the distance, growing steadily louder.

"So here's what I'm going to do: I'm going to go kill a Regent, take his house, and then run this city. And if you try to stop me, I'll do the same to you."

Adrian's gut twisted in pain. He didn't know how Garrick would react, but he guessed it would be with fury. Instead, Garrick's posture softened, the corners of his mouth turned down, and his eyebrows lifted high. Adrian's words had actually hurt him.

Good, Adrian thought, though the sick feeling in his stomach disagreed. He climbed onto the window ledge.

"Wait!" Garrick called out in a panic. Adrian ignored him and hurled himself over the edge, landing hard two stories below. The impact was rough, but his body absorbed it without trouble. He hit the narrow alleyway between the packed houses, then sprang up to catch the top of a tall gate, locked for the night. Garrick's voice still echoed from above, but Adrian quickened his climb to escape.

No sooner had he hit the ground on the other side of the gate than the police arrived. Adrian cloaked himself in the darkness, just as he had done hundreds of times before, and the officers ran past, completely unaware that their criminal stood only a few feet away. It was too easy.

Adrian strode along the road in silence, heading away from the flashing red and blue lights of the police vehicles. A few windows flickered with light as he passed. Adrian didn't mind—what were they going to do? The shadows obscuring his figure warped around him, causing the streetlights overhead to blink and stutter.

He didn't have a direction in mind. Just away. Somewhere he could recuperate alone.

The telltale chirp of a bat dashed those plans. Adrian set his jaw and waited for Garrick to appear directly behind him.

"Wait," Garrick said again, more softly this time, raising a cautious hand. Adrian responded by drawing his gun.

"Don't make me call your bluff," Adrian seethed. He doubted a single bullet would kill him, even if it pierced his heart. But it would get the point across. "You can't talk your way out of this one. That won't work on me. I'm done! I'm done with you!"

Garrick held his hands up at his sides. That aching, pained look returned to his face, but he didn't interrupt or try to smooth things over.

"I've always just been a neck for you to feed on. And I took it because I needed you! I'd be dead on the streets right now if it weren't for you! I..." Adrian's arm shook as the words caught in his throat. When was the last time he told Garrick, "I love you," out loud?

"You're not just—"

"Don't," Adrian warned, holding the gun steady. "Don't lie to me anymore."

"I'm not lying," Garrick whispered.

"Yes, you are! You lied about Raymond! You lied about Val! You lied about loving me!"

Garrick's eyes drifted downward in shame, and his arms fell limp at his sides. "I never lied about loving you."

"Is that what you call always putting me second? Always saying yes to everyone else but no to me? Well, I don't have to put up with that anymore. I don't need you anymore. So give me a damn good reason not to shoot you right now!"

Just do it, Adrian thought. Don't give him time to weave together new honeyed words to placate him. No lies, no false promises. There was nothing Garrick could say that would make Adrian change his mind.

Slowly, Garrick walked forward until his chest touched the end of the muzzle, as if daring Adrian to shoot him.

"Okay," he said, his voice barely a whisper. "I'll help."

Adrian fumbled backward. He clenched his jaw, trying to keep his frustrated tears from spilling out. Of all the things Garrick could have said, Adrian was prepared to dismiss any of them as empty words. Except, maybe, "I'll help."

"No, you won't!" Adrian cried. "Why now?"

Garrick looked up with tired, weary eyes and opened his mouth to speak, but the shout of an officer cut him off.

"Freeze! Put the gun down!"

Right, shouting in the middle of the street, less than a block from the police, was a bad idea. Still staring Garrick in the eyes, Adrian slowly lowered his arm, knelt to the ground, and delicately placed the revolver on the pavement. Raising his hands beside his head, he stood once again. Garrick slowly raised his arms, too.

Zero rounds. No gunshot wounds. Standing in the middle of the street with no cover, facing an unknown number of police. Was it harder than going toe-to-toe against an Elder? Hard to say. He'd have to find out, or die trying.

Just let the officer get close, and then he'd jump on his neck. Re-summon his shadows, get low...

Garrick stared at him with the same blank expression that had met him outside Thea's hotel room, the one that had threatened him the night Adrian discovered he was a vampire. And Adrian just stared back.

Then, every light as far as Adrian could see extinguished, drowning the city block in darkness, broken only by the thin sliver of light offered by the crescent moon. The world faded into the dark grayscale of Adrian's night vision, pierced by two red eyes glowing with hellfire. The officers shouted in panic, and over Garrick's shoulder, Adrian saw several fumbling with flashlights just as dead as the streetlamps.

Those red eyes darted to his right, and Garrick turned. Ink-black clouds that even Adrian's night vision couldn't pierce swirled up from beneath Garrick's feet, forming a tendriled cloak around his figure. The officers—who shouldn't have been able to see in this darkness—stumbled back, screaming in terror at the eerie apparition. One fired her gun, the shot going wide as Garrick calmly advanced toward the group.

First, he seized the nearest officer, the one who had first pointed his gun at them, and twisted his head to the side, sinking his teeth into the man's neck. The next closest officer, the trigger-happy one, aimed her weapon a little too close to Garrick. He lashed out, first striking her wrist and knocking the gun from her hand, then slashing at her neck. She collapsed to the ground with a groan. A third officer tried to flee but managed only three steps before stumbling. A writhing shadow snaked out, grabbed his leg, and dragged him back toward the police car, where he eventually stopped struggling. A fourth officer simply cowered on the ground, and met Garrick's fangs with little resistance.

When all the police were subdued, the lights flickered back to life, revealing the swift carnage but none of the shadows that had caused it. The female officer groaned from the pavement, and for a long moment, Garrick simply looked down at her, watching her weakly kick her legs. He checked his watch, waited for what felt like an eternity, and then, only once she was still, placed a palm over her neck.

A tremor ran through Adrian's legs. He took a small step back, torn between the urge to flee and the paralysis of fear. Garrick walked toward him, eyes locked on his like a wolf's, and Adrian knew that running was no longer an option.

He stopped within arm's reach and held up his hand, gripping Adrian's knife. "You dropped this," he said, rotating it so the handle faced Adrian. After a moment's hesitation, Adrian took the knife with shaking hands and slipped it back into his empty pocket.

"Are... are they...?"

"No, not dead," Garrick answered with an uncomfortably flat affect. "That'd be too easy. Besides, the police hold grudges for generations. Better to give them a ghost story they can't explain than martyrs."

After Adrian failed to come up with a response, Garrick continued, "As I was saying, you want to kill an Elder. You're going to want my help."

"But..." Help? Now? After everything he went through, all the fights, now he wanted to help?

With a long, drawn-out sigh, Garrick's weariness returned. He dropped his shoulders and eyelids. "I'm sorry," he whispered. "I know I've been stubborn and pushed you... but I swear, you're the most important person in my life. Please..." His arm lifted but stopped short of reaching out to him. Instead, he simply turned his palm upward, inviting Adrian's hand into his. "Have me back?"

It had to be a trap, Adrian thought. He stared at Garrick's outstretched hand, arms trembling and eyes brimming with tears, desperate to take it in his own. After all these years of begging for support, now it was finally offered? Now that he was ready to burn the world down?

"No," he protested. "You're just saying what I want to hear again. What's the catch?"

The corner of Garrick's mouth lifted into a crooked half-smile. "Smart man," he muttered. "No catch. You want to raise Hell? I'll help."

Adrian knew that if he were smart, he'd turn around and run as fast as he could. Instead, he lurched forward, grabbing Garrick around the shoulders and holding him tightly. He buried his face in the crook between neck and shoulder and wept, releasing all the pent-up tension and anger in ugly sobs muffled against Garrick's collar. Garrick responded with a soft stroke along his hairline, and another down his side.

Adrian couldn't let him go. He wanted his freedom. He wanted his love. He wanted it all.

"I love you," Garrick whispered into his ear. "Let's go kill a Regent."

32
NIGHT 8 - ADRIAN

Adrian woke in Garrick's bed. They hadn't done anything. Adrian was far too exhausted for that. He had shed his blood-soaked shirt but fell asleep on his stomach with everything else still on, even his shoes. Garrick, at least, had the good sense to get comfortable beneath the bedsheets.

Garrick lay on his back, eyes still closed. After their fight the previous night, Adrian thought he looked at peace, though that could have been the unnatural stillness of vampire sleep. The dead never rested in frustration or anger.

His eye winked open beneath a lifted eyebrow. He looked

over at Adrian without turning his head, then closed it again, this time with a small smile on his lips. Oops, caught staring.

Adrian flipped onto his back and inched closer. "Morning," he said.

"Evening," Garrick corrected. Adrian knew what time it was, but morning, to him, was whenever he woke up. That hadn't changed in the forty years he'd been a vampire. Back when he and Garrick regularly shared the same bed, that had been their way of greeting each other. Morning. Evening.

"Did yesterday really happen?" Adrian asked.

"If not, then I had the craziest dream that you were in."

Adrian picked up Garrick's hand and laced their fingers together. With his pinky, he traced the ring on Garrick's finger. For a brief moment, everything felt all right. Garrick loved him. He had promised to help Adrian on his crazy suicide mission. It all seemed too good to be real. In the heat of the moment, all Adrian had needed was Garrick's reassurance. But now, he needed more.

"We need to talk."

Garrick sighed deeply, then turned to lie on his side facing Adrian, his arm braced beneath the pillow to support his head. Adrian mirrored the motion but kept his arms crossed in front of him. God, where to start?

"When you talked to Joseph, you didn't confront him about killing Raymond. You just told him not to kill in front of others. Why?"

Garrick looked away, and Adrian could see the wheels turning in his head once again. He almost snapped at him to cut it out but held back, allowing Garrick one last chance to be honest. He deserved that much, at least.

"Let's back up and address the bigger secret I've been keeping from you," Garrick said.

Adrian frowned. He could recall multiple times he'd caught Garrick in a lie, but none stood out as more significant than the others. Unless, of course, it was the lie about Garrick loving him. If Garrick truly intended to keep his promise, then Adrian no longer believed in those doubts.

"You're aging too fast. Healing wounds isn't something you learn at forty. Most pick it up around eighty."

What? Aging too fast, was that possible?

"That shadow trick you love doing so much? You learned it at twenty, but most can't manage it until forty. I thought maybe you had some innate magical talent that gave you a head start, but you've been aging at twice the normal rate."

"But... what does that mean?"

"If it were just about magical powers, then this would be cause for celebration. But aging faster also means less time before you become an Elder."

It took Adrian a moment to absorb what Garrick had said. An Elder—the point at which Adrian would go mad, and Garrick would have to put him down like a rabid dog. Theoretically.

"But... no. What?"

Vampires became Elders two hundred years after they were turned. If Adrian was aging at twice the normal rate, that meant he'd only live to be one hundred. His life was almost halfway over.

"Why?"

Garrick shrugged. "Everyone's different. Two hundred years is just an approximation. Some are early, some are late."

"By one hundred years?" The wheels in Adrian's head began spinning rapidly. How could that be possible? "No... there's got to be some way to slow it, right? Should I stop using magic?"

Garrick took Adrian's hand and held it gently. "I'm sorry," he said.

This whole time, the secret Garrick kept from him was Adrian's own death. He always knew it would come eventually, but this soon?

He still had sixty years left. Perhaps it was best they had

this conversation now, rather than in forty years. One hundred years was still at the upper end of a normal mortal lifespan. Had he never learned of vampires, he would have been ecstatic to know his fate was to live so long. And with someone he loved, and a roof securely over his head? Could he really ask for more?

Yes, he could ask to live as an Elder, like Garrick, Joseph, Owen, and Linh. But that was a difficult conversation, and his heart had already been shattered enough times in the past two days. It could wait.

Sensing that Adrian's emotions had calmed, Garrick continued. "So, to answer your earlier question: Raymond was only one hundred and forty years old, but he was already showing signs of becoming an Elder. It's not an easy conversation to have."

Had Raymond been showing signs? Adrian hadn't known him very well, nor did he even know what to look for. Raymond hadn't seemed like he was going mad. But if it was true, that would explain why Garrick hadn't been upset with Joseph for the murder, except for the method.

"But still, you couldn't have just told me?" Adrian asked.

"I..." Garrick paused, thinking over his answer. "I know you think I have a reputation for being well-spoken, but that doesn't mean I like to speak freely. Raymond was accelerated in age. Not as much as you, but still a far cry from two hundred. That would invite questions. Questions that I..."

Another pause. Adrian held his tongue, forcing himself to be patient.

"I know I should have told you sooner, but I was afraid. Six hundred years of watching my loved ones die or go mad. You'd think it would get easier with time. But it only makes the anticipation worse.

"And to address an earlier accusation—it doesn't excuse what I did, but... that's why I sought Val out. I first noticed ten years ago, and I panicked. Being with you, it was impossible not to worry."

He squeezed Adrian's hand a little tighter. "I know I've already apologized a lot for that, but... I'm still sorry."

That was an old wound, one that hadn't healed as much as Adrian initially believed. So it was easier to lie to him and seek comfort in Val's embrace than to simply talk to him? But what else was there to do than to gracefully accept, or turn him away? Worse, as a hypocrite.

"I'm sorry for cheating on you." Adrian wanted to say more, but he couldn't think of anything that didn't sound like a deflecting excuse. He had been so sure Garrick's love was a farce, and that made it feel okay. But read the situation all wrong.

"Thank you," Garrick said with a smile. "It'll take time before I fully forgive you, but... I'll get started on it right away."

Painfully honest. And it was a relief.

Adrian turned his attention to Garrick's chest. Next question.

"How did you really get that scar?" he asked. "Did you have a heart transplant?"

"Technically, I didn't lie. I did get into a fight with another Elder. Though, I suppose I omitted the part where he cut me open and tried to take my heart." Still gripping Adrian's fingers in his, Garrick pulled their hands closer and traced the scar. "I know a thing or two about heart transplants. Too much. It's not a part of my life I'm proud of."

Suddenly, everything snapped into place. Garrick—the leech doctor, the physician, the surgeon. No wonder Owen had accepted another, more powerful Elder into his city. He wanted to learn from him.

Adrian slowly brushed his thumb against the back of Garrick's hand. It was only sundown, and he was already exhausted. If only he could spend the night resting in his arms, forgetting everything that had happened, and was still happening.

"Are you really going to do this?" he asked. "You were so against betraying Owen before."

"I've been the man you want me to be," Garrick said. "I don't like it. I'll do it, but I've been down this path before. It's never as clean as you expect."

"Why not?"

"It's so easy to look at the people above you and think, 'This is so simple. Why doesn't Garrick just do this one little thing that would make all my worries go away?' Then you get into that position and realize there are twelve different problems with your simple solution. Meanwhile, you now have dozens of people below you asking why you're not doing their simple solution. You must be too stupid or too evil to do it."

The spite in Garrick's voice sent a chill down Adrian's spine. It was the spite of centuries of accumulated experience, the likes of which Adrian couldn't begin to imagine.

"If we do this, you're in charge. You're the one who makes the hard decisions."

Adrian stared down Garrick and nodded. "Wouldn't have it any other way."

Garrick smiled at that. Deep down, he approved. Despite how hard he had tried to steer Adrian away from that path, he was proud of him. Adrian smiled back.

But one last thing still nagged at him.

"Do you really not have Madness?"

The smile faded from Garrick's face. He waited a moment, not with a look that searched for the right words, but one that braced for the answer.

"All Elders have Madness. Even me."

Adrian's heart sank. The last drop of hope that he might be an exception like Garrick was dashed. It had been unlikely before. Now it was impossible.

"What's your Madness?"

"Something subtle. Something I can suppress well enough for the lie to work. If we do this, you'll see it."

"Why did you lie about it?"

"I didn't think you'd love me if you knew."

Adrian frowned. What could possibly be so bad that it would cause him to fall out of love with him, yet still be something he could hide? His first thought was the lying, but Garrick seemed so refreshingly honest now, staring into his eyes like he did when they first fell in love.

"Bet," Adrian said. "We'll see about that."

Garrick smiled again. He reached over, drew Adrian's head close, kissed him on the forehead, then nuzzled him against his shoulder.

And then, as tenderly as the moment had begun, it ended. Garrick sat up and swung his legs over the side of the bed.

"We should get up," Garrick said as he pushed himself up. "Your girlfriend will be awake any minute now."

"She's not my girlfriend," Adrian mumbled, following Garrick off the bed.

"No? It seemed like you two got along well."

Garrick pulled a clean shirt out of the dresser and held another one out for Adrian, since his clothes were in another room.

"I told you, I was just…" Adrian paused to reconsider his feelings. It was difficult to think back to two nights ago during his tryst with Thea, like revisiting those moments would be cheating on Garrick all over again. But he knew the feelings had been sincere, at least at the time. He had greedily indulged them in some vain hope that, when the dust settled, he'd still have her love to salve the pain. It wasn't fair to her, or to anyone caught up in Adrian's failed plan.

"I'm sorry," he said again. It wasn't directed specifically at Garrick, but the crushing guilt on his shoulders needed acknowledgment. Maybe then the weight would start to lift.

"Do you love her?"

Adrian tried to identify the tone in Garrick's question. At first he flinched, as if being accused, but after replaying it in his mind, he realized there was a layer of curiosity instead.

"Maybe," he admitted. "But I killed her. Can you still love someone after that?"

Garrick didn't respond. His gaze dropped, distant again, and Adrian wondered if he'd stirred a memory within him. At six hundred years old, Adrian wasn't his first.

"Not that it matters," he said quickly. "She'll hate me as soon as she wakes up."

They moved into Adrian's room. Lying flat on his bed was Thea—eyes closed, skin pale, her chest still. Adrian pulled up a chair and sat by her bedside, while Garrick took a seat on the other side of the room.

"I have to admit," Garrick said, "this isn't what I intended when I told you to fix the problem."

Adrian stared forlornly at Thea's face. "She won't be a problem anymore if she can't hunt during the day."

Within a few minutes, Thea's eyes shot open, and she sat up straight, as if waking from a bad dream.

"What? Where?"

Adrian held out his arm, sleeve pulled up above the elbow, and Thea latched onto it like a starving wolf. It took only a few seconds for her to snap out of her instinctual hunger and shoot Adrian the dirtiest, ice-cold stare he'd ever had to endure. He looked away in shame.

Thea pulled her teeth from his arm and ran a finger over two newly elongated canines.

"What?" Her voice wavered. "How... you!"

Adrian went over his cover stories. He had thought plenty about them the previous night. He could lie. Say Owen shot her and the rest of the hunters, and Adrian heroically saved her the only way he could. That would work for about ten seconds, until Thea talked to her sister. He still had no idea what Melissa knew. It was possible she didn't know anything, but Adrian didn't think that was likely.

He could confess everything. Tell her about the plot to use the hunters to take out Owen and his followers. That would ensure Thea hated him, but telling the truth might help smooth things over. Not by much, but an honest would-be murderer was better than a dishonest one.

"Um..." Adrian was stuck. If only he could figure out what Thea knew first.

"Start talking!" Thea commanded. "What did you do to me?"

"Made you a vampire." Well, that was an easy enough question to answer. "You... were shot."

"What?" So she didn't remember that part. Adrian figured the shock of it might be affecting her memory. "By who...?"

Thea slowly furrowed her brow as she stared at him. She knew.

"Adrian," she growled. "Tell me. Everything."

"How much did Melissa tell you?"

Thea's confrontational stare dropped instantly. "No..." she whispered. "She was telling the truth?"

Those words ripped his heart out. He hadn't considered the possibility that Thea trusted him enough to doubt her sister. Not that it would have mattered, the truth would have come out anyway. At this point, it was better to be wholly honest, no matter how much it hurt.

"I needed to kill Owen. There's a good chance he's Striga, and even if he isn't, he's a narcissistic bastard..." Adrian stopped and sighed. He was procrastinating the real point. "Elder vampires are difficult to kill, but even Elders are vulnerable during the day. I thought if I led the hunters to his house, they'd take care of it. And... yes, I knew Melissa slept there too."

Thea's jaw trembled, hanging partly open. The sense of betrayal spilling from her face was too much for Adrian to confront, and his guilt kept him from giving her the attention she deserved. And damn it, he wasn't even finished.

"Why didn't you just ask me to help? Wait, how did you even know where to find us?"

"I did," Adrian answered, his hand hovering over his pocket as he instinctively reached for his phone. "Remember? I asked if you were willing to kill Owen. You said no. And I couldn't risk you telling Melissa. As for the other question…"

Adrian decided to just show her. He pulled out his phone and brought up the location tracker. "Remember when you handed me your phone at karaoke?"

Staring at his screen in growing horror, Thea slowly pushed herself off the bed, opposite the side where Adrian sat. "You… you were just using me the whole time."

No, he wasn't. Adrian felt something genuine for her. He had been fully prepared to do anything after the fallout of Owen's death, whether that meant embracing her as a vampire or letting her go to live out her life as a mortal. But no, that wasn't the full picture either. He had genuine feelings and still used her. He chanced a sideways glance at Garrick, who sat at the end of the room, chin resting in his palm as he silently watched the confrontation unfold.

He could keep his feelings to himself. Thea didn't need excuses, and Garrick didn't need his infidelity.

"Yeah," Adrian confirmed, and left everything else unsaid.

Thea stared at the floor, shoulders tense, fists clenched, eyes brimming with tears of anger. Silently, she grabbed her belongings from the foot of the bed and walked toward the door. She didn't look at him as she left, and Adrian made no attempt to stop her. The room fell silent in her absence.

Adrian collapsed onto the bed face-down. He groaned into the mattress, then turned his head to face the back wall. Garrick sat there patiently, in the same position as before.

"I feel like shit," Adrian said.

276

"That's how it is sometimes," he replied. "Not to interrupt your wallowing, but what are our next steps?"

"I don't know," Adrian complained. "I know I made a big show of it last night, but I have no idea what I'm doing."

"If you'll allow me to make a suggestion, we should find a new place to stay in the short term. This hotel isn't safe for us anymore."

"That's a good idea." Adrian got up from the bed. Strategizing his next steps might help take his mind off how morally ugly he felt in the moment. "I'll let you decide where the safest place for us to stay is. I need to make a call."

Garrick nodded and retreated into his room. Adrian picked up his phone and dialed Val's number. He still hadn't heard back from her. Given everything that had happened, he feared the worst. His stomach dropped as the call rang four times and went to voicemail again. Val's pre-recorded message played, instructing him to leave a message. Adrian had the grim realization that this might be the last time he'd hear her voice.

"Hey," he said, the single word trailing off as he tried to figure out what he wanted to say. "I just... I just need to know you're okay. I don't know what happened, and... Garrick and I made up, actually. Things between us are better than they've been in a long time. Just... give me a sign you're okay."

Adrian stood up to pace around his room and pack the few articles of clothing strewn across the floor, but he sat back down before making it halfway. In two days, he'd lost two of the three people he loved, and it was only by the grace of God that he hadn't lost the third. All for what? To destroy the goodwill of even more people around him?

He waited for Val to reply, but she never did. Disheartened, he stood and gathered his belongings. A few minutes later, Adrian emerged from his room with his pack slung over his shoulder, joining Garrick, who had his own bag in tow.

"Should we pack Val's things?" Garrick asked.

Adrian shook his head. "She can come pick it up once we're out of here," he said. He realized his answer assumed she was still alive, but what would they take? They'd already left behind everything but the essentials, and he didn't need her clothes as a memento.

The two walked outside to a thirty-year-old sedan parked in a nearby space. Adrian remembered when Garrick had bought the damn thing. Their lifestyle didn't require much driving, so it hadn't accumulated too many miles for its age, but thirty years was still pushing the poor car's limits. Adrian worried the drive from Los Angeles to San Francisco might be the vehicle's last.

They entered the car with Garrick in the driver's seat. Adrian took one last look at the old hotel. Moving once again, though he felt no attachment to the place this time. The car felt more like home than the building ever had, and Adrian desperately wanted to be rid of it, too.

"Can I get a motorcycle?" Adrian asked.

Garrick slotted the key into the ignition but looked up at Adrian in disgust before turning it.

"What? No, they're far too dangerous."

"For us?"

"Being a vampire doesn't spare you from having your brain matter smeared across the road."

"I promise I'll wear a helmet," Adrian protested.

Garrick looked Adrian in the eyes and sighed. "Fine, but only after you get your license. In fact, it's probably a good idea for you to learn how to navigate the process of getting your own government documents forged."

Adrian beamed. He really did enjoy Thea's motorcycle.

He didn't ask where Garrick was going. Adrian wasn't sure if one type of hotel was any safer than another, or if the opposite side of town was better than a place just four blocks away. They drove in quiet contemplation for over half an hour.

Garrick pulled up to a small, shabby motel on the outskirts of the city. They parked near the front, and Adrian accompanied him into the main lobby. Garrick began to pay for a room but paused, glancing at Adrian for guidance. Adrian held up a single finger.

"One room for the night," Garrick said. "Not sure how long we'll be staying, so we'll pay nightly, if that's all right."

The two received their keys and returned to the car for their belongings, then entered their room. Adrian first noticed the two twin beds. He deflated a little, but he told himself it was for the best. His relationship with Garrick was still rocky, and he didn't need it to be tumultuous. Still, what a shame it would have been if there had only been one bed.

Garrick walked to the window and examined the thin cellular shades.

"Is that going to be enough?" Adrian asked. Throughout his entire vampiric life, he had only ever lived in residences with full blackout blinds.

"Potentially," Garrick said, "but I'd rather play it safe."

Adrian looked around to see if there was some way to block out the window—something to hang a blanket on, perhaps—but nothing obvious existed in the room. He then considered curling up under the covers, but the twin-sized bed didn't offer much space. There was no room beneath the bed either.

As Adrian contemplated their predicament, Garrick grabbed a pillow and the bedcover and walked into the bathroom. Amused, Adrian followed and found Garrick setting up a nest of pillows and blankets in the shower. The bathroom was windowless, so there was no danger of sun exposure. Still, it appeared to be a rather uncomfortable solution. Adrian crossed his arms and leaned against the doorframe.

The shower was lined with stone tile on two walls and glass on the others. It was just long enough for Garrick to lie flat, though with a slight bend in his knees. At least it wasn't fully enclosed, as the bathroom already felt suffocatingly small.

"There," he said. "Don't give me that look. Compared to a wooden coffin, this is far more luxurious."

Adrian raised an eyebrow. Had he really slept in a coffin before?

"This is certainly one solution."

"You're free to come up with your own. Sitting upright in the closet might be more comfortable."

"No." He'd do it if he absolutely had to, but a pillow nest in the shower still sounded like a far better option than the tight space of a closet. He changed the subject. "I'm hungry. You?"

Garrick got out of the shower. The two walked out of the room and onto the street. The motel sat on a lonely stretch of road, flanked only by a gas station and shuttered businesses with iron bars over the windows and doors. The streets were understandably empty of pedestrians, a far cry from the bustling city blocks near Owen's hotel.

"What do you think?" Adrian asked. "I mean, there's no one around to interrupt us if we do find someone out here. I guess we could stake out the gas station…"

"Hm…" Garrick scanned the darkness. "This way," he said, and began walking toward the gas station. Adrian followed. As they approached, Adrian saw two men walking toward them on the sidewalk. Probably not worth it. He wasn't sure he could scare off a full-grown man by shouting, "Boo!"

The two men stopped short. Their sudden reaction startled Adrian, but then he noticed a ribbon of shadow covering both their eyes and ears. Adrian glanced at Garrick, who smiled back at him smugly.

"There we go, that didn't take too long." He walked up to the men, still as statues, and patted one on the shoulder. "Drink up."

Adrian cautiously approached one of the two men and leaned in for a bite. The man didn't move, didn't even grow weak as Adrian drank. Adrian stopped himself before he was fully satiated and moved on to the second man. Between the two of them, he felt full enough to keep both himself and Garrick going for another day. And he still had plenty of time to hunt later, if need be.

Adrian freed himself and joined Garrick behind the two men. Suddenly, the men sprang to life again, stumbling slightly and looking around in confusion. They turned toward the two vampires but looked past them, and then continued on their way.

"What... how?"

"The irony of getting old is that by the time you've gained enough power and experience to do something with ease, it's too late to use it for yourself."

Adrian frowned. "Me. I still need to hunt. Couldn't you have joined me and helped out?"

Garrick recoiled. "Well, you needed to learn to be self-sufficient." Adrian could tell that Garrick knew it was just an excuse.

Adrian calmed himself. Garrick liked to subtly flaunt his power, but the emphasis was on "subtle." If he had to guess, Garrick had his reasons for keeping his abilities hidden in the past. Getting angry wouldn't make him any more likely to show off in the future.

"Well, that was very cool. Could you teach me to do that?"

"Ah, hypnotism is quite advanced. Most people don't begin to learn it until they're around one hundred and fifty years old. So even though you're advanced, that's still... what, thirty years? Now, if you want to know how to still your venom so you don't knock out your victim, that's actually quite simple. It's just that most vampires don't have any use for it, since you don't want your victim squirming and screaming."

Garrick's confident demeanor returned, and Adrian sighed in relief.

"I've been practicing healing. I can stop an open cut fairly quickly now."

"Good. Maybe you can work up to larger cuts. Under my supervision, of course."

Adrian gazed up at the pitch-black sky. He was far enough from the center of the city to see one star. One single star shining through.

"Now what?" Garrick asked. "Do you still plan to over-throw Owen?"

Adrian steeled himself, tightening his fists in his pockets to tap into that anger once again. With Garrick finally behind him, it was all too easy to lose his drive, to slip back into old habits.

"Yeah," he said. Val was still missing. Either she needed his help, or she was dead, and Adrian wasn't above taking revenge.

"Then, can I suggest we think about this strategically instead of charging in guns blazing again?"

"...Sure." His raid on the hunters the previous night was fueled by desperation and anger, and now that he had the clarity of hindsight, it was really quite stupid. Poor Garrick had been right to worry about him.

"Any suggestions?" Adrian asked.

"Not without more information," Garrick said. "Sounds like a lot has changed in a short time. You killed the hunters, and the police have likely taken any other silver weapons into custody. So we're on our own as far as committing war against another Elder. I know my powers are impressive, but they're no..." Garrick sighed, "silver bullet, as they say. I need a drink."

Adrian tilted his head, exposing his neck. Garrick studied him a moment, making sure he understood Adrian's inten-tions correctly.

"You sure? I can just take a moment on your arm…"

"Come on, Dracula," Adrian teased. "Get personal."

Garrick shook his head in exasperation, then leaned into Adrian's neck. Adrian hugged his shoulders and waited impatiently for Garrick to finish. Finally, Garrick pulled his head away, but he lingered in Adrian's embrace, letting his forehead brush against Adrian's hair. Adrian rested his gaze into Garrick's blue eyes.

"We should get married," he said.

"Excuse me?"

"It's legal now."

Garrick snorted. "None of my marriages were ever blessed by God or government. Didn't take you for the marrying type."

"Why not?"

"You never mentioned it."

"Was marriage different back in the Dark Ages? You're supposed to ask me with a ring."

"Yes, actually." Garrick smiled and leaned in close, not quite kissing him, but teasing their lips. "Your parents are supposed to offer me a dowry, and I'm a very expensive man. I won't consider marriage for anything less than three cattle."

Adrian's mouth pulled into a smile, and Garrick lightly nipped his lower lip, trying to kiss him through his laughter. Adrian relaxed, his breath stilled beneath Garrick's touch. He had missed him, his tender moments, so much.

When Garrick finally broke away, he lifted his right hand and pulled the ring off his finger. He handed it to Adrian, brushing it against his shoulder.

"Wait, this is yours," Adrian protested.

"So keep it safe until I get you a proper one, all right?"

Gently, Adrian slid the ring onto his own left hand. It was a little loose, but not so much that it threatened to slip off. The ring comment had been a joke, but now, seeing it on his hand… Adrian leaned into Garrick's chest, holding him possessively, running his thumb over the rim of the metal band. Garrick was his. His savior, his world, his love. And now, with the ring as a reminder, he knew the reverse was true too.

But Adrian couldn't shake the question that would put everything into perspective, his lifeline amidst the confusion. Just what had happened two nights ago?

33

NIGHT 6 - VAL

I'm turning my phone off now.

Val snickered at her teasing. It was too easy with Adrian. He had the easier part of the plan, so she was happy to get a few laughs at his expense.

How do you get a group of vampire hunters to attack a specific place at dawn? Witchcraft, of course. However, not knowing who the hunters actually were made casting the required spell a bit difficult. But if she could break into their house, she could anchor the spell there and affect anyone who resided within.

She could also leave a fake note from "Striga" if that failed.

The heart within her chest pinched and ached terribly, but as far as Val could tell, she had come out of the procedure feeling more powerful than before. She spent her morning practicing the spells Adrian knew, like warping shadows and healing wounds. It would take practice, but she felt an energy coursing through her that she hadn't noticed before, an energy that flowed directly into her magic.

The location Adrian sent her to led to a two-story house in an area that was almost suburban, if only the houses had more space between them. Each had a small, almost laugh-ably sized front yard, with an arm's-width alley on either side and around the back. A wooden gate, about her height, blocked access to the rear of the houses.

No lights shone through the windows, which meant the hunters were likely out, searching the streets for vampires to shoot. That was good. Val was prepared for danger, but only if it became necessary.

Val walked up to the front door and turned the handle. It was unlocked, and she breathed a sigh of relief. She had cast a spell to ensure one of the hunters left the door open, and it seemed to have worked. Good news for her witchcraft, too. Though she wasn't trying to compare, part of her couldn't help but wonder if this meant she was more powerful than Adrian—making her the third-most powerful vampire in the city, behind Garrick and Owen. She had brought Adrian's lock picks just in case, but she hadn't had much time to prac-tice. Thankfully, she didn't need them.

The inside of the house was dark, with no sign that anyone had noticed her entrance. Good, but she still had to keep her eyes and ears open, just in case.

Val stalked into the living room and dropped her bag on the large sofa. She rummaged through it for paint, candles, anything she could lift from the craft store to set the scene.

Just as she grabbed a can of spray paint and started to shake it, she heard a sound. A footstep? Val waited through several long, silent seconds for any other movement. Nothing. Just the old house creaking. She was being paranoid.

And that was her last thought before a sharp blow to the side of her head sent everything into darkness.

———

When Val came to, she was slung over the shoulder of someone much bigger than herself. She faced down at the pavement, her arms dangling, wrists tied. She couldn't tell whether her captor was spinning or if it just felt that way.

After a minute spent clearing her head, a voice spoke beside her.

"She's awake. Should we knock her out again?"

"Nah, not unless she starts causing trouble."

The voices were familiar, but before she could identify her captors, her attention was drawn to the cloth gag shoved into her mouth. Val moved her jaw in an effort to push it out, but, as expected, it was bound tightly. Her wrists and ankles stung with each bounce on the man's shoulder as he walked.

"Should we leave her out back?"

"Just dump her once we're inside. I don't want her escaping."

The fog clouding her mind finally lifted, and she recognized the voices as belonging to Seth, Devin, and Nora. How had she ended up with them? Had they come to her rescue? But how would they have known? And being tied up and slung over Devin's shoulder—this was clearly not a rescue. She craned her head to see Seth standing by the back door of the mansion, watching through the glass pane. His gaze flicked back to Val, and he gave a sinister smile. He pursed his lips to silently hush her, but instead of bringing a finger to his mouth, he completed the motion with the barrel of a gun.

Seconds later, Sophia opened the door. She saw Val and looked visibly confused but didn't ask any questions. Seth pressed a second gun into her hands and darted inside. Devin followed, and then Val suddenly found herself hitting the floor, slamming her head and shoulder onto the cold tile. She let out a pained whimper, waiting for her wits to return before assessing the situation.

When her eyes refocused, she saw that her wrists weren't merely bound by nylon rope. Barbed wire wrapped around them as well, cutting into her skin. But the wire looked brighter than usual. Silver. It was made of silver. That explained the burning, beyond the usual pain of the cuts. Val tried to wiggle her wrists free but found her arm strength lacking.

Two gunshots rang out from the sitting room. Val listened, trying to get a sense of what was happening, but the commotion was too frenzied to make sense of. Despite the pain, she rolled onto her elbows and knees and tried to push herself upright, but between the head injury and the silver barbed wire wrapped around her ankles, she collapsed to the floor again. Instead, she crawled, inching forward like a worm, toward the sitting room.

Melissa sat crumpled on the floor, clutching two bleeding wounds in her stomach. Nora quickly bound her wrists with rope and wire, just like she had with Val. Seth and Sophia scanned the room's entrances, likely searching for the man of the house.

"Owen!" Seth called out. Then, to Val's amazement, he vanished. She thought she saw a small animal scurry away from the spot where he had stood just a moment before.

It didn't take long for Owen to burst into the room, gun in hand, firing haphazardly in their direction. Val flinched at the sound. Devin returned fire, shielding his head with one arm, while Nora and Sophia ducked for cover.

And then, as if out of nowhere, Seth reappeared, shoving a

large device into Owen's side. It snapped and sank metal teeth into the Regent, releasing a sickening spray of blood. Owen stumbled and collapsed to the floor. Seth froze in horror, while Devin ran up, kicked the gun out of Owen's grip, and surveyed the damage with admiration.

A bear trap. Though the device was covered in dark red blood, Val imagined it, too, was coated in silver. Whether that was even necessary, she wasn't sure. Even as Owen lay on the floor, the powerful force of the trap continued to snap his ribs. Owen wasn't dead. He flailed, weakly, but Val wasn't sure that was a kindness anymore.

"Fuck me," Nora whispered, peering out from behind the sofa.

"These hunters don't fuck around," Seth muttered. He wiped the blood splatter from where it was heaviest on his face and arms, but nothing short of a shower was necessary to completely remove it. He walked to the other side of the room, picked up his gun, then collapsed onto the sofa and rubbed his eyes.

"Should we tie him up?" Nora asked.

"Better safe than sorry."

Nora bound Owen's wrists with the barbed wire as well, though Val didn't think it was necessary. Melissa sat nearby, scowling, while Sophia walked over to speak with Seth.

Val wasn't sure whether she should reveal herself or try to quietly slip out of the sitting room and, hopefully, out the door. She doubted she could get far in her current state. As silently as possible, Val shifted her tied hands toward her pocket and delicately pulled out her phone. Having her hands bound in front gave her just enough dexterity to unlock the screen and type a quick message to her first contact: Adrian.

Help.

Unfortunately, she wasn't able to type any more before Seth snatched the phone out of her hands. He glanced at the screen and scowled, then shoved it into his own pocket. Catching Devin's attention, he gestured toward Val. "Behind the back, will you?" Seth clapped his wrists together behind him to mime the position. "Sit her down and take the gag off. Then watch the door for any rescue attempts. Shoot first, ask questions later."

Devin picked Val up off the floor and set her in a chair opposite the couch. He cut the silver wires from her wrists before wrestling her arms behind her back and twisting new ones into place. Then, as instructed, he removed the gag. Seth leaned back, arms resting on the back of the sofa, his face smeared with Owen's still-wet blood.

"So," he said, "which of us wants to ask, 'What the hell are you doing here?' first?"

Val looked over her shoulder at Owen, crumpled on the floor. "I think I know what you're doing here," she said. "And technically, you brought me here."

Seth rolled his eyes. "What were you doing at the hunters' house?" he asked.

"What were you doing there?"

"Okay." Seth leaned forward and pointed the gun at her. "I just saw what happens when you snap a bear trap around a man's ribs. I'm not going to be fazed by whatever the hell this does to you."

Val stared down the barrel of the gun, frozen in fear. It was clear now that whatever friendship they once had was gone.

"I wanted to kill Owen," Val answered slowly, choosing each word carefully to avoid provoking Seth into firing the gun. "Like you."

"How did you know where the hunters were staying?"

Val carefully reviewed the answer in her head, trying to determine what information was safe to share and what might put her in even more danger.

"Adrian met one." Melissa could vouch for that information being true. "Became friends."

Seth's reaction was a surprise. She had expected anger or disgust at the revelation that a fellow vampire had been associating with a hunter. Instead, he appeared confused. Before Val could figure out why, Melissa growled from the corner of the room.

"What did you do to them? The hunters?"

Seth raised an eyebrow at the intrusion, then pointed to Sophia. "Sit her up here," he commanded.

Sophia pulled a chair next to Val and dragged Melissa onto it. Her side was red with blood, but the wounds seemed to have stopped weeping.

"Why do you care?" Seth asked.

Melissa bit her lip, and Val could see her making the same mental calculations she had thought through just a moment ago. Val knew why Melissa cared but gave her the courtesy of revealing that information on her own.

"My sister is one of them," she said, choosing honesty. She quickly added, "She went looking for me after I disappeared. She only joined the hunters to find me and isn't a threat. I tried to send her away, but she insisted on staying."

Seth's eyebrows slowly furrowed. He looked Melissa up and down. "Wait," he said, "Thea's your sister?"

Val frowned. Had they mentioned Thea's name to Seth before?

Seth leaned back, his eyes darting around as he thought. Something about the situation had set the gears in his head turning, and Val was desperate for him to share. He looked at Melissa, then at Val, then back at Melissa.

"So, at some point, your sister, Thea, met Adrian, and they became friends. Adrian got the location of the house from Thea and then shared that information with you." He pointed at Val. After a pause, he pulled Val's phone out of his pocket again. He glanced at the screen, then scrolled slightly.

His eyebrows lifted, and his lips spread into a wide, amused grin.

Val sat as stone-faced as possible. Somehow, Seth was putting the puzzle pieces together, and found it incredibly entertaining.

"Hey, Val, what's Adrian up to tonight?"

Val didn't reply. She could feel Melissa's eyes on her, a subtle rage simmering just beneath the surface.

Taking her silence as an answer, Seth turned his attention back to Melissa. "To answer your question, the hunters are safe and sound, as far as I know. Getting drunk at bars, buying drugs, who knows. Thea split off to do her own thing tonight, though. I didn't listen to the explanation, didn't care. I suspect she's having a good time.

"Back to you." Seth pointed toward Val. "What were you doing at the hunter house?"

Val picked her words carefully. "We were going to get the hunters' attention and then lead them here so they could strike during the day."

Seth nodded mockingly. "Good plan. Almost like I could have come up with it. Two problems. First, wouldn't that also kill one of us in this room?"

Val glanced over at Melissa, glaring daggers into the side of her head. Seth didn't believe there was an actual problem with the plan. No, judging by the way he looked at Melissa, this was about making sure she understood the consequences.

"Sure would," Val said, staring directly into Melissa's piercing scowl.

"Second, I thought I told you not to go after Owen."

"Sure did. But I wanted him dead just as much as you do. You should've told me you were planning something. Maybe we could've worked together. Besides..." Val paused, once again calculating what she wanted to reveal and what to keep hidden. "It wasn't just about Owen. I was going to send them after Garrick too. That's why I had to take the opportunity while Adrian was busy. It wasn't just about keeping Thea distracted so we could strike Owen, I needed Adrian out of the way, because he'd never agree to killing Garrick."

Seth stared at her, then his amused smile returned. "You're more devious than I gave you credit for," he said. "Not because I actually believed that, but it was a good story. You must have considered it to think on your feet that fast. I might have believed it if you'd had more time to prepare."

Val frowned. Well, at least he didn't seem angry about the lie.

"Or prove me wrong," Seth taunted before pulling out his phone. "What room number is he in?"

Suddenly feeling cornered, Val sank into her chair.

"What's the deal, Val? I thought you were all about revenge, but apparently that only goes as far as your own nose. Joseph killed your boyfriend, so he qualifies. Owen pissed you off, so he qualifies. Garrick's killed people. You know that, you just don't know their names. You want the power to kill an Elder so you can what? Take his place and be a slightly less shitty person than he is? You think you know better than he does which people deserve to have their skulls caved in?"

Val remained silent, unable to defend herself against Seth's condemnation. Revenge was supposed to be simple, uncomplicated. She hadn't thought too hard about what came after, but yes, that was the idea. She, or Adrian, would make a less shitty Regent. Was that really so hard to achieve?

Melissa answered before Val could respond. "I'll tell you, but I need to make sure Thea is safe."

Though he seemed annoyed that Melissa had deflected his accusation, Seth nodded. "Fine. But only because I like her."

Sophia retrieved Melissa's purse and handed over the phone. Seth took it and turned on the speaker. After four rings, the only response was Thea's voicemail message.

"I think she's a bit busy," Seth teased. Melissa scowled and nodded toward the phone, motioning for him to bring it closer. Seth obliged, making sure to hold her arms down so she couldn't knock the phone out of his hand. After Thea's message concluded, Melissa began to speak.

"Thea, please call me back as soon as you get this," she said, her voice suddenly losing all aggression. "Don't go back to the hunters, it's not safe. And..." She paused, her anger returning. "And I swear to God, if you're sleeping with Adrian right now!"

Seth lurched forward in an effort to stifle his laughter. Only after he hung up the phone did he allow himself to make a sound, placing his hands on his hips and cackling fully.

"I genuinely wasn't expecting today to go this well," he said. He turned, beaming at the two women. Val didn't share his delight. "All right, I did all I could. What room are they staying in?"

"Rooms one hundred one to one hundred three," Melissa growled, trying not to lash out at Seth's mocking tone.

"Thank you." Seth dropped Melissa's phone onto the sofa next to Val's, then picked up his own. He tapped the screen and held it to his ear. Unfortunately, they wouldn't get to hear his personal conversations.

"Hey, this is Striga," he said. "Need you to check out a hotel on the corner of Atlantic Avenue and Broadway, in the Pacific Heights district. Rooms one-oh-one through one-oh-three. I'm going to be busy past sunrise, but... I live here, man. I'm not putting my life on hold just because you extended your visit. Okay, good. I have a good feeling about this one. And do me a favor—leave the heart intact, throw it into a cooler with some ice, and bring it back to the house... Black market stuff, don't worry about it... You think I can pay San Francisco rent driving rideshare? ...Cool, talk to you at sunset."

"Wait..." Striga—the mole, the hunter double agent—was

Seth. Val's mind raced as she sifted through all the information she and Adrian had gathered, trying to piece together who Striga could be. Everything had seemed to point to Owen, or maybe Melissa. But Seth?

"Surprise." Seth said in a flat tone, holding out his hands and shaking them in mock enthusiasm.

"But..." Val glanced over at Melissa.

"Oh, she helped, but it was mostly my idea. Would you care to explain?"

Melissa didn't reply. The muscles in her jaw clenched in defiance.

"Or not. Someone was in hot water because Summer slipped through her fingers. So I stepped in to help. I offered to contact some vampire hunters who could subdue her and recover the most important part of her." Seth drew a cross over his chest. "Tracking Summer wasn't the hard part, it was taking her alive. She was an Elder and dangerous. We needed some crazy mortals with silver weapons to get the jump on her. Unfortunately, I should have specified that I wanted her alive—not just any vampire alive. Adrian got in the way."

Adrian? So that night, when he'd first been attacked by the hunters, they had actually been stalking Summer. If Adrian hadn't been there, then maybe Summer would have... No, she still would have been killed, just after Seth and Melissa recovered the most important part of her: her heart.

"But then, why go after Adrian?"

"That part was originally Melissa's idea," Seth said with a shrug. "You'll get a more accurate answer if she's willing to share."

Melissa rolled her eyes. Val hadn't expected her to divulge the information, but surprisingly, she spoke. "Adrian's powers. He's never had a heart transplant. Garrick told Owen that on the first night, after his fight with Tyler. I was able to confirm there was no scar while my sister played nurse," she said, a note of spite in her voice. "Owen was curious about why he was aging so fast, so he wanted to investigate. We weren't planning to kill him, but Garrick would never have allowed Owen to cut him open. That's why Garrick was also a target—we were just waiting for him to finish tutoring Owen."

So they weren't wrong. Striga wasn't just Seth; he was Seth, Melissa, and Owen, all under the same username. Even if Seth was the one specifically running the account, he was taking orders from Melissa, who in turn took orders from Owen.

"Oh, so you've known for a while that Adrian and Thea were working together," Seth said. "And you didn't think to tell me?"

"You would have tried to kill her and you know it. Or Owen."

"So, if you and Melissa were working together..." Val glanced down at the gunshot wounds and the silver barbed wire wrapped around Melissa's wrists.

"I'm not here to run errands for Owen." Seth leaned forward, peering through strands of black hair crusted with drying blood. "This was just a convenient excuse to get hunters into the city without Owen freaking out. I was always going to direct them to this house, at least until a bigger threat walked into the city."

"A bigger threat?"

"Who would have thought that on the very night I was ready to set my plan into motion, a six-hundred-year-old Elder named Garrick Leach would appear?" Seth scowled. "What was I supposed to do? I couldn't play my hand on a pathetic new Elder like Owen and have nothing prepared for Garrick. As soon as he'd realize the hunters were a real danger, he'd go into hiding—or maybe he'd slaughter all of them himself, catch them when they least expected it. No, I just had to wait and keep the hunters busy while I modified the plan."

"So, you're after…"

"Steal the silver weapons for Owen." Seth wiggled the gun in his hand. "Then send the hunters towards Garrick the next morning. And Adrian, but sounds like they're not exactly sharing a bed any longer."

"Adrian?"

Seth must not have heard Val, as Owen groaned at the same time she asked her question. Seth's attention snapped to the Regent, and he waved Devin over.

"Throw him in the closet," he said. "It's a little late at night for heart surgery. Then keep these two bound." He gestured to Val and Melissa. "Don't want them causing trouble. Not until this is all wrapped up with a bow."

34

NIGHT 7 - VAL

Val spent the day locked inside a windowless bathroom, her hands and legs still bound by silver barbs. She stared at the bleached white walls, tub, sink, and toilet, lights on, blasting her vision with torturous brightness until the night's dark magic waned enough for sleep. Val woke to the same sterile sight, then squeezed her eyes shut, trying to blot out the light with a darkness more befitting of her mood.

Garrick was dead. That fact left her feeling oddly numb. He had been her friend. A problematic friend who often acted purely out of self-interest, their relationship built on a strange foundation of attraction and lies, but she had never felt that he wanted to hurt her. And yet, he had warned her: if she found herself in trouble as a result of her reach for power, he wouldn't come to her rescue.

But how long would that have lasted, anyway? Seth wasn't wrong that there had always been a layer of conditionality to Garrick's goodwill. The night he made her a vampire, he told her that one day she would need to take over Adrian's responsibilities. Blood. She was his spare, in case Adrian ended up dead. Anyone could be a spare. It would only take one helpless homeless man to replace them.

Now Garrick was dead. Owen was captured. She was no one's spare, and no one's friend.

The door opened, and Sophia dragged Val out of the bathroom. She was deposited back onto the same chair Seth had interrogated her in before. A moment later, Devin entered the sitting room with Melissa in hand. Seth, dressed in his pale blue sweater, paced the length of the room with a phone pressed to his ear. At some point during the early morning, he had found time to bathe and wash the blood from his skin. He appeared unhappy.

"What do you mean there was no one...? Well, try again tomorrow morning. Don't worry about it, I... It's good information, I promise... Bah!" He hung up and threw the phone onto the couch.

Val didn't speak, but based on the side of the conversation she could hear, it sounded like the hunters had failed to kill Garrick. Her heart leapt in relief. He had survived. Was that cause for celebration?

Seth continued to pace, rubbing his eyes, until something made him stop. He reached into his pocket and pulled out Val's phone.

"Oh, looks like Loverboy's awake," he said, his mood brightening. A second later, he pulled Melissa's phone from his other pocket and held it up. "And what coincidental timing! It's Thea."

Seth didn't wait for Melissa's demands and brought the

phone over by her head. He answered it, immediately switched to speaker, and hushed everyone in the room.

"Melissa?" Thea's voice echoed through the speaker.

"Thea?" Melissa glanced around the room, as if Seth's command to stay silent wasn't threat enough.

"Oh, thank God. Is everything all right?"

Melissa glanced up at Seth for direction, and he silently shrugged. "Things were a little chaotic last night, but I'm safe," she said. "Where are you?"

Val's phone, in Seth's opposite hand, began to vibrate. He checked the screen, then showed it to Val and Melissa. Adrian was calling. Seth smirked and let it ring.

Poor Adrian. He didn't deserve to become the entertainment.

"I'm at the hunter house."

"Bullshit," Melissa said, scowling as she looked from Val's phone to Seth's bemused face. "What were you up to last night?"

"Nothing. Was up late and went to bed at sunrise."

"Thea, I know you're with Adrian right now."

"What? No. Why do you think I'm with Adrian?"

"The entire damn room you're on speaker with knows you two slept together."

A pause. "No," Thea insisted. "I didn't sleep with him last night! Look, does it matter? I'm an adult, I can make my own bad choices."

Seth shrugged in agreement, and Val was certain Melissa was about to ignore the call and rip his throat out herself.

"Well, I'm not with him right now, so tell me whatever you want."

Seth nodded his approval. It was unlikely that Thea had put herself on speaker in front of Adrian, so even if they spoke openly, it shouldn't matter. And if it did, Val figured, Seth didn't really care.

"My night was pretty exciting too. One of your hunters

turned out to be a vampire all along. Apparently, he was using you to get his hands on a stash of silver bullets—two of which are currently lodged in my gut."

"Hey, Thea," Seth cut in. "It's Striga. Did you have a nice night?"

The other end of the line was silent.

"Listen, can I call you back?" Thea asked. Val could hear the sudden horror in her voice.

"I thought you weren't with him?" Melissa asked, mockingly.

"I'm not, but this isn't a conversation suitable for public."

"That's fine," Seth answered in Melissa's stead.

"Okay, call you back soon."

The room went quiet, save for Melissa shifting uncomfortably under the weight of everyone's attention.

"You should lighten up on your sister," Seth said, poking the bear. "Good for her, honestly. Let her have some fun. Bet you'd feel a lot better if you got laid for reasons other than power grabs."

Melissa lurched forward and fell face-first onto the rug as her legs caught on the silver binding. Seth bellowed with laughter, and Val was just glad that, for now, it wasn't her, Adrian, or Garrick under scrutiny. Devin picked Melissa up by the scruff of her dress and dropped her back into the chair just as the phone rang. Seth answered on speaker again but didn't offer it to Melissa.

"Talk now?"

"What do you want?" Thea hissed from the other end of the line.

"Easy now. Like she said, your sister is safe, but we're not exactly friends. I wouldn't lose any sleep if something unfortunate happened to her."

"Fuck you."

Seth smirked and waited a beat before continuing, likely stopping any further taunts to remain amicable.

"Listen, I'm going to need a favor if you want to keep Melissa in my good graces. Two, actually."

Thea's voice lost its harsh edge, now sounding helpless. "What is it?"

"Don't worry, it's your specialty. I need two vampires taken care of. You can kill them both, but I'd prefer if you kept their hearts intact and brought them to me, wrapped up nicely in a cooler full of ice."

"What? Gross!"

"Just extra credit, keep it in mind. The first vampire I need you to kill is named Garrick. Tall guy, late forties, aging blonde hair. I'll send you the location of his hotel room after this call. Just a heads-up: he's old, even by our standards, so I'd advise against engaging him at night.

"The second vampire, you're not going to like."

A pit opened in Val's stomach. No, he wasn't going to suggest...

"Loverboy is on my hit list, too."

"Fuck off!"

Seth's smirk widened, revealing sharp fangs beneath. "Hold up, I think this decision will be a little easier once you hear what I have to say. I've got Adrian's friend Val here, and she had some very interesting things to say about your little date last night."

Val squeezed her eyes shut. No, this couldn't be happening. She should have left Adrian out when she told Seth about her plans the previous night. And now, that information was the knife held to his throat.

"He needed to keep you occupied while Val leaked the location of our headquarters to the other hunters. Know why he never mentioned that to you? Because your sister sleeps here, and she would've been one of the casualties if it had worked."

The phone remained silent for several seconds, causing Val to wonder if the connection had been lost.

"But don't take my word for it," Seth continued. He held the phone by Melissa's head.

"It's true," she growled. "He was using you to kill me."

"Shut up!" Thea screamed. "You're lying! You never liked him, so why should I believe any of that? What happened in the last five years to make you such a bitch?"

"Excuse me?"

"Hey, hey, calm down." Seth picked the phone back up to his lips and turned his back on Melissa. Yeah, the last thing he needed was Thea telling his blackmail to go fuck herself. "I'm willing to bargain. Remember that extra credit? If you bring me Garrick's heart, I'll let you keep Adrian alive."

"You'll 'let' me?"

"Well," Seth rolled his eyes and scowled down at Melissa. "I'll keep your sister alive, but I'm starting to question whether that's even a persuasive argument anymore. So either bring me both Adrian's and Garrick's ashes, or bring me Garrick's heart, and I'll keep your nighttime affairs a secret from our hunter friends. I'll even convince them to leave Adrian alone, if you keep him alive."

The other line was quiet, except for a few uncertain groans.

"Take some time to think it over, and call me back when you have an answer. Feel free to ask me any questions about proper vampire hunting. I don't want to see you dead on the pavement wearing a necklace of garlic."

Seth hung up, and only then did Val start shouting.

"Why Adrian?" She wanted to appear threatening, but the words came out as a plea. "He didn't do anything!"

"He's an Elder," Seth answered. "There are no innocent Elders."

"What? No! He's only forty!"

"And yet, he's an Elder."

"No! He can still drink mortal blood."

303

"Can he?" Seth searched her face for any sign of decep-
tion. "Not for much longer."

"What do you know?" she spat.

Seth glowered down at her, his patience wearing thin. Val
bit her tongue, remembering her place as his prisoner. But
Seth didn't snap at her. Instead, his attention flicked upward,
over Val's shoulder.

"Impeccable timing, Nora."

"Been here a while. Just didn't want to interrupt."

Val twisted her neck to see Nora standing by the front
door, arms crossed in a relaxed pose. Now that her presence
was known, Nora crossed the foyer to the sitting room,
walked past Val without so much as a glance, and stood
shoulder to shoulder with Seth. With a sly smile directed at
Val, Seth leaned over and bit Nora on the neck. The woman
made no attempt to struggle beneath his fangs.

Seth was an Elder. No, the heart transplanted into his
chest had belonged to an Elder, and as a result, Seth's age had
lurched forward. Val turned to Melissa to gauge her reaction
and found surprise. She hadn't known either.

When Seth was finished, he sneered, blood still clinging to
his teeth. "I know a few things about being an Elder," he said,
then nodded at Devin. "Speaking of which, where's our least
favorite Elder Regent? Go grab him, will you?"

A moment after leaving the sitting room, Devin reappeared, dragging Owen behind him, the bear trap still
clamped around his midsection. He dropped the Elder on the
floor to Val's right. Today, Owen was slightly more mobile—
able to prop himself up on his knees, kneeling and hunched
as much as the trap allowed despite the ongoing torture. The
blood on his suit had mostly dried, except for a few fresh,
bright red specks from the reopened wounds. His arms shook
uncontrollably.

"All right, who wants his heart? It's a painful procedure,
so there's no shame in refusing."

"Wait," Owen wheezed. "You've never done this before. If you don't know how to keep a non-Elder heart alive—"

Seth sneered. "I think there will be plenty of opportunities to give myself a proper heart once I'm done with you Elders."

"No. I'm talking about my heart."

When the room fell silent, waiting for an explanation, Owen began to laugh. Each breath rasped like the stutter of an old engine trying and failing to start, ending in a sickening gurgle as fresh blood spattered from his lips.

"I'm not... an Elder," Owen coughed. "Not by age."

"You're lying," Seth snapped. "You're just trying to stall for time."

"Then feed me mortal blood and see how long I survive."

Seth knelt down to grab Owen by the chin and look him in the eyes. Val tried to determine for herself whether Owen was lying. If he was, he was very convincing. He let out a few more strained chuckles, seemingly unbothered by Seth's intimidation, and it appeared Seth had come to the same conclusion. He stood, stared down at the weakened man, and fidgeted. The small movements—a twist of his foot, a brush of hair out of his face—offered little relief from the fury quickly growing inside him.

"This whole time," Seth said softly, before the anger built to a crescendo. "This whole time, and I was stronger than you? I could have done this years ago!" He kicked Owen in the face, sending him tumbling to the ground again. "Get him up! On his knees! I'm doing this the proper way."

Seth walked behind Owen and cocked his gun as Devin grabbed him under the arms and lifted him up.

"Wait!" Owen tried to shout, though his words barely rose above a rasping breath. "You'll want to keep me alive!"

"And why's that?" Seth asked, lowering the muzzle to the back of Owen's skull.

"Why did I give you a heart stronger than mine?"

Seth hesitated to pull the trigger. The gun held steady, but

Val could tell the question hit on something Seth had been wrestling with.

"In the basement," Owen continued, "behind my locked door. If you don't like what you see, you can kill me then."

Seth waited, then lowered the gun. An exaggerated eye roll punctuated his self-disgust at listening to Owen, but Val was glad he had decided to stay the execution. Curiosity gripped her mind. What could Owen possibly offer that would spare his life? And she was relieved she didn't have to witness a murder mere feet from where she sat.

"Pick him up. Let's go see what's so great in the basement," Seth groaned. "Nora, Sophia, keep an eye on these two so they don't cause any trouble."

Grabbing him under the arm once again, Devin dragged Owen across the room and disappeared into the kitchen, leaving the four women in awkward silence. Val had no interest in breaking it, knowing that any further conversation would only make things more uncomfortable.

Unfortunately, Nora didn't agree.

"You didn't know Owen wasn't actually an Elder?"

The question was directed at Melissa. She paused to think, then shrugged.

"No, I'm with Seth. Had I known, I would have tried to overthrow him sooner too. It's not like Owen really runs things. The bank accounts, government documents, internal accounting—that's all me. Honestly, if you want your transfer of power to go smoothly, you'd better make sure your leader doesn't get too trigger-happy around me. Not unless you want to start guessing passwords."

Nora leaned her head back in a full belly laugh. "You're a slimy little weasel, aren't you? You truly have no loyalty to anyone, except whoever's dick happens to be dangling above your head. You must be so disappointed that Seth has no interest in women."

"Absolutely hurt," Melissa said, not rising to the taunt.

Despite being bound by the silver wire, she sat a little straighter and swept her feet to the side of the chair. "I have talents, and it's a shame they're going to waste on men who don't fully appreciate them."

"Well, Seth isn't the only one in charge around here."

Val caught Sophia's glance, and it was a strange feeling—going from being dragged around as their prisoner to sharing an uncomfortable moment.

"Can you two, like, get a room?" Sophia groaned.

"She has a point, though," Nora said. "She's not the slightest bit loyal to Owen now that he's nearly dead, and we do need access to his money."

"I can't believe she got to you." Sophia rubbed her eyes.

Melissa smirked and angled her chin high. Based on the way she carried herself, the silver barbed wire no longer appeared to be a binding, but rather jewelry worn proudly around her wrists and ankles. The lack of mobility was of little consequence, with Devin carrying her wherever she needed to go.

Val hated the envious feeling bubbling within her. As she bounced between conflicting emotions—power, revenge, self-preservation, and loyalty to her friends—Melissa seemed to have her life in perfect order. Of course, it was easy when that order consisted only of herself, Thea, and no one else.

Val wilted. Where would she be if she hadn't made vengeance her top priority this past week? She knew all the stories and sayings about revenge: It won't make you feel better. It won't bring him back. She knew them all. She didn't listen. Maybe a little patience would have gone a long way.

Seth reappeared in the sitting room with Devin right behind him. Owen was nowhere to be found. At first, Val assumed Seth had shot him in the basement after calling Owen's bluff for a few more minutes of life. But the excitement beaming from Seth's face suggested otherwise.

"Nora, Sophia, you have to come check this out."

307

The two women, just as surprised as Val, hopped off their seats and followed Seth back to the basement, while Devin lifted Val over his shoulder and carried her to the bathroom. Val didn't protest. She knew it wouldn't accomplish anything. And despite having more pressing priorities, her biggest disappointment was not getting to see what was so great in the basement.

She lay helpless on the white tile once again, alone with only her thoughts to torment her. She wanted her revenge. She wanted her friends. And she had lost both. She waited for someone to retrieve her from the bathroom once they finished ogling whatever was in the basement, but no one came.

35
NIGHT 8 - THEA

The first thing Thea thought to do was call Melissa and tell her everything. But the thought of the conversation made her sick. The last time she had spoken to her sister, she'd gotten chewed out about her private love life. And now that Melissa had been proven right, Thea knew she'd never hear the end of it. She would, of course, tell her that she was now a vampire eventually, but she didn't need any more crap added to her already full plate.

It took her an hour to walk all the way back to the upscale hotel, where her motorcycle was still parked. The sky had fully darkened, and hotel guests passed by, chatting and smiling among themselves. Loneliness had been a constant companion over the last four years, yet watching the crowd of people hurrying to dinner or strolling arm-in-arm along the road made Thea feel violently ill.

She'd never feel the warmth of the sun again. Never.

Thea rode down a major street with no particular destination in mind. The road along the edge of the peninsula was the most scenic, but it reminded her too much of the ride from two nights ago. She weaved back into the city and followed a major highway that stretched the length of the landmass, then turned around to ride it again. She only stopped when she realized she was famished.

Thea found a spot to park her motorcycle and sat on the curb, her head in her hands. The vampiric hunger didn't feel like normal hunger. It wasn't a pain in her stomach but a clawing sensation that spread through her entire body. She couldn't ignore it the way she could push through ordinary stomach growls.

Eat first, Thea thought, mourn later. She looked around. It was still early enough that a steady stream of pedestrians moved along the major roads. She figured she'd have to jump one, much to her distaste. In weighing the pros and cons of becoming a vampire, the need to take blood from innocent people had been a major con. Some hunters believed that becoming a vampire switched off the part of your brain that knew right from wrong. Melissa and Adrian seemed to suggest some truth to that, but Thea didn't feel any different now. How annoying, especially now that her life depended on it.

Annoying? Was there no other way to sustain herself? Whether vampires could live off animal blood was a hotly contested question on online forums. Some insisted they could, others disagreed. Based on what Thea had seen, vampires needed human blood. Why else would Adrian and Melissa bother with the much more dangerous alternative? Even Adrian had admitted he was in a tight spot that day they went to the karaoke bar.

Thea grumbled at the thought of Adrian. He used her. He used her as a means to hurt her sister. Yet he had seemed so genuine that night, and the nights before. Ugh, he probably hadn't been thinking beyond his own nose. This grand plan Striga told her about probably wasn't even that complex.

She pushed those thoughts aside and turned her attention to the more pressing matter at hand. Parking lots were good places to find people. Thea got up and stood by her motorcycle, pulling out her phone in boredom to scroll through the hunter forum. She visited the site reflexively, though she now recognized the irony in it.

A car drove into the lot and parked. *Perfect*, Thea thought. A single man got out of the vehicle and walked toward her, completely oblivious to the threat she posed. Thea kept her eyes on her phone as he approached, her heart racing and palms sweaty. Just a little closer…

The man walked past, and Thea didn't move. She was too paralyzed to follow him. Burying her face in her hands, she let out a frustrated groan. *Come on*, she thought. *This is your life now. This is how you survive.* She tilted her head back and sighed.

Thea watched as a family of four walked by, then a young couple. She couldn't target them either. She considered other options—maybe a nightclub or stalking the streets—when a single woman walked past. Thea glanced over her shoulder to make sure they were alone, then trailed the woman to her car. She thought she was being quiet, but just as the woman reached for the door, she spun around with a canister of mace pointed directly at Thea's face. Thea jumped, raising her hands to her chest.

"Walk away," the woman warned.

"S-sorry!" Thea took several steps back and watched helplessly as the woman got into her car and drove off quickly.

Thea sat back on the curb and pulled her knees to her chest. Turns out, she made for a terrible vampire. Tears welled in her eyes, and she angrily wiped them away. *Pull it together,* she thought, *vampires don't cry about how alone and confused they are.*

She jumped when she felt a hand on her shoulder. Kneeling beside her was a man about ten years her senior.

"I'm sorry, is everything all right?"

Thea scrambled to her feet and wiped away her tears again. "Y-yes, I... Well, you see... I just found out my boyfriend cheated on me... and..."

The man shook his head. "I'm so sorry," he said. "You're too good for him! You deserve someone better."

Thea nodded. "D-Do you mind if I ask for a hug?"

The man opened his arms and embraced her. Thea sucked in a breath, something she realized she hadn't been doing this whole time, and let out a long sigh as she clutched him back. Then she bit his neck.

Blood didn't taste any different now that she was a vampire, but it had lost its repugnant qualities. The metallic flavor was suddenly pleasant on her tongue, making it easier to suck on this random man's neck. When she was finally full, she pulled away and realized she was holding up the man's full weight as he fell unconscious. Thea looked around to make sure they were still alone, then set him down by a nearby car. She ran.

Thea hid in a nearby alley, paralyzed by the thought that someone had seen her and was now chasing her down, demanding to know what she'd done to the poor, innocent man. But after a minute passed, she realized she'd made a clean escape. It had been a rocky start, but her first night as a vampire had been a success. Now, she had the rest of eternity to go.

No wonder every vampire she'd ever met was an asshole.

Figuring she should put some distance between herself and her victim for the next hour, Thea wandered the city. Now what? Should she call Melissa and tell her everything that had happened? She glanced at her phone and read the messages she had received while lying dead on Adrian's bed. Striga had sent two, asking whether she had come to a decision about hunting his vampire for him. Melissa had sent none, but that was likely because she was Striga's prisoner. Thea bit her lip, hoping Striga hadn't been hasty with his threats.

She was still mad at Melissa, but that didn't seem so important after the whirlwind of the last two nights. Still, she couldn't bring herself to work for Owen. Thea wasn't up for violent revenge against him, but she sure as hell wasn't going to work for the man either.

How did Owen fit into all of this? He must have sanctioned it. Since when did Melissa become such an idiot, thinking that following someone like him would end well? He killed their parents. He wouldn't think twice about betraying her once the circumstances changed.

When she returned to the parking lot, the man was gone. She left on her motorcycle once more. Step one, getting something to eat, was complete. Step two would be to find shelter before sunrise. That shouldn't be too difficult. She had managed to get a hotel room at the last minute, and she was a vampire now. A dingy motel in the shadier parts of town wasn't nearly as dangerous as it used to be. But at some point, she'd need to figure out how to spend the rest of her vampiric life in a way that didn't involve rotating between different motels.

This would be a lot harder if I didn't have Mom and Dad's money, she thought. She silently thanked her parents for being wealthy, then groaned at herself for how that sounded. She would have preferred her parents alive, of course, but given the circumstances, she appreciated the several million dollars in her bank account. It was enough to buy a motorcycle, enough to quit her job, and enough to buy a house in San Francisco.

Well, it would be enough to buy a semi-decent condo in San Francisco. *Maybe I should move to a different city.*

But first, she needed her belongings. Thea hadn't brought much, just whatever she could fit in a backpack while riding across the country. But even vampires needed clothes. She rode out of the lot and drove back to the hunter house, rehearsing multiple cover stories in her head to explain why she had been gone so long and why she had to leave so soon.

That proved unnecessary when she arrived to find the house surrounded by police vehicles, the door kicked open and taped off. Thea stared, wondering what had happened, but quickly thought better of it and continued riding. After putting several blocks between herself and the police, Thea pulled out her phone and searched for local news.

It didn't take long to find. "Five Dead in Fatal Home Invasion," read the headline. The news article was sparse on details, other than noting the primary suspect was a white male with dark hair. So, literally half of San Francisco, but Thea placed her bets on Striga. She breathed a little easier, metaphorically speaking, knowing the police were looking for someone who wasn't her. If they hadn't realized yet that she'd been staying in that house, they would soon.

In the meantime, what was she to do with her life? She could buy new clothes and a phone charger from a supermarket, then find a hotel, and then... what? Do the same thing again tomorrow, and the day after, every day, for eternity? That sounded boring. She also had no idea how to be a vampire. Were there any rules she didn't know about? The last thing she wanted was to accidentally find herself dead because it turned out vampires secretly needed to sleep in a coffin once a month, or something ridiculous like that.

Thea looked at her phone again. She'd have to address the most pressing issue soon or risk losing her last lifeline in the vampire world. Even if that lifeline was being a total bitch.

She tapped Striga's phone number and held the phone to her ear.

"Hey, there you are!" Striga's irritating voice called out. "I got worried for a minute."

"Is Melissa still alive?" she demanded.

A few seconds later, Melissa's voice sounded through the speaker.

"Thea! Oh, thank God, where were you?"

Thea didn't answer the question directly. "I'm guessing I'm on speaker again?"

"Yep," Striga replied.

"I was teaching your mom to swing both ways, since she regrets having you."

The line went silent. Got him.

"Anything else you'd like to report?" Striga asked, and Thea could tell her quip got under his skin. She smiled. Don't dish what you can't take.

"Did you take my laptop with you when you went on your murder spree, or did you let the police confiscate it?"

Again, Striga went silent. "What?" He sounded genuine.

"You…" He didn't kill the hunters? "The other hunters are dead. Did you check the news?"

A few seconds passed before she heard him mutter a curse under his breath. "That wasn't me. Sorry to disappoint."

Huh, perhaps it was a drug deal that had gone horribly wrong. Maybe Thea got lucky and dodged a very lethal bullet by getting screwed over by Adrian.

"Is that all you wanted to ask?"

"Uh, no." Thea did her best to shake off her nerves surrounding the situation. She was a vampire now. She'd never have to meet up with strange men online again. "Got your heart."

"Wait, really?" Thea tried to gauge Striga's reaction. She had no idea if he could actually check on the status of this

Garrick guy, but he sounded genuinely surprised. Maybe priming him with a successful insult had lowered his guard.

"Yep. Where am I supposed to bring this?"

"I'll send you the address."

Striga hung up, and a minute later, he sent a text with an address. Thea realized it was in the neighborhood he had pointed out when they first arrived. What had his plan been? Probably to use them to take out a rival vampire.

Thea rode to the mansion and parked nearby, steeling her nerves. Striga was holding Melissa hostage. He probably worked for Owen, the man who had murdered her family. Walking in and shooting wildly was unlikely to accomplish anything, but she had nothing left to lose. Maybe it was the heartbreak, or the uncertainty of her new, shitty vampire life, but Thea felt oddly accepting of the possibility of death. She drew her gun, rang the front doorbell, and held the weapon at head height.

The door opened. She squeezed the grip, and Melissa stood in the entrance. At the sight of the gun, Melissa flinched back, and Thea quickly dropped her arm.

Holy shit, how close had she come to shooting her own sister in the face?

"Th-Thea!" Melissa stammered. "You're…"

"You're…" Thea looked her sister up and down. "You're looking quite free."

"Is Thea here?" Striga's voice echoed from inside the mansion. "Bring her to me!"

Melissa stepped aside, allowing Thea to enter the foyer. Neither sister said a word about the near-accidental homicide.

The inside of the mansion was decorated with modern sensibilities. Solid, angular furniture greeted her, nothing like what she expected from a vampire's home. Though slightly upscale, everything felt oddly normal. A part of Thea felt disappointed by the lack of cobwebs and gothic décor. Striga sat on a black leather sofa farther inside, near large windows that overlooked the city. He stood and waved her over excitedly.

"All right, where's the heart?"

Thea glanced back at Melissa. Although she had a curious pattern of cuts and bruises around both wrists, she was clearly not his prisoner. The Hollywood-style rescue operation was obviously no longer necessary.

"I lied. Figured you'd be familiar with the concept."

Striga looked down at her, his shoulders heaving in a sigh, though he still wore the same mild-mannered smile.

"Okay." He pulled a gun from his pocket and shot her in the stomach. "I only gave that a fifty percent chance of working, anyway."

Thea clasped her stomach and hunched over in searing pain. Melissa screamed behind her, and Striga shouted in response. Something about her being a hunter, dangerous. Thea's legs shook, but she didn't lose her balance. Slowly, the pain subsided, and though the sleeves of her jacket were stained with dark red blood, she straightened up, ultimately unharmed.

Striga held his gun menacingly to Melissa's face, but both turned their attention to Thea, their eyes wide with surprise as she shrugged off the bullet.

"Oh." Striga lowered the gun. "So..."

Thea pulled her lips back in what was meant to be a smile, but her unbridled disgust twisted it into a sneer. Either way, it revealed her fangs.

"What? How?" Melissa asked.

Thea hesitated before answering. "I asked. That's what I was doing with Adrian."

It wasn't so much the need to defend Adrian that caused Thea to lie, but rather the tension and casual violence that made her fear any additional reason to hate him might spark another explosion. She needed her sister to be calm. She needed someone to be calm.

"Why?" Melissa asked, unable to hold back her spite.

Thea stared her in the eyes. Was it really that difficult to guess? Her sister was a vampire. Her only friend, before he betrayed her, was a vampire. She simply shrugged as a response. Melissa could be left wondering. She didn't need to waste her time explaining herself. Not like she could go back, anyway.

Melissa opened her mouth to protest again, but Striga cut her off with a shrug and said, "Well, welcome to the family." He walked back to the couch and picked up his phone.

"Plan C, then."

He walked out of the room, leaving the two sisters alone. Thea checked her bullet wound again. Now that the initial shock had worn off, there wasn't as much blood as she expected. That was one bright point about the new condition thrust upon her—hard to kill.

"Where's Owen?" Thea asked. That was one thing she could focus on, getting revenge for her parents. Or at least seeing the man responsible.

"Seth locked him in the basement," Melissa answered. "Don't worry about him, he's not in charge anymore."

Seth... That was probably Striga's real name. He was obviously in charge now.

"Cool. I'm gonna... get comfortable, I guess."

Melissa hesitated, hovering nearby protectively, but Thea could tell she had other matters on her mind. Thea sat on the leather couch, leaned her head back, and closed her eyes to rest, which seemed to put her sister at ease. Melissa walked away, and only after she had been out of sight for a full minute did Thea get up to look for the basement.

Sneaking through the mansion as quietly as she could, Thea checked the kitchen, a long hallway, and every door she came across. After growing discouraged—each room turning out to be an office, bathroom, or master bedroom—she finally reached the end of the hallway.

The far room was a large utility area, built of concrete and simple laminated tile. A washer and dryer sat against the back wall, next to a basin sink. Shelves lined the sides of the room, stocked with spare bedsheets and towels. Two doors were positioned haphazardly on the walls. Thea opened the first to find a closet crammed with cleaning supplies, but the second was locked. It was the only door in the mansion she'd seen that could be locked with a key, suggesting it had been custom-installed specifically for that purpose. Why, Thea wasn't sure, but Melissa had said Owen was locked up somewhere. This door seemed like a good bet.

Thea stared at the lock, wondering what to do next. Sneak through the mansion looking for the key? Instead, she placed the muzzle of the gun against the lock and fired twice. No one had come running when Seth shot her, so she figured gunfire was common enough not to warrant investigation. The metal lockbox blew apart, allowing her access to the concrete stairwell on the other side.

Calling the depths beneath the mansion a basement was an understatement. The locked door concealed nothing less than a dungeon, with its rough rock walls and hastily strung incandescent bulbs dimly lighting the narrow hallway that led to a larger chamber. Only two bulbs illuminated the entire underground level, one at the hallway entrance and another at the center of the inner room. But that was all Thea needed. Even the dark corners and harsh shadows seemed faded now, no longer offering cover for whatever once tried to hide in the darkness.

Sitting against the wall to the right was a man, his wrists and ankles bound with nylon and a thorny twine that reflected the light as he twitched. Thea recognized the wire as silver. Carter had brought it to San Francisco. At first, she thought Owen was wearing some kind of cage around his midsection, but then she realized it was Noc's bear trap. His pale suit displayed the bloody damage the trap had caused, its beige fabric splattered with red like a canvas. The man's head snapped up as she approached, his eyes primal, like those of a starving animal.

Thea guessed this was Owen, and she felt a pang of disappointment at his appearance. It was, of course, unreasonable to make assumptions about what the murderer of her parents might look like, but she had always imagined him as large and imposing—a cartoonish kind of evil. Instead, he was neither handsome nor ugly—average height and broad, but lacking the fat or muscle that might make him intimidating. His bald head added to his nondescript appearance, as if Thea could put a wig on him and he'd transform into every man she had ever seen on the street and then immediately forgotten.

But still, she raised her gun and approached slowly. Many an evil man looked like a dipshit.

"Who are you?" Owen wheezed, his voice strained. Having a bear trap clamped around his ribs would do that.

"Thea Fowler," she answered. She offered no further explanation, waiting to see if Owen recognized the last name. His eyes narrowed and then unfocused.

"Melissa's sister," he said, finally remembering. "Out for revenge?"

Thea remained silent. Yes. Yes, she was, and here she stood, in front of the man who had ruined her life. One of them, at least, but the first. She held a gun aimed at his head, loaded with silver, and all she had to do now was pull the trigger and it would all be over.

Already? Thea's revenge plot had ended just as quickly as it began. She hadn't expected her target to be bound and waiting in a dungeon. She thought there would be some attempt at a fight, an escape, or at least for Owen to beg for his life. Instead, he sat like a trussed pig awaiting the butcher.

"Did you kill my parents?" Thea didn't entirely understand why she asked. At this point, it was obvious that he had.

"They got too nosy," Owen answered. "Would have killed you too, just to be safe. But you were on the other side of the country at university. I didn't have the strings to pull for that one."

Thea gripped the gun tighter. "It's silver," she warned.

"Silver doesn't matter when it's your brain matter being blown out."

"You don't seem to be afraid."

"I'm dead already." Owen peeled his lips back in a laugh, blood staining the whites of his teeth. "I convinced Seth to keep me alive in some vain hope that I could escape, but realistically, I'm not walking away from this. Maybe it's better to get it over with sooner rather than later."

Thea wanted to fire the gun. She had no reservations about killing him. At least, that's what she thought. But this wasn't the revenge she had imagined. There was no satisfaction in killing an imprisoned man, no emotional catharsis to be found. Letting out an aggravated sigh, she lowered the gun.

"You're too soft," Owen said. "You won't last long if you can't get your hands dirty."

It took Thea a moment to realize he was referring to her vampirism. "You can tell?"

"Just assumed if you were here. Who turned you?"

Thea kept her mouth shut. Not because she wanted to protect Adrian, but because she saw no reason to give Owen the information. Just because she no longer had the will to kill him didn't mean she suddenly trusted him.

"Doesn't matter, just curious if Garrick had anything to do with it."

"No. Not with me, anyway," Thea stated indignantly.

"You'll be working for him soon. Or for Seth. It's hard to say."

"I'm not going to work for anyone."

Owen just laughed. "You will, or you'll make a mistake and get yourself killed." He paused, waiting for Thea's reaction. She gave none. The thought of spending the rest of her life—however long that was—working for the monsters who had destroyed her future made her sick.

"...I would like to see you succeed, though," Owen continued. "Figuratively speaking. It's going to be hard to watch from Hell. Most vampires are idiots. They tell themselves they don't need to worry about finding vampire necks to feed on, until it's too late. They tie themselves to their Regents for safety, but in doing so, they rob themselves of the ability to make it on their own. I was smart. I got out early. I'm not a real Elder; I'm only eighty years old. Nothing is stopping you from biting the necks of your friends now. If I could do it all again, I'd start earlier. Learn how to wrap lesser vampires around your little finger while you still have the option to fall back on mortals."

Thea stood in silence. She didn't know why Owen was giving her this advice. She wasn't even sure if she wanted to take it. After all, she hated him. Right?

"Why are you telling me all of this?"

Owen shrugged his right shoulder, the one not clamped by the savage device. "I don't care one way or another. Wouldn't mind seeing Seth brought low after doing this to me." He pointed at the bear trap. "I made a mistake keeping you alive. If Seth hadn't beaten you to the punch, you probably would've found me and killed me in my sleep. My fatal mistake was underestimating you. It'd be nice to know that mistake went on to become a complete nightmare for the rest of vampire-kind. Might make me look a little less pathetic."

Thea hated herself for it, but she found herself contemplating his words. She didn't need his permission or want his encouragement, yet it was strangely empowering to hear

322

someone affirm that her refusal to ever work for a vampire as vile as Owen was not just commendable, but the right choice.

"How do I become a Regent?" she asked.

"Just convince other vampires to give you their blood," he said. "Most pay them, usually by covering rent, utilities, maybe an allowance for nice things. Some just hand over cash. Others make grandiose promises about how they'll change everything if you simply offer them your neck. And some," Owen chuckled weakly, "some do truly vile shit when they get desperate. Everyone's got their own method. Get creative."

"What are you two talking about down here?"

Thea jumped when she realized Seth had walked up behind her. She had been so focused on Owen that she somehow missed the sound of the basement door opening. Straightening her back in a false show of confidence, Thea crossed her arms in front of her, as if Seth were intruding on important business rather than her failed attempt at revenge.

"Just corrupting the youth," Owen quipped.

"Uh-huh. Well, hurry up. I need something from you."

"We're done," Thea cut in. She needed time to process Owen's words and had no intention of doing so in front of Seth.

"Okay. Cool." With that, Seth pulled his gun from his pocket. Thea flinched and looked away just as the gunshot rang out. Shaking, she slowly turned her head back and immediately regretted it. Owen hadn't been lying—vampires really couldn't survive a gunshot to the head, and now she understood why. She thanked her better nature for not shooting him earlier. Though she didn't feel sorry for Owen, the thought of inflicting such violence with her own hands sickened her. She hoped he was wrong about her not surviving long as a vampire without the stomach for it.

Unbothered by the gore, Seth pulled on a pair of gloves

and wrenched the bear trap open far enough to remove it from Owen's lifeless body. The trap snapped shut again, and Seth slung it over his shoulder, fresh blood dripping down his back. He turned and walked away, paying Thea no mind as he left her in the basement.

After waiting a few haunting moments to ensure Seth was out of the stairwell, Thea placed one foot in front of the other, doing her best to imitate a normal walk. Allowing herself to run would make the terror real. Slowly, she ascended the basement stairs, walked back into the laundry room, crossed through the rooms to the foyer, and exited the mansion. She didn't announce her departure.

She didn't know how she felt about her talk with Owen, but she knew damn well she couldn't stay.

Thea hadn't gotten far before Melissa ran out of the mansion to chase her.

"Thea!" she called to her. "Where are you going?"

Thea turned, searching for the words to answer. It was so strange, seeing Melissa act normal. She hadn't seen Owen's head blown off his shoulders, but the dissonance between their emotions made Thea feel alien. How could she possibly begin to explain herself when there was no common ground between them anymore?

"Away," she whispered. "I... I can't stay here."

"Don't be ridiculous," Melissa scolded. "It's not safe for a new vampire to be out on your own."

Thea's jaw hung parted in disbelief. She shook her head and took several steps back. "He shot me," she said.

"I know." Melissa squeezed her eyes shut. "But Seth is the new Elder now. It's better to stay on his good side—"

"Don't," Thea spat. Tears welling in her eyes, she tried to stare down Melissa, to figure out what had happened to drain her backbone after five years of being gone. But all she saw was her sickly older sister, slowly losing hope in her hospital bed—and maybe that girl never recovered.

"Good luck with him. I'm not coming to your rescue." Thea turned and walked back to her motorcycle, uninterrupted this time.

36

NIGHT 8 - VAL

T hat was enough wallowing.

Val did not murder Tyler in cold blood and rip his beating heart from his chest just to lie around feeling sorry for herself when things got tough. This was exactly the kind of situation an older heart was meant to handle.

What could she do? Val didn't know exactly how old Tyler's heart was, and she wasn't sure if Tyler did either. But he could use shadows and heal quickly. Shadows didn't seem like they'd be much help in this situation, unless she could somehow give them mass to help wedge the silver wire off. Quick healing was a boon, however. Even if her escape plan caused serious damage to her hands and feet, it wouldn't debilitate her for long.

Serious damage, like... breaking her hand? Val bit her lip. That was a painful solution. Best to put a pin in it and keep brainstorming.

What did she have around her? She was in a bathroom, and a nice one at that. Clean, roomy, without the clutter that made a room feel lived-in. There was a sink, a toilet, even a bath. She could fill the basin with water, which would accomplish... She had water. Keep thinking.

There were lights, a rug, and a large mirror above the sink.

Glass. Sharp glass, if she shattered it. Silver was soft, wasn't it? That sounded right. Silver jewelry was delicate. Val stood, slowly to keep her balance, and stared at her reflection in the mirror. Before, it had blurred slightly, like her eyes were unfocused. Now, it was like a Val-shaped cloud, the details blending together in soft colors. She concentrated, and her reflection flickered. If she held still and stared, it disappeared completely —but as soon as she relaxed, it came back. The silver digging into her skin was likely to blame. No matter. Blurry was good enough. If Val could see her own eyes in her reflection, she'd likely lose confidence in what she planned to do.

Val leaned back. This wouldn't be nearly as painful as Garrick cutting open her chest and performing heart surgery, but for some reason, the memory of it filled her with even more fear. She didn't want to feel that pain again. Suck it up, Val. Don't chicken out now.

Wasn't this how Tyler nearly died? A blow to the head? And now she was about to inflict the same injury on purpose? Maybe her new heart wasn't as old as she thought.

Val sucked in a breath, closed her eyes, leaned back, and...

You're a goddamn witch, Val thought as she opened her eyes.

Turning around, Val felt for the faucet handles and turned

on the water. Then she closed the drain so the basin would fill. What did water have to do with casting a protection spell? Not much, but being surrounded by the elements was better than nothing. When the sink was full, Val turned back around and peered into the water.

"By the powers of the universe, from—"

The sound of a gunshot shattered her concentration. A woman began shouting, but from inside the bathroom, Val couldn't tell whose voice it was. She froze, listening intently, trying to figure out what had happened. The shouting soon faded. Best to get out of here quickly.

"By the powers of the universe," she repeated, "from the celestial above to the earth below, protect me in what I am about to do—in mind, body, and spirit. So it shall be done."

Imagining the sink as a pure lake of crystalline water, Val dunked her head and then leaned back, letting the water drip down her neck and over her shoulders. She drew a long breath, filling her lungs with air, and exhaled. She grounded her feet against the Earth and stoked the flame in her heart.

Then she smashed her head against the mirror.

Val didn't remember hitting the floor, but she found herself staring up at the ceiling, surrounded by glass shards. Her hair was stuck to the tile floor by a puddle of water, tinted red. But she was alive, and that was what counted.

She found a large, sharp shard and grabbed it, then began working on cutting the bindings. The angle made it difficult, but after a minute of experimentation, Val knelt down, the glass pointing downward, and used her shoulders and knees as pivots to saw through the silver barbed wire. After several minutes, testing her patience as she was unable to check her progress, the pressure around her ankles finally gave way, and she could stretch her legs independently again.

Cutting through the binding on her wrists took a bit more time, thanks to the awkward angle. But eventually, it too gave way, freeing her from her constraints.

Val pressed her ear against the bathroom door, listening for anyone who might object to her escape attempt. Convinced the area was clear, she slowly opened the door and peered out.

No one was posted to guard the door. Good.

Mimicking what she'd seen Adrian do, Val warped shadows around her feet to muffle the sound. She was surprised at how easily it came to her. Her new heart was already paying off.

Val stalked down the hall, looking for an exit. She was on the second floor and would need to descend the stairs. No one had bothered to turn on the lights, so Val twisted the shadows around herself as well, just in case.

After a minute of cautiously stepping down the hall, she stopped when she heard Devin and Sophia talking. They were at the bottom of the staircase, near the opening to the foyer, blocking her exit. They appeared nervous, possibly because of whatever had caused the gun to fire. Val balled her fists instead of cursing and tried to determine whether she could sneak around them or if it was better to hide until they dispersed, risking someone realizing she had escaped the bathroom and her bindings.

Devin and Sophia ended their conversation, and Sophia began to turn toward the stairs where Val was lurking. Val ducked back into the hallway before Sophia could see her and retreated. Her options were to return to the bathroom or hide in the guest room. The guest room seemed like the better option. She ran, hoping to make it before Sophia turned into the hall, opened the door, and slipped inside. The hinges squeaked, and Val panicked at the noise that might have given her away.

The guest room was minimally furnished, with just a bed, a wooden nightstand, and a small dresser that wouldn't shield her from view through the doorway. The bed stood too high to hide under, and a pair of blackout drapes over a window on the far wall were bolted shut.

Was her heart strong enough to handle standing on the roof? Only one way to find out. Val looked up and jumped, kicking her feet up as a surge of magic pulled her not back to the ground, but to the ceiling. She landed with one foot hitting solid roofing while the other plunged straight through the drywall.

Perhaps she ought to have checked the ceiling material first.

Sophia must have heard her fumbling. Val lay flat against the ceiling, spreading her weight as much as possible, and rolled above the doorway. She covered her hole with a blanket of shadows just as the door opened beneath her and Sophia poked her head in. If the lights had been on, the swath of darkness would have stood out against the white walls, but the near-pitch-black room disguised her makeshift patch. As long as she didn't scrutinize the smudge on the ceiling too closely, she'd be safe.

Another gunshot. Though it wasn't terribly loud from their position in the mansion, Sophia jumped. "Son of a…" she muttered. "What is Seth doing?"

She turned and closed the door, leaving Val alone in the room. Val waited nearly a minute to make sure Sophia didn't raise any alarms about her escape, and then decided it was safe. This time, being careful to use the shadows to muffle any sound from her movements, Val dropped from the ceiling and landed on the sturdy floor.

The window, did it open? Val yanked the blackout blinds from their bolts in the wall, revealing a large window that spanned nearly the entire length of the wall. But there was no way to open it.

Great. Val cautiously opened the guest room door once again and confirmed that Sophia was no longer in the hall-way. Making sure to mute herself, Val crept down the hall once more and descended the staircase. She was so close to the exit.

And then she stopped. What had been so great about the basement?

She could leave all this behind. For better or worse, she was free. She didn't have much money, but she had enough for a bus ride, a few cheap motel rooms, and a new phone. With careful planning, she could go anywhere she wanted. She could put everything behind her and start over fresh—a ten-year-old vampire with a heart of indeterminate age.

Or she could stay in the city and watch from afar to see how the pieces fell. Perhaps Seth and her old friends would emerge victorious and establish a new order in San Francisco. After things settled down, she could return and bargain for a place among them. Given how they treated her—and how she treated them—it wasn't likely they'd put it all behind them to work together again, but opportunities might still present themselves. Would Seth's hatred for Elders stop at San Francisco? He might find the information she had about the Regents in Los Angeles useful.

Or she could head in the opposite direction. If she truly wanted revenge, what better way than to return to Los Angeles at Joseph's side? It wasn't her he hated, and she had information on Garrick and Adrian's whereabouts. He'd be interested to hear that San Francisco was now in a volatile state. For all his wanton violence, he wasn't an idiot. He was smart enough to survive territory wars against Linh, and he knew an opportunity to extend his power when he saw one. And once he finally thought he had it all, Val would be behind him, a silver-toothed bear trap in hand.

Or she could turn around and find out what was in that damn basement.

Pushing a cold breath through her teeth, Val turned around and peered down a long hallway. The basement was somewhere in that direction, based on where Seth and Owen had disappeared earlier. There wasn't much room to hide; she'd have to be quick.

She sprinted. A large utility room stood at the far end of the hallway, and Val made a snap decision to check it first rather than open every door along the way. But after three long strides, she heard a door creak open from the utility room, and a harsh light spilled across the floor, along with a human-shaped shadow. There was no time to think, only to act on instinct. Val wrapped shadows around her entire body, pressed herself against the wall, and prayed.

Seth emerged at the end of the hall. It wasn't very wide, so Val pressed herself as flat as possible. Even if Seth couldn't see her now, he could easily bump into her, or notice that one area was more shadowed than the others, or...

Val felt her back melt into the wall behind her, like lowering herself into a cool, still pool of water. She leaned back until only her face remained above the plane of wood and drywall. She didn't dare push farther, but it was enough. Seth walked by innocently, the metallic bear trap hanging from a thick chain slung over his back. Val didn't move until she was sure he was out of sight and sound. Then, gingerly, she stepped a leg out from the wall.

Until a second girl rounded the hallway, and she slipped back into her shadow again. Val didn't recognize her, but thankfully, the girl seemed lost in her own thoughts. She walked by without a second glance.

Val stepped out of the wall. Had she melted into her own shadow? She'd never seen Adrian or Garrick do anything like that. But it wasn't a stretch, considering the powers she knew she had. Control shadow, become shadow.

Murdering Tyler for his heart had never felt better.

Once inside the utility room, the basement door was easy to spot. The girl had left it open, and the stark concrete walls hinted at dark horrors within. Perfect.

Val didn't realize how true that thought was until she

reached the bottom and saw the true horror. Owen's body lay crumpled against the side wall, half his head blown open. Val snapped her head away and fought to steady her shaking legs.

No. No, she looked back. Owen's head was blown open, blood and brains oozing down past his ear. It looked familiar. The universe had given her this—a little reminder of what mattered in this hellhole of a world. A bit of justice, finally delivered.

She smiled. Joseph would be next.

The rest of the room was unremarkable. The stone walls were uneven, as if they had been hastily chiseled by hand. The floor was merely a slab of concrete. And beyond that, there was nothing. No powerful artifacts, no lab filled with rusty medical equipment, no horrors beyond Val's imagination. Just an empty room.

"Seriously?" Val spat. She risked coming down here for nothing. Nothing except the opportunity to gloat.

A hole in the far wall caught her attention—only an inch high and half a foot wide, just below eye level. Val peered through it and saw only a darkness that even her night vision couldn't penetrate. She tried to melt into the wall again, and after a moment of fumbling with her chest and cheek pressed against the cool stone, she finally slipped into the solid pool. This time, she went all the way—head, feet, shoulders, hands —until the world was divided. Above, harsh stone and incandescent light; below, darkness. And Val stood flat in between.

She almost panicked. The sensation of flatness disoriented her. Where was the hole? She fumbled around in that in-between space until she found a small area that folded. Was that it? She tried to step into it somehow but quickly realized that, despite being flat, she was not any smaller. Stepping through the hole now would be just as difficult as it had been originally.

She pushed herself back into the world and kicked the

wall. Surely, there had to be a way to manipulate her shadow and make it smaller, but how?

Footsteps interrupted her thoughts. It was too dangerous to practice new magic here. Val pressed herself against the wall again as Devin appeared. He didn't flinch at the sight of Owen, just swore and muttered Seth's name. He rifled through Owen's suit jacket until he found a wallet, then returned upstairs.

Val reformed and took one last look at the hole. Garrick could get through it by turning into a rat or something. Maybe he could teach her how to make her shadow smaller.

That was assuming Garrick was still alive. As of two nights ago, he was, but had Seth succeeded in getting the hunters to attack him during the day? No, she couldn't imagine Garrick, a six-hundred-year-old Elder, falling to a few mortals. Would he still care for Val after his promise not to help following the heart surgery? She honestly didn't know. Garrick cared for her, but he did not suffer fools. And Val was, perhaps, acting a little foolish.

Adrian, though. If there was one thing she could count on, it was him acting the fool. Thank God someone did. They had agreed to become Regents of San Francisco. Would Adrian run from the city, tail between his legs, because his plan didn't work out? No. She'd already seen him do that once. He wouldn't do it again.

Assuming Seth didn't kill him first.

37
NIGHT 9 - ADRIAN

Adrian lined up a shot and sank the four-ball into a pocket but left the cue ball in a bad position. Unfortunate, but he wasn't playing seriously anyway. Having the pool table to help relax his mind was better than pacing around their hotel room, even if it was slightly riskier. He doubted the other vampires would come this far south, where the population was sparse and the nightlife consisted of a small bar barely big enough for its own pool table.

Light glinted off the metal band around his finger as he pulled his hand back from the felt. Adrian didn't want to think of himself as a sap, but he had spent the waning minutes of the previous night staring at it, running his thumb over it while lying in Garrick's uncomfortable nest of blankets and pillows in the shower.

"I think I know what your answer is going to be, but I feel the need to offer it anyway," Garrick said as he leaned over the table to take his shot. He struck the ball but didn't pocket anything. "We could simply move again. I won't make you take any orders you don't want."

Adrian missed Los Angeles, but realistically, it was the worst place for them to go. If Joseph even caught a whiff of their return, he wouldn't stop until he drove a stake through both his heart and his head.

"Like you said, the other Regents aren't any better. And if we're going to fight, someone young like Owen is our best bet. Besides, we can't just leave Val behind."

He was still holding on to the hope that Val was alive. Adrian leaned over for another shot but paused, then straightened up.

"Are you really okay with fighting Owen now?" He hated bringing up the subject again, but it still seemed too good to be true. "Is it really that you hate running cities that much?"

Garrick sighed and leaned against his pool cue, resting the butt on the ground by his foot. "Yes," he said, "but it's complicated. I won't refuse if it's necessary." He paused, and Adrian waited patiently for him to explain. Garrick stared back, then gave in. He opened his mouth, searching for words again.

"I can't hide my Madness, not while running a city. The pressures, the responsibility, the criticism... If I just keep my head down, it's fine. But..."

When Garrick didn't pick up his trailing thought, Adrian pressed further. "How do you keep it suppressed?"

Until this morning, Garrick had insisted he was immune to it, a one-in-a-million coincidence. Now Adrian knew he had merely been tempering his Madness, just enough to make the lie believable. Still, it was better than every other Elder he'd met.

"I wish it were so simple that I could teach you," he said, picking up on Adrian's implication. "But part of it is that you don't even realize what you're doing. No—more like, you know, but you just don't care. It's that voice in the back of your head, justifying everything you do against what you were taught about right and wrong. A coil around your heart, keeping it from feeling the way it used to."

There was something chillingly mundane in Garrick's description. What struck Adrian after being turned was how normal he felt. In stories, vampires were often heartless monsters, and a small part of him had worried he'd become one upon waking. But maybe the stories were true—they just came with a two-century delay.

"But how do you keep it in check?"

Garrick shrugged. "Practice. Introspection. Four hundred years of experience."

"What's your Madness?" Adrian asked. "Not violence or paranoia like Joseph and Linh, obviously."

Garrick stood motionless, staring downward through the floorboards, lost in thought. His lips remained parted, as if he wanted to respond but couldn't shape his thoughts into words. Then he closed his mouth, unable to find anything that could push past his filter.

"I'm sorry," he whispered. "Not today."

Adrian slowly leaned over the table to take his next shot. His bridge arm trembled with a surge of emotion he didn't want to acknowledge. He couldn't be disappointed in Garrick, not after all the shit he'd put him through, but even a ring didn't mean he'd be trusted with all the man's secrets.

No matter. Adrian was going to become the next Regent of San Francisco anyway. He could shield Garrick from the stresses of running a city, and even if he couldn't, he would love him regardless.

Adrian took his shot, wildly missing his target. But what disappointed him more was the realization that he couldn't reasonably promise unconditional love. His imagination conjured up many unlovable actions—and Garrick was a powerful man, capable of all of them.

His phone vibrated in his pocket, snapping him out of his thoughts. Adrian's muted heart skipped a beat when he saw the caller. Val. He hastily answered.

"Val?"

"Hey, Adrian."

The voice on the other end was male, and definitely not Val's. Adrian gripped the phone tightly, shooting a look of intense disappointment at Garrick, who watched him from across the table.

"Who's this?"

"Seth." A brief silence followed. "You bit me at the bar."

"Oh." Wasn't he one of Val's friends? "Where's Val?"

"Don't worry, she's doing just fine. Your girlfriend is too, by the way. I met her last night."

"Why are you calling from Val's phone?"

"All right, we'll skip the small talk. Come to the mansion, I want to speak with you face to face."

Adrian stared at Garrick. Of all the powers vampires were said to possess, telepathy would have been extremely useful right now. He couldn't put Seth on speaker for the entire bar to hear.

"Why?"

Seth huffed. "Look, I'm trying to be nice. I don't want to start threatening people, because then I might have to follow through. So come on over, and let's have a chat."

"Where's Owen?"

"Don't worry about him. He's been taken care of."

Taken care of. Dead? Just what had happened over the past three nights?

"If it's all the same to you, I'd rather have this talk over the phone," Adrian said. "Just finished cocktail hour."

"Ha, you're funny. Meet me in a few hours, or I might get impatient. Bring Garrick. Oh, and Adrian?"

Adrian groaned. "What?"

"Did you tell Garrick about sweet blood yet?"

Adrian furrowed his brow, continuing to stare at Garrick, who watched him in return. Garrick gave no indication that he'd overheard anything. Though why it mattered, Adrian wasn't sure.

"No." By the time it was worth mentioning, their relationship had already taken a turn for the worse. There was always something more important to talk about instead.

"Pro tip: keep that one to yourself. Mansion. Two hours. Don't make me do something neither of us wants."

Seth hung up the phone, leaving Adrian under Garrick's curious gaze. Sweet blood? What did that matter? He and Val had already linked the odd-tasting blood to Owen's heart surgery, assuming it was a strange byproduct. Why wouldn't he want to tell Garrick about it? Maybe Garrick knew something that could give them an edge. Seth was just trying to scare Adrian.

"What's going on?" Garrick asked as Adrian lowered the phone from his ear.

"I'm not entirely sure," Adrian muttered. "That was Seth, one of Val's friends. Sounds like he's in charge now. I don't know if Owen's still alive."

Garrick frowned. "That doesn't clarify much."

Adrian tried to remember as much as he could about his meeting with Seth and Val's conversation on the beach. He hadn't told Garrick about either encounter, or any of the information he'd learned.

"I don't know much about Seth, other than he had a heart transplant to increase his age."

"Him too... Do we know how old his heart is?"

Adrian shook his head. "He also wants us to come by the mansion for a talk. It's almost certainly a trap."

"I know you're not a fan of walking into homes that have been turned into traps." Garrick shifted, as if he wanted to say more but then thought better of it. "It's your call," he said. "Whether we walk straight into it, ignore him, or try to renegotiate. If we rescue Val, that'll be your win. If she dies, that's your responsibility. And if we die..." Garrick hung his head and leaned over the pool table. "If we die, then Hell better have a good marriage counselor."

A good-humored smile lifted the corners of Adrian's mouth, but it was a somewhat terrifying thought. He'd been quick to blame Garrick every time he bent at the first sign of conflict. Now, he didn't have that excuse anymore. How much of a hypocrite would he be if he folded under Seth's threats?

Besides, this was Garrick, the man who had walked through flames without fear the last time he'd been caught in a trap. What could Seth possibly do to harm him?

"We're rescuing Val," Adrian stated. "And I'm going to sit real pretty on Owen's leather sofa when this is all over."

Garrick sighed, shrugged, and did his best to maintain a good-natured smile.

Adrian tapped the pool table with his cue. "Now take your shot. I want to finish up our game before we go see that demon marriage counselor."

Garrick returned his good-humored smile, adding a roll of his eyes as he leaned over the table. As he carefully lined up his shot, Adrian felt his own smile fade. Once again, he had failed to mention sweet blood. He told himself it wasn't because of Seth's warning. It just wasn't important right now. Adrian thumbed over Garrick's ring again, lying to himself that's all it was.

38

NIGHT 9 - ADRIAN

There was something oddly enticing about standing on the roof of a house like a hawk, perched and scanning the ground for prey. From his current vantage point, Adrian couldn't see any movement inside the mansion, roughly twenty yards away. The lights were off, but that wasn't unusual for them. Shadows wrapped around his figure, just in case Seth was on the lookout for them too.

No wingbeats alerted Adrian to the arrival of an owl, which morphed at the last second into Garrick. He planted his feet on the square rim of the roof and caught his momentum with an outstretched hand around the roof's corner. Keeping low, Garrick carefully sidestepped closer to Adrian, careful not to alert the house's occupants to the trespasser above.

"Anything?" he asked. Adrian shook his head.

"Almost certainly a trap, then. If he really did just want to talk, I imagine there'd be some sign of life inside."

"He's got the home-field advantage," Adrian said. "Even if we know it's an ambush, he still has the upper hand. The question now is how he plans to spring it."

Garrick let out a heavy sigh, resting his elbows on his knees like a gargoyle. "I suppose it's too late to request that we turn this into a rescue mission rather than a full-on firefight?"

"No, you're right. Let's go back to LA and fight Joseph instead. I left my favorite pool cue there."

Adrian chuckled to himself, knowing Garrick shot him a disgruntled look without needing to check. He took the revolver from his pocket and inspected it again. Six bullets loaded. Safety off.

"You know I don't like guns."

Adrian frowned. "You had one."

"Good for impersonal killing at a distance, which is rare for us. Not an impossible scenario, but still uncommon. I have a feeling this will be a very up-close and personal fight. And mine didn't have silver bullets."

Adrian snapped the cylinder back into place. "All the more reason to bring this one."

Garrick hummed. "Always assume that whatever weapon you bring will be used against you."

"Always assume your opponent will use every tool at their disposal."

Garrick looked up at him from under a furrowed brow, but a hint of a smile betrayed his amusement. "Since when did you become such a wise guy?"

"Where do you think I got it?"

Garrick shook his head and stood, stretching his back in the process. "No balconies. Our options are the front door, the back door, or breaking a window. And before you get any ideas, breaking a window is a great way to lose the element of surprise and suffer many lacerations."

"Speaking from experience?"

"I was young and foolish once, too."

"We'll go in the back, then. Seems more... sneaky that way."

"Yes," Garrick said flatly. "More sneaky."

Garrick grabbed Adrian by the arm. But instead of being pulled closer, he felt his body dissipate and was hit by an intense wave of vertigo—until, suddenly, he found himself standing on the pavement again. Garrick still held his arm as he regained his balance.

Dissolving into misty shadows sounded a lot more fun than it actually turned out to be.

They rounded the back of the mansion, jumped the fence, and slowly made their way to the rear door. Adrian remained cautious, watching the windows for any sign of movement, but the mansion seemed just as lifeless as when he first started prowling it. Garrick inspected the edges of the door for a gap and shook his head. They'd have to break in the loud way. He backed up and, with a single powerful kick, smashed the door off its hinges.

Adrian dashed, gun drawn, into a dark and silent house. Garrick strolled into the back sunroom, unbothered. After a moment spent inspecting their surroundings, Garrick nodded toward the kitchen. He silently led them through the room, and without incident, they entered the large, open sitting area where Owen hosted his many gatherings.

Adrian wasn't sure what to expect of the mansion's interior since their failed coup attempt, but the furnishings appeared undisturbed. If there had been a fight, the victor had been kind enough to set everything back in its place, as if nothing violent had transpired. A splatter of blood staining the drywall suggested otherwise.

The window on the right wall overlooked the San Francisco Bay, a small cluster of lights in the distance outlining the water's edge. Adrian's eyes darted to the corners of the room —the twin couches, the far sitting chairs, the serving table. It was unlikely they'd catch Seth and his cronies by surprise. He listened for any telltale movement that might signal the start of an ambush.

Suddenly, Garrick pulled Adrian into a bear hug as two gunshots shattered the silence. The movement was so abrupt that Adrian barely had time to register what had happened before Garrick released him and glared over his shoulder. Obscured by the darkness, Seth stood by the back window with a pistol raised, though Adrian could have sworn he hadn't been there a moment ago. Seth shrugged and tossed his gun carelessly to the ground.

"Well, color me impressed," Seth taunted. "Not many Elders would jump in front of a bullet like that. Maybe he actually does like you."

Adrian ducked out from behind Garrick and raised his own gun, but Seth's figure dissolved into the surrounding darkness. He waited a moment, scanning for movement, but couldn't find any sign of the other vampire.

Garrick let out a grunt and then stood up straight. He stretched out his arm, as if all he had suffered was a light cramp. It would have been more strategic for Adrian to take the bullets, and he wished Garrick had let him.

With the gun still raised, Adrian slowly surveyed the sitting room once more. Seth was hiding somewhere, and Adrian hated waiting for him to make the first move.

Garrick grunted, drawing Adrian's attention, and he noticed him looking up at the ceiling. Following his gaze,

Adrian saw Seth clinging there, red eyes staring down at them. Suddenly, Seth transformed into a large owl and dove, talons outstretched, toward Adrian and Garrick. Adrian raised his gun to shoot, but someone grabbed him from behind, yanking his arm to the side.

His assailant bit into his neck, and panic surged through Adrian's body, giving him just enough time to think and act before the venom clouded his mind. He lurched forward, tearing the fangs from his neck, then slammed his head back into his attacker's face. His skull connected with a satisfying crack, followed by a shout of pain as the man loosened his grip just enough for Adrian to dart forward.

Adrian fired blindly behind him as he clutched the wound on his neck. He stumbled slightly as the room began to spin. Brain and blood were the two things vampires still needed to function, and a severed carotid artery denied the first of the second. Adrian wouldn't have time to check if his healing was working. He just hoped that when he took his hand away, the bleeding would stop.

A few paces away, Devin—his face smeared with blood from a broken nose—knelt on the ground, one arm cradling a bullet wound in his leg. He'd walk it off in a minute, but better than the bullet missing entirely.

Adrian felt something brush his back and instinctively threw himself to the floor. Nora tripped over him but bounced back to her feet quickly. Adrian tried to regain his footing as well, though far less gracefully, wobbling as his head struggled to clear from the venom.

That accounted for three of Val's four friends. Adrian risked taking his eyes off Nora for a moment to check his surroundings for Sophia. He spotted her halfway out of cover behind a wall leading into the dining room, a kitchen knife in hand. She ducked back into the other room when Adrian raised his gun.

Adrian backed up against the window to guard against

any more surprise attacks. Each of his assailants took cover behind pieces of furniture, varying their positions to avoid getting shot. To his right, a bear and a giant snake took turns swiping and snapping at each other. Adrian couldn't tell which one was Garrick.

The wobbling stopped, a good sign that his emergency healing had worked. Adrian passed his gun into his left hand and drew his knife with his right. There wasn't much time to waste. The silver in Garrick's back would eventually take its toll. If he could just put two rounds into Seth, that would even the odds.

Then the giant snake struck suddenly, snapping Nora between its fangs, lifting her into the air, and hurling her against the wall with a sickening crack. The unexpected change in target seemed to stun everyone in the room, except for the large bear tearing into the serpent's tail. The snake didn't seem to care and immediately lunged at Devin. He jumped out of the way just in time.

The shift in the battle's momentum gave Adrian a moment to catch his breath and gather his thoughts. Then he sprinted straight toward the bear. Shooting a bear with a metal as soft as silver didn't seem promising. Shooting a bear directly in the face probably would, though. Adrian hoped Seth was too focused on hurting Garrick to notice his approach, but before he closed half the distance, the bear looked up and growled. Adrian raised the gun and fired, but Seth shifted out of his large form just in time to dodge the bullet.

As a human again, Seth charged at him, and Adrian braced for impact. But just before Adrian made his move to intercept, a large snake tail whipped around and flung Seth into the window, shattering the glass. Seth's limp body fell beneath the broken pane.

Adrian sighed in relief. Two down, two young vampires left. Sophia darted out from behind the sofa and stabbed the snake midway down its body. The snake hissed and spat in response. Adrian rushed to intercept, but before he could reach her, Devin stepped in his way. Devin grabbed Adrian's gun hand, but Adrian twisted around and buried his knife in Devin's side. Breaking free of Devin's grip, Adrian spun around to see Garrick—now shifted back to human—holding the kitchen knife.

Adrian turned to confront Devin and end their fight, only to find Nora standing right beside him. Nora? Before he could question her sudden appearance, Adrian was tackled from the side and felt his body grow weightless, dissolving into mist. Panic surged within him, but he couldn't express it. Moments later, he found himself lying on the ground, several yards from where he had just stood. Garrick knelt protectively over him. Along with Devin and Nora, Seth stood nearby, seething with anger, before vanishing back into the darkness.

"Something's wrong," Garrick said.

"Seth being an Elder was unexpected," Adrian responded.

"Not that. They're healing too fast, especially the younger ones."

Adrian stood up. "Any idea why that is?" he whispered.

"They're drawing from some source of magical power."

"Owen?"

Garrick furrowed his brows, keeping his eyes on their opponents, though Adrian could tell he was deep in thought.

"Maybe. Maybe not. But we'll be here until sunrise unless we stop it."

Adrian tried to think, but Garrick's voice echoed in his head. Wait, since when could he do that?

I'll keep the Elder busy. You go find the power source and shut it down. I think it's coming from below.

"How can you... Are you sure?"

Garrick nodded. Adrian swore under his breath, unsure if Garrick could hear it inside his head. He didn't even know the mansion had a basement.

347

Adrian darted to the left, back into the kitchen. A gunshot blasted overhead, and he ducked behind a table, his ears ringing. Damn guns, he had imagined his would be more useful than this.

Adrian stood and hurled a kitchen chair toward the entrance. It smashed against Devin's shoulder, but the smaller Sophia darted out from behind him to continue the chase. Some of the chair's debris must have struck Devin's leg wound, as he dropped to his knees in renewed pain. Nora yanked the gun from Devin's hands and continued firing.

Aiming for the edge of a window to maximize his chances of hitting a stud, Adrian kicked off the side wall and flipped onto the ceiling. He ran a few strides, then flipped back down to the other side of the kitchen. A few gunshots followed, but none came as close as the first.

Adrian had to think fast. The right hall would bring him back around to the foyer and the staircase leading to the second floor. He could safely assume the basement wasn't in that direction. Left it was, into a part of the mansion he'd never explored before. He took a risk and ran into the first room off the hallway, only to find himself in what appeared to be Owen's study. The only other door in the room opened to a small closet. To avoid the inevitable flurry of bullets, Adrian wrapped shadows around himself and dashed toward the study's exit, pressing against the wall behind the door hinges —just as it opened and Nora stepped in, gun raised. Adrian slammed into the door, striking her shoulder and outstretched arm. Then he shifted his gravity again and crashed through the drywall to the other side.

Lying on the floor of the hall, Adrian drew his gun and fired at a dazed Nora and a very surprised Sophia. The gun clicked. The lack of a gunshot made everyone pause, and the corner of Adrian's eye twitched, as if laughing at the absurdity of the moment. He should have known better than to trust this dingy revolver.

Adrian got back on his feet, but the hallway was straight, making him an easy target if he simply turned and ran. Nora regained her senses enough to raise her gun again, and Adrian instinctively raised his arm and turned his shoulder in defense.

A mass of shadows slinked around the corner and materialized into Val. Her fangs sunk into Nora's neck and a kitchen knife slashed across Sophia's face. After another stab to Sophia's side for good measure, Val turned toward Adrian, her face lighting up with joy and relief at the sight of him.

Adrian mirrored it back. Thank God, Val was alive. And, surprisingly, not Seth's prisoner. He opened his mouth to speak, he had so many questions, but they weren't safe yet. Devin rounded the corner into the hall and charged toward them, a broken steel pipe in hand.

Adrian grabbed Val's hand and pulled her down the hall with him to the last room—a laundry room covered in white tile, with a door in the corner whose lock had been blown out. That was promising.

Adrian waited until Devin nearly caught up to him, then raised the gun at the last moment. Devin knocked it out of his hand, and Adrian grabbed the pipe with his other hand at the end of his swing. They struggled for a moment until Devin dove for the gun. Good. With the broken, sharp end pointing down, Adrian drove the pipe through Devin's midsection, piercing the tile beneath him.

"Is that the basement?" Adrian asked, ignoring the violence and snapping Val out of her shock. She nodded.

"Come on!" Adrian darted to the door and flung it open. A staircase descended into the earth, flanked by stone walls on either side. This was definitely the way to the basement.

Adrian ran down the steps two at a time, with Val close behind him.

"You came back for me!" Val said, and Adrian noted the genuine happiness in her voice.

"Seems like I didn't need to!" he replied.

"You're a day late, but I appreciate the thought."

Adrian beamed, relieved that his gambit hadn't been for nothing. But he couldn't afford to celebrate yet. He still had a power source to find.

39

NIGHT 9 - GARRICK

G arrick watched as the three younger vampires left to chase Adrian. He frowned, having assumed at least one would stay behind to help their Regent fight. Still, it confirmed he was right about the power source.

"Looks like it's just us now." Garrick sat on the couch, still watching Seth out of the corner of his eye. If Seth were smart, he'd go after Adrian as well. But the young Elder had focused on him for the entire fight, so Garrick figured it was safe to disengage briefly. He rotated his arm, stretching the muscles in his back. One bullet had hit him in the shoulder blade, the other in his gut. Neither was true silver, judging by the absence of the intense fire that usually accompanied the pain. Cheap bullets. He didn't care to let Seth in on his discovery.

Seth kept his hands raised like a boxer, waiting. Garrick could tell that his inaction irritated the young Elder.

"Oh, relax. We both know this fight is going nowhere. Have a seat."

Seth lowered his hands but remained standing. He stared at him, glowering.

"Have you considered simply working alongside me instead of fighting?" Garrick offered. "You've clearly won their loyalty. That's promising. Elders don't often work together, but there's no reason we can't. I haven't held real territory in a hundred years, and I'm not looking to. You could use an Elder with experience to mentor you."

Seth scoffed. "I'm not looking to work together," he spat. "And I'm not an Elder. Once I'm done with you and Adrian, I'm ripping this heart out of my chest and putting a proper one back in."

Garrick furrowed his brow in confusion. "You want to go backward? Why? You've already accomplished what every vampire hopes to achieve at your age. You have three loyal followers willing to offer their necks to you."

"Friends," Seth clarified. "They're my friends."

"Friends—until they need vampire blood too. Then you'll need four more friends. Then eight."

Seth laughed at that, which made Garrick pause. He expected Seth to be angered by his logic.

"I know what you're trying to lead me to," Seth jeered. "How many friends have you killed? Probably a lot. Probably enough to know you should only keep one sucker close at all times. Hard to be friends with people when you know that one day you won't take your fangs off them until you've drained their life away."

Garrick sat in silence, his hands clasped in his lap, thumbs slowly circling one another. So young, yet Seth had already contemplated his existence more than most. Young vampires didn't always survive their first week, often unable to face the harsh necessities of their continued existence. Young Elders faced two trials: the first against the current Elders, who stamped out potential threats before they could grow; the second against themselves, struggling once more to endure the demands of their prolonged lives.

His Madness coiled around his heart like twin vipers, shielding it from Seth's accusations.

"So instead of taking their blood slowly over a century, you'll take their heart in one go," Garrick stated, his voice flat. "If it helps you sleep in the morning."

"I'm sure I can find someone better off dead to take it from. And once there's no one left, I'll be happy to lay down my own life when the time comes."

Garrick's mouth contorted into the facsimile of a smile.

"I always enjoy listening to young Elders justify their Madness."

That statement successfully drew a reaction from Seth. He flinched, as if every muscle in his body wanted to snap and lash out, but was restrained by some better nature. He stayed silent just a moment too long. A twitch of the eyes, the rustling of clothes, a faint tinkling of metal. Garrick twisted in his seat to look behind him, and the sudden rush of motion near his head caused him to raise an arm in defense. The back of his hand brushed against steel, and a violent snap filled his ears. He opened his eyes to see a bear trap clamped around his forearm, bending it slightly askew beneath teeth glistening with his blood. His mind froze at the sight of his own body so viciously warped, but experience kickstarted it again before the pain could fully choke out his thoughts.

A swell of magic tugged at every fiber of his being, weaving him into mist and siphoning him away from his seat on the couch—until it reached his arm. There, it stopped cold. The threads of Garrick's being were yanked back into the shape of his physical body, his arm still clamped in the silver teeth of the bear trap.

Then the pain hit him.

Garrick cried out but quickly stifled it into hisses between his clenched teeth. Pain won't kill us, he had taught Adrian. Just leftover signals from a time when their bodies were more fragile. Ignore it. Protect what's important.

"Good enough," he heard Seth say over the ringing in his ears. "Hand me your gun, I'm out of ammo. And figure out where that knife went."

Garrick stood, cradling the bear trap in one arm. Dark tendrils of shadow twisted around him, contorting into horrid visages that screeched, wailed, and scraped at the walls.

A red stain splattered in front of him as a gunshot echoed through the room, causing the shadows to shatter. His vision blurred, darkening at the edges, and a thick drop of liquid ran down his face, between his eyes. The surrounding sounds blurred together, difficult to parse.

One... two... three... He blinked. He flexed the fingers of his free arm and swayed his weight back and forth. Impressive that he remained standing. Must have been a small caliber.

Garrick turned his head to look over his shoulder and met the horrified faces of Seth and his friend, the woman with the darker skin.

Adrian had better hurry up and find that power source.

"What are you?" Seth whispered.

"Old."

With trembling hands, Seth pulled a small plastic device from his pocket. It took Garrick a moment to recognize it as a simple cigarette lighter.

"Whatever you're thinking of doing…"

Seth dissolved into the shadows once again, though it wouldn't stay dark for long.

40

NIGHT 9 - ADRIAN

I t wasn't until Adrian reached the bottom of the staircase that the vertigo kicked in. The adrenaline from the fight above had kept him from fully considering the implications of entering the basement—not until he was already beneath several feet of solid earth, his only exit behind him, trying to kill him. A single bulb bathed the room in a harsh yellow light, highlighting every crook and crack in the cramped space, which was barely large enough for him, Val, and the half-disintegrated corpse in the corner.

Corpse? Why was there a *corpse* down here? What danger lurked in the stairwell that—

"Wait, where's Garrick?" Val asked. She stood by the far wall, next to a rectangular indentation.

Garrick? No, he was still fending off Seth. Adrian needed to find the power source. If he found it, he could shut it off. Then he could leave.

"Power source," Adrian choked. "Where...?"

"Are you okay?" Val asked. "Are you hurt?"

"I'm fine," he lied. His heart hammered in his chest, its throbbing filling his ears. He wasn't going to turn tail and run, not while Garrick needed him. He looked around again. Power source... where was it? In the corpse?

Val pointed at the hole in the far wall. "It's through here," she said. "Can you fit?"

Through the hole? Adrian leaned over and peered through, but saw only darkness. The hole was only about an inch thick, so there was likely another room on the other side. His muscles tensed at the thought of somehow squeezing through and becoming trapped in an even smaller, darker space. He reached his hand through the cutout and gripped around the stone, as if grabbing hold of the darkness might make him feel safer.

If he were an Elder, he could change his body to fit—a mouse, a spider, maybe even the dark mist that Garrick had forced him into minutes ago. Was there another way? He tugged at the stone, thinking he might be able to break it free, but it held steady.

The pounding in his ears grew louder until it drowned out all thoughts. How was he supposed to concentrate like this?

"Do you hear that?" Val asked. "Or feel it, I guess?"

Val heard it? Was his heartbeat that loud? No, it was something else. Adrian flexed his fingers again and tried to focus on the pulse. Now realizing it wasn't coming from within his own chest, he grew curious. An energy. The power source. Could he use it? The others had increased their strength with it. So could he.

Adrian closed his eyes, shutting out the outside world. Waves of energy washed over him in rhythm with his own heartbeat. A living organism, though not alive in the way mortals or vampires were. Something simpler, yet extraordinarily magical. With each beat, the walls around them shuddered, as if the mansion itself had a heart.

Could he reach out to it? Focus his energy like Garrick had taught him with healing? He imagined himself as a flame, his own energy radiating heat. Thinking of it that way, the other side of the wall became a blaze of magic. And he could touch it.

The sensation of gripping cold stone vanished, and Adrian opened his eyes to see his hand dissolve into a cloud of black smoke. He jerked it back, and it reappeared.

Yes, he could do this.

"Hold on." Adrian extended his other arm, and Val took it without question. He reached through the hole again and focused once more. It was easier the second time, now that he knew it was possible and recognized the sensation that followed. He spread that strange numbness up his entire arm, over his head and chest, and extended it to Val.

Then he was mist. Formless, yet still aware enough to move through the solid world. The hole yawned open like a great archway, and he pulled himself and Val through until they were fully within the bounds of the other room. Then he released his hold on that energy, and his body snapped back into place.

Once through to the other side, the darkness gave way—but only slightly. Adrian could barely make out the four walls of the chamber. Shadows still clung to the corners, slithering out from behind the outlines of tables and tool benches littered with bladed instruments and glass jars. He shifted his weight, his feet ready to spring away from the darkness that threatened to smother him. The pounding of his heart intensified, drowning out the sound of Val's footsteps as she slowly explored the chamber. Adrian raised his hands to cover his ears but stopped a few inches short, unwilling to look like a fool.

He needed to find the power source. Only then could he leave.

A plodding of footsteps snapped his attention to the back corner of the room, to his left. They weren't alone. Adrian pulled his knife and rushed toward the faint silhouette of a person. His arm struck something solid before his blade could find flesh. Instead, something sharp pierced Adrian's gut.

Up close, Adrian saw Melissa standing in front of him, blocking his attack with her arm. He raised his hand to strike again, but a sudden pressure in his side knocked him to the ground with unexpected force. Melissa stood over him, her nails sharp as claws and dripping with his blood.

He pounced. His body melted into the darkness and surged forward, reemerging directly in front of her. She slashed at his face with sharp claws, but they did little to halt his assault. He slammed her into the wall, bit her neck, and threw her to the floor. Dropping a knee to pin her chest, he grabbed a fistful of hair to wrench her head back. Instead, the hair slipped away with little resistance, giving Adrian a brief moment of confusion.

Melissa raised a hand to protect her bald head, wrapped in a velvet headband. She used Adrian's hesitation as an opportunity to snap at him.

"Where's Thea? I know she went back to you."

Thea? No, she hadn't spoken a word to him since the night before.

"You tried to kill me!" Adrian spat. He tossed the wig aside and pulled his fist back. His punch landed against Melissa's raised arms.

"Adrian!" Val's voice made him hesitate. No, it was clear now. Melissa was Striga and had tried to have him killed. She was trying to kill him now. He raised his fist to strike again.

"Adrian, wait!" Val's hand gripped his shoulder firmly. "She's not a threat anymore. Just—"

"What?" He whirled around and stood, violently knocking Val's hand away. "She tried to kill me! She tried to kill us! She—"

"I know. It's just... your eyes are glowing red."

His eyes? No, no, that was impossible. They only did that when one was an Elder, and their Madness...

"No..." Adrian shook his head. "No, no, I'm not... I'm not mad, I'm not. It's the room. It's..." This stupid chamber and its suffocating darkness that he could just leave if he had that fucking power source!

"I know." Delicately, Val pulled him into a hug. Light at first, then firm as his shaking subsided. "I know you're not mad. This power source is making us all a little stir-crazy. I just don't want you to do something you'll later regret."

The power source? No, that's what he *needed*. Once he had the power source he could leave, go back to Garrick...

"Seth is Striga, okay? Seth is trying to kill you."

Seth? But, how? Why? He couldn't think right now. But... she was right about Melissa. He already regretted trying to kill her once and making an enemy out of one of his only friends. Melissa wasn't acting like a skilled fighter, despite getting the jump on him.

Val tugged on Adrian's sleeve and led him to the back wall. They approached a table holding a large bowl and a dozen smaller glass jars, each filled with a dark liquid. A quick breath confirmed Adrian's suspicions about the contents, as his nose filled with the stench of iron. Looking closer, he realized the bowl was the same vessel Owen had used to collect blood—now completely full. The surface of the pooled blood rippled in a rhythmic fashion.

After observing it for a few seconds, Adrian pulled back his sleeve and reached inside. His hand brushed against something repulsively fleshy, pulsing in sync with the waves of energy he had felt earlier. He grasped the entity and pulled it out, revealing a human heart. Beating.

"How...?" Val asked. Adrian studied the heart, but he had no answer.

"The heart of an Elder Vampire," Melissa said, walking up beside him. Adrian jumped at her sudden appearance but made no move to fight again. In fact, she seemed oddly calm, despite their altercation just moments before. "This is your power source."

How was the heart still beating? Was it something innate about the heart itself, or was some other magic keeping it alive? With every throb in his hand, Adrian felt a wave of magical energy course through him. The weariness from the previous battle faded, and Adrian felt not only strong, but almost incorporeal. The material world, once so solid and fixed, now seemed elastic, moldable. Before, he had merely existed within the universe. Now, the universe bent to him. Changing it would be trivial, starting with himself, molding his body into any shape that could still sustain life. The walls, once solid and imposing, were now nothing more than malleable liquid.

Finally, Adrian relaxed. Not even the Earth itself could trap him down here. He was free to leave at any time, through any door. Even one he made himself.

"How do we stop it from giving power to everyone?" Adrian asked.

Melissa shrugged. "Never had to do that before. Kill it?"

"You're being awfully helpful," Val muttered.

"I'm just hiding down here until a victor is decided. I don't care which of you wins. Just promise me you'll keep Thea safe if you do."

That was fine with him. Adrian focused on the heart again. He couldn't kill it. Doing so would drown him in the choking darkness once more. It would mean discarding a major weapon against Seth and jeopardizing their safety. It would mean giving up his revenge against Joseph and his chance to return home to Los Angeles. So what if he suffered a little Madness?

The heart fluttered, and instinctively, Adrian knew it was starved of fresh blood. He drew his knife and made a long cut along his palm before grasping the heart once again. The physical touch created a link. He could shut off its power to Seth and his friends, as if it were his own heart.

"Let's go," Adrian said. He nodded to Val, then looked over at Melissa and gave her a polite nod as well. He didn't trust her, and he hadn't forgiven her, but he had no reason to believe she'd harm him at the moment. He had bigger problems.

Adrian took Val's hand in his and returned to mist. With the heart firmly in his palm, the transformation was effortless. Together, they flew out of the dark chamber, through the small hole in the wall, and rematerialized on the other side.

That's when Adrian heard the gunshot.

Val's head snapped back in a spray of blood, and Adrian instinctively caught her falling body, even as his mind froze, unable to process the sound and horrific sight. Standing at the entrance to the basement was Devin, gun raised. His gaze was fixed on the spot where Val's head had been, as if he too were paralyzed by the chain of events. Then, his eyes flicked to Adrian's, and he shifted the gun ever so slightly, read-justing his aim directly at Adrian's face.

Looking down the barrel of the gun unleashed an anger within Adrian, overriding any fear he might have felt. He charged at Devin, lurching to the right just in time for a second bullet to whiz past his head, then leaped for Devin's neck. He bit the man, then immediately yanked his teeth away before kicking him off his feet. Devin hit the floor and clutched his wound with his left hand. Adrian delivered a sharp kick to his face, the shock of which made it easy to wrest the revolver from Devin's right hand. He first aimed it at Devin's head, then shifted his aim to his heart and fired. Make him suffer a few extra minutes.

He ran back over to Val and skidded to the ground by her side. She had landed on the floor, head twisted upward, and lay unmoving. The bullet had struck the right side of her head, exposing shattered pieces of bone and what Adrian thought was brain matter. His stomach lurched, but this time, he couldn't look away.

"No, no..." he choked out, then delicately placed a shaking hand over the wound. Could his healing magic, even with the Elder heart, work on something as destructive as this? Adrian checked Val's wound again. He couldn't tell if his healing was having any effect. He gently tilted her head upward, and her eyes, though unfocused, moved slowly around the room. Still alive, though just barely.

"Here, take this." Adrian pressed the Elder heart to her chest. Val was in no state to hold anything, if she even understood his words at all, so Adrian tore the front of her shirt, turning the neckline into a messy V-cut.

"Sorry," he muttered, uncomfortably shoving the heart into her bra. Perhaps having it close to her own heart would improve the healing. Adrian lifted his hand away and instantly felt the power wane. Yes, having the heart in contact with skin and blood helped it focus, but it meant less power for him.

As a final precaution, Adrian took out his knife and began cutting a strip of cloth from his shirt, until he realized it would be quicker to just take the whole shirt off. He folded it a few times, then hastily tied it around Val's head. Slipping his jacket back on, he tucked the knife into his pocket. Then, he carefully picked Val's body up in his arms. Mindful not to jostle her, he stepped over Devin's body and out of the basement. He hurried up the stairs, only to find that the universe wasn't finished with its assault.

From the open doorway at the top of the stairs, smoke spilled out onto the roof of the hall.

41
NIGHT 9 - ADRIAN

Crawling on the floor wasn't an option for Adrian as he held Val to his chest. The smoke stung his eyes, but unlike the last time he found himself inside a burning building, he simply shrugged off the pain. It was a relief that Nora and Sophia weren't waiting for him at the top of the stairs, ready to restart their fight. If they were smart, they would have run as soon as they noticed the fire.

Garrick... He needed to find Garrick. He was Val's best chance for survival. Adrian ran back through the utility room, past the unused bathrooms, and found himself face-to-face with a wall of flames. He tensed and hesitated. He could run through the flames, but… No, magic was made for problems like this.

He looked down and placed his fingers back on the Elder heart. He felt his body dissolve again, quickly enveloping Val as well. Then he floated across the flames, unharmed.

The hallway burned for about five yards, then cleared just before reaching the sitting room where the previous battle had taken place. Garrick was nowhere to be seen. Panic rose within Adrian, and he nearly dropped the mist state, until he realized it would be much easier to remain in mist form than to keep switching in and out. He floated to the other side of the room, trying to get a sense of where Garrick might have gone. Perhaps to the place where the fire had started.

Adrian tried to think, to observe—especially since Val wasn't bleeding out in this form anymore—but he found it difficult to hold a thought for very long. His mind fogged over, and a sense of calm, of selflessness, tugged at his consciousness. That feeling of being more than the material world returned, but without the commanding presence from before.

Adrian lurched with a brief sensation of vertigo and stumbled back into solid form. Ah, that's why no one stayed in mist form for too long. He snarled at his rude reentry into the real world and shook his head to clear the smoke from his eyes again.

"Garrick!" he called, but there was no answer.

The panic boiling up inside Adrian made his stomach churn. He wasn't escaping this time, but going deeper in. Adrian rushed down a hallway and came across an empty guest room. He kicked open the door to a closet filled with spare linens. The back exit was deserted, and he didn't see anyone out on the lawn.

Returning to the sitting room, Adrian considered checking the dining room on the other side of the mansion, but the fire made him hesitate. If he wasn't careful, he'd find himself trapped. Again. There was no guarantee Garrick was still in the house, and while finding him was Val's best hope, getting them both killed wouldn't help anyone.

If Adrian wanted to go deeper into the house, he'd need all the magical power he could gather. That meant taking it from the Elder heart, and not using that magic to keep Val alive.

He looked down at Val and didn't see any signs of life. That didn't tell him much—she'd barely shown any to begin with—but her half-closed, unmoving eyes were concerning. Adrian adjusted his grip to place a hand near her head and tried healing magic again. If it would just keep her alive a little longer...

Adrian held Val a little tighter and remembered the night he was saved. The screams of his crew echoed in his mind— their voices filled with rage at the man who betrayed them— as Garrick had carried him past, damning each of them to a fiery grave. He stood paralyzed, torn between the competing thoughts: dropping Val's body, taking the heart for himself, and running unencumbered into the flames—or running with her out the door without looking back, and nothing but hope for Garrick's survival.

The ring on his finger glinted in the light of the flames around him.

"I'm sorry..." he trembled. "I tried."

Slowly, he knelt and lowered Val's body to the floor. He cursed himself, cursed Seth, cursed the universe, and said goodbye. His fingers brushed around the heart, but he hesitated to take it from her skin.

He needed the heart. He needed it to move around the mansion as mist again. And while he liked Val, he loved Garrick. Of course between the two of them, he would pick Garrick.

But he couldn't. If he had the power himself, he wouldn't

have to choose. He could save both. An Elder wouldn't have to choose.

Adrian scooped up Val again, sprinted to the front door, kicked it open, and ran out into the cold, open air. Struggling to steady his trembling arms, he laid Val down on the lawn a safe distance from the house and scanned the sky. Maybe Garrick had escaped and was circling the mansion, searching for signs of him.

He wasn't there, and Adrian knew he would have to go back in.

I'm not mad. Not yet. Please, not yet... Adrian choked back the last of his protests. Then, using the power contained entirely within himself, he dissolved into mist and returned to the mansion.

With newfound resolve, he rushed up the stairs into the thick, black smoke. He felt the pull of losing himself in the swirling dark, but resisted it. He focused on an area where the smoke was densest and moved closer. It appeared to be pouring out of one of the guest rooms.

Though it was difficult to see past the haze, Adrian could make out the outlines of two people standing in the room, the smoldering fire casting an eerie glow that highlighted their figures from below. Closer to the back stood Seth, his shorter, aggressive build and long black hair giving away his identity. Near the door, hunched and kneeling, was Garrick, a bear trap clamped around his arm. He appeared to be trying to pry it open with his free hand, but it wouldn't budge. A line of blood spilled over his fingers and along the teeth of the trap.

Seth raised a gun and fired several rounds into Garrick. The Elder didn't attempt any magic to escape. Instead, he simply raised his arm to protect his head. He shook, and Adrian realized just how badly his shirt and pants were torn and soaked with growing red stains. Seeing him in such a state filled Adrian with protective rage, and he shot forward, returning to his solid state just in time to knock Seth off his feet.

Not wasting his momentum, Adrian clasped one hand around Seth's gun hand, pinning it to the ground, and placed the other over his face. Fighting through the man's flailing, Adrian leaned in toward his neck, only for Seth to dissolve beneath him. Adrian followed the motion of the shadow to his right, where Seth reappeared, eyes glowing red, gun raised. Adrian misted, dropping the state just in time to lunge for the gun again, but Seth retreated into his own mist. Adrian lunged again in a deadly, magical game of tag—and realized Seth was laughing.

"Looks like you've learned a new trick," he taunted. "How's it feel? This power?"

Adrian snarled. He still had the gun in his pocket, apparently working despite the earlier misfire, but he had lost count of how many bullets remained. Then again, Seth didn't know either.

He pulled the gun and aimed, causing Seth to dissipate again. Taking a split second to determine the direction of his retreat, Adrian grabbed his knife with his other hand and whirled around to stab where he assumed Seth would reappear. The knife struck something solid, and Seth flinched as the blade landed just beneath his ribs. He misted again, but this time Adrian reached into the cloud and misted as well.

Fighting someone when neither held a physical form was an odd feeling. Adrian could feel Seth push and tug at his essence, and a second later, the two tumbled to the floor together, straight into the flames.

Ignoring the searing pain, Adrian held Seth's head to the fire. Seth tried to turn to mist again, but after their shared experience, Adrian knew how to keep him within his grasp. He drained the mist of its power and slammed Seth back down. Seth cried out, and after a moment of struggling against the flames, looked up at Adrian.

"Mad Elder," he seethed through clenched teeth.

"Shut up!" Adrian wrestled the gun away and pressed it against Seth's forehead.

"You should be turning that on him," Seth said. Adrian frowned, then realized he was talking about Garrick. He looked up to see Garrick kneeling by the door, eyes wide and watching.

"Don't bother saving his life. He won't extend that kindness to you!"

"Shut up!" Adrian cried again. "I'm not mad!"

"Using Thea, slaughtering hunters, sounds pretty mad to me! If you're not mad, then you're just a terrible person!"

The gun trembled in Adrian's hands. No, he couldn't listen to Seth. He was just trying to get into his head.

"Go on, sane vampire. Kill me, take my heart, and justify it to your Elder later. I'm sure he'll agree next time his fangs are on your neck, draining your life away!"

"I'm not mad!" Other than the uncontrollable trembling, Adrian was paralyzed with fear. He shouted his protests not just to Seth, but to himself. His life had been so short. He couldn't bear the thought of being executed by the man he loved. Garrick loved him too. He wouldn't kill him. He wouldn't...

Adrian lowered the gun. He knew the smart move would be to kill him now, before he had time to recover and attack again, but the lion gnashing for violence and control in his heart stilled. He didn't need it, not anymore.

A hand brushed his shoulder, and Adrian jumped. Garrick knelt beside him. "It's all right," he whispered. "I know."

With his good, untrapped hand, he brushed the gun away from Adrian's grip and pulled him in close as he stood. Adrian clutched his shirt tightly, desperate for the man's protection.

"I don't want to die..."

Garrick leaned his forehead against Adrian's and brushed

his fingers over his scalp, soothing his trembling. The two stood together, shutting out the intense heat and the flames dancing around them.

"I know," Garrick whispered.

Then he grabbed the back of Adrian's coat and, with a surprising burst of strength, lifted him off his feet and threw him out the window.

Adrian flew backward, suddenly exposed to the cool night air. He fell as if in slow motion, then all too soon slammed into the dirt below. He thought he had lost consciousness, and when he finally became aware of the world again, he was lying on his back with Val's limp body several feet away.

Adrian lifted his shoulders off the ground, doing his best to ignore the screaming pain radiating down his spine, and saw the mansion engulfed in flames. The exterior wall, the one with the window he had burst through, crumbled.

"Gar..." he cried weakly, unable to finish the man's name. A lone sob escaped his lips.

He raised Hell, and he alone was victorious.

42
NIGHT 9 - GARRICK

S orry, Adrian. Tough love was necessary, sometimes.

Off to Garrick's left, Seth cackled, his laughter punctuated by coughing fits caused by the thick smoke around them. The flames that had licked at his skin and clothing eventually died out, but not before searing part of his face an angry red.

"Fucking liar," Seth rasped.

Seth didn't seem to be in any shape to continue fighting, so Garrick knelt once again to tend to the bear trap clamped around his arm.

"Adrian's a good man," he said, a tender smile on his lips. "Not much, though. Just a little good. He tries. But that's why I love him. I can't love a truly good man, because me? I'm not a good man."

He placed the trap in front of him on the floor, its teeth angled upward, and positioned his foot over the jaws.

"I like power, and I learned long ago to never apologize for that."

Steeling himself for the pain, he stomped down on the trap, severing the remaining muscle, skin, and bone. Taking a moment to let his body protest the act of self-mutilation, Garrick picked up the severed half of his arm. Carefully aligning the thumb and bone splinters, he pressed the two halves together and reached for his rapidly depleting well of magic to heal the seam.

"You know what I said when I found out I'd become an Elder?" Garrick continued. "'Finally.' I was ready for it. I'd gone mad long before I earned the title. Crossing that threshold just made it official."

He twitched each finger in turn, testing the healed connection in his limb. It was weak, but recovering from an injury like this would take time.

Seth scoffed. "Is that what you'll tell him when he's struggling beneath you, begging for mercy? Or will you stake him in the morning, right after he falls asleep? No, it's what you'll tell yourself after you cut off his head and take his heart as a memento."

Garrick's Madness flared, hissing and spitting like chained vipers. He smothered it as he always did, but deep down, he knew it was only a matter of time before they escaped. It had been a short, beautiful forty years during which he'd managed to keep his Madness locked away.

Would Adrian still love him when he saw it?

His contemplation was cut short by Seth cackling once again. What an aggravating man. Getting under people's skin seemed to be a natural talent of his. Garrick knelt down, pinning Seth's chest with his knee.

"You made me lose a lot of blood today," he growled. "I think it's only fair I take some back."

Adrian

Val still had a pulse. Adrian pressed two fingers beneath her chin, counting the faint heartbeats. They were slow, even by vampire standards, but it was enough. Somehow, some way, he had managed to save her life.

The second heart, pressed against her breast by her bra, still beat. Its rhythm had weakened, but it was still alive. Adrian reopened the cut on his palm and resupplied the heart with blood, causing it to pump with new vigor.

Now what? Adrian was tired and starving, but they weren't safe out in the open like this. He wasn't sure why the fire department hadn't arrived, but he considered it a blessing that he didn't have to add running from the authorities to his to-do list. Their original hotel was the closest, and he still had his room key.

Adrian rubbed his eyes and felt his arms begin to shake. No, not yet. Grieving could come later, once they were safe at the hotel. But he hesitated to pick Val back up. It was just a little farther, but the distance felt impossibly long.

Adrian lifted his head, his eyes heavy, but he snapped alert when he saw someone halfway between him and the mansion. At first, he thought his mind was playing tricks on him. But when Garrick—covered in soot and blood, limping toward him—locked eyes with Adrian and let out a small, defeated sigh, Adrian lost all control and ran to him. He collided into Garrick's arms and held him tight, digging his fingers into the back of his shirt, just in case letting go meant losing him forever once again.

Garrick softly clasped him in return and leaned his head against Adrian's, resting it on his shoulder.

"I'm tired," he said. "Let's go home."

43
NIGHT 9 - ADRIAN

They returned to Garrick's original hotel room. Val remained unconscious, but Garrick confirmed she was still alive. He cut his palm and let the blood pour into her open mouth to help the healing along, then took an interest in the Elder heart near her breast.

"You found this beneath the mansion?" Garrick asked, taking the heart in his fingers for a closer look.

"That was the power source," Adrian said. "There were jars of blood near it too, so maybe there were others. But this one was in that big ritual bowl Owen used."

Garrick's eyebrows lifted, but he didn't look surprised. Instead, a flicker of curiosity tugged at his lips.

"Do you know, like… what that is?" Adrian wasn't sure how to properly phrase his question. It was a heart, beating, highly magical… but how?

"The heart of an Elder vampire, torn from its owner's chest, still beating. I didn't think Owen already possessed one."

"Do they all do that?"

"Ostensibly. Not that I've seen it done many times." Garrick continued to observe the heart, spinning it between his fingers and rubbing it with his thumb. Then he placed it back near Val's breast. "Research on vampire hearts is sparse, as you can imagine. Elder hearts even more so. But you already know how hardy Elder hearts can be. They're quite good at keeping themselves alive."

Adrian frowned. Had he? He went down the list of Elders he knew, trying to recall if any of them had been stabbed or shot in the heart. Then he realized. Adrian brushed his fingers over his left breast.

"No," he protested. "No, it doesn't make sense. I can still drink human blood."

"Is it difficult for you to feel full on it?" Garrick asked.

Had it? Sure, he'd had his accident on the beach, but that didn't mean anything on its own. Val had made a comment before then, and true, there were a few times he'd stopped before feeling satisfied, but he was being careful. He couldn't tell just from thinking back. Was there a pattern he simply didn't want to see?

"When you bit Tyler, was his blood sweet?"

Adrian bit his lip, unable to bring himself to answer. Seth's warning rang in his ears. No, sweet blood was connected to the transplants. All three of the vampires whose blood he had tasted had undergone a transplant.

But those had been the only vampires he'd bitten since the incident with his heart. Had it all been a coincidence?

Garrick took his silence as confirmation. "That sweet

flavor comes from the magic in our blood. Once you start needing that magic, you become sensitive to it. It's the most reliable indicator of our transition into Elders."

"But…" Adrian trembled. "You said I still had sixty more years."

With that statement, Garrick showed genuine distress. "I don't know," he whispered. "I'm sorry, Adrian. I truly thought you did. Even when I saw your heart heal that fast… I didn't think it was possible."

Garrick pulled him into a hug, squeezing him tightly. Fear and uncertainty plagued Adrian's mind, but he tried to relax in Garrick's embrace. He was so tired.

"What's going to happen to me?" Adrian whispered. "I promise I'll keep the Madness in check. I won't become like them."

"I know," Garrick said, soothing him. "It's an hour until sunrise, and I'm a little filthy. Let me take a bath, and we'll talk about this in the morning. Okay?"

Against his shoulder, Adrian nodded. Garrick let him go and disappeared into the bathroom. Adrian let out a long, calming sigh. He should probably clean himself too, but he couldn't bear another painful shower. How much longer until the running water started to sear his skin off?

Instead, he quickly filled the sink with soapy water and washed himself off with a wet towel. Then he sat by Val's side in case she woke up. They still had Adrian's shirt wrapped around her head as a makeshift bandage, since pulling it off might restart the bleeding. Adrian, and the Elder heart, had spent a lot of magic healing her, but he didn't know how much damage remained. The memory of her lying on the ground, a hole in the side of her head, made him feel sick. He rubbed his face, then pulled the revolver out of his pocket.

He pushed the cylinder open. Only one bullet remained, and it wasn't in the firing position. He had assumed the beat-up old gun had jammed and had been careless about retrieving it. But it was possible the bullet had been defective instead. After all, they were silver bullets, probably bought online from some shady source. What was really amazing was that five of the six bullets had actually worked.

Never bring a weapon you don't want turned against you, Garrick had warned. Adrian closed the cylinder and set the gun on the nightstand. If he hadn't brought it, if he'd been more careful, Val wouldn't have nearly died.

Adrian pulled up one of the high-backed antique chairs from the far side of the room. He didn't want to sleep in his own room tonight.

He placed his elbows on his lap and rested his head in his hands. His body ached and weighed heavy, drained from the blood he had used during their fight in the mansion. How was this happening already? He tried to calm his racing mind, but it kept circling back to the Madness. How had Garrick described it? A coil around the heart, a voice in the back of the mind, twisting the sense of right and wrong. Was that what Adrian had been feeling? Were his recent actions truly so contemptible? He closed his eyes to rest. This kind of self-reflection required a clear mind.

The click of a misfired gun snapped his eyes open.

The first thing Adrian saw was the barrel of the revolver pointed directly at the side of his head. Then he saw Garrick, holding the gun, his eyebrows raised in surprise as his eyes darted from the weapon to Adrian. Both men froze, their gazes locked.

Fear swelled within Adrian until it felt like the walls around him were closing in. For several agonizing seconds, he couldn't move, despite his mind screaming in silent terror. Finally, he stumbled out of his chair, eyes wide and mouth agape, and scrambled across the floor. He let out whimpers not yet fully formed into screams.

Garrick inspected the gun, then tossed it aside at his feet. His face twisted in pain as he raised a hand to rub his eyes.

"No, no, please…" Adrian pleaded. Garrick tried to kill him. He was only alive because of that damn faulty bullet.

"I'm not mad! Please! Just give me a chance!"

At first, Garrick didn't respond and kept his face warily in his hand. Then he looked up and wiped the last remnants of emotion from his face. Expressionless, he walked toward Adrian with all the fervor of a man asleep.

The door was only a few feet to Adrian's right. He ran for it and pulled the handle, but the chain lock kept it from opening fully. Before he could fumble with the lock, Garrick slammed him against the wall with his forearm and sank his fangs into Adrian's neck. Instinctively, Adrian tried to shove him away, until he remembered his magic and misted through the crack in the door. He reformed and stumbled into the hotel hallway, doing his best to run despite an over-whelming wave of vertigo. As he approached his hotel room, he glanced over his shoulder just in time to see Garrick reform out of his own dark mist. Adrian realized he left the key to his room, not that it would have mattered.

He sprinted down the hallway and out the front door, afraid that at any moment Garrick would grab him from behind and sink his fangs in again. He ran a block before glancing over his shoulder to see how close Garrick was in pursuit.

Standing at the entrance of the hotel, Garrick looked up at the sky, its color a deep indigo. He lowered his head to look at Adrian but didn't follow him.

Adrian continued to run. Sunrise was in half an hour. He needed to find somewhere to hide before then. Someplace the sun couldn't reach, but also where everyday people wouldn't stumble upon a seemingly dead body. He ran past office buildings, closed stores, parking garages. Time was running out. He would have to pick a place to hide and pray it was abandoned.

Adrian misted to slip into a closed building, hoping it

contained a rarely used closet or basement, but he immediately stumbled to the ground, his body barely deforming before snapping back. He rose to his feet slowly, but the world was spinning. He tried to take a few steps before dizziness overtook him, sending him crashing to the cement sidewalk again.

He was spent, but he couldn't give up. Giving up meant death. He tried to push himself to his feet again, but the effort was weak.

Suddenly, Adrian's emotions caught up with him. Garrick tried to kill him. Garrick, the man he loved and had believed loved him in return. He didn't have the strength to do more than softly sob. Amid the cracks of his anguish, he briefly considered pulling his overcoat over his head in a last-ditch effort to avoid the encroaching sunrise, but his will to survive had gone numb.

Adrian gave up and closed his eyes.

44

NIGHT 9 - VAL

There was no sorrow on Garrick's face when he reentered the hotel room. Nor was there fear, surprise, or anger when he noticed Val standing on the other side of the bed, pointing the revolver at his chest. Tears streamed down her face as she held the gun with both hands—one gripping the handle, the other steadying her trembling aim.

Garrick closed the door behind him and waited, keeping his eyes on Val's rather than the gun.

"Well?" he said, as if bored. "Are we going to see if it works this time?"

Val didn't fire. Her first memory since waking up was of Garrick taking this gun from the nightstand and pointing it at

Adrian's head. She hadn't fully followed what had happened, or what they'd said. Hell, she didn't even know what had become of Seth, Melissa, or anyone else at the mansion. All she knew was that Garrick had tried to kill Adrian with this gun. For some reason, it hadn't worked.

But even if it had, Val wasn't sure it would actually pose any threat to Garrick. His nonchalance confirmed that. But what was she supposed to do? Pretend it hadn't happened?

Losing patience, Garrick turned and walked toward the sitting area. He picked up the chair, lying sideways after their earlier scuffle, and dragged it to the far end of the room.

"Sunrise is in fifteen minutes," he said. "You can take the bed."

He rotated the chair so that it faced the door, not directly at the bed, but positioned so Val remained in his line of sight. He sat with one elbow resting on the armrest and his head in his hand, his thumb rubbing his temple.

Val finally lowered the gun, but she remained standing. She watched Garrick with disgust, though he seemed content to sit and sleep for the rest of the night.

"Where is he?" she demanded. "Tell me you didn't…"

Garrick opened his eyes and stared at her, his gaze unwavering. He remained silent. A fresh pain tore through her chest, and she raised the gun again.

"Seth was right," she spat. "It was all fake, wasn't it? He loved you! And you—"

"I'm six hundred years old." Garrick cut her off as he slowly rose from his chair. He walked toward her calmly. "If I saved everyone I loved, then Adrian would have died on the side of the road forty years ago, unloved by anyone."

He stopped just inches from the barrel of the gun. Gently, he placed one hand over the top, then forcefully pulled it from Val's grip. He opened the cylinder, let the single defective bullet fall out, then, with both hands, tore the cylinder from its hinges. Both halves of the gun dropped to the floor.

"That night, when I took you in as a vampire, I told you that one day you'd have to take over Adrian's duties. This is what I meant."

He returned to his chair and closed his eyes. Val trembled, stuck, trapped. She couldn't stay with this betrayer any longer, but where was she supposed to go? She had no car, no house, no job, less than eight thousand dollars in her bank account, and now a brutal head injury, the extent of the damage still unknown. Sunrise was ten minutes away, and even if she had a plan, Garrick would never let her go. He needed blood. Vampire blood. Her blood.

"Too good for revenge?" Garrick said, almost as if he could read her mind. "That's not the Val I know. You still have an Elder you need to kill. It's a good thing I know a thing or two about powerful hearts."

Val didn't respond. She didn't even allow herself to think, just in case he could read her mind. She focused only on her anger, how much she hated him, so that when his serpent's tongue tried to charm her later, she would remember this moment.

And Garrick smiled at that. He winked open an eye, and something in his mad brain approved.

"Rest up, we have a lot of work to do tomorrow."

45

NIGHT 10 - ADRIAN

Abare drywall ceiling greeted Adrian when he woke unexpectedly. He was still on the hard ground, though this one was covered with thin carpet. A lingering sweetness filled his mouth.

He blinked twice. Somehow, he wasn't dead, or the afterlife was a lot more mundane than he had expected.

Slowly, Adrian sat up and looked around. He was in another hotel room, similar to the one Thea had brought him to before. The room was immaculately clean, and although he'd been left on the floor, a lounger was placed in front of a large window overlooking the city of San Francisco. The sky still held some light, but its hue had deepened to the navy

383

blue of dusk, darker than the brighter shade it had been when he passed out.

Continuing to look around, he jumped when he realized someone was sitting on the bed, her back against the headboard. Thea watched him, wearing a loose-fitting T-shirt and slacks, her phone in hand. Adrian stared, utterly confused.

"Hey," Thea said, then returned her attention to her phone.

"Hey?" Adrian waited a moment to see if Thea would say anything more. She didn't. "Um, where am I?"

"Hotel room."

Adrian glanced around again. Yeah no shit.

Thea pointed to the nightstand beside where Adrian sat. "That's for you," she said.

Adrian stood up to see what she was pointing at and saw a glass full of red liquid. He pounced on it and greedily drank the entire glass, spilling some in his fervor. It was sweet, but only slightly. Just enough. Adrian glanced back at Thea and noticed a bandage wrapped around her palm.

"Thanks," he murmured. "Where... why am I here?"

"Got a little concerned when you didn't answer my text. I kind of thought you'd be happy to hear from me. Then I remembered this." She waved her phone in the air.

Confused, Adrian felt around in his pockets for his phone and looked at the screen to find two missed texts from Thea.

Hey, need to talk to you. Call me?

?

Based on the timestamp of her texts, Adrian had been far too concerned with Garrick nearly murdering him to notice his phone buzzing. But how had she found him in so little time?

Right, the GPS feature. Adrian never shut it off.

"Why were you out on the street so late?" Thea asked.

Garrick… Adrian's spirit drained from his body. He wanted to drop to the floor again, to reacquaint himself with the feeling of being dead, but he had enough sense to sit on the window lounger instead. Though his better nature was repulsed by the thought, part of his heart wished Thea hadn't rescued him and instead left him to his bright, sunny grave.

Thea watched him, and her face slowly darkened with growing concern. "Um, I wanted to talk to you about something."

Adrian didn't respond, but his full attention gave Thea permission to continue.

"I need help."

"With what?"

Thea sucked in a breath and let it out in a strained sigh. Adrian noticed her chest continuing to rise and fall, a quirk of new vampires who hadn't yet broken the habit of breathing.

"You may have noticed," Thea continued, finally looking back at him. She pointed to her mouth. "I've got a new life trajectory. Kind of got forced into the vampire career path. And I'm not following in Melissa's footsteps. I'm not sucking up to shitty Elder vampires to survive. So, I'm the Elder vampire."

Adrian held her gaze for a moment, then let out a single, huffing laugh. That sounded familiar, and Thea had only been a vampire for a few days. She was asking the wrong person. How well had that worked out for him?

"You can't just be an Elder," he said. "That doesn't happen until you're…" Adrian trailed off. Until you're two hundred, give or take one hundred sixty years. "It's an age thing."

"Well, yeah, with the powers and all. But I'm going to have other vampires working for me, not the other way around."

Adrian regarded her suspiciously. "And how exactly are you going to do that?"

Thea shrugged. "Buy a house. Build some influence."

She said it so casually, like it was easy and anyone could do it. He was about to protest, but Thea spoke up first.

"Look, I have money. I don't need to depend on others. But what I don't know is much about vampire life. And that's where you come in."

Adrian frowned. She wanted him to be her mentor?

"Don't think this means I'm forgiving you," Thea said with a scowl. "But I need someone who knows how to vampire. All the little rules about what I can do, how to interact with other vampires, who I should trust... that kind of thing. Melissa doesn't believe in me. And, well, you're kind of the only other vampire I know. I don't really trust you when it comes to..." She lifted her hands and waved them around. Not in any way that suggested she was trying to say "romantic affairs," but he knew what she meant. "I still think you're my best shot. So, I'm willing to keep things professional. You help me become a badass Elder vampire who doesn't take shit from anyone, and I'll do the same for you. Deal?"

Adrian paused to think. So much had happened in just a few short days. He thought he was finally free—taking control of his life, ruling the city with the man he loved, before being betrayed. Now he was... free. Working with the woman he had once loved, before betraying her, overlooking the city mere inches from a terrifying, lethal drop. What more was he owed?

"Deal."

Acknowledgments

First and foremost, I'd like to thank you, the reader, for taking a chance on a new author and her debut, self-published novel. If you liked this book, please leave a review on Amazon, Goodreads, or wherever else you may have bought it. Reviews are immensely helpful for new authors like myself to break into the world of authorship, so that I may write more books like this one. If you did not like this book, then please also leave a review. Otherwise, if I only have 5 star reviews, people will think they all came from my mom.

I'd like to thank my friends—the "Epoch" gang—for getting me interested in the World of Darkness tabletop games, where I discovered how cool the vampires were, even though they all preferred the werewolves.

Thank you to my beta readers: Brentyn, my sister, my mother, and my grandmother—all for the support and excitement you shared with me while writing this book. Thank you to my dad and brother-in-law for your support as well, even though it was only for the first few chapters. I promise I'll make an audiobook as soon as it makes financial sense to do so.

A big thank you to the baristas and bartenders at the local coffee shops and social club. This book was powered by iced chais, cocktails, and your always friendly presences.

Moderate thank you to all of the companies that didn't hire me during this process. While I appreciated the extra time to devote to my book, my wallet is feeling a little tight, and I could do without the stressful interviews that went nowhere. Special shout out to Greg, who refused to help me look for a job because "The last guy who came to me for a job wrote a bestselling book, and I want to be 2 for 2!" So, here's hoping you keep that streak.

A cautious thank you to the psychic in Arizona, ten years ago, who told me I should get out of tech and programming, and that I was going to be a successful writer and meet the president. You've been right so far, but talk about a serious monkey-paw situation on that last part.